Lola Moore has always loved reading and writing from a young age. Having gone on to study and briefly practice law, she now enjoys writing fiction with a passion for the romance genre. When she's not working, writing, or spending time with her family, she's usually engaged in reading a book. She believes that a good book is entertainment for the heart and mind.

Her hobbies, besides reading and writing, are cooking, organising, watching films, and socialising with family and friends. Lola lives happily in the South East of England with her husband and two daughters.

Dedicating this book to my family and to God.

Lola Moore

EARTH ANGEL

AUSTIN MACAULEY PUBLISHERS™

LONDON • CAMBRIDGE • NEW YORK • SHARJAH

A CIP catalogue record for this title is available from the British Library.

ISBN 9781398445758 (Paperback)
ISBN 9781398445765 (e-Pub e-book)

www.austinmacauley.com

First Published 2022
Austin Macauley Publishers Ltd®
1 Canada Square
Canary Wharf
London
E14 5AA

I would like to thank my parents, siblings, and daughters for always believing in, and encouraging me.

I would especially like to thank my wonderful husband for his patience and immeasurable support on my writing journey of this book from start to finish.

Finally, I would like to express my gratitude to God for the inspiration, the gift and ability to make this story and book a reality.

Chapter One

It was cold and the thick darkness was broken by bouts of illuminated blurry streetlights. The distant sound of a passing car briefly cracked the silence of the quiet one-way street. The hardness of the ground was a catalyst for the cold that crept into his bones. RJ coughed and a sharp pain tore through him. Damn! He lay quiet for a couple of minutes, and then finally attempted to sit up. He winced as a much sharper pain soared through his left side. He paused for a few seconds and then, with a gust of aggressive resolve, pushed himself onto his feet in a slightly crouching position. More excruciating pain! He shuddered. Finally, but slowly, he stood up on his feet and steadied himself. The pain just wasn't going away.

RJ's eyes focused and he looked around. Where was Danny boy? Sudden panic came over him. He reached for the side where the pain was emanating. The thick crimson liquid that oozed from the deep cut was soaking through his grey T-shirt and hooded top quickly, covering his left hand. He looked around again. No sound, just the night lights from the houses along the street proved that other humans existed in the world. He studied the ground and concluded that the blood could only be his alone. He had to find Danny. Where was he? Was he okay? RJ could not bear to think of what might have happened to the young lad. Looking down at his side again, RJ realised that the cut might be deeper than he initially thought and that he was losing quite a lot of blood. Slowly but painfully, he began his walk towards any sort of help. He needed it and fast, but he was not about to go knocking on a random house at this time of the night, he thought as he staggered a little. Suddenly, he heard it. It was faint, almost unreal. Was it music… singing? It sounded beautiful, almost angelic. Was it the sound of angels? Was he dying? 'Yeah right', RJ sniggered to himself. Didn't angels belong in heaven? If there was a heaven, there was no way he'd be headed there.

Even he had to admit that to himself. That was ok, though. He had long accepted that.

He gradually made his way towards where he thought the sound was coming from. He must have been walking forever. RJ was not sure how far he had gone, but he sensed that he was getting weaker as his steps slowly lost their pace. The lights had started to go blurry again. Or was that just his vision? He could not hear the singing anymore. The soft sound of voices could be heard and then some car doors shutting. More sounds: car engines starting and then pulling off. RJ tried to stagger to where he perceived these sounds were coming from. He did not know where he was or where he was going. He began to feel very faint. His feet hit some steps. He turned, and through a hazy glaze, was bathed in light pouring from a point at the top of the steps. He instinctively mustered all the energy he had left to climb the three steps that led to… heaven? *No way*, RJ thought as intense darkness gently took over and the pain subsided.

Eva stepped out of the inner church office. From the silence, it seemed the choir practice was over. She glanced at the huge Elizabethan church clock. It was ten forty-five pm. They had finished later than usual tonight. It was about time she started heading home herself. James, the parish secretary stepped out from another inner room.

"Don't worry, James. I'll lock up," Eva said to him.

James gave her a 'thank you' nod and turned to leave through the church's back door.

As Eva moved around ensuring that the hymn books were properly stacked in place, she could not help feeling at peace and at home in this small old Anglican Church. St Benedict was built in the 19th century on the ruins of the original Norman church. Much of the old church had disappeared now, and what was left was a smaller refurbished one that embodied a lot of the old stones and hints of its historic architecture. It currently had about 100 congregants spread over two services every Sunday and one mid-week service on Wednesdays. St Benedict's main vision was outreach; with its current focus on the youths, especially the gangs that were strongly posing a problem in the neighbourhood. Being part of the church felt like being a part of one big peaceful and loving family. She had made up her mind to always be a part of it, to serve the church and help people discover the joys of the Christian faith and being members of such a wonderful community of love.

Eva suddenly felt chilly and pulled her cardigan more snugly around her. She frowned. That was weird! The windows were hardly ever opened. During the summer, the cold stone walls of the church ensured the inside remained cool. The installation of central heating a few years back kept the church warm when the weather was cold, especially during the winter. So where was the draught coming from? She looked searchingly around. It didn't take her long to discover the source. The double doors of the church's main entrance had been left wide open.

The last chorister to leave must have forgotten to close them. She sighed and made a mental note to put a notice regarding this in the next church bulletin. Eva made her way quickly to the entrance. She grabbed hold of the hard-wooden doors and was about to push them shut when she noticed something from the corner of her eyes. There was a figure sprawled on the doorstep. She almost screamed in fright, but suddenly realised that it was an unconscious body. She let go of the doors and stepped out onto the steps. The lights from the inside of the church shone bright enough to reveal the blood on the steps and the body it was flowing from. Eva's hand immediately went to her mouth as she moved hurriedly to kneel beside the seemingly lifeless body of a man.

"Oh no! Please don't let him be dead, God. Don't let him be dead," she whispered to herself in terror.

Hospital food never tasted better, RJ thought. Or was that because he had been practically unconscious for about two days and had been drifting in and out of consciousness? Usually, baked potatoes and vegetables were not his favourite, but they seemed quite tasty with the chicken in creamy white sauce. RJ had his last forkful, placed the cutlery back in the plate and then settled back into the hospital bed. He could not wait to be out of here, though. He had loads to sort out. He had to find Danny. What could have happened to him? The dull throbbing from his left side was the best he was going to get from the pain killers he had been given. The experienced elderly Asian doctor, who he presumed stitched him up, had explained how lucky RJ had been. Apparently, the sharp blade that had pierced him just below his ribs, had surprisingly managed not to hit any vital organs. Still, RJ had lost quite a lot of blood and was very lucky to have been brought here before it was too late. He even got a private room. Seems, for some unknown and baffling reason, he had been given a guardian angel.

There was a knock on the door and a lady dressed in the nurse's blue apparel came in. She smiled at him. She was not particularly pretty, but her smile was warm. RJ smiled back.

She blushed.

"Looks like you have some visitors," she informed. *Damn!*

Two police officers walked in through the door that had been left open by the nurse. Dressed in the full uniform and regalia, their presence would have intimidated anyone. The nurse nodded at them as she wheeled the tray carrying his empty dinner plate and cup out of the room.

"Hello, RJ," said the bulkier of the two officers.

"Constable Fischer, what brings you here this fine Friday evening?" Fischer looked RJ over.

"Oh, just a presumed case of assault occasioning in bodily harm." RJ looked him squarely in the eye.

"I don't know anything. All I remember was taking a little walk after leaving the pub on Wednesday night and then… nothing."

The two officers stood staring at him in silence.

"I must have blacked out 'cos, it was only after I woke up that I realised I had been stabbed. I tried to find help but was out again at some point."

Fischer's stare revealed the fact that he wasn't buying RJ's story. The other police officer took out a note pad and began making some notes.

"So, are you missing any valuable effects?" asked Fischer. RJ was quiet.

"Just trying to find probable cause," the second officer stated. RJ understood all that.

"Look, I couldn't even tell you. I might have had a little too much to drink that night, anyway. I wouldn't even know if any money was taken out of my wallet."

"So, you didn't see anyone… don't remember anything… didn't get into a disagreement with anyone recently?" Fischer threw the last one in there.

"Don't know. Can't recall," RJ answered, looking straight at the door.

Fischer looked like he was going to ask something else, but then said instead.

"If you remember anything or come across any useful information, please don't hesitate to contact us. I believe you know where to find us."

RJ nodded without looking at them.

The two officers walked to the door. Fischer paused at the door as the second officer stepped out of the room.

"You were lucky this time, RJ; you might not be next time." And with that, he left the room and shut the door.

RJ heaved a sigh of relief. He looked round the hospital room and wondered where his mobile phone was. He had several calls to make. He wanted to get out of bed and search, but his muscles and bones felt too heavy to make the move. *Must be all the bags of blood they pumped into him,* RJ thought to himself, knowing full well that it was because his body was recovering, and he had not exercised his muscles in a couple of days. It was not like him. He liked to keep fit. Voices outside the room put him on the alert. He made out that of Fischer's and a female voice, probably a nurse. He strained to hear what they were saying but could not make it out. Why wouldn't Fischer just go? The sudden thought that he might be coming back in to ask him more questions made RJ lie back in his bed. He did not have time to pull the covers over his body to give the full impression of having fallen asleep when the door was opened again.

RJ slammed his eye lids shut. He heard the door close, then… silence. Was it Fischer? Maybe that smiley nurse had come back in again. The silence was deafening. RJ couldn't help it any longer. He opened his eyes just enough so he could to peer though his eye lashes, but still appear to have them closed.

A lady stood there staring at him. She was black… no, mixed race. A mass of beautiful brown curls of varied shades covered her head, fell around her face and onto her shoulders. Her eyebrows were full and perfect. She had big light brown eyes under long curved lashes. Her small but pointy nose had a couple of freckles on them. Yet, the rest of her creamy beige skin that he could see from her face and neck was spotless. The bottom pink lip of her small pouty mouth was slightly fuller than the top one. She was simply beautiful. It took all of RJ's strength not to move. Instead, he continued to study her.

Her 5'4" height went well with her slender physique, and she had all the right curves in all the right places. Her fitted white blouse hung nicely over black trousers tucked into a pair of black knee length boots. The lady just stood there, with a black coat hanging from her right arm, looking quietly at him. Lady? No, this was an angel!

Eva felt like a thief as she stared at this stranger whilst he slept. He was a tall man who obviously looked after his body and ensured he kept fit. Nice build, proportioned muscles, and that full head of black hair reminded her of Damon Salvatore from *The Vampire Dairies*. She had only seen a few episodes of Season one before she had decided it wasn't for her.

Eva hadn't noticed how he looked the night she found him on the church steps. All she had thought to do was ensure that he stayed alive. She had checked his pulse and heartbeat to confirm that he was still breathing, and then had hurriedly called for an ambulance. Everything had happened so fast. She had also called Reverend Bainbridge, and he had approved the use of some of the church's welfare fund to get him a private room. Eva had not seen him since he was brought into the hospital last Wednesday night. Due to the nature of his injuries and the circumstances surrounding it, the hospital had found it necessary to contact the police. The constable had identified the mystery man as 'RJ something'. They apparently knew who he was. She, on the other hand, was yet to know anything at all about him.

Eva wasn't sure she should remain in the room since he didn't seem to be available to talk now. However, she could not stop looking at him. His perfect jaw line and cheek bones made him very good to look at. He had a small scar at the top of his left eyebrow that added some character to his face. His breathing was remarkably quiet for a sleeping man. She suddenly felt uncomfortable. She ought to leave. It was wrong for her to stand here and watch him sleeping. Eva turned around and walked towards the door. She would come back when next she had the chance… before he got discharged from the hospital, she thought as she reached for the door handle.

"You're not big on hello and goodbyes, are you?"

Eva was startled as she had not expected to suddenly hear RJ's voice behind her. She slowly turned back to look at him. Had he caught her staring at him?

He was sitting up in bed, hands folded across his chest and watching her with the deepest and bluest eyes she had ever seen. *Heavens,* she thought. The man was incredibly good looking!

She walked uncomfortably towards his bed but made sure she stopped at a reasonable distance.

"You're awake."

Eva wasn't sure if she was feeling embarrassed because he had been aware of her staring at him or by the fact that she found him quite attractive.

"Very perceptive," RJ stated with a smile.

Eva licked her lips; a habit she displayed whenever she was in discomfort or lost for words.

"Well, you were supposedly asleep half a second ago," Eva gently blurted out a little defensively.

"Possibly," he responded almost immediately.

Eva studied his face but could not find any sign of annoyance. Nonetheless, she felt she owed him an apology.

"I'm sorry. The officers had just left your room, so I wasn't expecting to find you asleep." When he did not respond, but continued to stare at her, she went on…

"My name is Eva. I'm the one who found you and called the ambulance."

An unknown look flickered across his face, and he raised an eyebrow. There was an awkward five second silence that seemed like forever to Eva.

"I thought I was dying. So, I was saved by an angel, after all," he finally said.

"Angel? Hardly! You could have died. However, thank God you didn't," Eva said slightly amused, slightly serious.

RJ then said something which she did not quite catch. It was almost a whisper. "I'm sorry, what did you say?" she asked curiously.

The look in his eyes was unexpectedly soft. "Earth angel."

Eva did not have time to react to that when there was a firm knock on the door and in walked a doctor followed by two nurses.

"I'm afraid it's time for the rounds. Visiting hours will have to end at this time," the doctor said. His name tag read 'Dr Omash'.

Eva nodded in understanding. She will have to come see him again another time. As the doctor faced RJ and began scanning through his medical chart, one of the nurses was setting up the drip bag so she could hook him up to an IV. Feeling intrusive, Eva walked quietly to the door.

"Thank you," she suddenly heard RJ say as she opened the door. This was the second time he was catching her unawares.

She turned to look at him and was overwhelmed by the genuineness in his eyes. She responded with a short nod and then left the room.

15

Chapter Two

Daniel was a skinny lad that looked a little small for his age. He was seventeen and would be turning eighteen in a few months' time. Being eighteen meant one... and only one thing to him.

Freedom! Freedom to buy alcohol, to get into certain clubs, to be his own man. However, with freedom came boldness and courage, and he did not have plenty of those. Having been raised in an orphanage and three foster homes, Danny had not had the easiest life. Two of his foster homes had been hell on earth, between deadbeat foster parents who worked him to the bone, to drunken ones who had beat him to the bone. He had finally run away and was subsequently taken in by a notorious gang. The first foster home was where he had encountered true kindness. Unfortunately, the image of the sweet woman who had fostered him, from when he could remember, hanging from the ceiling fan when he was just ten years old had remained with him till this very day. From the little he heard and remembered of the conversation between two social service workers, her estranged ex-husband had killed her for some reason and tried to make it look like a suicide. Life had taken a turn for the worse for him after that, and he had not experienced kindness again until he had met the leader of the gang. They were like his family now, but then, chaos had ensued and now he didn't know which way to turn.

Danny was worried now. In fact, he was more than worried, he was scared. He felt he had to do something but did not know what to do. He reached into his jacket pocket and pulled out a mobile phone. It still had the dried spots of red on it, and Danny wondered why he had not bothered to wipe them off. Not having a phone of his own since it was recently confiscated, Danny felt he had better hang on to this. Flashbacks of the awful night kept replaying in his head and he dropped his head into his hands as he sat on one of the steps leading up to the council flat that the gang occupied for now.

Hearing footsteps from within the building, and then making their way down, Danny hurriedly put the phone back in his jacket pocket.

"Danny boy," Nick called out. His tone was a mix of mockery, mischief, and playfulness. Danny tensed as the big boned guy settled himself beside him on the step. Nick Payne's neck and arms were covered in tattoos of everything and nothing in particular. The metal ring that went through his left eyebrow made his questioning look aggressive.

"Look, no use thinking 'bout 'im. 'E 'ad it coming, and 'twas for the best. I'll look after you now. I told you I would. I 'ave great plans for the gang. Things are going to be different now, you'll see. I 'ave so much more to offer than he ever 'ad. That's why it's best you stick wiv me… wiv us," Nick said, his voice not coming out as gentle as he'd intended. When Danny said nothing, Nick put an arm on his shoulder and asked in a very hushed tone,

"Am I going to 'ave trouble wiv you, Danny boy?"

Danny tensed even more, and then his shoulders dropped. He gave Nick a shy but brief glance, and slowly shook his head.

Danny gave him a gruff pat in the back, "That's my boy," he growled with humour.

"I could go with you to the hospital tomorrow, if you'd like?" Joyce asked Eva as they both made their way out of the Church after dropping off the printed church bulletin for the coming week.

Ever since Joyce Hutton had joined the St Benedict Church three years ago, Eva and the forty-year-old had forged a unique bond despite the good thirteen years between them. The older quirky black American and her English husband had moved to England from Seattle ten years ago after her husband had suddenly announced that he missed his country and wanted to move back home. He had lived in the United States for twelve years where he met and married Joyce. Joyce, being the good wife that she was, supported her husband and moved back with him. Eva found the woman to be God fearing, yet fun and laid back.

"That's nice of you, Joyce. I would really appreciate it," Eva replied with a smile.

"Plus, you did mention that he was a cutie… which I have never heard you say before, so I am curious. Just want you to know that it is not purely selfless," Joyce said with a half grin.

Eva shot her a playful scolding look. "I said he's an attractive man, Joyce. It was mentioned only as descriptive."

Joyce looked at her and nodded with mock agreement, "Hmm hm."

Was it possible that when she talked about this RJ mystery man with Joyce, she expressed a bit too much? That she found him attractive certainly did not mean she was attracted to him. Or did it?

"Look…" began Joyce, "… I have known you a while now and never heard you talk about a man with that intrigued look in your eyes. Plus, you're young and single, and it won't be out of place for you to see something you like."

Eva gasped, a blush rising to her face. "Oh please. You're wrong, Joyce; I don't know enough… or anything about him for that matter, to like him at all. Who knows what his story is?"

"Well, I'm just saying. I have been praying to God, for almost two years, to drop a husband at your feet, and it might be that He literally has. God does answer prayers, you know." Joyce retorted opening the door to the driver's seat of her Audi A4 that was parked next to Eva's Vauxhall Corsa.

Eva sighed. It always amazes her how everyone was so eager to have her find someone and get married. Her mum was the worst culprit. Eva, on the other hand, didn't give it much thought. Yes, she would love to be married, but she knew it would happen in God's time. In the meantime, she was focused on the Church and the youth group, plus her hopes to go to Africa on missionary work. Her plan was to do that for six months to a year, then return to England. Where would a husband feature in that? It would work out better after she was back from her missionary work.

Eva rolled her eyeballs and smiled warmly at Joyce. "On that note, I'm off to have dinner at my parents now. I have no doubts that there will be more on that topic coming up. We will leave after church service tomorrow. I'll drive," she said.

Joyce chuckled as she nodded, then waved Eva goodbye, and got into her car.

"Tell me again, why you have to go visit that man in the hospital?" Evan asked watching as Eva rearranged the stacked plates in the dishwasher.

"Errr… because that's where he is," Eva responded and changed her position from bending to crouching so she could better sort out the plates.

Evan gave her a 'not-so-impressed-with-your-humour' look. "Seriously, you don't know anything about the fella; what he could be involved in. There are a few of those rogue gangs around. You cannot tell them from the regular guys these days. Who knows whose toes he has stepped on for his life to have been intended as the price?"

The kettle whistled its signal, and Rachel Knowles proceeded to make five cups of tea. She glanced up at intervals to view the exchange between the love of her life and his identical twin sister. Well, almost identical. Evan was several inches taller than his sister, had short cropped curly hair compared to his sister's mass of curls, and had the expected masculine features, physically and facially. There could be no doubt, however, that the two were siblings. Having come out fifteen minutes before Eva, Evan liked to think of himself as the older sibling.

Rachel wasn't particularly pretty. She was a little on the plump side, but she had a warm disposition and sweet smile that beautifully transformed her face… her whole appearance in general. One couldn't help but fall in love with her. She always thought how lucky she was to have Evan as her boyfriend. He was absolutely gorgeous, and she could not deny that she worried about losing him to the countless pretty women out there. It also helped that he was a man of faith from a family of faith. They had met in church, and Rachel believed God had orchestrated their relationship. So, she did not understand why they had been dating for two years, and he was yet to even mention the word marriage to her.

"He could have been robbed, Evan. The word of God teaches us love, remember? Now what sort of person would I be to help a person who could have died, and not follow up on his recovery?" Eva responded, finally straightening up from her task. She gave Evan a quick glance and saw the hidden irritation on his face because she had rearranged the dishes he had already taken the time to stack. He had not done it right, as usual. However, instead of telling him that, she would rather appreciate the fact that he had done it at all, and just redo it. Knowing Evan as well, he would not express his irritation that she had redone it.

"Yes, remember the story of the good Samaritan in the Bible? I think it was somewhere in Luke chapter 10?" Rachel joined in and handed Evan and then Eva a cup of tea each.

19

Evan nodded, "I do agree. However, you still need to be careful. Promise me you will be?"

Eva gave her brother a reassuring smile. It warmed Rachel's heart at how protective Evan was of Eva. Apparently, he had always been like that, ever since they were both little.

"Dinner's been over for almost thirty minutes, are you three coming to watch 'goggle box' with us or what?" Abigail Da Silva called out from the sitting room.

"And what's happening with our tea?" Timi Da Silva called right after her.

Rachel hurriedly carried their cups of tea to them in the sitting room. They were both seated beside each other on the settee facing the television. They were a close and loving couple who had brought up their children in the Christian way. Timi Da Silva was of African origin and had moved to the United Kingdom to further his education in his early twenties. As an engineer, he had done very well for himself and had a comfortable home. His wife, Abigail was the daughter of the Pastor of the church he attended back then. She was a blonde hair and blue-eyed Yorkshire lass from the York country town, and more talkative than her quiet husband.

Evan and Eva joined them in the sitting room, and they all settled down to watch the programme that Timi and Abigail seemed to be addicted to.

Chapter Three

"He discharged himself?" Eva exclaimed disbelievingly. She turned from the nurse to face Joyce with a look of shock. Joyce had the same look on her face due to the information they had both just received.

The nurse checked the records again with a perplexed look on her face, "That's what it says here. Against the doctor's advice, I might add."

There was a pause as Eva was still trying to process this information. How was that even possible? With the kind of injury he sustained, he should be hospitalised for another week or two. The wound was deep; he lost a lot of blood and could have died. As Eva remained dumbfounded, Joyce took the liberty to thank the nurse for the information and pull Eva away by the arm.

Eva shook her head still confused as she and Joyce made their way towards the entrance of the hospital. "Why… why would he do that? Can he even do that?"

Joyce shrugged. "Well, I guess so. He's an adult and not a prisoner." She looked at Eva and pulled her close to give her a half hug. "I know you felt responsible for him, but you've done all you can. All that's left is for you to pray for him. That God heals and watches over him."

Eva nodded. Joyce was right. However, a part of her could not help feeling a bit worried and disappointed. Eva would have liked to see him again. She did not understand why; she had spoken to him for less than five minutes, and she didn't know him at all. Her disappointment did not make any sense. No! Joyce was right; she could only commit him to God's hands and then forget about him. Sighing, Eva tried to brighten up and gave Joyce a smile of agreement. In no time at all, she would forget all about the handsome mysterious stranger. She was sure of it.

RJ was lucky that he had some money in his wallet. He wasn't surprised though, as he had to believe that the 'what's yours is yours' code still stood on some level. He might not have his mobile phone anymore, but he could at least use a pay phone. He stopped briefly as he took a deep breath and exhaled in an attempt to rid himself of the nauseous feeling he had. He couldn't even stand up to his full 6'2" height due to the pain from his side. Yes, he knew he had left the hospital too early, against the doctor's wishes, but he had to find Danny boy. He had to keep him safe. He knew if he had to settle some scores, he needed to get himself well first, but time was of the essence. He looked around to see if there were any phone booths in the area. RJ shivered; the weather had to be about ten degrees. He only had a slightly thick small sized black T-shirt on. His pair of jeans were the only item of clothing that he had found laundered and available. His white T-shirt and hooded top were nowhere to be found. The hospital must have written them off and discarded them due to the irreparable damage from his blood. He was not proud of it, but he had stolen into a room where a middle-aged man was fast asleep just so he could ruffle through the small travelling bag that he had his clothes in. RJ found the black T-shirt and decided not to take his coat as well. He had quietly apologised to the sleeping man.

Obviously, the T-shirt was not protecting RJ much from the cold. Everything was hitting him all at once: the pain, the nausea, and the chill. He felt weak, but he had to keep on going. He needed to get to his pad but wondered if it was safe. He wondered where his motorbike was at this moment.

"Damn you, Nick," he swore under his breath.

RJ thought hard about where to go and what to do. He might as well get a cab. It had been a while since he had used one, but he was not about to make things even more complicated by walking or using any other form of transportation. No, the cab was quicker and more discreet. He suddenly spotted a phone booth right across the road and heaved a sigh of relief. It was an effort to cross over, but he made it. He noticed someone already in the booth and two other people waiting to use it. RJ gritted his teeth. Just his luck! He would have to wait his turn.

After five minutes had gone by, RJ wondered what was going on. He studied the man in the booth who was dressed in a dark suit and talking rapidly and angrily into the phone. RJ then looked at the other two people waiting. They did not appear bothered or in a hurry. One was a woman who might be in her late 40s. She was busy scrolling through what seemed like her phone photo gallery.

Did she not have any credit or data? The other person was a young man who had been riding his bicycle; he had his headphones on and was obviously engulfed in whatever beat he was listening to. RJ looked at the man in the booth again and could not take it anymore; he had run out of patience. There were a lot of terrible things in this life, and one of them was inconsiderate people who were oblivious to the trauma their self-centred existence caused others. He walked past the other two as quickly as his pain would let him and opened the booth door. The man on the phone stopped talking and turned to RJ with a frown on his face.

"Do you mind?" the suited man asked in confusion.

This distracted the other two from what they were doing, and their focus switched to RJ and the man.

"As a matter of fact, I do mind. I think you've talked enough," RJ responded, trying to keep the look of pain from his face. He hoped he had not opened up the stitches.

The man's face took on an aggressive look of disbelief, "Excuse me?" he almost shouted.

"Yes, you are definitely excused," RJ responded coolly.

"But clearly I haven't finished," the man shouted, his eyes darting to the other two outside in a bid to elicit some sort of support. The two just continued to watch.

"Yes, you have. Save the rest for face-to-face," RJ replied; his tone steely.

The two engaged in about a ten second staring contest; the man angrily at RJ, and RJ steadily at the man. Within that short time, the man's expressions managed to change from that of anger to curiosity, and finally fear. He hurriedly told the person on the other end of the line that he would see him later and put the phone down. Without making eye contact, he quickly left the booth.

RJ nodded in satisfaction. He was nothing if not fair and so gave way to the woman as she was up next to use the booth, but she suddenly turned and walked briskly away just as the young man hurriedly got on his bicycle and rode off. He watched them leave with a look of innocence on his face. He then shrugged, went into the phone booth, and closed the door. It felt better in there as it shut out a bit of the cold. He then took a deep breath and proceeded to punch his mobile number in. He did not know what to expect or who was going to pick up, but it was worth a try. The number on the other end rang several times, and just as RJ was about to put the phone down, it was picked up. RJ stilled and said nothing.

He was waiting to hear the voice at the other end of the line. No word came, but he could hear breathing.

RJ decided to take a chance. "Hello."

The breathing quickened. "R… RJ… is that you?" Danny's shocked but hushed tone came back barely audible.

The office was about 1,250 square feet. Its walls were a rich bone china pale blue, and the grey stone marble tiles did not miss a reflection. On the left side of the office was a sitting room area that boasted a plush rug of a darker shade of grey to the tiles, including white leather sofas; a three-seater and two two-seaters. Several beautiful abstract paintings graced the left and right walls of the office, and behind the massive rectangle telluride black and reddish-brown executive desk, was simply a wall-to-wall glass window that overlooked the river Thames. However, the most prominent furniture in the room was the Yaros Keymat Diamond Panasonic screen that occupied the vast part of the right wall of the office.

Constable Fischer never ceased to be impressed by the sheer magnificence and luxury of the office. He stood, as he always did, in front of the huge desk while Alexander Fairchild sat quietly in his swivel chair behind it. He was dressed in an expensive Armani suit with an unreadable expression on his face.

Alex finally broke the long silence. "You say he was admitted last Wednesday?" Fischer nodded.

"How bad is this wound?" asked Alex.

"Bad, but he'll live," Fischer replied.

Alex gave a slow nod. "So he discharged himself yesterday against doctor's orders, and now you don't know where he is or might be?"

Fischer coughed. "Not yet. He hasn't been to his house, but we're keeping a look out." Alex sat back in his chair.

"Keep me updated," he ordered calmly.

"As always," Fischer said, taking that as his cue to leave.

"One more thing," Alex called out and Fischer turned around as he got to the door.

"Next time, don't wait five whole days to inform me about anything pertaining to Rhys." Fischer took the scolding in stride, nodded once, and left the office.

Chapter Four

Rachel followed closely behind Eva as she walked into the office kitchenette, which made Eva almost scream when she unexpectedly turned around.

"Goodness, Rachel! You startled me." Eva clutched her chest in relief.

Rachel's expression took on an apologetic one. "Oh, I'm so sorry. I didn't mean to frighten you. Just didn't want to miss you."

"What's up?" Eva asked, much calmer now as she turned to open the fridge and grab the ham and tomato sandwich she had made this morning.

"I guess you're not going out for lunch today?" It was more of a rhetorical question.

Eva shook her head. "I was planning to have my lunch at my desk; I have a deadline."

Eva worked in the marketing and advertising department of a publishing firm and thoroughly enjoyed what she did. She was very good at IT, specifically digital creation. Her brother Evan was equally good, but had chosen to go into core IT, working in the telecommunications industry. A year ago, there had been an opening for a marketing assistant role, and since Rachel had awesome administrative skills, Eva had helped her get a job in the company even though she did not have any marketing experience. It did help that Rachel was a fast learner with a super personality. She had thought that it would be a bit awkward working with her brother's girlfriend, but so far, she had been proven wrong.

"Maybe I can call you later tonight to talk about it?" asked Rachel, not wanting to keep Eva from her work.

Eva thought about it and decided she could spare a few minutes. "That's okay. What is it; are you okay?"

Rachel smiled. "Yes, I'm fine; nothing to worry about."

Rachel looked like she was wrestling with how to say what she wanted to say, or whether to say it at all.

Eva frowned and placed a hand on Rachel's shoulder. "Come on, Rachel, you can talk to me. What's bothering you?"

Finally, Rachel said, "I know it's not the place or time to talk about this, and maybe I shouldn't even be bothering you with it."

"Okay, just tell me what it's about, and we can discuss it further later tonight?" Eva leaned back on the kitchen counter near the sink.

Rachel took a deep breath. "I don't know where my relationship with Evan is going." She sounded distressed.

"What? Where is this coming from, Rachel? Did Evan do or say something?" Eva straightened up in concern.

Rachel shook her head. "It's what he's not doing that I'm worried about."

"How do you mean?"

Rachel looked candidly at Eva. "Eva, you know how desperately in love with your brother I am, right?" She continued when Eva nodded in confirmation. "I just want to know how he feels about me. I mean, I know how he feels about me, it's just… I'm not sure if he feels as strongly as I do, or if we want the same thing."

Eva looked slightly uncomfortable. "Are you talking about marriage?" Rachel nodded uneasily.

"Aww, Rachel, have you tried talking to him about this?" asked Eva, her heart going out to her.

"Hey, Eva, Rachel," greeted Adam Tomilson from the sales department, walking in just as Rachel was about to reply to Eva.

Rachel smiled at Adam in response, obviously unable to carry on her private conversation with Eva. Adam did not even notice as his attention was solely on Eva.

"Did you have a good weekend?" he enquired as he proceeded to make himself a cup of tea.

"Yes, thanks. You?" Eva responded, then quickly addressed Rachel. "Later then?"

"Yes, later," Rachel replied with a masked smile on her face and left the kitchenette.

Adam turned to Eva. "I had a busy weekend; had to babysit my young nephews. We did swimming, cinema, lunch and milkshakes; in no particular order."

Eva chuckled. "That's nice. How old are they?"

"They're nine and six. A bit of a handful, but it was great fun," grinned Adam.

"I'm sure it was, especially for you," Eva joked.

Adam smiled at her. He was not a bad looking man and was a couple of inches taller than her. "Right, I'm headed back to my office." Eva informed, making her way to the door.

"Errr, Eva, a group of us from work are off bowling on Friday after work. It will be nice if you could join us." Adam hurriedly said, his eyes almost pleading.

This was not the first time Adam had invited her out. She did not want to jump into conclusions about what he was up to as it was possible that he was only being friendly. After all, so far, he had not asked her out on a one on one. It was always with a group of others. However, it seemed more likely every time. Usually, Eva refused politely as she fortunately always had something else planned. She really did not want to lead him on, plus, she was not sure it was wise having a relationship with a colleague. Then again, it was almost rude to keep saying no, so she decided to be a little more positive.

"Can I get back to you by Thursday?" she asked.

This was more than he had ever received, and his eyes shone with hopeful joy. "Of course. I'll remind you on Thursday." He grinned.

Eva could not help but give him a genuine smile. He was a nice and decent guy from what she knew about him so far. He was good at his job and was not like some of the jerks at work. Who knows, she just might go along on Friday and get to know him better.

As she left the kitchen, her mind went to Rachel, and she made a mental note to give her a call tonight.

"I really think you need to discuss this with Evan, Rachel. You can't get yourself all worked up over something you haven't discussed with him yet," Eva said.

Rachel sighed. "The fact that he isn't even thinking about it is what worries me." Then she went on, "I'm afraid to bring it up in case he gets upset and it causes a strain that ruins our relationship."

Eva understood what she was saying and was glad she had rung Rachel that night as she had promised; it was clear that she was in deep distress about this.

"I totally understand your concerns and fears. However, how do you know he isn't thinking about it? He might not have brought it up yet, but you can bring it up too. It's something you both must want and discuss. Besides, if he gets upset about it, then that kind of tells you where he's at, doesn't it?"

There was silence at the other end of the line, and Eva knew Rachel was pondering on this. She looked at the time and saw that it was getting quite late, so she added, "I wouldn't mind finding a way to broach the topic with Evan, find out what he's thinking, but I really think you need to be the one doing this first."

Rachel remained silent.

Eva was sure Evan loved Rachel, so she did not think he would be upset if Rachel brought up the topic or could be averse to marrying her. "Pray about it before you talk to him. Place the burden in God's capable hands and stop worrying… please."

That seemed to work as Rachel sighed again. "You're right, Eva; that's always a good idea. Thank you for listening and being so supportive."

As Eva got ready for bed that night, she could not help wondering why Evan had not brought up marriage with Rachel. Was he not ready? He had a great job, lived in a lovely semi-detached bungalow that he could afford to pay rent for easily as he did not have the financial burden of children to worry about. Eva was renting too; she lived in a nice but somewhat spacious flat not too far from where her parents lived. There was no way Evan would be dating Rachel without the intention of eventually marrying her; she was almost sure of it… or was she?

The woman walked in the room with a Burger King bag in her right hand. She had a nice figure but looked older than her years. Her once pretty face had more lines than it should. She walked up to the bed and tossed the bag at RJ.

"Here you go," she said, watching him as he caught it and placed it beside him on the bed he was sitting on. He thanked her. "You need me to change the dressing on your wound?" she asked when he slowly clutched his side.

He shook his head. "I've already done it, thank you. Although, not as well as you've done it these past three days. Just took some more pain killers; they should be kicking in soon."

The woman looked satisfied to hear that. RJ opened the bag and pulled out a 'double-bacon extra-large' with fries. From the way he bit into the burger, it was obvious he was ravished. After wolfing down three mouthfuls, he reached for the cup of tea that had been sitting on a small writing table by the bed. Once he had taken a few gulps, he looked up at the woman who stood in the middle of the room watching him.

Lisa stared at his handsome face; she could not help herself. After five years, she still had not gotten over the crush she had on RJ. In fact, at some point, she was in love with him. Four years ago, when she worked the streets, RJ had been very helpful in getting her out of a lot of dangerous situations. She had wanted out of that life, and he and his gang had come to her rescue when the people she worked for threatened her. He was like her knight in shining armour; tall, gorgeous and in control. How could she not fall for him? She wasn't ashamed of how she had thrown herself at him. He had not taken advantage of her, which had made her want him even more. He was quite a lady's man and it had hurt her when he rejected her advances time and time again. However, over the years, they had become friends, and while she was not quite in love with him anymore, the crush stubbornly remained.

Lisa had later landed herself an honest paying job cleaning houses, which she did for two years before gaining employment working in a factory. She still worked there till today, and rather enjoyed her job. It was hard work, and she was very hard working.

Now that he needed her help, she certainly couldn't say 'No' to him… she didn't want to say 'No' to him. She was ready to do anything to help him. He needed a place to stay, and she was ready to put him up in her small flat for as long as he wanted. He looked at her with those deep blue eyes, wanting answers.

"My brother, Charlie, said your home is still being staked out, but he was able to sneak through the back door without being seen. He managed to grab some clothing and other things you asked for. He will come by later with them."

RJ sighed in relief, but then looked up at her again, "Did he say who was staking out my place? Was it the police or the men?" he asked.

Lisa frowned, "He didn't say. I assumed it would be some guys Nick is paying. Why would the police be staking out your house; what did you do?"

"Nothing; never mind." RJ shrugged it off. "I was just curious. They came to question me at the hospital; I just wondered if they were still looking for me to give a statement or something."

Lisa knew that RJ was not telling her everything. There had always been a mystery around him. She had never pried, and she was not going to start now. She sighed and asked, "So what are your plans now?"

"I told Danny to find your number on my phone. He's supposed to make contact when he gets the chance. Nick watches him like a hawk, so I don't know how he's going to manage that."

His voice suddenly took on a dangerous edge. "I will deal with Nick later; I just need to make sure Danny is safe; find a way to protect him."

"You really should give yourself an opportunity to heal properly first. I can get Charlie to do some snooping, find out if he's heard anything about the gang. I'm sure he wouldn't mind. You've always been good to him. It's the least he can do." She had added the last bit because she knew RJ would be thinking of Charlie's safety and refuse. He had refused Charlie going over to his place to help get a few things, but she had insisted.

RJ nodded reluctantly, "Just tell him to be careful, okay?"

Lisa nodded too. "Don't you worry. Eat up; I want to check the dressing on your wound. I have a feeling you haven't done it right."

RJ chuckled as he turned his attention back to his unfinished meal.

Chapter Five

Their team lost, but it was a good game. There had been two teams with five of them on each side. Eva made a mental note to brush up on her bowling. She hadn't thought she would have as much fun as she did, and really needed to get out more. She loved taking part in church activities and anything to do with charity or volunteer work, but she really needed to do a lot more socialising outside of that. She got to see the fun and quirky side of her colleagues; not to mention how charming Adam was.

"Are you joining us for a meal and drinks at the White Horse... my treat? It's only around the corner from here." Adam asked as they swapped their bowling shoes for their original ones.

Eva was certainly hungry, but she had planned to do some work organising the soup kitchen the church's hospitality committee was planning for next week. She had some left-over curry and rice she was planning to have as she worked on her laptop.

"Not tonight, sorry. Maybe another time...?" She replied, feeling tempted. Adam could not hide his disappointment.

"Big plans tonight?"

Eva shook her head. "Not really. My church is organising a soup kitchen next week in the youth hall, and I'm on the planning committee. I have to go through the budget, put together the meals, assign chores to the serving team, and get the printed flyers out."

Adam looked surprised. "Whoa! Sounds serious. So, you're a Christian? I really shouldn't be surprised. It's just that... you don't look it."

Eva turned to face him with a beaming smile. "How do you mean?"

Adam paused, trying to find the right words. "It's just, you look so... well... beautiful. You're classy and trendy."

Eva frowned. "You think Christians are ugly, tacky and unfashionable?"

Adam looked uncomfortable; obviously unhappy that he had begun this line of conversation.

He was saved briefly by their colleagues calling out to them to signal they were heading to the pub. Eva waved and Adam did a hand gesture back to communicate that he would be joining them in a bit.

Facing each other again, Adam did not know what to say. Eva was not upset with him and smiled again to reassure him.

"Thank you for the compliment, Adam. However, believing in God, accepting the sacrifice of His son, and striving to live a life characterised by love, doesn't mean you cease to be human or can't live an abundant life." When he remained silent, she went on, "People are individuals, everyone with their different personalities in the church, the mosque, the workplace, football team, within the family. You'll find people of all categories everywhere. Christianity isn't a cult; it's a belief, a faith. Besides, nobody is ugly on the outside. True beauty and ugliness can only be found on the inside."

Adam sighed, then smiled back at her. "I stand corrected. Anyway, I think you are beautiful inside and out."

Eva blushed slightly. "Thank you. Any chance you might want to stop by at the soup kitchen next week… to see what we do there?"

He looked sceptical. "Thought it was all about feeding hungry people?"

"Yes, definitely. It's also about reaching the troubled youths, the gangs out there, plus the homeless and runaway teens; offering them an avenue to get advice, shelter, food, a hot meal, warm blankets and clothing," she replied.

Adam considered this briefly, then shrugged. "Sure, why not."

He figured he made a great call judging by the beautiful smile that suddenly appeared on Eva's face.

"Great. We will be distributing flyers all through next week. I'll give you one on Monday."

He nodded, and they began moving towards the entrance. "I better head off to join the others before they order without me."

Rachel was nervous and deep in thought. She had prayed about it and decided today was the day she was going to bring up the topic with Evan – about where their relationship was going. She had invited him over to the three-bedroom house she shared with her two closest friends. Since her two friends were going to be away for the weekend, she thought she could have the kitchen to herself and make her version of a Thai Green curry with rice for lunch. He had arrived thirty minutes ago straight from his usual Saturday morning cricket game with a few of his old university mates.

Her hands shook a little as she emptied the water from the bowl of uncooked rice and turned on the tap to fill it up with water again for more washing. Her movement, though slightly shaky to the keen observer, was almost automated as she thought of how she was going to bring up the marriage issue with Evan. She must really love him for her to be as bothered as she was. She did not want this to put a strain on their relationship. Once again, she emptied the water from the bowl of rice.

"Gosh, babe, do you think the rice has been washed nearly enough times?" Evan asked as he watched her, his hands folded across his chest as he leaned against the kitchen counter.

She did not care much for his sarcasm, at least not at this moment. She had not even realised that she had washed the rice more times than was necessary.

"Just making sure I got as much of the starch out as I could," she responded, trying to cover up her unease.

She had meant to bring it up during lunch, but he was enjoying it so much and kept complimenting her that she did not want to ruin the mood. Once the meal was over, she was hoping they could settle down in the living room so she could find a way to ease into it.

However, just as they made their way into the living room, Evan pulled out his phone from his back pocket. "What do you think about us going to the cinema this evening? There are a lot of good films showing this weekend," he said, scrolling though the Odeon site from his phone.

No! No! No! That was not going to work. "That would be nice, but I was thinking more like just having a nice quiet day indoors spending time with each other."

He paused what he was doing and gave her a questioning look. "What's up? I get the feeling there's something on your mind."

This was it; her opportunity. "Do you ever think about the future?" she asked. He finally got off his phone and gave her his full attention.

"Of course, I do. Don't you?"

He did? Rachel could not believe it; how easy it seemed to be going.

"Yes, definitely. You know how much I like to know where I'm going and plan ahead," she replied.

Evan frowned. "Oh, come off it. So why are we almost always late to functions? You make the plans and yet keep me waiting forever for you to get dressed!"

She waved that off. "That's different, and you know it."

"Really? You tell me where we're going, you give me the time to come pick you up, I get here, and you're not ready. It's either a debate on whether you should let your hair down or pin it up, if the ankle boots go better than the knee length ones, or if the blue dress makes you look slimmer than the black." He shook his head disbelievingly. "No way could you have planned ahead."

Rachel stared at him. His tone wasn't serious, but she knew that he was, nonetheless. She was a little annoyed with him, especially as he was preventing the conversation from going where she wanted it to go. Besides, she always did plan ahead. She planned all the dress, shoe and hairstyle options. She only needed his help in deciding which option was best, and that could only be done when he was actually there.

"Well, shame on me for wanting to look good for you," she replied coolly.

At that, Evan's light brown eyes shone with warmth. He smiled, moved closer to her on the settee, pulled her into his arms and kissed her gently on the lips.

"I'm sorry I upset you, babe. You always look good to me," he said in that sweet tone of voice that always worked its magic on her.

She relaxed, smiled, and wondered if it was still possible to get back on track with their discussion.

"Come on, let's go see a film at Odeon. Go get yourself ready. I need to stop by at mine first to get changed. You can pick a film on the way."

Rachel sighed and got up slowly. It seemed she had lost her window. She must admit, it would be nice to forget about that burden for now and just relax and have fun with him. A little voice in her head told her she was being a chicken.

As she made her way out of the living room and upstairs to her bedroom, she heard him yell after her, "How about if I always arrive an hour earlier than you scheduled so we can get you sorted sooner? At least, that way, we wouldn't be late getting to functions."

Seriously? Rachel could have smothered him with one of the settee pillows if she had still been in the living room. Evan could be so infuriating sometimes;

the infuriating man that she loved with all her heart and wanted to spend the rest of her life with. She sighed loudly and slammed her bedroom door a little loudly behind her to send him a clear message on what she thought about his suggestion.

"You know you can stay at my place for a while, give Lisa here a breather," Ben Sharpe said; his flirty grin at Lisa not lost on RJ. Ben might be close to fifty, but he was still as tough as nails. It was to him that RJ had sold the pub he used to own, 'The Three Lions', although he still had some equity in it. RJ had opened the pub to distract him from his gambling addiction back in the day. That was a past he had planned never to revisit, and the pub had helped him to overcome that.

"I ain't complaining, am I?" Lisa retorted as she handed both men a bottle of beer each.

RJ smiled at Lisa. "Thanks, Lisa. However, at some point, I'm going to have to go stay somewhere else. I wouldn't want you to get caught in the middle of what's to come." He then turned to Ben with more seriousness "If you don't mind, I'll take you up on that offer when the time comes."

Ben nodded. He was good for it, and he would always have RJ's back.

Lisa joined them on the old worn sofa in her small living room.

"Charlie says Nick and Meltdown are definitely planning something, but he wasn't able to find out more. Two members of the gang have been hanging around the strip club he frequents," she informed.

Ben cursed. "I still can't believe Nick Payne would stab you in the back like that. I knew he was getting too big for his boots, but never thought he could step to you like that. His stab was meant to kill you, 'cos he knew he'd be in trouble if you survived."

"I did, and he is." RJ said in a steely voice.

"Charlie says some of the men are still loyal to you. The two men at the strip club seemed to be, but you can't be too sure." Lisa stated.

RJ nodded.

"Anyway…" Ben moved forward on the sofa. "I just think it's a stroke of luck that you were found…"

"More like a miracle." Lisa interjected. Ben looked sceptical at the term 'miracle'.

Lisa gave him a genuine look. "Look, I'm not a religious person myself, but that was definitely a miracle… literally. RJ saw lights, heard angelic music, and was practically saved by an angel."

Ben looked at RJ and laughed. "Really? You were bleeding out… probably on your way out, you were obviously delirious and seeing… hearing things."

RJ leaned back in the sofa. "I don't know if I was delirious or not. Maybe I was imagining the singing and lights, but the angel… the angel was very real."

Ben stared at him in disbelief. "What do you mean real?"

"She came to see me at the hospital a couple of days later, I think." RJ replied.

The chuckle that came after was from Ben. "You sure you weren't still delirious?"

RJ looked at him pointedly with a side smile. "I'm sure. Trust me; I have her face etched in my memory. You can't forget that face…" he trailed off; his eyes lost in some other world.

Lisa had seen him get that look before… when he had first told her about the encounter. She could not help but feel a little jealous of this angel, but not as much as she felt gratitude to her for saving RJ's life.

Ben looked like he was struggling to keep what RJ was telling him in perspective. He took a swig of his beer and decided to try a bit of sarcasm to bring things back to earth; literally speaking. "So, did she have wings… or maybe a halo?"

"Stop it, Ben." Lisa scolded with partial seriousness. "She was real; he spoke with her."

RJ's attention came back to Ben, and he also took a drink from his beer bottle. "No. No wings or halo; just a sense of peace and… well… something else about her." Plus, she had been… was absolutely beautiful. She seemed perfect, but how would he know this about her? He knew nothing about her. Maybe it might have been his imagination after all. Maybe he dreamt her up. Maybe Ben was right.

"Anyway…" RJ stood up slowly. "… I'm getting bored sitting indoors doing nothing. It's a Sunday; I need to get out there."

"You need to fully heal." Lisa warned, getting up to assist him. Ben got up as well.

RJ cursed. "Will you please stop fussing, the pair of you. I'm healing, but I could damn well do with some exercise, okay?" His voice was laced with frustration.

"Okay, okay." Ben threw his hands up in surrender. "But you could certainly do with a cane to support you for the time being. Lucky for you, I have one lying around somewhere."

Joyce loved having a part time job as a secretary. She enjoyed what she did, but mostly, she liked that she had the other half of the day to do whatever she wanted. Right now, she was happy to be giving out the flyers for the soup kitchen their church was organising. She had parked her car by the church and was taking a nice walk around Brixton road, dropping flyers where she could; handing them over to young lads who should be in school on this bustling Monday, but weren't, and people who appeared homeless.

She turned a corner and noticed a group of men smoking outside a kebab shop. There were probably five or six of them, but she was not really counting. It did occur to her that they might be a part of a gang, but Joyce was not scared. She had seen her fair share of gangs in Seattle, and in Atlanta where she had gone to university. The gangs were even worse out there. She walked right up to them. "Hello, fellas; you alright?"

They turned to her with curious expressions on their faces but said nothing.

She lifted up the flyers for them to see. "St Benedict church is organising a soup kitchen this Saturday. Hot food, warm blankets, stuff from the food cupboard if you boys are interested?"

Two of the men turned away, deciding that she offered nothing of interest to them. The tallest of the lot took a deep drag of his suspicious cigarette and raised an eyebrow as he took one of the flyers from her to study.

"Where are you from?" asked one of average height with a raspy voice.

Joyce got asked that question a lot when people heard her accent and was only too happy to oblige with an answer.

"Seattle," she replied with a smile. She got nothing but a curious stare… "It's in the United States. I'm from the United States," she elaborated.

The guys suddenly nodded in pretentious realisation. The tallest of the men gave her his full attention. Joyce noticed the deep scar running from his cheek to the edge of his earlobe.

"This Saturday, eh? Hot food?" he asked, seemingly sceptical.

Joyce was about to respond when another one of them with a shiny bald head interrupted her.

"Oh yeah, I know that church. You had something like that last year, didn't you?" he asked. He spoke quite well, like he had gone to school at some point in his life.

"That's right." Joyce nodded.

The bald guy turned to the tall guy. "Definitely for real, Meltdown." He confirmed as he took out one cigarette from the pack in his leather jacket pocket.

The tall guy with the scar called Meltdown, seemed to consider this. Then he spoke up to get the other guys' attention. "Hey, any of you lads fancy getting some free hot food on Saturday?"

They all seemed to shake their heads and he turned back to Joyce. "Well, that's that. 'Preciate the invitation though."

Joyce gave them a questioning side look. "You going to pass up free food stuff too?"

One of the guys who ignored her when she first approached turned to her in irritation. "Do we look hungry to you?"

Joyce was taken aback. This was the last thing she wanted; to upset them and scare them off. "No, no, I apologise. I didn't mean it to come across that way. Everyone likes free stuff... even me." She said quickly with a little laugh at the end.

"I'll go," came a voice that got all their attention. Joyce hadn't noticed the young man in the group until now. He was quite obviously the youngest of them, probably in his teens. He was about 5'6" tall with dark brown eyes and wavy dark hair that could do with a bit of a trim.

Meltdown raised his eyebrows. "Really?"

The boy had both hands dipped into his back jeans pocket, like he was trying to warm his hands from the cold. He seemed shy as he leaned forward, took out his right hand from his back pocket, and reached for the flyer Meltdown was holding.

"I've never been to one. Would be nice to see what other free stuff I can get besides a hot meal." He said this gently as he studied the flyer now in his hands.

It broke Joyce's heart to see a teenager like him hanging out with the likes of these men. He should not be here; he should be in school. He spoke well too. Where were his parents?

"Oscar, you'll go along with him on Saturday." Meltdown said authoritatively taking a deep drag of his cigarette that was nearing its finishing point. "Just to make sure he's safe," he added on second thought, and Joyce knew that was for her own benefit.

Joyce guessed the bald man was Oscar, because he nodded and then playfully placed his hand on the boy's head and ruffled his hair. She was glad the boy would be coming. She really hoped he could make it. They were going to be giving out some leaflets which included numbers for help lines and some encouraging scriptural passages.

The lad kept his eyes on the ground and shyly shuffled his right foot on the ground. Joyce smiled.

"What's your name?" she asked.

He raised his eyes up to look at her without quite raising his head. He then turned his eyes to Meltdown who was busy lighting another cigarette. Meltdown looked at him, gave Joyce one last assessing glance, then gave a short nod.

The boy turned to her. "Daniel. My name's Daniel."

Chapter Six

Nick Payne kicked repeatedly and violently at the front tyres of the black Ducati V4 S. He was full of frustration and rage. He wanted to destroy the bike as he hoped he had destroyed the owner. The bike had been hidden away in a business partner's garage. He planned to take it apart and sell the parts for whatever they can get. He just had not gotten around to it yet. He had a deal going down in a few weeks but had this terrible itch that he still could not scratch away, and it was driving him mad.

He finally stopped kicking as the bike toppled to the side. He turned to the four men in the garage with him, panting as perspiration beaded his forehead. He was not a very tall man at 5'5", but his mean look, and stocky stature still made him appear formidable. Nick's hands instinctively went to his hair to ensure every strand was still in place. His hair was one of his prized assets, along with his countless body tattoos. He kept it in a '70s style that he got from his favourite character 'Danny Zuko' in his favourite movie of all time 'Grease'. It was odd that he combed his hair like that and spent a fortune on hair gel, but no one dared say anything about it. The only person who had constantly made unappreciated jokes about his hair was RJ.

"RJ!"

He growled under his breath and then took deep breaths to compose himself. Finally, he turned to the four men standing in front of him in the garage.

"So 'e definitely ain't been to 'is pad? You sure you checked all the morgues, 'ospitals, every newspaper, an' that you asked 'round?" he enquired; a gruffness in his voice.

The men did not respond as they gave each other uncertain looks.

"What?" asked Nick. "Will one of you fuckin' speak up?" he shouted when they remained silent; obviously afraid to speak.

"Hey, boss." Meltdown called, as he joined them in the garage. "We shouldn't assume that Brixton is the only place to look. We might not find anything here, but then there's the whole of London, and it's a big place."

"Plus…" he went on, "We need to be careful about what questions we're putting out there. People are beginning to ask questions of their own, and we need to come up with answers for them. If anyone should know his whereabouts, people expect it to be us."

Nick sighed in exasperation.

"I thought we told people that 'e's missing an' we're trying to find 'im. We're supposed to make 'em think that any one of our enemies could've kidnapped 'im or taken 'im out." Nick asked as he waved his hand to dismiss the other men standing there. They turned and left quietly.

Meltdown nodded. "Yes; that's what we're doing, but how we go about it is also important." Nick put a hand across his face and slides it down with another heavy sigh.

"What if 'e's alive? What' if 'e survived? We might 'ave a big problem on our 'ands. 'E'll be coming for us." Nick said, more to himself than to Meltdown.

Meltdown folded one arm across his side, rested the elbow of his other arm on it and stroked his stubbled chin.

"There's no way he could have survived that. The knife went in pretty deep. He was passed out, it was late… in a secluded area, and would have bled to death." Meltdown said.

"If he was dead by the time his body was found, they wouldn't know who he is, would they? It might take them a while to identify him. Besides, not all deaths are reported in the newspapers or on TV." Meltdown reassured.

That seemed to offer Nick some sort of comfort, but then he said, "I should've done it be'er; dug that' knife into 'im several times to make sure. I should've watched 'im die."

"It all went down so fast. Danny boy flew into a panic and was out of control. We had to hurriedly get out of there and not create a scene that would have alerted people." Meltdown reminded him.

Nick looked away shaking his head in frustration. "Danny boy should've ne'er been there. But, oh no, god forbid that 'e is ever out of RJ's damn sight." Nick spat out.

Meltdown said nothing.

Nick turned to him again "You keep a close eye on 'im. We need to know we can trust 'im to get over this an' not tell the rest of the gang what' 'appened. RJ 'as too many people who are loyal to 'im. Those people are loyal to me now as long as they don't know the truth. Got it?"

Meltdown nodded. "Don't worry, boss. He seems to be cooperating. We're all he has. He's got nowhere else to go."

Reverend Bainbridge was getting ready to leave after their usual Wednesday evening service. Eva was heading home too. She normally liked to stay to help out with clearing up and getting some things organised for the coming Sunday, but she was tired. Last weekend had been very busy for her, and work had gotten really stressful of late. James had been kind enough to ask her to leave it all to him.

She had really enjoyed the sermon that evening. It had centred on service, not only in your local community, but reaching beyond… into other boundaries. Not just preaching the gospel but showing the gospel in service of love.

The choir practice had begun, and she heard the sweet familiar piano intro to the hymn 'Great is Thy Faithfulness', just before the beautiful voices of the choristers joined in, as she came out of the church and walked quickly to catch up with the reverend.

The seventy-year-old widower, who had lost his beautiful hearted wife to breast cancer four years ago, had gone through so many trials in his life, but had been able, through the grace of God, to come through it all with a stronger faith. If he had not been tested, how could he have been strong enough to preach hope to others who were going through storms in their lives? He was remarkably sharp and sprightly for his age despite the aging wrinkles on his face and the much-receded hairline of his completely white hair.

She got to him as he reached his car. Hearing footsteps behind him, he turned around. He smiled warmly at her.

"Great sermon today, as usual, Reverend," she said.

"Thank you, my child. We do as the Lord leads," he responded.

There was such a warm and peaceful air about him. He was a truly good man, and she found it easy to talk to him, to be encouraged by him, as did others too.

"You're leaving earlier than usual," he stated as he opened the back door to his VW Golf Estate and deposited his bag and some paperwork in the back seat.

"Yes, I'm feeling very tired. I want to have an earlier night," she replied.

He turned back to her. "I do really appreciate all your hard work in the Church Eva. You are doing a very good job, especially with the planning of the soup kitchen coming up on Saturday," he said with genuine gratitude in his eyes.

She smiled. "That's okay. I do enjoy it. All is finally set for Saturday. The doors open at twelve noon. We should be running till about six thirty pm, at the latest. There are two shifts, but I will be there all day," she informed him, knowing he would appreciate the update.

There were different church departments with their own heads to deal with specific areas regarding the running of the church and its achievement of its core goals. That way, the reverend was not bogged down with other matters but was free to focus on the spiritual growth of the church. He was, however, kept up to date and had the final decision regarding most things. Besides him, there were two other junior reverends that played their roles in the church.

"Brilliant! I shall, no doubt, be there once I have gotten Sunday's sermon and service planned out," he said, pleased that all was in order.

There was a chill tonight. Eva shivered and pulled her coat more snugly around her. She supposed it was expected, as they were smack in the middle of October and autumn had finally giving way to the winter cold.

"Your sermon got me thinking more about the missionary trip to Africa the Church was looking into for January next year. It's something I've been seriously considering." She decided to get straight to the point. She did not want to keep herself and the reverend out too long in the cold.

He nodded. "Yes, a number of you have expressed interest, and it pleases my heart to know this." He went on, "You must realise that it is for six months, and it will be in a local village there… where help is needed. We have not yet decided on whether it will be Zimbabwe or Kenya. We have forged some friendships in both countries, and our plan is to help them start up or grow their churches. The Kenyan village already has a church, but the one in Zimbabwe is struggling to build one, and I'm not talking about the building. I mean the people, because the people make up the church."

He paused for a bit and then continued, "We don't have enough people or church funds to put towards both right now. We will work on one for six months… probably even a year, and then the other the year after. We want to reach out to these people, feed the hungry, give to the poor, help the needy, encourage the broken hearted, be companions to the lonely, support the sick, uplift the faithful, bring back the lost, and strengthen the weak. It's what Jesus did, and what God has called us to do." He sounded so passionate, so lost in his vision, like he was on the pulpit.

Eva smiled as her eyes got teary; his passion was infectious as it was touching.

He then looked at Eve with gentle eyes. "You have to be sure it's what you want to do. You will be leaving the comfort of your home, family, and life for probably a year. What about your job? Is there a special person in your life, maybe? These are all things you need to consider."

Eva nodded. There was a lot to consider; a special person in her life… besides her family? Not at all. She thought about Adam, who seemed to seek her out every day at work this week and call her up every evening since last Friday night when she gave him her phone number just before they had said their goodbyes. He was a really nice guy, and she was beginning to like him a little. Who knew where their friendship might be a month from now? However, for now, it was nothing; nothing to keep her from being a part of the missionary work in Africa. Plus, she wasn't sure they were compatible. Would he embrace Christianity like she has?

"I still can't believe you haven't brought it up with Evan yet." Eva said as they walked back to the office after having a lovely lunch at Chiquito, a Mexican restaurant not too far from their office. Adam had wanted to take her out to lunch, but she had sadly declined since she already had plans to go for lunch with Rachel that day. She had, however, promised to go out with him for lunch the next day, and he had been happy with that. Rachel glanced at Eva. She still could not get over how much she and Evan looked alike and still managed to wear their genders so perfectly well; he was very male, and she was very female. Eva had her curly mass pulled back in a ponytail which showed off her delicate features and pretty face. Her clothes always seemed to flatter her perfect figure, no matter what she wore. Eva was a very modest dresser, but still managed to pull off a sexy look. Rachel knew she was insecure about herself, which made her even more insecure about her relationship with Evan. Evan was not just good looking, but a very hot guy. In fact, most times, she wondered what he was doing with her… why her? She wished she was a lot slimmer and not as curvy, had a pretty face like Eva, had Eva's figure…

"Rachel, are you even listening to me?" Eva's voice cut through Rachel's thoughts and Rachel felt guilty that she had been lost in her idolisation of Eva… her envy of her. What was wrong with her? It was so wrong for her to be having these thoughts and feelings. She did not want to feel jealous or envious, or whatever that emotion was. She admired Eva, but it would be a sin to idolise her.

"I just haven't been able to find the right time." Rachel replied, turning her attention back to the pathway and their walk back to the office.

She knew it was an excuse and that Eva knew it was too.

Eva sighed. "As long as the issue bothers you, there's no right time to bring it up. There's only the wrong time. Just don't bring it up if you two ever happen to get into an argument, because that would be the wrong time."

Rachel blinked. Eva was right. "You know, for someone who's had only one serious relationship in university, you are very good with giving relationship advice."

Eva grinned. "I did date David till way after Uni. It only ended about five or six years ago; thank you."

Rachel laughed. "Only? That's a long time to be single, Eva."

They both waited for a car to drive past, but then waved at the driver in gratitude when he stopped to allow them to cross over to the other side of the road.

"I got caught up in my walk with God, and haven't found the right person, I guess."

"I have heard about your relationship with David. Evan said you two were so close. What happened, and are you still in contact with him?" Rachel asked.

"We grew apart, I think. We both wanted different things. I wanted to be more involved in the church, and he wanted… well he didn't want that. It was a sad but friendly break up. He lives in Australia now. We don't communicate much, but I know he is still single, and has a daughter from a relationship that didn't work out." Eva answered.

They were almost at the office.

Rachel did not understand how someone like Eva could still be single. She knew there must be countless men constantly asking her out. She always managed to turn heads wherever she was. Rachel had noticed a few men do just that at the restaurant, and on their walk.

"What about Adam? He's not bad, and he seems to fancy you." Rachel said. Eva shot her a quick look that practically asked; how did you know about Adam?

"Pleassse; the guy is besotted with you. He has been for a while. Practically everyone in the office knows. He isn't hiding it." Rachel explained, giving Eva a 'like-you-didn't-know' look of her own.

Eva's face took on the look of a half-smile, half frown. "Nothing's going on. We're just getting to know each other; that's all. I do wish he would keep things private. Office relationships make me uneasy."

"Or maybe he makes you feel uneasy." Rachel joked. Eva slapped her arm playfully.

"Are you coming to our soup kitchen event on Saturday?" Eva enquired in a bid to change the subject as they approached the office entrance.

Rachel shook her head. "Unfortunately, we won't be there. Wish I could, but one of Evan's office co-workers is getting married on Saturday, and I'll be going with Evan."

As Eva held the office door open for Rachel to enter first, she could not help but wonder how Rachel must feel about attending weddings with Evan when she was so unsure about whether or not they will be having one of their own someday.

Lisa was panting heavily by the time she stood outside the door of her flat. She had run up three flights of stairs and she was exhausted. She could not remember the last time she had run like this. She was definitely not in shape. Granted, she was not slim, but she was not curvy either. She hurriedly tried to get her keys from her handbag with one hand as she clutched tightly to her mobile phone with the other.

She was trying so hard, but for some reason, she just could not get her key in the keyhole. "Wasn't that the right key?" she asked herself frantically still trying. Her bag suddenly dropped to the floor with a loud thud, and she swore.

Suddenly, the door was flung open.

RJ stared at her with concern. His eyes were wide, and he had a foreboding expression on his face. "Are you alright?" he said, stepping out to look to the left and right.

She nodded and shoved her phone at him, still trying to catch her breath.

Still looking suspicious, he bent down, a bit uncomfortably, to help pick up her bag which had its content spilt out on the floor.

"No. You take the call." She managed to catch her breath. "Too much time wasted already."

It was just as well that the call came in just as she got off at the bus stop that, lucky for her, was just a two-minute walk to the block of flats that she lived in. Ten seconds, if you are running, she noted.

RJ put the mobile phone to his ear. Silence! Lisa stared at him. "Hello." RJ finally said.

"RJ?" Danny's relieved but impatient voice responded at the other end of the line.

"Danny. Oh, my goodness; am I glad to hear your voice, mate."

Lisa breathed a sigh of relief that Danny was still at the other end of the line. Her marathon was worth it. Ben had helped RJ purchase a new phone, but Danny did not have that number yet.

She bent to pick up the contents of her bag from the floor as RJ went inside the house to have the conversation.

Once she had gotten everything back in her bag, she closed the door, used her key to lock and unlock the door, and it worked.

"Typical," she said, unlocking the door and entering the flat.

"Okay. Don't worry, I'll be there," she heard RJ say as she dropped her bag on the sofa and slumped into it. She needed to rest a bit, plus she wanted to listen in on the phone conversation. She felt she had earned it, even though she could only hear one side of it.

RJ stood in her tiny living room. His tall and well-built frame seemed to make her living room seem tinier than it already was.

"Yes, I'm fine. And you; are you okay?" asked RJ. "Oscar, eh? That's fine. We'll handle Oscar," RJ assured.

"I know the place. Between 1pm and 2pm. Got it. And Danny…" RJ started to say, and then paused.

"Okay, okay. See you on Satur…." RJ looked at the mobile phone, and then slowly gave it back to Lisa.

His eyes looked more alive than they had been these past few days.

"He had to get off the phone hurriedly," he said. "Thank you for that. You're a real gem, Lisa."

Lisa waved him off with her hand. "So, what did he say?" she asked.

"He said to meet him at some church in Brixton the day after tomorrow. I think I know that church. There's some charity thing going on there. They're going to be feeding hungry people or something like that. Anyway, obviously several people will be there, which will offer some distraction. He managed to get Meltdown's permission to go there. He'll be on Oscar's leash, but we'll find a way around that; not a problem."

"So, what exactly is the plan?" Lisa asked.

RJ walked to where his phone lay on a stool and picked it up. He could not yet stand straight to his full 6'2" height, but Lisa couldn't believe how fast RJ was healing. His sheer determination and inner strength had a lot to do with his speedy recovery. He still had pains and needed more time to heal properly, but he was doing very well.

"I'm going to give Ben a call now so we can strategize."

Chapter Seven

———∽———

"I must admit that when you said you wanted to take me out to lunch, McDonald's never even crossed my mind. Not that I mind." Eva laughed as Adam pulled into the fast-food drive-through.

He smiled. "I didn't say I wanted to take you out to lunch, I said let's have lunch together." He corrected with a mock frown.

She gave him a doubtful look. "Really?" she asked.

"Why would I take you out for an hour's lunch? I would rather take you out for dinner on the weekend. I want the office lunch time meal to be a casual one. That way, there's time to talk and relax without the fear of getting back to the office late."

"Ah, that makes perfect sense." She laughed again.

After they had gotten their orders, he parked in a parking bay and then indicated that they would be eating in the car.

Eva was perfectly fine with that.

"So, Eva, I've been meaning to ask; are you single?" Adam suddenly asked.

Eva finished chewing and took a sip of her diet coke. "I wouldn't be here with you, if I wasn't," she responded.

This made Adam smile broadly. "Are you implying that there's more between us than friendship?"

Eva gave him a 'don't-be-silly' look. "No. I'm saying that, if I wasn't single, going out to lunch with a male colleague and eating a meal with him in his car, would be very inappropriate."

"I see," Adam said, scoffing down fries into his mouth.

There was an awkward silence after that as they ate their meals.

Adam sipped the last drops of his drink, rumpled up the paper bag and then turned in his seat to face Eva fully. She was done with her burger by now and was only now eating her fries.

"So, were you born a Christian, or was it a conscious decision later in your life?"

Eva gave him a side look. "You make it sound like being a Christian is a kind of medical condition. Like you are either born with it or develop it later."

"Oh. My bad," he said apologetically.

She thought about it. "Hmm… I don't think anyone is ever born a Christian. You can be born into a Christian family, but being a Christian is a conscious decision that you have to make when you're mentally and spiritually responsible enough to do so."

He nodded in understanding. "So, your family, are they all Christians?"

She nodded as she put more fries in her mouth. "Yes, I come from a Christian home, and we all believe in the faith. When my brother and I were old enough, we decided to leave the old church our parents attend and find one that was more rewarding to us spiritually."

He went quiet, and she was forced to ask, "Have you ever been to church? Do you have any family members who are Christian?"

He looked straight ahead as he remained quiet for a little longer, and then spoke, "I have been inside a church for a friend's wedding, and then a year and a half later, for his son's baptism. However, I wouldn't say that I have been to church, nor do I have any family members that are Christian; at least, none that I know of."

Eva suddenly felt the need to invite him to her church to attend a service one Sunday. However, she thought she had better not, he had agreed to come to the soup kitchen, which was a start.

Eva checked to see if everyone serving food had arrived. It looked like they had. She felt comfortable in her stone washed jeans, fitted t-shirt, sneakers, and her hair in a neat ponytail. She was ready to take on the world.

The different foods were neatly arrayed on electric food warmers. They had chicken soup, beef stew, white rice, chicken curry, pork 'n beans, salads and sandwiches. They had extras of everything as they had contracted a caterer. That was the hot food section.

There was also the drinks section which was being manned by Josh from church. This section had countless packs of water and canned non-alcoholic drinks.

Eva smiled as she went past Joyce who was overseeing the food cupboard section; where they had a lot of canned foods to give away. Three items per person so that everyone got something.

There was a section that gave away warm blankets, old jackets and clothing that were still in good condition, thanks to the generous donations of many people within and outside the church.

The last section was the information and help section. There was a long table with tracts and flyers that had hot numbers for help, advisory lines, and websites. Mini Bibles were available for those who chose to have one. In addition, the people assigned to that table were ready to listen to people who needed someone to talk to. There was a register where they could fill in their names and details, should they opt to.

The youth hall was attached to the church but had its own entrance. It was days like this that confirmed how spacious it really was; it was able to accommodate so much and so many people. The heating was on, and soft gospel music played in the background. They were ready to open the doors.

There was something about the ambiance in the hall; something inviting, peaceful… almost homely about it. Friendly faces to meet you at the entrance, soothing music… and the lovely aroma of different foods hit him hard; his stomach growled in hunger. Danny heard Oscar whistle beside him.

"Damn! Is that beef stew I smell?" asked Oscar excitedly.

Danny turned to the older man and wondered. Was that all he saw, the food? Didn't he get something else from the vibe here?

Oscar gave Danny a short tap on the back. "I say we get our bellies full first, and then wander to the section with the clothing and canned stuff later. I wonder if there's any alcohol."

"This is a Church." Danny said, giving an oblivious Oscar an irritated side glance. He did not know much about churches and all, but he knew enough not to expect to find alcohol here.

"Whatever!" replied Oscar, making his way to the food section, fully expecting Danny to be right behind him.

Danny's eyes scanned the room. There were quite a number of people in there. He hoped he would be able to spot RJ soon, but he had to lose Oscar first. Not that the hall was big enough to prevent Oscar from finding him in a short period of time, but he needed to get him distracted long enough. Unfortunately, there was no alcohol. His only other weakness was a pretty woman. Oscar loved women, and the prettier, the better.

Danny looked around again, and then he spotted one. She was certainly very pretty; too pretty for the likes of Oscar, to be honest. She was talking to an elderly woman and then gave her a warm hug. Once she had finished with the elderly woman, he started to walk towards her. As he approached, she immediately noticed him and gave him the warmest and sweetest smile he had ever seen.

"Hi there. You alright?" she asked.

He nodded but didn't say more. Danny didn't like to talk much but preferred to remain in quiet observation.

"Are you here alone?" the pretty lady asked curiously. Danny shook his head shyly.

"You've never been to one of these before, have you?"

"No." Danny managed to say.

She looked directly into his eyes and smiled again. Danny was taken aback. It was weird, but he thought he saw love in her eyes; like she cared. How could she care about him? She didn't even know him. "My name is Eva, and you are?" "Daniel," he responded, feeling a little more comfortable around her. "Nice to meet you, Daniel." She patted him on his left arm.

"So, are you hungry? There's plenty of food."

Suddenly he felt bad for thinking of using her like this. She seemed so nice and did not deserve to have Oscar drooling all over her.

His silence made her ask, "Or would you prefer to talk?"

Danny thought about quickly making some excuse and moving on when he suddenly felt a slap on his back.

"Oi; I thought I told you before we got here to stick close." Oscar said angrily, one hand balancing a paper plate laden with food.

There was a slight pause when Oscar noticed that Danny was not alone. His anger disappeared and his face took on one of charm.

"And who's this gorgeous thing?" he asked, his attention leaving Danny and settling fully on Eva.

Eva smiled again. "Are you Danny's father?" she enquired.

Danny was not too happy right now. Why had he walked up to her? Why hadn't he left quickly before Oscar found him?

Oscar laughed. "His father? Do I look that old? Nah. I'm more like a big brother. Very big brother," he responded, putting emphasis on the last phrase.

Eva looked like she was trying to maintain her smile, and Danny was about to do or say something to get him and Oscar away from her, when he noticed something familiar from the corner of his eye. Was that Ben?

Danny looked harder. It was Ben. He was casually talking to two men and then glanced towards the information table. Danny followed his gaze, not concentrating on whatever conversation Eva and Oscar were having. There was nothing out of the ordinary about the few people around the information table. Two ladies, an old woman, two young guys and an elderly man were being attended to by the church people. However, there was something familiar about the elderly man's back. That was not the back of an elderly man. He had thought he was elderly because he wore a tweed cap and was holding a cane… like a walking stick. The man turned his face partially, and Danny caught a glimpse of his side view. RJ!

Relieved and overjoyed, he turned to Oscar and mumbled something about going to get some food. Oscar nodded without giving Danny so much as a brief look.

Danny made his way to where RJ stood at the table and then nudged him.

Rachel did not always feel beautiful, but today, she felt it. She was wearing a knee length purple two layered satin dress which complimented her curvy figure. The round neckline and three-quarter sleeves were made from flower-patterned lace. She had on thin black tights and glittery silver pumps that matched her glittery silver clutch bag.

Last night, she had put her hair in rollers and kept it on overnight, which resulted in its shiny full bouncy waves after a quick blow dry this morning. Make up, a set of white pearl earrings and a necklace, completed her look. She had paid special attention to her outfit and getting ready for this wedding. She did not really know the groom very well as they had met only a handful of times at office functions and another of Evan's colleague's birthday party. She had been feeling so insecure as of late that she just wanted to give herself a boost. Not that she was going to outshine the bride, but possibly try to be on a par with the other beautiful women that were bound to be in attendance as well, and possibly get Evan's undivided attention. She was craving for a wedding of her own so bad, that attending someone else's was a little uncomfortable for her. She needed to feel good about herself; to feel confident.

Evan looked just as handsome as she expected him to… as he always did. He didn't even have to try. Wearing a fitted midnight blue suit and tie, he looked very distinguished.

When he arrived to pick her up, he had not even noticed that she was ready on time… for a change. He had mostly stared at her and looked restless; like he was in a hurry to head off to the wedding venue. The ride there was uncomfortably silent, and Rachel wondered what was going on with him. So much for trying her best to look beautiful for him! He had not noticed beyond whatever it was that was obviously bothering him. It would be nice if he could share it with her, instead of acting like she did not exist. Did she not look beautiful enough for him?

Was there someone else? Was he thinking of breaking up with her? Her initial feel-good high had now dropped.

The wedding reception was at a lovely hotel in south Kensington. It was simply gorgeous and well decorated with an assortment of daisies and calla lilies on each table. The hall was a perfect venue for a wedding. The recently married couple had had a short wedding ceremony in Thailand during the summer, and this was the reception that had been pending. It was certainly worth the wait, she thought.

Evan was a different person once he had arrived and was among his colleagues. He either hugged the ladies or kissed them on the cheek. Rachel could not remember if she got a hug when he arrived to pick her up. They were all stunning in their beautiful size six and eight dresses, looking like they should be on the cover of Vogue.

Rachel sighed. This is exactly how she did not want to feel. She smiled and exchanged pleasantries with his friends, some of whom she had already met before.

When they were finally seated, he looked uncomfortably at her again. Rachel frowned. He was really making her feel uneasy.

She leaned closer to him. "Is everything okay?"

He nodded. "Sure. Why wouldn't it be? Are you okay?"

She nodded, sighed, and relaxed back in her chair. *Fine! Let him be like that then.*

She picked up her wine glass and decided to ignore him. Beverley, one of his beautiful colleagues, was sitting on his right side. She said something to him that made him laugh, and Rachel found herself getting annoyed. Luckily, Scott was on her side, and she knew he was single and quite notorious with the ladies. She also knew deep down that what she was about to do was wrong, but at this moment, she did not care. She turned to Scott, gave him a full smile, and began to flirt.

The food had been delicious, the music soothing and she had had more alcohol than she would normally have. She was not drunk. She was not even tipsy, but she was not as clear headed and sober as she should be. She chatted a lot with Scott, laughed a bit too much at the best man's funny speech, and could not be bothered about the annoyed, confused and even irritated glances and stares Evan threw her way.

"You seem to be having a great time," he stated sarcastically. He did not lean close, but she heard him clearly.

She gave him a very brief look, picked up a glass of water and said, "Aren't you?"

He studied her for a bit and then opened his mouth like he was about to say something, but then closed it again and shook his head wearily.

Rachel felt so frustrated with him. Why won't he just talk to her? He seemed to be having a better time with his work colleagues, particularly the female ones, than with her. He chatted with them a lot more.

Just then Scott, who had been away from their table for a while, came back. He had a bottle of champagne in his hands. Another one from the bar? Their table had had more than enough already.

He looked pleased with himself. "Now don't say I don't know how to keep a party going." He laughed with boyish pride as the others cheered him. Rachel stole a look at Evan. He did not seem impressed or amused.

Scott topped up the eager glasses of some of the others, plopped into the chair beside her and filled her glass as well. Rachel really did not want any more. Scott lifted his glass to Rachel. She glanced briefly at Evan. He had an unreadable but serious look as he glanced back at her. Her frustration suddenly got the better of her; she picked up her glass, turned to Scott and gave a big smile. "Cheers!"

RJ felt a nudge and turned quickly. Danny boy stood beside him with a pleased look on his face. Relief washed all over him. He grabbed Danny by the shoulder and looked him over. He looked well. Then he pulled him in for a big hug.

When they separated, Danny asked, "How's your wound?"

RJ let Danny assess him, and then chuckled. "Don't worry. I'm almost as good as new."

Danny shook his head in wonder. "It's unbelievable. I was convinced you couldn't have survived that."

RJ nodded. "You and me both." There was a moment of seriousness in the air; the realisation that that could truly have been the reality.

"Now you're stomping around like an old man." Danny half laughed, clearly trying to change the mood.

RJ grinned as he twisted the object of Danny's mockery in his right hand, his walking stick.

"Ben gave it to me. It keeps me steady for now and helps take the pressure off my side. I won't need it for too long."

RJ sighed and looked at Danny enquiringly. The lad was a few inches shorter than him, but did not have to bend his neck to look at him "So... where's Oscar?"

"Found a way to keep him preoccupied." Danny replied. He sounded both proud and guilty.

"How?" RJ asked curiously. He did not want to take any chances.

"I left him with a pretty woman." Danny said, his gaze automatically moving to an area in the room.

Instinctively RJ followed Danny's gaze. There was Oscar, with an empty plate in his hand, talking and laughing with his mouth full. His eyes held a glow of hunger, the kind you see in the eyes of an animal who had his prey in sight. RJ's gaze now extended to the poor prey. She laughed, a bit uncomfortably, at something Oscar said. He squinted and kept his gaze on her. He knew that face. For some reason, his heart skipped a bit. He froze. It was her, his angel... the angel.

Someone tapped him on the shoulder. "Hey, RJ."

He turned to find Ben beside him. He and Danny were looking at him curiously.

RJ tried to give them his full attention, but the awareness of Oscar and the woman weighed on him like a massive rock.

"My men are all over this place like a rash and it seems Oscar's the only one here with Danny boy." Ben informed.

Danny nodded. "Meltdown trusts Oscar completely. I think he kind of trusts me too… a little."

"I guess he figured a church event was nothing to be too cautious about." Ben concluded.

RJ looked over to where Oscar stood with the woman.

"We need to find a place to talk. We don't know how much longer he will be with the woman." RJ said.

He felt a little uneasy about Oscar talking to her. Watching them together stirred a flame of anger within him. Damn! Calm down. He told himself. He did not really know her. Oscar was a monster, and she was an angel. He needed to get her away from him… or maybe him away from her. Either way, he was only trying to protect her from things that she should not and didn't need to be a part of. That must be why he felt uneasy. Yes, that was it!

"Murdering Oscar wasn't part of the plan." Ben said.

That got RJ's full attention. What in the world was Ben talking about?

"I never said we had to kill Oscar. What are you on about?" asked RJ confused.

"Well you certainly look like you'd like to," retorted Ben.

RJ quickly looked at Danny to reassure him. "No one has plans to kill anyone, okay?" "Not unless we have to." He added under his breath looking towards Oscar.

Danny sighed. "I can see you don't like that he's talking to Eva. I feel guilty too. She seems super nice… and too fit for the likes of him."

Eva! Her name's Eva, he thought. At that point, Oscar laughed loudly, and RJ had had enough. "Okay. We need to get him away from her." RJ said suddenly.

"Why? He's hardly going to hurt her… and certainly not here?" Ben asked in a 'don't-be-ridiculous' tone.

"Probably not, but I'm more likely to hurt him… and definitely here." RJ said as he started to make his way to where they stood.

Ben and Danny quickly followed him. "What has gotten into you, RJ? This wasn't the plan." Ben hissed.

"Change of plans," RJ replied, not breaking a stride even as he used his walking stick.

"Don't, RJ. He thinks you're dead." Danny exclaimed in a whisper.

"Well, Oscar's favourite series is the 'Walking Dead'." RJ retorted.

They were almost close, and then RJ suddenly paused and turned to face Ben and Danny. He felt he owed them some explanation.

"It's her," he said.

Danny and Ben exchanged confused looks. RJ didn't know how to explain it.

"It's my… the angel."

Danny and Ben stared at him, totally lost. RJ opened his mouth to say more…

"I thought I recognised you. Daniel! Right?" The female voice was cheery, loud, and strongly accented.

The black woman had a very boisterous disposition, and he could tell straight away that she was American. Well, the American accent helped too.

As the three of them had been caught unawares, they had no immediate response. She smiled at Ben then at RJ, and her eyes finally settled on Danny boy. RJ and Ben looked at Danny as it seemed he obviously knew who she was.

Danny shyly scratched his forward. "Yes. Thank you for the invite."

"I hope you're enjoying it. I see you brought some more of your clan. Have you had something to eat?"

The woman said so much so fast.

RJ stepped forward with a smile of his own. That smile that weakened women at the knees. "Why, hello, and what's your name?"

She smiled right back, not immune to RJ's winning smile. "Joyce."

He nodded. "Joyce! Lovely name. Joyce, would you mind showing Danny here to the food section? He was just saying how hungry he is as he didn't have any breakfast this morning."

"Of course, I wouldn't mind. Poor thing must be starving." Joyce said, grabbing hold of Danny's arm and leading him away, unaware of the upset look he shot RJ.

Now that he had gotten Danny away for the time being, he said to Ben "That's the lady who saved my life."

"Who? The Joyce woman?"

RJ shook his head impatiently. "No, the woman talking with Oscar." Realisation dawned on Ben's face. "Ah… she's the angel."

RJ nodded. "I'm sorry, but I feel the need to get her away from Oscar."

Ben looked at where Oscar stood with the woman, thought about it for a few seconds, then said,

"Fine. You approach him alone. I will be close by, should you need me. I hope you know what you're doing."

"Of course, I don't know what I'm doing, but thank you. It's good to know you've got my back, either way," RJ responded.

Chapter Eight

—————～————

Eva was beginning to buckle under the strain of her forced smile. The Oscar guy was coming on a bit too strong, and she desperately needed to get away from him. She had tried to get to know more about him; to see which areas he might need help and offer guidance. However, it seemed that he needed help in all areas. He came across as having had some sort of education though, but Eva had not been able to get any information out of him except the impression that he lived a somewhat reckless life, and that he thought he was funny and God's gift to women. He wanted to know everything about her; what she did for a living, where she lived, and even asked her if she was 'hitched'. Eva knew she did not want to spend any more time talking to him. She had other things and people to tend to. Besides, she wondered if Adam had arrived yet. Forgive me Lord, she said in her head as she realised, she was no longer paying attention to what Oscar was saying.

"Is this friend of mine bothering you, by any chance?" A tall figure joined them.

The first thing Eva noticed was Oscar's reaction; it was that of sudden and raw bewilderment… and of unadulterated fear. She then turned to look at the man who had brought this on. It was her turn to look shocked, probably not for the same reason as Oscar. It was him; the injured man she had rescued on the church steps. What was his name again? RJ. The constable had mentioned it, she recalled. She did not think she would ever see him again. Somehow, she had not forgotten about him. He had been somewhere at the back of her mind. She had only seen him twice, and he had been sprawled on his back both times. This was the first time she was seeing him standing. Her assessment of him the first time was nothing compared to her assessment now. He was tall and even more attractive than he looked when she saw him at the hospital. Was this lust she was feeling? God help her; she was having all the wrong feelings today. She looked him over. He seemed to have recovered… or almost recovered, judging from the cane he held in his right hand.

"The fuck is this?" Oscar forced out in alarm and trepidation, breaking the awkward silence.

RJ put his left arm around Oscar's shoulder and gave him a friendly smile, which made Oscar freeze again.

That Eva was uncomfortable was an understatement.

RJ then turned to look at her; his deep blue eyes taking the breath from her. He appeared to be waiting for her to say something.

"Well… err, no. No, he wasn't bothering me," she replied, then noting Oscar's apparent discomfort, went on, "Although he's clearly bothered by you."

"Is he now?" RJ asked with an undertone as he turned to look at Oscar again. The bald man remained silent, unable to speak.

Eva frowned. What was going on here?

"Please excuse us; Oscar and I need to have a chat." RJ said.

Eva took a step back. "By all means, go ahead," she replied somehow managing to tear her eyes away from RJ, turn and walk away from the two men.

That was the most awkward situation she had ever been in; RJ's sudden appearance from nowhere, and the smiling, but threatening air about him. Then there was Oscar who looked like… well who looked like he had seen a ghost. There was something about RJ that seemed dangerous. She should be staying far away from him, yet why did she find herself attracted to him? Lord help me, she prayed. She had to get the odd encounter out of her head and focus on what today was about. She should also look around to see if Adam had arrived. He might be here somewhere looking for her.

RJ led Oscar out of the hall with his arm still around his shoulder. Ben and a couple of men trailed behind them. Once outside, they walked to where a black Hyundai SUV was parked at the side of the road, several feet from the church. RJ opened the door to the back seat and guided Oscar in, and then joined him through the other side. Ben got into the passenger seat in front, and the other two men remained outside.

Oscar slowly turned his head to look at RJ. Despite the 10-degree weather, beads of perspiration appeared on his forehead.

"Aa… are you real?" he asked, his face pale, his body stiff.

RJ sighed. "What do you think?"

Oscar gasped. "But… but you're dead."

"How do you know that?" RJ asked curiously. Oscar opened his mouth, and then shut it.

"Well?" RJ enquired again; his icy stare not wavering.

Everyone knew that when RJ asked a question, he always expected an answer. He always got it; one way or another.

Oscar relaxed a bit as reality dawned on him. Slowly he rested his forehead in his right hand.

"It's what Meltdown and the boss…" He paused suddenly and went on "… I mean Nick told us. They said some masked men ambushed you guys that night and that they took you and swore you would probably be dead by the next morning."

He turned again to RJ, his face contorting to one of unbelief, amazement and then relief as his eyes got a little teary.

"We didn't want to believe it. It's been almost two weeks and we hadn't heard anything. Nick had some of the men ask around. He offered a reward to anyone who could find the bastards who took you. He has threatened fire and brimstone on the people responsible for it. We have been searching everywhere we can." Oscar lifted his head to look at RJ again, as if to reassure himself that he was actually there in the car with him.

RJ was silent; the kind of menacing silence that one should find uncomfortable.

Shakily Oscar continued. "Meltdown said it was likely you were dead anyway. So, we have been searching at the morgues, hospitals, and the news for anything at all to, at least, confirm your death. This has devastated the men."

At that, RJ corked his head. "Has it? Has it really devastated the men?" he questioned with unhidden suspicion.

Oscar frowned in confusion. "Of course it has. Why wouldn't it? We just didn't know how or even want to mourn you… not without certainty… not without confirmation… a body. But deep down, we knew. At least we thought we knew."

Oscar assessed RJ, his eyes settling on the cane that propped on the edge of the seat beside him.

"Are you alright? Were you hurt? Where have you been?" Oscar asked all at once.

"Stabbed and left for dead, but miraculously survived. I've been recuperating." Oscar was left dumbfounded.

RJ relaxed in the seat and took a deep breath as he contemplated. He caught Ben's eyes in the rear-view mirror. This was the only indication that the man was even in the car. He was quiet, but RJ knew he was very alert. Moving his hand, RJ pressed the window switch, and when the glass was halfway down, he spoke to one of the men. "Go check on Danny boy. Make sure he's ok. Reassure him, if necessary."

The man nodded and left. Once the window was back up, RJ relaxed again in his seat.

"Oscar, I have never had any reason not to trust you. Yes, you have messed up in the past with your inability to stop when a woman says stop, or to understand that her no means no.

"You needed help, and I was there for you. You assured me you have changed, and as far as I know, you haven't done anything to make me question you."

Oscar listened quietly as RJ went on.

"You told me that you dropped out of school because you just couldn't afford your education; that you ran up debts that you still hadn't paid… the college… people…"

Oscar looked humbled as he cut RJ off gently. "You helped me pay off my debts and offered to pay for me to continue my studies in engineering if I ever wanted to go back to college some day; that it was never too late."

Slowly RJ turned to look at him. "Have I ever given you any reason not to trust me?"

Oscar turned towards RJ, his eyes getting teary again. He put his hand on his chest. "RJ, you have and will always have my loyalty."

RJ gave him a level look and said, "We weren't ambushed that night, I was!"

Oscar jerked back, astounded. He looked away, and then towards Ben, who turned to him, his eyes confirming the myriad of unbelievable thoughts crashing around in his head. When Oscar's eyes met RJ's again, they held hurt and anger.

Oscar shook his head slowly in disbelief and finally put voice to his conclusion. "Nick and Meltdown?"

The number of people was beginning to dwindle now, and it was time to start packing up. Eva found that her muscles ached from being on her feet since the break of dawn, and she yawned. It had been a successful day. It was good to see a lot of hungry people fed, and those who lacked in one way or another, get replenished. So many needy people out there and it was great to be able to be of help and encouragement to them. Reverend Bainbridge had stopped by briefly. He had prayed for those who needed it and helped counsel some who were lost. They had packaged whatever food was left into plastic and foil containers and given them to those still left. Eva smiled as her eyes met the equally tired ones of Joyce as she carried a carton past. The young lad, Daniel had obviously left by now. Eva noticed that he had spent quite some time in Joyce's company.

She wondered where he was now. Was he with Oscar? Where was Oscar? Slowly her mind went to RJ again for the millionth time that day since he appeared from nowhere. The man was such a mystery to her. There was something interestingly dangerous about him, and try as she might, she couldn't get him and his beautiful blue eyes out of her head. It wasn't that she hadn't been attracted to men in the past since David. She had her fair share of men coming on to her strong and men who were too shy to make any move, but it was quite apparent how they felt. It was more to do with the fact that her taste had changed considerably. Men who seemed honest, sincere, and amiable, men who worked hard, men who had respect for women, men who had a love and appreciation for God as she did. There were few men like that. It was very difficult to find a man with all those qualities, and to be honest, she had not really been looking. She had not given it much thought until recently. There was Adam, who had not shown up today, and there had been no word from him to inform her that he wasn't, nor to explain why he hadn't. Then she dared not to even think about RJ. Why he even came to mind on this train of thought, she had no idea. She knew nothing about him to attribute any of what she looked for in a man to him. Why had he been here today? He did not seem like the hungry homeless sort... or was he? Was he in some sort of trouble? That would not be farfetched; after all, he was almost killed nearly two weeks ago.

Eva helped carry some boxes into a van outside and then came back in to help the other members of the church with putting the messy hall in order. She loved doing things like this, helping people... organising things for people. She smiled to her herself as she recalled when she was a little girl; how she always said she wanted to be a nurse. Curiously, her dad had questioned why she had chosen the nursing profession instead of that of a doctor, while stating clearly that there was nothing wrong with being a nurse. She had tried with her nine-year-old mind to explain how nurses did more than doctors. Doctors treated, but nurses nursed and cared for the patients. They got to know the patients more and on a deeper level than the doctors and were better able to encourage them and put a smile on their faces. She remembered seeing the pride in her dad's eyes as he nodded in understanding. She had not gone into medicine, realising as she got older, that there were other ways one could help people.

It's not that she was perfect. She had not been an easy teen; not always wanting to go to church every Sunday with her parents, and she had preferred to hide herself up in her room with her nose buried in one novel or another. Her mother had concluded that she was moody, but she had been shy and preferred her own company. Evan had been the outgoing one, school athlete, and the boy that tended to get himself into one scrape or another: some of it from either defending or protecting her. It was in university that she came out of her shell fully. She became more outgoing, more creative, and more independent. In her first year, she partied a little too much, and even lost her virginity to a guy she dated for only a month. The beginning of her second year, David waltzed into her life, and they hit it off big time. At some point just before they graduated from university, she had reconnected with her faith and God, to the joy of her parents. Her deeper walk with Christ made her look back in regret at some of the decisions she had made. However, she was not looking back anymore. She was forging ahead and looking to make a difference with her present and future.

It was 7:40 by the time they were all done clearing up and loading things in the different cars they came in. The group said a prayer together just before the hall and church were locked up and they began heading to their respective homes.

As Eva walked to her car, she felt an arm come around her from the side and pull her into a friendly hug. Eva already knew it was Joyce. Her fruity scented perfume always gave her away. Eva hugged her back.

"It was a really good day. Do you know how many people filled those forms?" Joyce asked rhetorically. "It's good to know that people are willing to get help; that they are reaching out."

Eva smiled. "It was a great success; thank God. Some people looked like they hadn't eaten in days; God help them. I think we also ran out of warm blankets and clothing. I really wish we had more. Too many homeless people." She sighed.

Joyce gave Eva a little shake, their side hug remaining intact as they walked on. "We're doing what we can, and even if what we have isn't enough, prayer is always more than enough."

Eva nodded and they broke their hug as they stopped beside Joyce's car, which was not parked far from Eva's.

Then she suddenly felt compelled to mention. "I noticed a lad named Daniel with you for quite some time today. I'm curious about him."

Joyce adjusted her handbag strap on her shoulder. "Yes, Danny. Not a talkative one, but rather sweet and bright. I made sure he went away fed and stocked up with canned foods. I even gave him extra."

Eva was glad to hear that. "Just curious about his living arrangements. He came with this rather questionable bald guy named Oscar."

"Oscar? Funny, I didn't see him at all. He was appointed to bring Daniel and keep him safe, but Daniel came with two other men."

Eva found this very curious. "How do you know Oscar?"

"When I was distributing the flyers, I came across this group of guys. They could be part of a gang or something. Daniel was the only one who expressed a willingness to attend the soup kitchen, so some scary looking guy, who I assume, is their leader, kind of just told Oscar to chaperone him. However, like I said, when I saw Daniel, I saw him with two other men, not the Oscar fella. I assumed they were other members of the gang. They looked a little different though."

Eva could not help feeling sorry for Daniel. It was not hard to believe that it was a gang, and that Daniel was somehow one of them. The London gangs ranged from people of all ages, depending on how young they could suck the helpless, homeless, and naive youngsters who are looking for some responsible adult guidance, but have nowhere to go and no one to turn to.

Joyce suddenly gave a mischievous grin. "Though, I must say, one of the men was certainly easy on the eyes."

Eva rolled her eyeballs, and Joyce smacked her playfully on the arm.

"Oh please, I can appreciate some of God's beautiful creation, can't I? Ian knows this; I say things like this in his presence all the time. It doesn't mean I don't love him."

This made Eva laugh. It was true though; the sort of relationship Joyce had with her husband, Ian was such a close and trusting one. The two of them were a fun and hilarious pair, and they were made for each other.

"Anyway, you won't believe who I saw today?" Eva asked Joyce, knowing she could never guess.

Joyce's curiosity was roused. "Eva, unless it was the Lord Jesus himself, don't keep me in suspense, girl."

The woman never ceased to bring laughter to Eva's heart. She knew she had better not waste time about it or Joyce would explode with anticipation.

"The man I discovered bleeding on the church steps about two weeks ago; the one who discharged himself too early from the hospital."

Joyce put her hands on her waist in surprise. "Really? What are the odds? How was he? Do you think he was looking for you to thank you?"

Eva shook her head. "He seemed to have healed or be healing incredibly well. To be honest, I don't know why he was there. The encounter was quite weird. I think he was there to speak with the Oscar guy."

"The Oscar guy?" Joyce repeated.

"Yes, Oscar obviously wasn't expecting to see him, and looked scared out of his mind. Then he asked me to leave so he could speak to Oscar, and I never saw either of them again for the rest of the day."

Eva could imagine Joyce's brain going into Miss Maple mode. Her eyes narrowing and expressing the mental investigation that was taking place with the speed of light.

"What if Oscar knows something about what happened to him? Ooo oooh wait. What if Oscar was the one who stabbed him, and he was back to take revenge?"

Eva sighed. "I don't know Joyce, but you really should lay off the 'whodunnit' dramas a tad bit."

"Girl, don't knock 'em till you've tried them." Joyce replied, feigning annoyance.

The sound of footsteps coming their way broke their conversation. They turned to see who it was.

For the second time that day, Eva was taken by surprise. She and Joyce watched as RJ walked towards them, his swagger broken now and again by his reluctant reliance on a cane. Speak of the devil!

It was another quiet drive back to her place. It had been a beautiful wedding, but somehow, Rachel had not been able to enjoy it; not like Evan thought she had. He had acted strangely today, or was it her imagination? Was she so consumed with this whole marriage thing that she was seeing and perceiving things that weren't there? Was this an excuse to be annoyed with him? No! It had not been her imagination. It was not her imagination that he had been quiet on the drive to the wedding. She certainly was not imagining the silence right now. It had not been her imagination that he hadn't even kissed or hugged her when she had come out all dressed up. Neither was it her imagination that he had not paid her any compliment at all, after all her efforts to look beautiful for him. Yes, granted, she had spent most of the time today talking with Scott, but Evan had started it by ignoring her and giving the other ladies more of his attention.

By the time he pulled into the visitor's parking space by her home, Rachel was relieved. She was knackered, probably brought on by drinking more alcohol that she was used to, and from the mental and emotional turmoil she was going through.

He turned off the engine, and she turned to him. "Thank you," she said, not feeling very grateful.

He nodded but said nothing as he stared at her for a long moment. *Gosh; not this again.* Was he waiting for her to say something? She had nothing to say. Was he ever going to say something? Rachel had just about had enough and was about to say goodnight and get out of the car, when he said, "You looked really beautiful today."

What? Really? Now he says it! Why did he say it? Did he really think so or he figured rightly that it was what she wanted to hear? Was it because she had been lightly flirting with Scott most of the time? He always knew what to say to get her to relinquish her upset and smile at him again. For a few seconds, she struggled to let things go and just hug him; to feel his reassuring arms around her. No! She thought again. Not this time. It wasn't going to work this time. He already messed up her mood, messed up her day, and frankly, the compliment had come a bit too late.

She tried to smile. "Goodnight," she said, and then opened the door, got out of the car, and walked to her front door without looking back.

"Why, hello again," Joyce said with a beaming smile at RJ as he joined them.

Eva's head quickly turned to Joyce. "You know him?" she couldn't help asking.

"Yes, he's the other one of the two men who came with Daniel today." Joyce responded. "Where is Daniel now?" she asked.

RJ, who had been watching Eva all this time, finally turned his focus on Joyce. "He's back home now. Thanks for taking good care of him."

"It was my pleasure. So how can I help you?" Joyce said, her wide smile not wavering. Eva wondered what Ian would have to say about this.

"Oh, you've already been a big help today. I just wanted to properly thank my angel here," he said the word 'angel' like it was a term of endearment.

It was Joyce's turn to look at Eva. Eva could just imagine the thoughts going on in Joyce's head. To quickly dispel the contemplation that he was some secret boyfriend that she had not told anyone about, Eva said "He's the one who left the hospital before he was discharged."

Joyce's eyebrow shot up in surprise. "Oh! Oh, I see."

RJ chuckled "And what do you see?"

Joyce shook her head. "Oh nothing. I just didn't realise that it was you."

"There's no way you could have," he said.

RJ then turned to Eva again, and the three of them stood in awkward silence. However, Eva was not sure RJ felt the least bit uncomfortable.

Finally, Joyce broke the silence, "Well, I need to head off now. It would be nice to put my feet up. It's been a long day."

Eva smiled at Joyce. "It sure has. Great work today. See you tomorrow. If not, then Wednesday."

Joyce waved at them both as she walked to her car. RJ raised his hand in a brief wave back.

Turning his attention back to Eva, he smiled. Her heartbeat quickened, and she chastised herself.

He was the one Joyce had been talking about all starry eyed, and now she understood why. There was something about him.

"Well, do you want to just stand there, or are you going to say something?" she asked.

He chuckled. "I realised we never got to properly introduce ourselves, and I never got to say a proper thank you."

"Well, maybe if you hadn't run away from the hospital, we would have gotten that over and done with by now," Eva replied.

"Trust me; there was no running in my condition." The sarcasm in his eyes glared at her.

"There was no way you should have left in your condition either, but you did," she retorted.

"You seem angry."

"Why would I be?"

"I'm sorry."

"Why are you sorry?"

"Because, right now, I feel like I should be." RJ's sarcasm had been replaced with a serious expression.

Eva turned away from his uncomfortable gaze. "You don't owe me anything." A subtle gasp escaped from RJ. At least that was what Eva thought it was.

"Of course, I do. I owe you my life. For now, all I can offer is my sincere gratitude."

Slowly Eva met his gaze again. Then she said, "You already thanked me before... at the hospital, and you're welcome. However, the church was responsible for you having your own private room. I can't take credit for that."

"Do I need to make a donation to the church?" The sarcasm was back.

"You don't have to. I'm just making a point that I don't deserve all of the credit."

"Gosh, are you really this modest? A private room didn't get me to the hospital on time and save my life."

Exasperated, Eva looked him squarely in the eye, her heart beating faster than it was supposed to. "What do you want from me, RJ?"

He suddenly smiled at her use of his name. He seemed almost surprised that she knew or even remembered it. *Oh Lord; that beautiful smile, those deep blue eyes.*

"I would like to take you out to dinner some time."

Take her out to dinner? She already knew deep down that he was not hungry or homeless, but he had come to the soup kitchen, and it was not to see her.

"Why did you come to the soup kitchen today?" she enquired.

He frowned. "I'm sorry, was that a yes or a no?"

"I didn't realise you had asked a question. You were merely making a statement."

71

"What are you, an English teacher? It was a hidden question in the form of a statement."

"Okay, my answer is no! You have already thanked me. You don't have to follow it up with dinner."

He stared at her, shaking his head incredulously. "I know I don't have to follow it up with dinner. However, I want to."

Eva gave him a helpless look. "But I don't know you."

"A good way to get to know someone would be over dinner, I should think."

"You know what? Your sarcasm has won me over. I'll think about it."

He gave a rich laugh. "I find yours rather endearing."

She said nothing. He was really making her feel even more uncomfortable. Her blood pressure was going up and she was not her usual calm self. What if he had come into her life for a reason? Maybe God needed her to do or say something that could help him in some way. What sort of Christian would she be if she failed to see an opportunity to serve? He scared her, though. For some reason, it was not her life she was worried about.

Her mind worked frantically as he stood there watching her with mixed curiosity and amusement on his face. How could she honour his request, get to know him, and still keep it respectable? It finally came to her.

She met his eyes again with much difficulty. His blue eyes could stare anyone down... or over.

"Since you like attending charitable events, I have one coming up soon that we could meet at."

His eyes narrowed. "What sort of charitable event?"

"It's a big ball and fundraiser for charitable causes. We usually get funding every year from the same source for whatever project we have planned out. I'm representing the church this year. It's usually a big, beautiful affair; food, cocktails. Hope you have a tux... or at least a suit."

RJ did not seem happy with this suggestion. He looked away as he considered her suggestion...

"How soon is this charity ball?" he asked without looking at her.

Eva wondered why he seemed so perturbed by the idea.

"Two weeks from today. You get to mingle with the rich." She did not know why she had thrown that in there. Maybe he might find it an attractive prospect. Was part of her hoping he would not say no?

"I know how these things are." His fast reply almost sounded like a snap. Eva had not expected that. What had she said wrong?

"That's fine," he finally said.

"I don't know the exact time or venue, but I can get the information after service tomorrow," she explained.

He seemed distracted suddenly. He looked at his watch. "I have to go."

"How do I get the information to you?" she asked, hoping she could get him to attend service tomorrow.

"Don't worry; I'll come get it when I can," he replied.

She stared at him, not knowing what to say or do. Should she give him her mobile number? She was not sure if she wanted him to have her number.

"Are you going to get into your car?" he asked.

Oh? Eva had not realised that their conversation had ended. What an arrogant and annoying man.

Okay, if that was what he wanted. "Well, goodnight then," she said.

He nodded and then watched her as she unlocked her car, got in and started the engine. As the car inched forward, she gave him a small nod, which he returned, and then she drove off.

Chapter Nine

He had to leave, but not before he had ensured that she had gotten into her car and was safely headed home... or wherever it was she was headed. To a boyfriend maybe? He had scanned her finger and had not spotted a ring. As he made his way back to where Ben was waiting for him in a parked car on the other side of the road, he could not help but marvel at how difficult she had been. Goodness, was everything all about charities and church that she could not just go out with him to a nice restaurant to have one lousy dinner? He had seen from her eyes how fast and hard her mind was working to find an alternative to his proposal. He smiled to himself. At least she had agreed to do something with him, and he was happy with that. But man, she was beautiful. She might not be married, but a babe like that could not be single; surely. He suddenly felt a pang of jealousy. Damn! What was it about this woman that got him excited and unfocused? He figured it was because she had saved his life, and this had brought about a connection. Maybe, it was the mystery of her that made it worse. He probably needed to spend some time with her to get over her 'aura' before he could finally move on. He had a lot going on in his life right now and did not need any complications. He was supposed to be a dead man, and he wanted... no, needed to remain so until the time was right.

"Well?" Ben asked as RJ got into the passenger's seat. Ben was at the wheel of the car. He had since relieved his men of their duties for the day.

"Frustrating woman," replied RJ.

Ben laughed. "So, will it be possible to scratch this developing itch?"

"Depends on your definition of scratch." RJ said.

Ben was such a safe driver, RJ thought as he observed how he kept to a reasonable speed. Ben drove like he reasoned and acted; cool and calm. RJ, on the other hand, was more of an adrenaline guy. He loved his speed and the excitement. Right now, he missed his power bike. He wondered what Nick had done with it; probably pawned the parts by now. He knew Nick too well. It had been hard letting Danny boy go back there with Oscar, but he had to. That was the only way to keep the fact that he was alive hidden. Besides, if Danny obeyed and kept off Nick and Meltdown's suspicious radar, then he was good. It was Oscar he had given the dirty job to spy on Nick and Meltdown. He needed to know what deal they were planning and when. He didn't really want to task Danny with the dangerous job of spying. Oscar would do a much better job. RJ wanted to know all of Nick's plans, where he was going, and how many men were loyal to him. Oscar had been shocked to find out what Nick and Meltdown had done and was only too willing to oblige. Danny wanted to help though, so he was given the important duty of keeping an eye on Oscar. One of the ideas they had was a cheap looking tracker wrist band, which he had asked Danny to wear. That way, they would always know where Danny was.

He could not wait to be alive again; being dead or playing dead was a real pain. He could not wait to be out and about openly and freely. He could not wait to be back in his own house; not depending or relying on, nor hiding from anyone. It would all happen soon enough. He just had to be patient. He had to know what Nick was planning and catch him unawares.

He would also like to be able to take anyone to dinner if he wanted to. He had asked Eva out to dinner but had not really thought about when and how he was going to accomplish that. Probably a posh restaurant just outside of London? That way, the chances of Nick, of any of the men, seeing him will be remote to none. He smiled to himself; fat chance of that happening. Trying to get her to have dinner with him had been difficult enough.

Her suggestion of the charity ball was a bad idea though. He was not happy about it, but at least he would get the chance to spend some sort of time with her. He gave a low groan that elicited a quick glance from Ben. Yes, Ben was undeniably right; the woman was a developing itch.

The sound of bone connecting with bone permeated the room. The muffled moan was pregnant with pain and fear. The small room, which was cluttered with books and papers, had a wooden desk with stacks of files and folders on it. It was dim as only the table lamp light glowed. The only window in the room was tiny and the rusty shutters were closed, totally blocking out the morning light from outside.

A man was tied to a chair. Blood slowly trickled out from the broken skin on his fast-swelling left cheek. His moist eyes gave the plea that his handkerchief stuffed mouth could not express.

Nick was seated in the only other chair in the room. He was quiet as he stared seriously at the helpless man on the opposite side of the table from him. Meltdown, who was standing beside Nick, gave a nod to the muscular man who stood over the source of the moaning. At this, the muscular man pulled out the cloth from the whimpering man's mouth.

"Please, please. My clients could be here at any minute." The man begged, sobbing. The tears flowed freely now.

Nick leaned forward in his chair. "You mistake me for someone who cares, Gary."

"I don't have the money available for you now, but I promise…"

"Well, you should 'ave thought 'bout that' before embezzling' your client's money. Now we kept our end of the bargain, Gary. 'Tis time for you to keep yours an' pay up… in full." Nick said in a voice that left no doubt that he meant business.

More tears streamed down Gary's face. "B… but your boss, RJ said I had till the end of the month to pay," said Gary, his eyes darting to the muscular man standing close to him, aware that he could hit out at him again any second now.

This seemed to set Nick off. "I'm the boss, ME! And the agreement was three months. This is the third month," he shouted, standing up.

"Ye-yes, yes, but… it should be until the end of the month…" Gary began hysterically but was silenced by a harsh blow to the side of his head. He groaned out loud in pain as his chair rocked, almost tipping over…

"I want my money in full by the end of this week. This week! You hear me Gary?" Nick barked.

Gary nodded quickly; tears managing to seep through eyes that were shut in an attempt to block out the pain.

The muscular man undid the ropes that held Gary's hands tied at the back of the chair.

Nick then began making his way to the door leading out of the cramped office of the small accounting firm; stepping on and crushing the spectacles that had dropped on the old and worn carpet earlier. He gave Gary one last look, then walked out with Meltdown and the muscled man close behind him.

Oscar and two other men were waiting outside for them when they came out. Nick turned to them.

"Otty, John you go collect from that ol' bag that' runs the Chinese takeaway down the road. She doesn't open 'till noon, but she'll be there prepping. Don't take any of her lip, you hear? Oscar, you come wiv us; we 'ave a meeting wiv the Oktapod in 'bout twenty minutes. I need as many men on ground as possible."

Otty and John obeyed immediately, while Nick and the other three men headed off for the planned meeting.

The five Albanians that joined them in the garage were calm looking. Nonetheless, they had a fierce aura about them. Their leader, Guri sat at a table opposite Nick. Their men stood behind their respective bosses.

Guri spoke first in a deep and strongly accented voice.

"Your facilities for cuckooing are acceptable. You definitely have the demographic for South London. The agreement is that you put down a quarter of a million to buy in. We take only cash. Once the money has been received, we organise training for your men when you are ready. We will support you with acquiring and supplying the equipment and ingredients, as well as with any serious problems where we absolutely need to step in. Generally, you are responsible for taking care of your own shit. Secrecy is of utmost importance; there is no room for recklessness, or we will have to take severe action. Here, in this business, you are an extension of Le Oktapod. We will, of course, take our fifty percent that is due monthly. This must not be below a certain amount, which we will finalise later. I will be coming personally to collect at all times."

Nick shifted uncomfortably in his chair "Fifty percent is a whole lot to take as your cut," he stated.

Guri leaned back in his chair meeting Nick's stare with a harder one of his own. "We stated this before. We are not here to bargain, but to set out and summarise."

There was a long silence, and it looked like the two men were trying to stare each other down. Suddenly, Nick grinned and reached over the table to offer the other man a handshake. Guri slowly reached his hand out and accepted the invitation.

"We'll 'ave the money ready for you by next week. Me an' my men are working 'ard to put it together," Nick informed.

As both men stood up, Guri suddenly looked curious. "I've been meaning to ask; what happened to RJ? We approached him many many times on joining us, and he was very quick to say 'no'. In fact, his 'no' was very determined and seemed unshakable. I am surprised, but glad that you guys have come around."

Nick looked down for a bit and cleared his throat before he looked up again.

"Yes, I was trying to convince 'im, 'n 'e was finally coming 'round, but some fucking bastards attacked us one night, an' that was it."

Guri shook his head in regret. "If it were us, we would hunt down the unfortunate souls and make them pay good. We are fiercely loyal and will not tolerate anyone disrespecting or hurting one of our own. It is a code we live by and value it in other organisations."

They all began walking towards the now opened garage exit as Guri continued. "Once, we made an example of one who dared to test our code; it happened to be a Judas in our midst; a traitor. We hunted him down, gutted him like a fish and fed him to the seagulls."

There was silence as everyone stopped walking. Then Guri laughed, patting Nick on the back.

"Next week," he said as he and his men departed. There was no smile on Nick's face as he watched them leave.

Eva knew Adam had been trying to get her attention or hoped to get her alone. It was as obvious as the sun shining at night. She was just way too busy to make it easy for him. She had not been to the office kitchenette since she went in there to drop her sandwich in the fridge that morning. Besides getting up a couple of times to chat to a few people in her department, she had been at her desk the whole morning. She felt bad because she had not done a tea run yet. She sighed; she would have to do it after lunch. Plus, she had to go to the kitchenette to get her sandwich anyway. Adam constantly finding a reason to be in her department and wondering here and there, trying to catch her eye was a little annoying. Did he not have any work to do? She paid no attention to him. Yes, she was a little annoyed with him; probably not as annoyed as she ought or wanted to be. He did promise to be at the soup kitchen but did not show up.

However, that was not why she was annoyed with him. It was the fact that he had not felt the need to call, text or something to let her know he would not be there, or to explain why he hadn't shown up. Eva paused typing and sat back in her chair; taking a break from the proposal she was creating. Who was she kidding? How many times had she thought about Adam that day? Yes, she had at some point, but his absence was soon totally forgotten. In fact, one person had occupied her mind most of the day from the moment she saw him again. RJ! If she had to be truly honest with herself, he was the reason she was in a mood she could not explain. It was not fair to take out her moodiness on Adam, even if he did deserve it. She sighed and decided she might as well do the tea run now.

Sure enough, Adam walked in as Eva poured a dash of milk into the strong tea requested by Maggie, whose desk was across from hers.

Eva pretended not to notice as she concentrated on making the other five cups. "Eva?" Adam called; his voice weighed down by a heavy conscience.

"Hey, Adam. You okay?" she asked, not pausing from what she was doing.

"Not bad. And how are you? How was your weekend? Did Saturday go well?" he enquired.

She nodded. "Very well, thank you."

She put the carton of milk back in the fridge and proceeded to stir the four cups of tea and two coffees.

He quietly watched her for about a minute as she methodologically prepared the hot drinks, and then said, "I couldn't make it. Something came up. I apologise."

Eva picked up the tray of drinks and turned to him. "Hope it wasn't anything serious or of concern?"

"Oh no; nothing like that," he replied.

Eva smiled to gesture that he was in her way, and he moved aside for her to go past him with the tray.

"I'll ring you later," he said as she left the kitchenette.

Eva nodded. Oh now, he could call her! What happened to Saturday or even Sunday? He could not even be bothered to explain what happened, and he had clearly just said it had not been anything serious. Careful, Eva! You are in a mood, and he's not the cause of it.

Back at her seat, she tried to analyse why RJ had her in a mood. It was not so much that he was infuriating, it was more to do with how he made her feel. How did he make her feel? Vulnerable, confused, unsure of herself. It did not help that there was this great cloud of mystery surrounding him. Plus, why did he have to be so damn handsome? That was it, wasn't it? She was attracted to him, and she did not want to be. She was annoyed with herself for feeling that way. Goodness! Eva decided to put all thoughts of RJ out of her head this Monday morning and focus on her work. She will talk about it with God in prayer later tonight; let Him deal with it.

Rachel watched as her mobile phone began vibrating again for the third time, and she ignored it for the third time. It was Evan again. She was dying to pick it up. They had not communicated at all on Sunday, which was unusual for them. She had a good long think yesterday, and decided she was going to take a small step back emotionally. Maybe Evan was too content with the way things were that he did not see the point of getting married. Maybe she gave him too much of herself. If she held back, maybe he would want more? She was going to spend less time with him and use the extra time to hit the gym. In addition, she should look into dietary plans. Probably if she lost some weight, or looked a little prettier, he would be proud to marry her. Maybe she should dye her brown hair red? Weren't red haired women supposed to be sexy? She would try auburn; yes, that was a good colour. Having a facial done too, would not be so bad. She needed to pay more attention to her looks. One of her house mates was big on Botox and lip fillers and had always recommended it to Rachel. That was not something Rachel had ever been interested in, but now she was desperately considering it. She guessed it would not hurt to investigate it; not that she had made up her mind yet. Maybe, probably, whatever; she needed to be decisive about it. Even though something inside her was telling her not do to this, she decided to make a stand and take the plunge.

Rachel would normally talk to Eva about this sort of thing, but she already knew what 'little miss perfect' would say, and it would not be the affirmation she wanted. Besides, Evan was Eva's brother, maybe she really should not be discussing him with her like she did. It probably made her uncomfortable. One thing she knew though, Eva was a good listener and would never betray her confidences.

Her phone vibrated briefly; signifying that another voice message had been left on her voicemail. Rachel looked at her watch. It was almost lunch time. She would listen to his messages and send him a WhatsApp message then.

"Hiya!" Rachel literally jumped at the sound of Eva's voice. She was more startled from the guilt of having just been thinking about her than from her suddenly standing beside her.

They both laughed at Rachel's reaction.

"Sorry, did not mean to sneak up on you. You were so deep in thought," Eva said.

"That's fine. Yes, I was. It's the awful Monday vibe," Rachel said.

"I know that feeling, I've been so lost in my own head all morning," Eva agreed as they both laughed again. "Just wanted to say hi. How did the wedding on Saturday go? Did you two have fun?"

Rachel smiled. She did not want to lie, so she was going to focus only on the truths. "It was absolutely beautiful. The bride looked stunning. How was the soup kitchen? Was there a large turnout?" she quickly changed the subject.

"Oh definitely; more people than we expected. Just knowing we were able to give to so many in need makes it all worthwhile," replied Eva.

"That's great. Glad to hear that Eva."

"I'm starting my lunch now, and about to go have my sandwich at my desk. Just wanted to say hello."

"Aww, I appreciate that. Thanks, Eva."

Rachel watched as Eva walked away and sighed. If only she could be more like her!

Charlie grinned from ear to ear. The twenty-four-year-old, who worked at the local Kwik Fit, stared hard at the two fifty-pound notes in his hand. He turned to RJ.

"For this, I could've cleaned and vacuumed your house too."

"I'm sure you could, but no need, Charlie. You have done so much already," RJ said, applying ointment to his healing wound.

"I put your mail on the dining table," Charlie informed and continued, "The Honda Accord's still parked on the road opposite your house, so whoever that is, is definitely still watching. But the Kia Niro, which reeked of the police, has finally disappeared."

RJ stood up straight, and buttoned up his plain black corduroy shirt as he took the information in.

"Is there anything else you need me to do for you RJ?" Charlie asked eagerly, still bubbling with appreciation.

RJ shook his head and smiled. "Not now Charlie; you have done more than enough. Thank you. I'll let you know if and when I need your help again."

Lisa was back at home from work and was fussing over dinner for Charlie when RJ left for The Three Lions. Ben had sent a car over to pick him up. He just couldn't be cooped up in the house all day. It was not something he relished.

When he arrived, he used the back entrance to get into Ben's private office. A short time later, Ben joined him just before the call came in from Oscar.

"In a week or so, we'll be doing business with the Oktapod. They have approved the location for cuckooing and agreed all the terms. All that's left is the buy in payment," Oscar reported.

RJ got up from where he was perched at the edge of Ben's office desk and began to pace. He was seething.

"Go on," urged Ben.

"We're all going to be dealing. Nick's already mapped out our locations."

RJ paused his pacing. "All of you? Including Danny boy?" His calm voice did not hide the rage beneath it.

"Yes, boss. He reckons Danny's innocent disposition and youth will be an asset."

"The fuck he does!" RJ exploded.

Ben raised his arms, motioning for RJ to calm down.

"To be honest, a lot of the men have mixed feelings about this. Some are excited, of course," Oscar added.

"And you; are you excited?" Ben asked Oscar as RJ began pacing again.

There was a brief silence before Oscar replied, "I wouldn't mind having easy access to meth. Not that I intend to use often. However, I don't fancy making or selling the stuff. And I think most of the men feel the same way I do. Danny boy is one of those that want nothing to do with meth. There's a small percentage that are all for it, though."

RJ stopped pacing again and asked, "Tell me, how much is the buy-in?"

"A quarter of a million," came Oscar's reply from the speakers of the hands-free phone box.

Ben and RJ looked at each other. Slowly RJ asked, "How does he intend to get that money?"

"He's been getting us to call in and pick up the loans all day. We'll be doing this for the next couple of days."

RJ clenched his right fist. He had heard enough. He didn't know what he would do if he heard anymore aggravating information.

"Thank you, Oscar. Please keep me updated as much as you can," RJ said in a restrained voice.

"Will do, boss," Oscar replied.

"One last thing…" RJ started, pausing to make sure Oscar was still at the other end of the line. At Oscar's 'Yes boss' reply, he went on, "Please find out who's staking my house and let me know when it ends."

Once they had gotten off the phone with Oscar, RJ turned to Ben. "First he tries to kill me, and then he goes around stealing my money so he can involve the guys in a dangerous business that I expressly forbade."

Ben looked annoyed too. "Can't keep count of that devil's horns."

RJ thought for a moment, then finally sat down in a chair. "Those men were counting on me. They were relying on me to do what's best for them."

"It's not your fault," Ben said.

RJ closed his eyes for a few seconds. By the time he opened them up again, there was fierce determination in the blue depths.

"I can't let the men down," he said.

Ben looked at him with confidence. "Don't worry, you won't."

Chapter Ten

———————∼———————

Rachel was tired when she arrived home that evening. She had worked later than usual and just wanted to have a light dinner and go straight to bed. As she came out of her car, she noticed Evan's metallic grey Mercedes C–Class coupe parked a short distance down the other side of the road. She could spot his car anywhere. He was lucky he found parking at this time on a Tuesday. She was a little thrilled to know he was waiting for her in the house. Evan was not in the habit of coming to see her after work during the week, unless they had something planned. Was it working? Was her step back already paying off? It had only been three days. However, it would be so much better if he did not see her until after she'd had her nails, hair and facials done at the beauty parlour where she had booked an appointment for this Saturday. She had also registered with the gym at the leisure centre. If only she could survive not seeing him for a month or so until she had completed her transformation. What was wrong with her? She was thinking like a silly girl from a teenage novel.

As she came into the house, the sound of soft folk music filled the living room from the Alexa device Sunita bought two years ago. However, she recognised the song from Karen's playlist. She and her two roommates could not be any more different. Rachel had known shy and private Sunita from the previous place she worked, where Sunita was still employed. They had both been looking to move to their own place but could not really afford the rent. Karen was the vain and worldly daughter of Sunita's mum's friend. She had needed a place to crash for a few weeks and ended up moving in permanently a year ago. Rachel was relieved that she had eventually moved in, and they could now split the rent three ways. As the house had three bedrooms, there was no real inconvenience at all.

Rachel heard Karen's flirtatious laughter as she walked into the sitting room. Evan was seated close to her on the sofa. She had a glass of red wine in her hand that she waved around as she rambled on about something. Rachel wanted to be angry, but she was too tired for that emotion. It would use up more energy than she had. That, and knowing what Karen was like; always flirting with Evan and was most likely the one who plopped herself conveniently beside him, made her hold back and sigh. Karen's annoying laughter-filled voice quietened as they became aware of her presence. She could sense Evan's eyes studying her as she turned to respond to Karen's acute observation.

"Oh, my Rachel; you look tired."

"Thanks."

Oblivious of Rachel's sarcasm, Karen went on, "Darling Evan, here has invited me to come watch him and his friends play cricket this Saturday."

"You know you're always welcome too, babe. I've always said that." Evan added quickly; trying to stop Karen on her callous path.

Rachel did not know what came over her. She was usually the pushover, the door mat, the one who always tried to please everyone and take their feelings into consideration. She would take so much and bend over backwards for all. However, after last Saturday when she ignored Evan, she felt more in control. She did not have to watch Karen always flirt with her boyfriend every time he came around. She did not have to be thick skinned while Karen made her usual sly remarks about her weight. She did not have to be the girlfriend who gave her all and never even got a hint of where all her investment was going. She did not even have to stay in this room and make conversation that she did not want to make. She slowly turned, walked out of the living room and up the stairs, leaving silence behind her.

Once in her room, Rachel let herself slump on the bed. She rolled onto her stomach as she held back tears that tickled the back of her eyes. She almost did not answer when she heard two hesitant knocks on her door, but finally called out, "Come in."

She knew it was Evan even before he walked into her room. He sat on the side of her bed and put a gentle hand on her back. This melted her on the inside, and she lifted her head up to look at him. He took her in his arms and held her tightly. It seemed minutes before he let her go. By now, the tears had escaped. Evan sighed when he saw them and tried to wipe them away with his hands. He gave her a minute to compose herself, and then asked, "You want to talk about it?"

This was it; her opening to talk about marriage. She debated. Was this the right time? How would he react? Should she be the one putting the ideas in his head? Isn't that something he should be thinking about too? What if he did not want to get married? This might just be the night their relationship ended. She knew that if he so much as said he did not know yet, or was not sure, she could not continue with the relationship.

Her silence must have been too prolonged because he asked again, "Babe, what's wrong?" There was a tinge of impatience in his voice. Rachel did not want to just jump right into it. She had to ease into the topic.

"I've been feeling a little fed up with the way things are?" she finally responded.

"How do you mean?" he asked with a frown.

"I want more. I want a change," she replied.

"I did ask you if you had some leave days left this year so we can take a little holiday to Ibiza or someplace sunny."

Rachel shook her head frantically. "No, that's not what I'm talking about."

Evan suddenly lost his temper.

"Then what are you talking about, Rachel? You've been acting all flirty, drunk, and weird since last Saturday. You won't pick up my calls; you walk out on Karen and me downstairs. And you're the one who's fed up with the way things are?"

Rachel sat up in bed in shock. "I was acting weird? Are you serious right now, Evan?" she responded angrily.

He got up from her bed. "I wasn't the one guzzling down wine and champagne like it was the last supper."

She could not believe it. "I had more than I would normally, but I wasn't drunk, and you know it." Rachel pointed her finger at him unable to control her anger. It was typical of him to exaggerate situations and make sweeping statements when he was trying to make a point, especially when he did not have one.

He folded his arms across his chest. "So out with it; tell me! What is Rachel Knowles talking about?" he asked in exaggerated curiosity.

How could she say it now? She was too annoyed with him, and vice versa. She was not sure she could ever bring up the topic now after this. He should figure it out himself. She lay back in her bed, closed her eyes and said nothing.

Evan stood there for about a minute before he said, "Fine! Have it your way, Rachel." She then heard the door slam behind him as he stormed out of the room.

Danny boy wasn't expecting to see Ben walk into the recreation room of the new house he and the guys had recently moved into. Apparently, it was to be the place where 'it' all happened; Nick's dream business that was supposed to rain big money into their lives. He had kept RJ updated as much as possible. So why was Ben here? He had also informed RJ that Oscar was keeping to his word, which was confirmed by Oscar's updates corroborating his. Of course, Oscar had even more information that Danny was not privy to which he faithfully passed on to RJ.

The other guys present in the room slowly stopped what they were doing as he strolled in coolly. The guys over at the pool table straightened up, while those watching TV turned their attention to him. They all knew him. They knew Ben was... or, in their case, had been a very close friend of RJ's.

Danny cast an inquiring side glance at Oscar. Did he know about this? It was annoying that they never told him anything. When will RJ stop treating him like a child? Oscar's eyes met his and then looked away, but not before conveying what looked like an appeal for Danny to relax.

It looked like one of the guys had ushered him in there to wait for Nick. Danny continued to stare at Ben who did not glance back at him, even though he was sure Ben was aware that he was in the room and looking at him.

"Gentlemen," Ben greeted with a nod.

Gentlemen? Only one person in the room was anything close to being a gentleman, and that was Ben. He was always so cool headed and mature. Some of the guys responded. This was the first time they were seeing Ben since RJ had disappeared. The silence in the room was awkward.

Nick finally shows up. He walked into the room with an air of authority as two of their hefty men kept a short distance behind him. If this was meant to intimidate Ben, it did not work. Besides, Danny was sure Ben's own men were probably outside the building, just in case.

"Ben! An' to what do I owe this great s'prise visit on this fine Wednesday evening?" Nick brought out his hand to the older man.

Ben took it and asked. "Nick! How are you and the fellas doing?"

Nick gave a flashing smile and stretched his arms apart. "You can ask 'em yourself."

Ben kept his eyes on Nick. "Any news about RJ?"

Nick looked like he was caught off guard as the sudden change of topic was too abrupt for him. Quickly, his expression took on a more sombre tone.

"I'm afraid 'e's gone. We 'ave looked everywhere. The filthy scums who did this are going to pay. One day, I'll get to the bot'om of this; I'll find the fucking murderers." Nick spat out. Some of the guys cheered at this.

Ben put on a downcast look. "RJ was a good egg. He will be sorely missed."

"For sure! 'Nuff said," agreed Nick with an emphatic nod.

"I certainly hope you catch those behind this. What about the police; any progress from their end?" asked Ben.

Nick coughed, clearing his throat. "Not a hoot. Useless lot! If you want' something done, you 'ave to do it yourself."

Ben nodded. "Please let me know if you need my help in any way."

"Cheers mate," replied Nick.

Finally, Ben brought out an envelope from his coat pocket.

"Hate to have to bring this up now, but my business hangs on it." Ben began, "RJ borrowed some money from me about three months ago. He was supposed to pay me back after two months. Due to our friendship, I extended the payback date. I have extended it further since his disappearance. Unfortunately, I now have to collect."

Nick frowned and remained quiet; digesting what Ben had just told him.

The room was quiet too as everyone seemed to be zoned in on their conversation. Suddenly Nick looked round the room with irritation. Immediately, all the men went back to what they were doing initially. Danny turned back to the TV, but he knew that, like him, the men's ears were still very much tuned into Nick and Ben's discussion.

"Why would RJ borrow money from you? 'E 'as... 'ad money." Nick's face was riddled with confusion.

"I don't know. As I didn't want to pry, I didn't ask. I trust RJ. I trusted RJ." Ben corrected himself.

When Nick said nothing again, but scratched his forehead, swiping a dangling curl away in the process, Ben stated, "I thought he told you everything."

Looking uncomfortable, Nick said, "'Cos 'e did. I must 'ave forgo'ten 'bout this one."

Fat chance, thought Danny.

"'Ow much was it again?" Nick enquired.

Ben handed Nick the envelope. Nick took it from him, opened it and read the content of the written and signed letter contained in it. As he scanned it, his face took on one of disbelief and shock; like he had just been kicked in the teeth.

"'Alf a million pounds?" Nick growled. This brought back the full attention of the men in the room.

"'Ow can this be? It makes no fuckin sense!" Nick looked from the letter to Ben's face and then back to the letter.

Meltdown, who had come into the room at some point, walked to where Nick stood, took the letter from him, and read it too. He sighed and gave the letter back to Ben.

"It's strange that RJ needed you to lend him that money. Very strange that he didn't tell us anything about it, but this is definitely Nick's writing and signature." Meltdown stated.

"Who knows why, maybe it was something he was ashamed to tell you lot about?" Ben said.

Nick looked very uneasy. He walked up to the mini bar and leaned on it, tapping his fingers on the top. "Thought you trusted 'im, why did 'e need to write that contract?" Nick queried, nodding his chin towards Ben.

Ben folded the letter and slipped it back in his coat pocket. "I did trust him. But I'm a businessman, Nick. I have a pub to run. I needed to cover myself in case of any eventualities. As it turns out, it's a good thing I did."

Nick growled again, but louder this time, and then slammed the top of the bar with his fist.

"Where are we s'posed to get that kin' o' money? We don' 'ave access to 'is account." Nick almost shouted.

"Well, I know he has a lot of people out there who owe him money. I'm sure it will all add up. If you can't get the money from them yourself, then give me their names and addresses, and I will get it done myself. But that money is mine, Nick." Ben said with an authoritative edge.

Danny looked on, wondering if Nick would go against the 'what's yours is yours' code. It would not surprise him.

Looking despondently down at his fingers, Nick quietly asked, "'Ow soon do you want it?"

"Yesterday, but I'll settle for Monday, next week; give you boys some time to round it up," answered Ben, beginning to make his way towards the door. At the door, he stopped and turned to look back at Nick. "You can throw in that bike of his, too. I'm sure it'll make up the count."

Nick remained still for several seconds, and then slowly nodded.

Almost immediately after Ben left the room, Nick violently started kicking every piece of furniture around him. "Shi'! Shi' shi' shit!!!"

Great! This is just what Danny needed; angry frustrated Nick making life unbearable for the rest of them. What was RJ thinking?

It was 10:22pm when Eva came out of the church. She had been rushing to finish and get home quickly; after all, there was work tomorrow. She had also been hoping to get some Netflix time before going to bed, but it didn't seem likely now. James had come down with a cold, so she had offered to get things packed away and locked up after today's service and the choir practice that ended twenty minutes ago. She had waited until all the choristers had left before she began turning everything off.

She pulled the big heavy doors shut and proceeded to lock it when a sound from a corner at the bottom of the stairs startled her.

"I was beginning to think you were planning on sleeping in there." RJ stated stepping out from the shadows and into the illumination of the motion light sensors that were on the wall on both sides of the double doors.

Trying to relax from almost screaming in fear, Eva stared at RJ. She could not believe how excited she felt to see him. She was probably mistaking unease for excitement. Looking down at his handsome figure as he stood there staring back at her, she was reminded of the first time she ever saw him. It was right on these very steps; his blood had stained them, and she had thought him dead. However, the blood had since been washed away, and here he was on the same steps, alive and seemingly very well. There was no sign of the walking stick he had with him the last time she saw him.

"How long have you been standing out here?" Eva asked, turning to finish locking the door and intentionally breaking the lock their eyes had been in.

"Too long," he replied.

"Why didn't you just come in?" She started walking down the steps.

91

He did not say anything as he waited for her to join him at the bottom of the steps. Once she was beside him, she asked again "It's cold out here. You really should have come in."

RJ ran his hand through his dark wavy hair. "I don't need to be in there," he stated.

Eva frowned. "Don't be silly; all faiths are welcome into the church."

RJ studied her face for a moment, and then said, "I don't belong to any faith."

"So, you're an atheist."

"I never said that," RJ said in a low tone.

She waited for him to elaborate, but when he did not, she said, "Well, the church welcomes everyone."

He appeared to consider this, and then gave her a curious look. "Do you have a life outside of the church?" he asked suddenly.

Eva had not been expecting that one. Why was he asking? She wondered how to approach this question.

"It depends. If by church, you mean God and my faith; the answer is, no. If by church however, you mean this building right here…" she said pointing at St Benedict "…then yes, I do. Why do you ask?"

"Well, besides the hospital, all the times I have seen you have been at this church. And yes, I did mean this building," he replied.

Oh please, she thought.

"Technically, you didn't see me the night I found you lying cold on the steps. Actually, you've only seen me three times, and one of them was at the hospital."

He looked amused as he watched her, a slow smile playing across his mouth.

"What?" she asked when he said nothing but continued to stare at her. When he looked at her that way, it made her feel all warm and tingly. The weather was cold tonight; could be the chill was getting to her.

"All I meant was that the night you saved my life, you were at the church. You were also an integral part of your church's soup kitchen last Saturday. Plus, you invited me to a fundraiser for the church, and here you are again at this hour; the last person to come out of the church." He said folding his arms across his chest.

It occurred to her then that the charity ball was why he was here to see her tonight. She had almost forgotten. To be honest, she had not thought he would go any further with that.

He was still looking at her; obviously waiting for a response. She did not really know what to say. She jutted her chin forward slightly "So what? You say that like it's a bad thing."

He laughed then; a rich and full laugh that made his eyes crinkle at the sides. She watched him, perplexed. He was laughing at her. He looked so handsome doing it, but still, he was laughing at her!

"I'm glad I amuse you," she said and began walking to where her car was parked.

"Come on, Eva, don't be like that," RJ said, following her.

He followed her until they got to her car, and then she turned to face him.

"For your information; not having a life outside of God means that I'm inclined to attend church services and fundraisers, inclined to help the church organise charity events, and guess what? They all kind of involve me having to be in the church often. Plus, I love it!"

He wanted to say something, but she put her hand out to stop him, and went on, "Having said that; I do go to the gym, I attend Zumba classes. I have an Odeon membership card, and yes, I use it. I hang out with my friends, attend soirees, parties, and I go on holiday twice every year."

She took in a deep breath when she finished, as she had foolishly neglected to do that during her unnecessary outburst. She did not have to explain herself to him. To be honest, she did not know why this conversation had worked her up a bit. While she was proud of her life and her commitment to God and the church, she didn't want him thinking she was boring and had no life at all.

RJ quietly watched her with a serious look on his face. She looked away. Relaxing a bit, she looked at him again.

"You okay? Have you calmed down now?" asked RJ, looking concerned.

Taking a deep breath, Eva said, "Why do people tend to put Christians in a box of no fun, boredom and death; like we don't live, laugh and love? God does not want people unhappy. He wants them to love, enjoy and do good to one another, as well as enjoy the good gifts he has given to all."

"Eva, I didn't mean to upset you. There is nothing wrong with you being a Christian or being involved in the church. I was just trying to get to know you better, and I guess… not put you in a box," RJ said softly.

When he spoke like that, he made her feel guilty for overreacting. He was apologising and had not really meant any harm. She looked at him, and for the second time that evening, their eyes locked. There was something about this man that scared and tugged at her at the same time, and she did not even know him.

A vibrating sound broke the surreal silence. Eva jumped. For a moment, she was not aware of what was making or causing that sound.

"It's coming from there," RJ informed, pointing to the handbag that hung from Eva's shoulder.

She hurriedly unzipped her handbag and rummaged for her phone. She did not find it immediately, but the caller was very persistent. Finally finding it, she quickly picked it up and put it to her ear before she had the chance to check who was calling.

"Hello," she answered.

"Hey Eva," Adam's familiar voice greeted her at the other end.

Aware that RJ was standing in front of her, Eva felt the need to hurry off the phone. "Hey, Adam; you alright?" she asked back, turning away from RJ, slightly.

"Hearing your voice, I am now. Hope I'm not calling too late?" he asked.

She quickly glanced at her watch. It was almost 11pm. It was late, but then again, she was not at home. Plus, she had another man standing right in front of her. She really needed to get home. After all, there was work tomorrow.

When she did not reply, Adam said, "I sense you have been avoiding me."

Had she been? Probably, but not consciously. He had given her the impression he was unreliable, which had kind of put her off. However, everyone deserved a second chance. She glanced at RJ, who was not even trying to hide the fact that he was listening to her side of the conversation or whatever he could get from the other end of the line. He just stood there watching her with his hands in his pockets.

"Tell you what, Adam, it is kind of late. Let's talk tomorrow, okay?" Eva said.

"Okay fine. Lunch?" Adam asked.

"We'll see," Eva replied. She was not sure, and she didn't want to promise.

When she finally put her phone away, RJ asked, "Boyfriend?"

"Work colleague," she answered. Not that it was any of his business.

Suddenly remembering something, she dipped into her handbag again and fished out the invite for the Charity Ball.

"Here's your invite. Lucky for you I picked it up from the church office today. It has all the information on there," she said, handing the fancy invite to

94

him. She was not going to mention that she had picked that up for herself alone, as she hadn't anticipated that he would actually be attending. There was another copy still in the office that she could swing by to pick up from church tomorrow evening after work.

He took it from her and studied it. He sighed, then looked at her. "Thank you."

She smiled in response.

"Do I get to pick you up?" he asked, smiling back knowingly.

Eva thought about that. Did she want him knowing where she lived? Maybe not!

"Err… why don't we just meet there? It starts at 7pm, and I will be parked and waiting at the venue's on-location free parking for 6.45pm."

He sighed. "Whatever you say, Eva. I'll be there."

"Can I give you a lift somewhere?" Eva asked.

"No thanks. I have my own ride," he replied.

He walked to her car and placed his hand on the handle of the door of the driver's side. She unlocked it and he opened the door for her. She quietly got in, and he shut the door. She wound down the window and said to him, "See you next Saturday?"

"See you then," he replied.

Chapter Eleven

"He's almost as good as new, it seems… but still bunking with that ex trick, Lisa Simms." Fischer said, moving his mobile phone from one ear to the other. He then waited patiently for Alexander Fairchild to respond. There was a clearing of the throat before Alex replied.

"It's strange that he is still at that woman's house and won't go to his. What are we missing, Fischer?" The cool, slightly raspy voice held a tinge of annoyance.

Fischer sighed. "I don't know yet, but I'm looking into it. He hasn't been hanging out with his crew either. Besides Lisa Simms, only Ben Sharpe has been to see him. He's been out a few times, but we try not to get too much into his business, in order to give him his privacy, as you asked."

Alex gave a curt laugh. "His privacy? Of course we are invading his privacy; we're just trying not to be too intrusive. Anyway, Rhys is too smart. If you go full on, he will spot you, so keep taking precautions and give him a break. However, something has changed, and I want to know what that is."

Fischer sighed again as he got off the phone. It was just like Fairchild to demand the impossible. How do they get all the information they need without invading RJ's privacy? Well, that was what Alex was paying them for. He looked up at his partner, Tom who was just about to head out of the busy office.

"It's a domestic. Some drunken idiot's beating up his wife and a neighbour's just called in. Kate and I are on it. You good?" Tom said, placing his police hat on his head.

Fischer nodded. "You go. Will update you on the call later."

Relaxing in his chair, Mark Fischer contemplated. RJ was stabbed and left for dead with still no probable cause or suspects. Of course, with the kind of life he led, there could be a few probable causes; only they had not found one yet. RJ refuses to give up the names of the culprit or culprits, does not go back home or to business as usual. In fact, he does not go back to his gang members at all. It was all a big mystery, but it was time to start looking for answers. He leaned closer to his computer and started typing.

Eva was just leaving her parents' house that early Saturday afternoon when Evan walked through the door.

"Hey sweetie, Eva and I made some apple crumble. It's just out of the oven… nice and hot as you like it. You want me to make you some custard to go with it?" Abigail said as her son walked over and kissed her on the cheek. Abigail was a feeder and loved to have her children, family, and friends over for meals.

"Honestly, Mum; he literally just walked through the door." Eva shook her head in amazement.

"Mmmm smells delicious. Custard will be good. I'm starving. Where's Dad?" Evan asked, giving Eva a hug.

"He's upstairs trying to find his pair of glasses. He's always looking for them. You better go check on him; make sure he's not up there trying to find himself as well." Abigail responded, disappearing into the kitchen.

"You go. I'm off," Eva said to Evan, moving towards the front door.

"What's the rush?" asked Evan.

"The rush? I've been here for the better part of the morning. In any case, I have a date tonight. Need to get my hair done, pick out what I'm wearing…"

"… a date? I haven't heard you go on one in a while. Must be special." Teased Evan.

"It's a guy from work. No butterflies yet but trying to see where it goes." Noticing that Evan had his cricket outfit on, she asked, "Why are you here? Thought you normally went over to Rachel's every Saturday after the game?"

The jovial look on Evan's face wavered. "I wouldn't say every Saturday. Besides. I think she's 'pmsing' or something. You know how uncomfortable that makes me. Better to steer clear of all that that unleashes."

Eva frowned and laughed. "Whatever. See you soon." She hugged Evan and yelled, "Bye, Mum, bye, Dad."

Lisa let Ben in and pointed towards the kitchen area of the open plan living room. Ben took Lisa's appearance in first before letting his eyes drift over to where RJ was slicing up tomatoes on the work top in the tiny kitchen.

"Hey, RJ." Ben nodded towards him before giving Lisa back his attention. "And where are you headed off to this evening?" He had taken in her heavily made-up face, the tight cleavage enhancing top and short leather skirt.

She gave him a 'mind your own business look' before swaying exaggeratedly away to her bedroom. He merely chuckled.

"You up for steak and kidney pie and some salad?" RJ asked; now slicing up lettuce.

"What? You baked pie? This whole situation has got you baking, RJ?"

"Look, you going to have some or not?" RJ asked again.

"Never had a combination of pie and salad before. More importantly, never had your cooking before."

"I'm taking that as a no then." RJ responded getting the medium-sized pie out of the small old beaten oven and then grabbing a plate from one of the cupboards. Soon he joined Ben on the couch with a plate of pie and salad.

Ben stared at RJ curiously as he dug into his meal. A minute later, RJ finally looked up from his food. Seeing Ben's face, he grunted "Lisa baked the pie, I made the salad, okay? So quit speculating."

Ben laughed. "To be honest, I was expecting you to say it was ready made store bought."

RJ shrugged. "Either way, I didn't make it."

"So, where's your misses going tonight?" Ben teased. RJ quirked an eyebrow.

Ben smiled again, stretching out his legs. "Oh come on, RJ. You two are living together, she baked you pie… it was a joke."

RJ sighed. "I convinced her to go out and have fun and stop fussing over me. My wound's healing nicely too. Hardly any pain these days. I can walk properly now. Still red and bruised and scarring, but not a problem."

"By the way…" Ben remembered. "…Oscar rang this morning; said Nick has pulled the trolls off your house. Not sure you should go running back there though, as you'll never know if and when someone will come checking," informed Ben.

RJ took this in. "Yeah, I know. That animal has really messed up my life." He sighed. "At least I don't have to keep sending poor Charlie anymore; I can actually sneak back there myself now and again."

Ben nodded.

RJ placed the almost empty plate on a tiny side stool. "Have you received the money yet?"

"That's one of the reasons Oscar rang up. They'll be stopping by the pub tonight to drop it off. I'll check that it's all there. It's obviously a large cash sum, so you need to schedule a meeting with your account manager as soon as possible," Ben replied just as RJ's phone started ringing.

RJ stood up to retrieve the phone from where it was lodged in his back pocket. He tensed when he realised who was calling.

"Danny boy?" he said, immediately picking it up. Ben sat up in his chair once he heard Danny's name.

"You do know you've left us with an angry Nick to deal with, right? What the hell, RJ!" Danny's quiet voice did nothing to hide the disturbed tone in his voice.

"Easy, Danny. Are you okay?" RJ asked, a concerned frown on his face.

"Yes, I'm fine, but Nick isn't. He's pissed off about losing the huge money he needed to buy into that drug business, and he's lashing out at everyone. I'm keeping a low profile now before it's my turn. It's really difficult to live this way."

RJ sighed in relief. "I'm sorry; I should have warned you, but we do have to be careful with communication. I hope you're being cautious making this call to me."

"Yes, I am. There's no one where I am at the moment," replied Danny.

"Okay good. Don't worry; Ben and I are brewing up a plan. Just hang in there. Contact us only when it's safe and if it's absolutely crucial, okay?" said RJ.

There was a brief hesitation before Danny responded, "Fine! But you need to let me know what's going on. Please, RJ, I need to know what to expect."

RJ sighed again. "I will try my best when it's absolutely necessary. The less you know, the better. Now bugger off the phone and stay safe."

When he was off the phone, RJ turned to Ben. "Once we've received the money, and we're sure Nick is desperate to make that money back one way or another, then we need to make our next move."

Ben nodded. "Is the lad okay?" he asked.

"Yes, he is," RJ confirmed "He's just worried that Nick's temper tantrum might hit him."

Lisa walked into the sitting room holding her handbag. "Are you boys done now? I need to catch a ride with you, Ben."

Ben stood up. "Where to?"

Lisa smiled sweetly at him "Where you're headed – the pub. I need you to buy me dinner and some drinks. Think you can handle that?"

Ben smiled back broadly. "With pleasure."

Le Vie Marine was a lovely seafood restaurant located on the north side of London. Eva had heard so much about it and was already beginning to see why. The elegant décor and sound of French jazz created a sweet ambiance that made you feel happy, eager to relax and eat good food. It was a busy night, but the tables did have reasonable spacing between them. Eva was relieved. There was nothing she hated more than restaurants that filled every space with tables, making it seem stuffy and crowded all in the bid to get more business for the night.

Eva sat in the chair the waiter had held out for her as Adam sat opposite her at the table for two he had reserved for them. She smiled at him as the waiter took their coats. Adam looked rather attractive tonight. He had on a nice shirt that he wore underneath a really classy thin jumper. His black khaki trousers looked smart on him. Eva had on a boohoo petite smock long sleeved tie-neck dress. The lemonade-coloured dress had gathers mid-sleeve and went very well with her strappy high heels. She wanted to be dressy but not overdressed, and she was glad about her choice.

Eva was having a really good night. The food was exquisite, the ambiance soothing, and Adams's company was turning out to be enjoyable. As she ate her seafood paella and he his seafood risotto, they talked about their families, the office and how they enjoyed their jobs. She found out that he was the last of three siblings, loved travelling, and was fascinated by Buddhism. She told him that she was a twin, that her father was a Nigerian born Briton and that she loved being a Christian.

Soon, the conversation became serious. "Not sure I have asked this question before, but why are you single, Eva?" Adam asked with honest curiosity.

She took a sip of her cocktail before answering. "For the very same reason you are."

"You realised that your girlfriend of two years was bipolar, and that the relationship wasn't working, so you broke up a year ago and have since been super attracted to only one person – a colleague at work who, at one time, didn't seem to notice you existed?" Adam replied with a half grin.

Eva was lost for words.

Adam sat back in his chair with a laugh. "I didn't think so."

His response took her by surprise, and there was a brief awkward silence.

"I actually thought your response would be that you just hadn't found that person yet, 'cos that would be my answer," she finally said, breaking the silence.

There was a second pause before they both burst out laughing at the silliness of the conversation. The realisation that he had practically told her that he was attracted to her was heavy in the air. Not that she had not sensed it; she would have to be a moron if that was the case. It was just the fact that he had said it out loud and now, they could no longer dance around it. The question is, how did she feel about him? She obviously liked him, or she would not be on a dinner date with him right now. Was there more though? Was she incredibly attracted to him… and only him? For some reason, the image of RJ infiltrated her thoughts. His handsome face, the way he annoyed and excited her at the same time. There was something about him that made her uncomfortable and yet comfortable. Why had her thoughts wandered to him? Here was a good-looking man who she knew and with whom she was having a lovely dinner, and she was busy thinking about a mysterious stranger who she couldn't' help but be drawn to… be attracted to. That realisation stunned her, and she tried to shake the thought from her head when she spotted something from the corner of her eye. She squinted a bit as she was sure she was not seeing right. Adam noticed her distraction and, following the direction of her gaze, turned around slightly in his chair. Four tables down to Eva's right, a familiar figure standing up, caught his eye too.

"Is that Rachel?" Adam asked.

Rachel could not believe it! What were the odds of Eva having dinner with Adam at the same restaurant that she was at? It almost seemed unlikely to be a coincidence; more like she was followed. She knew it was a ridiculous notion, and that it was her guilt weighing on her conscience. She had watched in panic as Eva, looking stunning as usual, and Adam were led by the concierge to their table thirty minutes ago. She was half expecting Eva to turn her head and see her. Rachel certainly didn't want to be seen! It was all she could do to not to grab her date by the arm and drag him out of there with her.

Patrick was the neighbour down the road who usually jogged past their house every Saturday morning. He was probably in his mid-forties and rather fit. She wouldn't describe him as handsome, but he did have a slight resemblance to the actor Benedict Cumberbatch. They had chatted several weeks ago when he stopped to help her move the compost bin that was annoyingly lying in the free space in front of her house where she was trying to park. She had thanked him, and they had spent about five minutes talking. Before he left, he had invited her to join him on his Saturday morning runs, and Rachel had said 'maybe' someday soon. Well, someday had been this morning when she decided that part of her makeover would be to start jogging on Saturday mornings to lose some weight.

Of course it wasn't surprising that she ran into Patrick on the path that people in that neighbourhood usually jogged or rode their bikes. She liked the way he was looking at her as they talked while sitting on a bench later on. He liked her; she could tell from his eyes and the way he smiled at her when she spoke. She felt attractive. That was it. That was what she was looking for. Something that made her feel good about herself, that made her feel attractive. Did Evan not make her feel this way? She was not sure. He used to, but then again, he had not really changed. She was doubting now because he had not even mentioned marriage once and had been really annoying her lately. Patrick was no Evan, but at least she wouldn't have to keep worrying about his faithfulness or whether or not she deserved him. If she were in a relationship with someone like Patrick, she would be more at peace, feel more secure. When was the last time Evan looked at her, like Patrick was doing now?

Those were the thoughts in her head when Patrick asked her to have dinner with him tonight. A bit too soon? Probably! However, he did mention that he had not forgotten the short time they had spent chatting weeks ago and had hoped that he would see her again. She suddenly found herself saying yes. Now here she was, in this nice restaurant, having dinner with a man she barely knew, who was not her boyfriend. Even though the food was good, and he was so charming, she had not been comfortable. As if to bring the point further home, in walks Eva and is seated some tables down to her left. She was thankful that she had her back to Eva, but it would have been better if Eva had her back to her.

As Patrick's voice floated around her like a haze, talking about how he was now focusing on expanding his retail business since his divorce almost a year ago, all Rachel was thinking about was how she needed to leave; that this was God's way of telling her something. That what she was doing was wrong. What was she doing? Trying to see if she could get over Evan if they broke up? That it could be easier being with someone else? She was so relieved when Patrick finally finished his lemon meringue and ice cream dessert.

Patrick sat back in his chair, satisfied. "You don't know what you missed. You should have had dessert and gone with my choice."

Rachel smiled. "It did look delicious. Pity I wasn't in the mood. I'm feeling rather tired."

Patrick quickly sat up. "Oh sorry. Where am my manners! Of course you're tired, especially after the run you went on this morning. As you're knew to it, you would feel tired. It would take some time for your body to adjust and get used to it."

Rachel gave another smile and a silent sigh of relief when Patrick signalled for the waiter and finally paid for their meal. All she could do now was hope that she and Patrick could get up and leave quietly without catching Eva and Adam's attention.

Chapter Twelve

"All done!" confirmed Meltdown, propping beside Nick at the mini bar of their recently acquired home. It had five bedrooms, two bathrooms, one guest toilet, a massive garage, kitchen, and a huge den that was also the TV room with the bar on the other side of it. There was another room which was used as the office and storage. It was also where the safe was kept. It was quite a comfortable home that they began renting only a few weeks ago and had moved in with all the guys. The remarkable thing about it was that it was an upside-down house. It was bigger on the inside than it actually looked on the outside. That was because most of the house was below ground. The bedrooms were on the ground floor and there was a flight of stairs that led underground to the rest of the house. The garage entrance was on the ground floor but sloped down to the underground floor. This made it the perfect house to cook drugs.

A friend of Nick's had informed him about a wealthy man who had moved to Spain on business but was looking for someone to rent his house for a few years until he returned. It was lucky and perfect. Nick had met up with the lawyer, signed the papers and assured the owner that the house was going to be well looked after.

Nick did not even bother looking at Meltdown or Oscar, who had come in with him and was now sitting in front of the TV flipping through channels.

Gruffly and reluctantly, Nick asked, "And the Bike?"

Meltdown stood up and made his way behind the bar to fix himself a drink and then poured Nick some more of what he had been drinking. "He wasn't too happy at first, but later agreed to use it to offset the difference." Meltdown replied before downing the vodka and then pouring himself another glass.

"I can't understand why that bloody RJ would've borrowed money from Ben. Almost like 'e knew this would 'appen. 'E was always a pain in my backside… even now that e's dead. I should've ended 'im ages ago." Nick rasped through gritted teeth. He had a wicked look in his eye that anyone who knew him could interpret as danger.

Suddenly Nick picked up his glass and threw it hard. It hit the wall and smashed into tiny pieces. Meltdown and Oscar were startled at the abrupt sound of shattering glass. However, they were not surprised as this had been going on ever since Ben had paid them a visit a few days ago. He checked the time on his watch. It was 10pm. The other guys would usually be in this room at this time, but Oscar gathered that the guys did not want to be anywhere Nick was at the moment. They were probably in the garage playing terrible poker or something. He did not blame them. Under normal circumstances he would have joined them, but he had to be here… to get any information he could.

"It was part of RJ's loan money that we used to pay the rent for this 'ouse three months in a'vance. I 'ave no idea 'ow we're gonna pay going forward. The solution for that would've come from our business wiv Oktapod. Now we don't even 'ave the money we need to buy into that. Guri will be 'xpecting the money sometime in the week, and we 'ave bloody nothing!" Nick screamed the last word like an animal.

Oscar got up and went to a corner of the room where they kept a brush and dustpan so he could clear up the mess Nick had made.

Meltdown sat back down on one of the stools, but sensibly leaving a little distance between himself and Nick. "We can ring Guri up and ask for an extension. If he does agree, he will give us a short time; a week probably, two weeks – max. Hopefully, it will give us some time to come up with something."

Nick seemed to relax a bit but still looked disappointed. "This is no way to start a business relationship, but we 'ave no choice. I'll ring Guri tomorrow, but we need to get that money fast, one way or another."

Eva's eyes slid to the bottom right corner of her computer screen as she typed. It was only 3pm. She sighed. What was it about Mondays that always made the hours go so slowly? She felt uncomfortable being in the office, seeing Rachel and pretending that she had not seen her having dinner with another man at Le Vie Marine on Saturday night. There was no mistaking Rachel with this man as they got up to leave. Thankfully, Adam had not dwelt on the fact that they had seen her too. She was glad for that, and they went on with their dinner as they had before, despite the weird and curious feeling inside her.

It had been a lovely night and Eva felt she could probably see their relationship becoming something more. He had given her a respectable peck on the cheek after driving her safely back home. Saturday was still obviously on his mind, she noted as he waltzed over to her department to chat with someone for the umpteenth time. He always tried to catch her eyes or hold her gaze. She found it funny and cute but decided to start pretending not to notice him. She had work to do, even if it seemed like he did not.

Her mind drifted back to Rachel. Why had she been out having dinner with another man on Saturday? Had she and Evan broken up? She did not think so. Evan would have said something. What was it he had said again when she asked why he had not gone over to Rachel's after his cricket game as usual? Something about her maybe 'pmsing' and needing to avoid her during that time. Eva had not thought much about it, but was he hiding the fact that they had broken up? If so, would Rachel be out with another man so soon after their breakup?

She would have thought Rachel would have told her about it. The feeling of dread she had felt when she saw Rachel at the restaurant suddenly came back. What if they had not broken up? Was Rachel cheating? How could she though? Rachel was crazy about Evan, and not too long ago, had been worried about Evan not having broached the marriage topic yet. Eva was really confused. More than that, she felt a sense of guilt. Did she make a mistake not discussing Rachel's worries with Evan? She should have been more supportive and encouraging. She just did not want to get immersed in their relationship; she figured they were mature adults who could work through their issues without any outside influence. She had prayed about it, but maybe she should have taken it more seriously. Unfortunately, she was stuck in a difficult place now as she could not let Rachel know she saw her that night, nor could she tell her brother what she had seen. Surely, she had to do something though, but what could she do?

RJ was late arriving at Ben's pub, but he had not been able to resist sneaking back into his house after such a long while. It was good to be back in his nicely furnished bachelor pad. He had missed it. It was nice of Lisa to put him up as she was, but her flat was quite small, and it had been nice to be back in his own spacious home… even if it was just for about thirty minutes. The place had been as neat and as spotless as he had left it. Charlie, being the good sport that he was, had emptied out the fridge of any perishable food items. There had not been much to do but sort out the post and grab some more clothes and shoes.

As he walked into the pub's office at the back, he heard the phone ringing. Just in time for Oscar's call. Not that much noise coming from the bar and restaurant as Monday nights were usually not that busy. He had received Ben's call on Saturday night to confirm the drop-off of his money, short of some thousands of pounds, but he could live with that. One of the best news was that his bike was dropped off as well. He loved his bike and was glad to have it back, even though he could not ride it for a while.

Ben gave him a 'you're-late' look as he hit the hands-free button on the phone box.

"He's a desperate man, RJ," Oscar informed. "He rang Oktapod today and asked for a two-week extension. Surprisingly, they offered him three weeks instead; on the condition that there would be no more extensions, or the deal's off."

"Good. Any ideas so far?" asked RJ.

"He's come up with a few. One of them is to rob a bank," replied Oscar.

RJ and Ben slowly exchanged looks, and then Ben threw his head back and laughed.

"Rob a bank? That's a bit ambitious, even for Nick," RJ retorted, amused.

"Well, he's not kidding, RJ, trust me," Oscar said seriously.

"What else?" Ben queried.

"Blackmail. According to Meltdown, vital information we have on our past loan clients could be used to blackmail them."

"Shit!" RJ put his head in his hands. "He wants to ruin my reputation, the prick! My clients come to me because they trust me."

Oscar went on, "However, kidnap might be the winner; snatch some rich man's child or wife and demand a hefty ransom. Nick's even proposing two simultaneous abductions, as he isn't sure he can get a quarter of a million pounds from one operation in the short time available."

RJ raised his head, an incredulous look on his face.

"The funny thing is, he's crazy enough to do it," Ben stated as a matter of fact.

"Oh he's crazy alright, if he thinks he will get away with either one of his ambitious evil schemes. I'm not going to let him drag the guys into a terrible life of crime. And there's definitely no way I am going to let him hurt anyone else... in any way," RJ stated in a quiet steely voice.

Ben looked thoughtful. "We need to get him to mess himself up without hurting anyone or getting the guys involved."

There was a brief silence, and then RJ looked at Ben thoughtfully. "I have an idea," he said.

"Eva? Shouldn't you be asleep?" Evan's sleep distorted voice held irritation. "Is everything okay?" he asked again, sounding more awake now but a little worried.

"Yes, all's fine. Were you asleep? It's only 11pm," Eva replied in surprise.

"Yes. Why are you not? It *is* 11pm, you know," he responded.

Eva giggled. She had to let it sink in that not everyone was a night owl like her, and shockingly, not even her twin brother.

"I'm sorry. Thought you'd still be awake, for some reason," she said.

"What's up?" Evan asked. She could hear him sitting up in bed.

"Nothing. Just wanted to catch up."

"Seriously, Eva? At 11pm on a Wednesday?"

Eva knew it was a bit weird. "Okay, maybe it's unusual, but I had you on my mind and decided to call. I'm sorry I woke you," she said.

There was a brief pause, and then a sigh, "It's okay. So, what's going on with you?" Evan asked.

"Oh, nothing much. Work's been a bit hectic. The date with my colleague last Saturday was actually really nice," Eva replied. This was the opening she needed.

"Was it? Are you saying you actually like the poor bugger?"

"Well, getting there. I don't not like him."

She heard Evan chuckle at the other end of the phone. "You sound smitten," he said sarcastically.

She laughed. "Not really, I see potential, I think. Adam is cute and really sweet, but that... erm... spark isn't there yet. That's not to say it won't happen."

"Are you trying to convince me or yourself?" asked Evan.

Eva sighed. Evan was probably right. Was she trying to convince herself? "Some of the best romantic relationships start off as friendships. That's what Adam and I are building."

"Okay."

"Okay? Nothing more to add?" Eva asked.

"What do you want me to say? I'm not a relationship expert," replied Evan.

"I know you're not. It doesn't mean you can't offer your opinion on it."

Evan gave a big sigh. "If you go into a relationship with friendship first in mind, then, to me, that's exactly what it is. Most romantic relationships that started as friendships weren't knowingly planned that way."

Eva thought about it for a few seconds. That actually made sense. She was taken aback. She knew she had asked Evan for his opinion on relationships, but she was not expecting him to be right.

"Wow... that... that was... err... kind of profound," Stated Eva.

"Did that really necessitate a stutter?" Evan retorted, feigning irritation.

Eva smiled. "That was how your relationship with Rachel began, wasn't it? You started off as friends."

She heard a slow breath intake from Evan. "Yes. It wasn't planned or expected. It just happened."

"Yeah. I remember thinking, she's not your usual type; not like that finicky model you dated before her. Rachel was... is a breath of fresh air."

The silence at the other end of the line said a lot. Then he said, "I'm different when I'm around her... better, I think. Her faith in God inspires me to grow in that faith."

It was Eva's turn to be silent. That was so true. Evan had always yoyoed with his Christian faith, but somehow Rachel had grounded him. That's why their parents loved Rachel so much. She was such a good and kind-hearted person. She thought about Adam; he wasn't a Christian at all. Could she bring him to Christ? She wasn't sure she could be with him otherwise. Suddenly, her mind drifted to RJ. He was definitely no Christian. RJ? What was wrong with her? Why, in the world was she even thinking along those lines? It's not like she was considering dating him. Maybe it was because she had a date with him this Saturday. No, not a date. It was a thank you dinner. Plus, a charity fundraiser didn't count as a date venue.

"So how is she?" Eva asked, trying to take her mind off RJ. Her question was really about their relationship.

"I... err... I haven't seen her in a few days. You know, busy lives," he replied uncomfortably.

Busy lives? Well, Rachel had certainly been busy. She knew her brother well enough not to expect him to open up about any issues in his relationship, unless she asked him outright, and she wasn't going to do that; not now! She knew all was not right with their relationship though, and Evan knew she knew. They had this connection where they did not have to say anything or much to convey a feeling or information to each other.

"How is she?" he asked quietly in return.

Eva had not spoken to Rachel in a few days herself. In fact, she had been trying to avoid her this week. However, she did see her, and she looked fine.

"She seems fine. Always hard at work." She tried to put a smile in her voice.

Rachel, sweet Rachel who loved Evan with all her heart, had gone out to dinner with another man. It seemed so unbelievable and so unlike her. Things must undeniably be very bad between them. One thing was for sure though, she couldn't tell Evan about what she saw!

Chapter Thirteen

———— ～ ————

There was always something about Fridays that lightened everyone's mood – the weekend. This week had been a particularly difficult one for Rachel. Having to deal with work, deal with her guilt about Patrick, avoid Eva whose face and presence added to her guilt, and having to deal with the pain in her heart – she missed Evan so much.

She knew how wrong it was of her to use Patrick to get her mind off Evan, and to see if she could get over him at all, if need be. It was not fair on poor Patrick, nor Evan. She loved Evan so much, but she had to admit that their relationship could well be over. He obviously did not feel for her as strongly as she felt for him, and probably did not intend on ever marrying her. It had been well over a week since she had seen or even spoken with Evan, and really did not know where their relationship stood. She knew she ought to let Patrick know the situation and let him down easy. However, she was dreading it. He would hate her, and she could tell that he really liked her.

She watched as a colleague rinsed up some mugs while she stood in the office kitchenette waiting for the microwave to warm up her lunch. She soon heard Eva's voice just outside, talking to Adam. Could the microwave not work any faster?

She had bumped into Eva yesterday and they had engaged in a six-minute conversation about work, the weather, and the most recent episode of The Housewives of Cheshire. Obviously, she had been super uncomfortable, looking for any signs to suggest that Eva might have seen her last Saturday night at the restaurant. However, Eva had said nothing to that effect, smiled a lot and kept asking her how she was doing. Rachel's mind had been put at ease at the confirmation she needed that Eva hadn't seen her that night, and since Adam had had his back to her as she had had to him, he definitely couldn't have seen her either. This knowledge hadn't taken away the guilt she felt, though. She had really wanted to open up to Eva about where she and Evan were now, and how she felt, but they had been interrupted by Adam, who joined them by the photocopier. Rachel remembered having felt a tinge of annoyance. She didn't know how Eva did it, but she had Adam following her all over the office like a love-struck puppy dog. Anyway, she had taken that opportunity to get away. If there was one good feeling she got out of that uncomfortable conversation, it was relief.

Adam and Eva soon entered the kitchenette. She and Eva smiled at one another. Just then, someone called Eva's name and she quickly stepped out to attend to the person.

"Hey, Rick, you make tea like my nana," Adam jeered jokingly at the tall black man who was busy making tea for what seemed like his whole sales team.

"Piss off; I'd like to see you make eight cups of tea in…" Rick checked his Smart watch "… less than three minutes."

Adam laughed. "Do you need a hand?"

"I will do. Can't carry all these hot mugs with just two hands," replied Rick.

"I can and have done," Adam said smugly.

"Yeah sure! Can't remember the last time you did a round," Rick quipped back.

The microwave chimed to signal that Rachel's ready-made Mexican beef chilli from Marks and Spencer could now be taken out. However, when she did, the bottom of the container still felt cold. Almost hissing, she shoved it back into the microwave to reheat for an extra minute and a half. Either the time given on the packaging was wrong, or the microwave was not working properly. She had really hoped to be out of the kitchen by the time Eva came back in.

"It's my parents wedding anniversary this coming Sunday. Those two have been married thirty-five years and still act like crazy love birds," Rick said.

"Nice," Adam replied, "Have you got any plans for them?"

"I was thinking a romantic dinner for two at a lovely restaurant."

"Oh, I know just the place," Adam snapped his finger excitedly. "Le Vie Marine; awesome place north of London that serves amazing seafood."

Rachel felt a bit uneasy.

Rick began shaking his head. "Don't want another Loch Fyne…"

Adam interrupted him. "No, nothing like that. Ask Rachel here, she was there recently. Trust me, you'll thank me, mate."

Rachel suddenly got a bitter taste in her mouth. What? Had he seen her?

She noticed that the two men were watching her, and realised they were waiting for a response. "Err, yes. Great." She managed to force out with a smile, while feeling like throwing up.

Oh No! He had seen her. That meant, so had Eva!

Adam turned to Rick with an 'I-told-you-so' look on his face, and Rick nodded in contemplation. Then between them, they picked up the cups of tea and made their way out of the kitchen.

Just then Eva entered in a rush, heading for the fridge. She smiled at Rachel. "Sorry, in a mad rush. Hope you're good." She grabbed her sandwich and left the kitchen. Rachel was not even sure if she responded to Eva or not.

She wanted the floor to open up and swallow her. Eva had seen her... all this time and had said nothing to her about it. The unexpected chime from the microwave startled her. Great! She had suddenly lost her appetite.

Eva was meant to be having a relaxing evening after such a long hectic week, and an exceptional busy day at work. Instead, she was coiled up on her sofa in front of the TV with a bowl of ice cream expressing her worries to Joyce over the phone about tomorrow and her meeting with RJ at the charity fundraiser. She felt a sense of dread and excitement at the same time.

"I wish you had told me sooner that you were going on a date with that handsome devil, I could have helped you find the perfect sexy outfit," Joyce said.

"I already have a lovely outfit fit for a charity ball, and it is not a date, Joyce," Eva said, rolling her eyes.

"Eva, do you even know what a date is? The venue doesn't define it. It's the 'feelings' and 'intentions' that do."

Eva took a deep breath. "Well, I'm going for the fundraiser. FairCorp is most likely going to be donating to the church, as usual. RJ is going so he can fulfil his gratitude obligation. I would hardly call that a date."

"Okay, if you say so, but that man is fiiinne. He's as sexy as they come. You can't tell me there's no attraction there?" Joyce asked.

Of course, RJ was a good-looking man... very good looking, but that was beside the point.

"Yes, but so what? He hardly seems the type that I should be attracted to. Besides, you're scaring me with all the 'sexy' talk."

Joyce laughed, and Eva could imagine her eyes dancing with amusement at Eva's reaction.

"Sexy is not what someone wears, Eva, it's what someone is, and sometimes, it takes the right outfit to bring the sexy out of a person." Joyce's warm voice always sounded like she was singing. Her American accent probably contributed to that.

Eva didn't know what to say to that, and Joyce continued, "We are Christians, Eva, not a cult. There is no 'type' for Christians. We are all individuals, and we all have our individual types. Giving one's life to Christ doesn't bring you under a 'type'. It's a choice, and one we pray everyone makes. We must be careful not to judge or be quick to condemn, Eva. It's still our job to help people see the light, last time I checked."

Eva sighed. Joyce was right, of course. Why did she have this wall up? It was because RJ scared her... a lot, and she did not understand why. She wanted to believe that his request for them to have dinner was so he could say thank you. In fact, she needed to believe that. There was no reason to believe otherwise or expect otherwise. After all, she might be strangely attracted to him, but that did not mean he felt the same way. However, she was going to stop judging him and truly try to get to know him better.

"You know..." began Eva. "You don't know RJ and have only met him once, yet you seem to really like him."

Joyce seemed to consider this before replying. "I don't know how to explain it; there's just this feeling deep in my spirit about him."

"What about Adam from my work. Any thoughts about him?" Eva asked.

"I'm not a Magic 8 Ball, Eva," Joyce chided, and they both laughed.

"I'm thinking of organising a games night," Eva said. It was an idea she had been toying with to help Evan and Rachel's relationship, and to get to know Adam better, to see how he fit in with her friends and family.

She explained further, "You and Ian, Adam and I, my brother and his girlfriend, Rachel."

Eva knew this would make Joyce happy; the woman loved being around people and having fun.

"Child, you know what I like." Joyce burst out, her voice full of smiles. "You know what would even be better? A movie night!" Joyce suggested.

Eva shook her head. "Oh no, Joyce. You and I have different tastes in films. I'll be playing the clarinet before I watch any of your crime dramas."

"Clarinet? Eva, it should be a crime to be so dramatic. I think you're going to love them just fine."

The rapid noise of a body rolling down the stairs was deafening. This was quickly followed by footsteps rushing to the scene. The figure sprawled at the bottom of the stairs did not seem fazed, though. He burst out laughing, even as blood trickled from the broken lip he sustained from the fall.

Danny and the other men who had rushed out from wherever they were, due to the loud racket, looked from the body lying on the floor to another figure that stood at the top of the stairs. Oscar, still looking a little shocked, put his hand over his mouth and asked with an unsteady voice, "Shiiitt, Otty, are you alright, mate?"

Otty laughed again as two of the men tried to help him up. Just then Nick and Meltdown walked in.

"What's going on here?" demanded Meltdown, not looking too pleased.

Otty was barely able to stand up properly as the two men tried to keep him steady. His shirt was stained with blood from the injury to his lip.

"Aahh that burst lip has gotta hurt," sniggered one of the other men called John.

Nick angrily looked Otty over. "'E pro'bly 'as a lot more 'urting than a cut lip. The twat's wasted."

Oscar began making his way downstairs. "So sorry, boys. I tried to grab him, but I wasn't fast enough."

Otty smiled broadly, showing teeth coated in a film of blood. "Happy days fellas, ha-ppy daayzzz." He then struggled to reach his jeans' back pocket. The two guys relaxed their hold on him. This enabled him to fumble with his pocket before he finally pulled out a thick wad of twenty-pound notes.

A whistle escaped from one of the men as Danny and the others stared in surprise.

"Where did you get that?" Meltdown asked, voicing the thoughts of everyone, except Oscar.

Otty managed to look smug, even in his drunken state "Won it... fair and squaaaarre."

"Bollocks! You must have nicked if off someone. We don't call you shifty Otty for nothing," exclaimed one of the hefty men holding him up. This provoked chuckles from most of the men.

Nick, on the other hand, was not laughing. He turned to Oscar. "You're sober, right?" When Oscar nodded, he asked, "Now tell me what the 'ell 'e's talking 'bout?"

Looking around at the men, Oscar swallowed, and then began to explain while they all listened quietly.

"Otty and I took the van to the garage to get the tyre changed this afternoon. While we were waiting, we overheard some guys talking about this new but restricted poker joint in Lewisham. It opens on Wednesdays, Fridays, and Saturdays at 7pm. It's supposed to be a guilty pleasure for some really rich businessmen who have nothing better to do with their money. According to one of the guys, saying the secret password gets you in. The bouncer lets you in on the belief that one of the rich blokes shared it with you…"

Suddenly Otty burst into song, "Weeee aarre… I aamm the champion… my frieennddss…"

Nick turns to the men steadying Otty and barks, "You best shut 'im up or 'e'll be singing wiv Freddy Mercury in a minute." Nick's clenched fist confirmed he was not joking.

John quickly passed a small hand towel to one of the men, who then gagged Otty. Once that was sorted, Oscar had everyone's attention again.

"One of the men said he was dating the daughter of this former politician who frequents the place. She told him what the password was. The weirdest thing about it is that these rich men are naff at poker. In fact, they're terrible. You only have to be remotely good…even basic to beat them. He said he had only just learnt to play poker but had since been there several times and had won a whole load of cash. The men don't seem to care how much money they bet or lose; the thrill for them is the possibility of winning…the mental adrenaline of the game." Oscar paused. All the men were incredibly quiet.

Daniel noted the seriousness and curiosity on the faces of the eight men standing there, besides Otty and Oscar. Even he was curious. Obviously, there was more.

"Go on," instructed Nick.

Oscar was a little uncomfortable this time as he went on "I know we didn't really tell you where we were going this evening, but Otty and I had to check out the place for ourselves. It seemed too good to be true. I'm really sorry Nick…"

"Go on!" ordered Nick.

Clearing his throat, Oscar continued, "We went there. At first, the plan was just to find out if it truly exists. Oh man, to our surprise, Nick... the flipping place actually does exist; these rich tossers started arriving from 8pm. Then Otty and I got it into our heads to try our luck. I'm not any good at poker, but Otty can, at least, hold his own a bit..."

The last phrase triggered an exchange of sceptical looks from the men with one or two appearing to consider this.

"Otty's rubbish at poker." Meltdown said firmly; saying out what the other men were thinking.

With that said, Oscar went on, "Well, he's better than I am. Anyway, we said the secret password and, just like that, we were in."

"Wait. Wait wait..." Nick's face took on an excited look of surprise. He scanned the faces of the men, expecting them to mirror his. He looked at Otty, and then Oscar with elation. "You mean, you know the password?" he asked in unbelief.

Oscar nodded.

Nick, trying to curtail the thrilled energy inside him that was threatening to explode, pointed at Oscar with a big smile on his face. "Tell me how this visit ends."

"The security seems tight, but once you say the password, act normal, follow the rules and play the game, there should be no problems. It's a maximum of ten players at a time and one dealer. We were there for about two hours. I didn't play, but I should have. Between us, we brought £250 to the table, and Otty won £2,500. We could have won more if we had stayed longer. Plus, we didn't want to gamble away our winnings. RJ always said to quit whilst you're ahead."

Daniel's eyebrows rose. Why did Oscar have to mention RJ? He quickly glanced at Nick who, surprisingly, had not noticed; being totally intrigued by what Oscar was saying.

"We were so excited that we went to the pub to celebrate our takings. The punk owes me about £500 from that. Anyway, I guess Otty got a little carried away with celebrating."

When Oscar finished, the men were in a buzz. Nick's smile had not wavered. He reached out and drew Oscar to him in a bear hug. "Awesome work Oscar. Fantastic." He let Oscar go and turned to Otty but seemed to think twice about hugging him too. "Take 'im to 'is bed. E's gonna be puking 'is face off before morning."

Daniel was happy too. Nick's mood had changed. It was cheerful and safe again. Initially he had been worried that whatever was going on with Otty and Oscar could make an already terrible situation worse. However, it had had the opposite effect. A sure way for Nick to make money – that's always good news.

As the other guys were busy bombarding Oscar with questions, Nick signalled to Meltdown, "Change of plans; let's talk."

Chapter Fourteen

———————〜———————

Rachel sighed! Who was she kidding? She had been sitting here watching TV with Sunita for an hour, but the truth is, her mind had been miles away. She didn't even know the name of the Netflix film they were watching, much less what was going on. Sunita had selected it and she had pretended to be keen to watch it. Karen had gone out for the night, so it was just the two of them at home. She turned to Sunita who was half sprawled beside her on the settee. The slow familiar deep breathing sound was the unsurprising evidence that Sunita had fallen asleep. This was typical; Sunita hardly ever watched a film to the end unless it was at the cinema.

Her pixie statured roommate's paternal grandparents had migrated to the UK from India in the 1960s. Her mother, on the other hand, had been an exchange student from India, when she met, and later married, her father in the UK. Sunita was a very quiet person but tended to be more open with her very close friends.

Rachel patted Sunita on the leg, rousing her from her sleep. Her roommate sat up, half asleep. She looked at the TV, shook her head, turned to Rachel, and smiled. Then she mumbled a good night, stood up, and made her way up the stairs and to her room.

Rachel was about to stand up to clear up their wine glasses and plates of cookies when her phone started to ring. She looked at the clock that hung on the wall of the dining table on the other side of their moderate living room – 11.40pm. The only person who could be calling at this time was either Karen, who might have forgotten her house keys yet again or... She dug her phone out from the side of the settee and saw Evan's name on the screen.

They had not spoken in some time, and she shuddered to imagine why he might be calling now. All day she had been thinking about Eva seeing her having dinner with Patrick and wondering what she was going to do. What if she had told Evan and that was why he was calling? She would not have thought Eva the type, but then again, that was her twin brother, and no one would blame her for looking out for him. Rachel had not been taking his calls before, and then he stopped trying. So why now? Her heart was beating fast. She could just let it ring and not pick up, but for some reason she swiped to answer.

There was an initial silence when she put the phone to her ear. "You there Rachel?" Evan finally spoke.

Rachel squeezed her eyes shut. She had no idea how much she had missed hearing his voice.

"Ye... yess," she responded. She still loved him like crazy. She did not think she could ever get over him. She just might have to. It was possible that he knew about her 'mess-up' and was calling to officially end their currently unstable relationship.

She heard him breathe a sigh of relief but said nothing. "How are you?" he asked.

"I'm err... I'm doing okay," she replied.

"Oh... okay. That's errm... that's good," he said.

The pauses were awkward, and Rachel felt extremely uncomfortable. "It's been a minute!" he said, chuckling slightly.

It's been too long, she thought.

"I guess," she said instead.

"Why though?" he asked almost immediately.

Why what? Why had it been a while since they had spoken or why had she gone out to dinner with another man? There was silence as Rachel did not know what and how to respond.

"Rachel, are you there?" He asked, confusion in his voice.

She released the deep breath she had been holding in, which answered his question.

"I really don't understand why? Please explain it to me. I'm going crazy here," he said. There was hidden emotion in his voice. Was it anger?

She knew then that Eva had told him. She understood but could not stop the furious feeling from rising within her. Eva should have minded her own business, she thought, even though something at the back of her head reminded her that Evan was Eva's business.

"Rachel, for pity's sake, answer me!" Evan was not holding back his annoyance anymore.

Rachel frowned angrily. "Eva told you, didn't she? Of course, she did." She laughed sardonically as she answered her own question.

There were a few seconds of silence before Evan replied, "What? What are you talking about?"

Rachel frowned again.

"Rachel, talk to me. What did Eva supposedly tell me?" Evan demanded.

"Bu... but you asked why?" Rachel enquired in a daze.

"Yes. I asked why we were fighting and not talking. I don't understand what's happening with us. Does Eva have the answer to that?" Evan seemed as confused and as curious as ever.

Rachel was shaking now. What had she done? Eva had not told him! Oh no!

"Dammit, Rachel, wha..." Rachel did not hear the rest of what Evan was about to say as she quickly cut the call off and tossed the mobile phone on the sofa. Thinking twice, she picked it up again and turned it off. She then buried her head in her hands and wept.

Eva's Saturday had started quite early, and it was going to be a busy one. Her list included dropping by at her parents', grocery shopping, going to the hairdresser's, and then getting herself all dressed for the fundraiser tonight. So far, she had managed to tick off two on the list. She was now hurriedly putting away the groceries so she could make it on time for her hair appointment. There was no hiding it; she was nervous and excited at the same time. It was not the first time she would be attending a fundraiser. She knew what she was feeling had RJ written all over it. She found that she was looking forward to seeing him again. It was funny that, even though she liked Adam, she never felt that way about him. The forbidden fruits always seem more tempting, she thought as she dashed to her room to get a few items together for her appointment. She was really cutting it close.

In the car, she caught a glimpse of herself in the rare view mirror. Her unruly mass of curls might need to be straightened for tonight. The ringing of her phone made her sigh impatiently as she grabbed it. It was Joyce. Eva was not surprised. She had felt the constant vibrating of her phone in her bag whilst she was shopping earlier. She suspected it would be the older woman. It seems Joyce was more excited about tonight than she was.

"Do you want me to come over and help you get ready this evening?" Joyce's voice was all bubbly.

Eva rolled her eyeballs. "No, thank you, Joyce. This isn't the American senior prom. I can manage."

"Well, it might as well be. I just want to make sure you look good," Joyce said, sounding a little disappointed.

"I will, Joyce, I promise. I'll even take photos," Eva said.

"Really?" Joyce seemed pleased.

"No. Of course not! Now I have to go, Joyce. I'm running late for my appointment at the salon," Eva said.

Once she was off the phone, she noticed several missed calls from Evan. In fact, Joyce had not even called before now. She saw a few text messages from him, too. *Strange!* It cannot be that much of an emergency, or her parents would have rung too. She would have to ring him back when she got the chance, she thought as she started the car engine.

Lisa Simms knew she could never have him, and she had accepted that a long time ago and moved on. That did not mean she could not take him in and admire him. She had stopped letting her mind ask the question 'what if' a while ago. He was a good man, her friend, and she would always be there for him. She just could not stop her eyes from roaming all over RJ's tuxedo clad form. The man was too beautiful for his own good.

The crisp white shirt with black buttons hugged his well-formed chest. It was tucked smartly into slim fitted black trousers. The black cummerbund around his waist was silk, which matched the black silk bow tie round his neck. Gold plated cufflinks held the cuffs of his long sleeves securely around his wrist. She could see the defined tone of his arm muscles through the sleeves. She had helped him trim the sides of his jet-black hair that morning. It was silky as it hung over his shirt collar at the back. She could not see the black socks he obviously had on as his trousers dropped over the shiny black masculine shoes that dawned his feet.

Lisa continued to watch him as he put on his tailored black coat with silk lapels. It fitted his lean figure. He adjusted his sleeves and made room for his Rolex to breathe. Then he neatly folded his clean white pocket square and placed it perfectly in the breast pocket. He looked like a million pounds. Earlier, she had asked him how much the tux had cost to hire when she saw it hanging in his room and was surprised when he informed her that he owned it. It was one of the things he had picked up when he snuck back to his place a couple of days ago.

She had known him a while, yet there was still so much she did not know about him.

He looked at her inquiringly with those cool blue eyes. "Well?"

"That angel better be worth it," she replied.

Sunita hurriedly stood up to answer the doorbell. This was the third time today. Once again, it was a delivery of a bouquet of flowers for Rachel. What was this all about? Had Evan upset her? Maybe that could explain why Rachel hadn't come out of her bedroom all day.

She hadn't even answered when Sunita knocked on her bedroom door several times between this morning and now.

Why couldn't Evan just have had them delivered all at once; this was a bit dramatic. Sunita was a little annoyed as she, once again, had to look for a vase for the new delivery. She filled it with water and nicely put the bouquet in it. She then placed the vase beside the other two on the dining table.

Hopefully, this was the last one. It was almost 6:30 pm, so no more deliveries!! She could not wait to cuddle back on the sofa and continue reading her romance novel. She had practically had the house to herself all day and she was loving it. Karen had come back home in the early hours of the morning, and it was usual for her to sleep the whole day once that happened. Rachel had not been out of her room at all, at least not that she was aware. Maybe she had come out to get herself something to eat and drink when Sunita had gone out for her run this morning. In fact, Rachel had recently started running on Saturday mornings too, so Sunita was surprised when she had not done so today.

The flowers were very beautiful. Evan must have really messed up to send three bouquets separately in one day. She moved to smell them. Her eyes fell on a small card looped through by a band.

All three had come with cards. She had made sure to leave the bands attached to the upper part of a stem from each bouquet. She had not thought to read the note in them earlier, but now curiosity made her check... wondering if Evan had written some kind of apology in them; something that could shed some light on what was going on between them.

"To: Rachel, I can't stop thinking about you. Please call me back. Patrick x."

Sunita's eyes widened in shock. Who in the world was Patrick? Was Rachel cheating on Evan? How could she? What woman in her right man would cheat on Evan? He was every woman's dream, and he loved Rachel! Sunita knew that there had to be more to this.

Just then Karen came down. Sunita quickly moved away from the flowers. "Goodness, you look rough." Sunita said going to settle back into the sofa.

"Thank you." Karen gave a sarcastic smile and then scowled. She had bags under her eyes and her hair hung wildly around her head. It was obvious she felt rough too.

Karen paused in front of the dining table on her way to the kitchen. "Wow. Who are these for?" she asked gesturing towards the flowers.

Sunita picked up her book, trying to sound casual "Oh, they're for Rachel." She said praying that Karen, like her, would assume they were from Evan.

Karen blinked and continued to stare at them. Sunita held her breath.

"Evan sent her all these flowers? Wonder what she's done to deserve it. Lucky, lucky Rachel." Karen finally said, her sarcasm reeking of envy. She then sauntered off to the kitchen.

Sunita let out her breath.

Nick and Meltdown stepped out of the rented limousine. A van parked right behind their ride, and four men came out. Oscar and Otty looked more presentable than the last time they were here. Like Meltdown, they wore black jackets over their T-shirt and jeans attire. Nick, on the other hand, wore his black jacket over blue shirt and black trousers. The other two men present wore their regular ensemble of T-shirt, saggy jeans, and leather jacket.

Nick patted his gelled slicked hair. Made sure the fold of his hair in front was still intact. Then he took in a deep breath of air.

"Do you smell that, boys? That's the smell of money, and I'm cashing in tonight." He smiled.

Otty gave a slight grunt beside Oscar. Oscar immediately turned to him. "You okay? You better get yourself together," he whispered.

Otty was still recovering from last night's drinking spree and tumble down the stairs. He was suffering from a strong hangover, a bruised lower lip, and grazed arms, hips, and thighs. Oscar felt bad for him. Nick had insisted that Otty be here, for obvious reason, which made sense. However, what Otty really needed was to be in bed, applying ice to his bruises and popping Ibuprofens. He had slept the better part of the day and had not had the chance to treat himself before they had to be here; the same place he and Oscar had made some cool cash last night.

They watched as several pricey looking cars arrived. Men dressed in expensive suits stepped out, some of them with beautiful ladies on their arms. There was some laughter and giggling from the ladies who, Oscar had no doubt, were high classed prostitutes. He watched them as they clung to the men they arrived with. The men all smoking cigars and creating a misty atmosphere as they approached the two huge bouncers at the door. Each of the men whispered something into the ears of one of the bouncers and he promptly let them in.

"You ready fellas?" asked Nick excitedly.

The five men nodded, and Meltdown signalled to the other two guys, who took their que to remain outside the building. Nick then began walking towards the heavily built bouncers at the entrance of the building with Meltdown, Oscar and Otty right behind him.

The ferocious looking bouncers studied the four men intently as they approached. Nick took out a cigarette and Meltdown retrieved a lighter from his back pocket and lit it for him. In front of the taller bouncer, Nick paused to take a huge swig of his cigarette and then let out a puff just before he leaned close to the giant of a man and whispered the password "Payback!"

Chapter Fifteen

Eva had planned to drive initially but decided to use an Uber last minute. There was no way she could have handled driving with her high heels. Besides, she could not risk dealing with traffic and getting frazzled. On the way to the venue of the fundraiser, she scanned the pictures she managed to take of herself in front of her bedroom mirror using her mobile phone. She sighed; the things she did for Joyce. She sent the three best ones out of the four she took and sent them to Joyce via WhatsApp.

The dress she wore was a long black satin mermaid dress. It moulded her slim waist accentuating her lovely figure on its way down where it gathered at her knees, and then cascaded down in folds. At the bottom, the colour of the dress fades into white with black and white tassels between the folds. The dress had very short sleeves that barely went past her shoulders and rested on the upper part of her arms. Her arms were bare from there on until just past her elbows where the long black satin gloves she had on stopped. Her neckline separated in the middle and dipped to her chest. But the artificial diamond clusters that sequined the edges created a covering in the middle, so she only showed off a decent amount of cleavage. Diamond drop earrings matched elegant diamond necklace and bracelet. Her long black high heeled shoes, that were buckled at the ankles and had two thin diamond studded straps across her feet, but just above her toes, were hidden away underneath the bottom of her dress. The plan had been to get her hair straightened, but the hairdresser had convinced her to celebrate her curls. So different sections of her hair at the front had been twisted stylishly and held back with small decorative silver pins, letting the rest of her beautiful curls fall back over her shoulders at the back. Her naturally long and thick eyelashes fanned her smoky-eye makeup effect. She had done her makeup herself and knew the colours that suited her pretty, delicate features.

It was almost 6:47pm when she stepped out of the Uber at Bloomsbury Ballroom parking. It was a lavish venue on the lovely Bloomsbury Square close to the West End and not far from the city. She saw many luxurious cars arriving and parking and many exquisitely dressed men and women coming out and making their way towards the entrance of the Victoria House building where the ballroom was. Some vehicles were chauffeur driven and had come to be parked after the owners were dropped off at the front of the building.

She had agreed to meet RJ here and that was why she had directed the Uber driver to the parking instead. Why in the world had she not exchanged phone numbers with RJ? Doing so seemed like a bad idea to her at the time, but she realised now that it was senseless that they had not. She was sure he thought so too. The phone in her hand buzzed. She hung her black satin shawl over her left hand, and quickly checked the message on her WhatsApp. It was Joyce:

"Ooo I'm soooo proud of you, Eva." This was followed by lots of love and heartfelt emojis.

Eva smiled before putting her phone in her black diamond studded clutch purse. How long did she have to wait for RJ before she deemed that he was not coming and had no way of letting her know?

She let her eyes span the parking area and was about to check her wristwatch for the time when she spotted him. She stood rooted to the spot and could do nothing but stare at him. RJ was a breathtakingly beautiful man, and he looked like he just stepped off a James Bond set. He was clean shaven, and his hair had seen a bit of a trim. She had once thought he might be a man who lived a little bit in the rough, but seeing him dressed like this, she was not so sure now. The tuxedo fitted him like a glove and looked like it belonged on him.

He was about ten feet away and had obviously spotted her too. Like her, he stood there for a while; not moving, staring at her. Finally, he began to make his way towards her. Her heartbeat quickened. Why did this guy have such an effect on her? She always seemed to lose control of her emotions… and her breathing whenever she saw him. Soon he was standing there right in front of her. The silence was overwhelming as their eyes drank each other in.

Inhaling softly, she forced herself to say something. "You clean up nice."

A slow delicious grin crept across his mouth. "And you're absolutely stunning," he replied.

The warm feeling that overtook her face was uncomfortable, and she looked down to hide her blush.

"You really are an angel, aren't you?" he said, making her look right back up at him. For a few seconds they were lost in each other's eyes. Deep sea blue meeting translucent light brown. She had to get herself together.

"I'm no angel. Angels are heavenly beings," she broke the silence once again.

"Well, I think you look heavenly," he said.

She smiled, and he smiled too.

"Well, earth angel…" he said pointedly. "…are you ready to go in?" he asked, crooking his right arm.

She smiled warmly and obliged with her left arm.

The ballroom was exquisite. The chandeliers, immaculately dressed waiters, the lavish décor, the lovely jazz music that flowed from invisible speakers. It was all bright and beautiful. Everyone was dressed in elegant dinner dresses and tuxedos. Some had white ones on, but most had on black. It was a plush atmosphere. There were several well-known figures in society and celebrities; people who worked on BBC TV, BBC Radio hosts and producers, business moguls and MPs. Eva also recognised a number of casts from EastEnders and Doctor Who, including a few judges and personalities from The Voice UK and Strictly Come Dancing. It always felt amazing to be here.

RJ pulled out a chair for her and she sat in it. It was a five-person per table set up. He took the chair next to hers.

"Isn't it amazing?" she said, her face aglow.

He seemed tickled by the look on her face. "How many of these have you been to?" he asked.

"This is the third one. They have it every year and it's always a different venue. My first was four years ago. We had four tickets then. The reverend, two other members of the church and I attended that one. The second year, we had four tickets again, but I didn't go. Last year, we got three tickets. Josh, Joyce, and I had the pleasure. This year, we got two. No one seemed to be able to make it. Joyce wanted to but changed her mind. The tickets are rather expensive, but we get them free, courtesy of our benefactor." Eva took a deep breath. She knew she was being a little chatty, but she did not know how else to control her nerves.

She studied his face. He looked very much at home in this environment and seemed rather unfazed by all the opulence around him. She noticed that his Tux was Gorgio Armani.

Renting it alone would not have come cheap. She felt guilty that she made him spend so much on a tux… one that fitted him so gloriously.

"So, tell me about yourself," she asked suddenly wanting to know more about him. He intrigued her. It was like there were two sides to him.

He leaned closer. "What would you like to know?"

His close proximity wasn't doing much for her thinking.

"Errm… where are you from? What do you do? Do you have family?" she asked in succession.

"Whoa! Slow down there." He laughed before he answered, "I'm from North London." He paused, and then went on, "I'm a money lender, and yes, I have some family."

Money lender? Eva was stunned. Did that mean what she thought it meant? Without giving it much thought, she asked in a whisper, "You're a loan shark?"

RJ tensed. "Did I say that?" he asked, defensively.

Eva was trying to get her head around it. Why was she surprised? Hadn't she always sensed there was something irregular about him?

"What you do is illegal," she stated, ignoring his response. Disappointment was evident in her tone.

When he remained silent, she went on, "Why anyone would go to a loan shark instead of a bank is beyond me," she said, shaking her head incredulously.

RJ cast her a side look and then asked coolly. "Tell me, how is a loan shark different from a bank? They both lend money to people who need it, and they both charge interest."

What? Eva stared at him, and RJ went on, "I think you will find that it does have benefits, which is why people go to them in the first place. There is none of the bureaucracy and tedious bank requirements."

A couple that just arrived took the two seats beside Eva. She smiled at them, and then turned back to RJ, lowering her voice once again to a whisper. "You say that, but loan sharks are awful when they don't get their money back as and when agreed. They charge really high interest and are known to be cruel monsters who hurt people and their families to get their money back."

RJ's tone matched hers. "Yes, you're right; that's why it's illegal. Albeit not all of them are terrible. I just wanted you to understand why people might be forced to go to loan sharks instead of the banks. I wouldn't have pegged you as the judgmental type, Eva. You need to be more empathetic with people. You are unaware of their circumstances and what makes them do the things they do."

That stung her. Was she being judgmental? She supposed he was right. Isn't that what she had tried to explain to people on many occasions? It was so easy to condemn others, especially without knowing much about their situations. She deplored that line of business, but she did not have to judge the people who solicited it.

Eva relaxed. "I'm sorry. I didn't mean to come across as judgmental," she said softly.

RJ looked at her and his eyes seemed to soften.

A voice came up on the microphone from a man standing on the stage. The speaker apologised for starting slightly late, announced that he would be the host for the evening and that the night was about to begin. He explained where the fire exits were, where the buffet table was, and then ran off the list of charities and their causes. The list included orphanages, poor communities in Africa, churches with major charitable programmes, homeless people and shelters, Cancer, Alzheimer, and mental disorder research, and more.

"Before we kick-start with a musical performance, I would like to call on the chairman of the annual fundraiser's organising committee, the CEO of FairCorp, Alexander Fairchild." The speaker announced, to which there was an instant round of applause.

Forgetting their talk about what RJ did for a living, she clapped along and glanced at RJ.

"That's our benefactor. God bless him," she said.

RJ seemed a bit tensed, but slowly joined the clapping. "You okay?" she asked in concern.

He cleared his throat and smiled. "Sure," he replied, reaching for the bottled water in front of him. He poured some into a glass and drank.

RJ could not get over how gorgeous Eva looked. She was breath-taking and he could not seem to take his eyes off her. The beauty she exuded rendered his annoyance with her at her reaction to what he did for a living very momentary. It was not the ideal setting he would have liked to get to know her. To be honest, he was not even sure it was a good idea to know her at all. However, they were here, and he desperately wanted to know everything.

Even though there was no major risk of Nick or anyone in that group seeing him here, there were other reasons that kept him from fully relaxing. Eva obviously loved being in this environment and was enjoying every performance.

He realised that he enjoyed watching her enjoying herself. After a couple more musical performances and a stand-up comedy act, the buffet table was now open. Watching the lingering laughter crinkle around her eyes and curve of her mouth made him take in a breath.

When they were both seated with their meals in front of them, he decided to ask questions of his own. It worked well for him too, as he did not like talking much when he was eating. Taking a sip of his champagne, he asked, "I think it's time for you to tell me something about you?"

She put a fork through a piece of lettuce and then squinted a little, thinking of what to say. It was obvious that she had just turned on her mental filter. He smiled.

"Let me see…" she began "… I'm from Yorkshire but was born and raised in London. My dad is originally from Nigeria. I have a brother who thinks he is older, and I work in marketing."

RJ laughed. "So, is your brother really older or he's just overprotective?" He would be very protective too if he had Eva as a sister.

"Maybe both?" Eva replied indecisively. "He was born fifteen whole minutes before me, he would say."

RJ was surprised. "You're a twin?"

Eva nodded.

"Interesting," RJ said fascinated. Eva was a very intriguing person. "So, are you similar in any way?"

"Nope. Well, maybe with looks, that's about it. I'm certainly the sweet and intelligent one. He would beg to differ, of course," she laughed, and he joined her.

"Ever been to Nigeria?" RJ asked curiously.

Eva nodded. "Only once. Evan and I were only ten years old, so we don't remember much. Except we were doted on by a lot of people. It was hot out there, and there was a lot of food. I would certainly like to visit again."

"I've been to Morocco and South Africa," he informed her. He remembered having a great time in both countries. Their culture was rich, and their warmth was touching.

"Really?" Eva's eyes widened in astonishment.

An elderly voice suddenly penetrated the steady buzz of chattering in the room. "Rhys? Rhys? Is that you dear?"

Sods! Just what he needed, RJ thought as an elegant and bejewelled elderly woman approached their table.

"Oh, my word, Rhys. It is you, isn't it? I haven't seen you in over... my goodness, a decade. Where have you been?" The woman chided, smacking RJ slightly on the arm. RJ noticed the sudden look of shock mixed with curiosity on Eva's face, but she said nothing.

He was not surprised that Betty Blythe would be at a function like this, but he had hoped not to bump into the likes of her. RJ stood up to acknowledge the old lady, bending to her five-foot two height so he could plant a kiss on both her cheeks.

The woman went on, "Look how you've grown; even more handsome. It does please me to see you here... like this. Your father must be so happy. He..."

"... Elizabeth Blythe, may I introduce you to Eva..." RJ Interrupted Betty with a forced smile, gesturing towards Eva. He had to do something to shut the woman up, but then realised he did not know Eva's last name.

There was a short awkward pause as the woman's eyes turned to settle on Eva curiously, waiting patiently for RJ to finish.

"Da Silva. Eva da Silva," Eva supplied for herself much to RJ's relief.

Betty Blythe's face took on one of intrigue and pleasure. "Oh charming. You're such a beauty, Eva. You and RJ are so well suited."

Eva suddenly looked agitated "Oh no Elizabeth; we're just..."

"... Eva please, call me Betty." Elizabeth interrupted.

Before either Betty or Eva could say another word, RJ leaned down and kissed the woman on both cheeks again.

"It was great to see you, Betty. Eva and I were just enjoying our meal. Please give my regards to Andrew." He was sure her husband was quietly seated at one of the tables, waiting for, but definitely not missing, her.

"Oh, dear." Betty frowned, taken aback. She cast Eva a helpless look and then briskly walked away from their table.

RJ sat down and caught Eva's look of disbelief. He knew what she was going to say but getting rid of Betty had been necessary.

"That was incredibly rude, RJ," Eva said, annoyed.

Eva did not know what to think. She was truly getting to know a little more about RJ. It seemed though that the more she knew, the more she didn't. She was still as confused and unsure about him as she was at the very beginning. His name was Rhys, and he could be really charming, looked absolutely fantastic in a tux, fitted into this environment like a glove, and he actually knew people… well someone from this world. This was a big surprise. On the flip side, he just might be a loan shark, and was just unreasonably rude to a sweet old woman he knew and who had come over to their table to say hello to him. Why was he so closed? Was it a good idea to be spending time with him? You're being judgmental again, a little voice told her. She sighed.

RJ hadn't responded to her reprimand but had proceeded to continue eating his food. She too had quietly faced her meal. The silence between them was one she had no intention of breaking. She had nothing to say to him if he was not going to answer to how he had behaved.

RJ finally leaned back in his chair and said, "Look, I realise I was rude, but she wouldn't leave otherwise; trust me! You don't know Betty Blythe."

Eva reluctantly turned to RJ. "And who is she?"

RJ sighed. "She's a London socialite that enjoys peering into everyone's business. She's a busybody."

"Well, I don't care who she is, it doesn't justify your rudeness," Eva said with irritation. "Besides, why would she be peering into our business, what juicy gossip can we possibly provide her?" Betty's wrong assumption that she and RJ were somehow together briefly came into her mind, but she failed to see how that would be of any appeal to the woman.

RJ leaned closer to Eva. "I might have reacted the wrong way. I apologise for upsetting you as a result."

Eva wanted to remind him that it was not her that he had been rude too but decided to let it go. He looked devilishly handsome looking at her like that. Yes, devil was the word. What the devil was she getting herself into with this man?

She let herself smile. "So… your name is Rhys." It was more of a statement.

The corners of his mouth turned into a grin. "Yes. And yours is Eva da Silva?" It was more of a question.

"Da Silva is of Portuguese origin. During the 1700s to 19th century slave trade, some Portuguese and Brazilian slave traders settled in the south-west coast; a place called Badagry Island in Lagos, Nigeria," Eva explained.

He seemed impressed and genuinely interested. "I think it's commendable that you know something about your heritage."

She fiddled with her napkin, a soft smile on her face. "Evan and I were always interested. If we weren't pumping our dad for answers, we were busy reading up stuff for information."

Eva continued to fiddle with her napkin and then realised something. She looked up at RJ. "I don't…" She stopped, catching him looking at her in the oddest way. Was it desire she saw in his eyes?

"… I don't know your last name," she managed to ask softly.

He seemed reluctant to let go of his thoughts. Finally, he exhaled. "Rhys Jared…"

Just then, there was an announcement informing people that they could start placing their pledges or cheques in the boxes at the four corners of the hall, and that the floor was open for dancing. The circular arrangement of the tables left adequate space in the middle for this. Slowly, people started to get up from their seats as the music from the invisible speakers was replaced by a jazz band that had set up on stage.

Eva stood up and RJ did as well, helping her with her chair. "I'm going to put a cheque in," she informed.

"Me too," replied RJ.

"Oh, you don't have to," Eva hurriedly said, worried that she was making him spend more money on this night. First the tux and now this.

"Nonsense! It's for charity and I'm here. Of course, I have to," he replied.

When she arrived back at their table, RJ was standing waiting for her, a glass of wine in his hand.

"I was wondering if you'd care to dance," he asked, putting his wine glass on the table.

Eva nodded with a smile. She placed her purse on her seat. She was going to be in incredibly close proximity with him, and she didn't know if she was looking forward to it or dreading it.

They soon joined the other dancers on the floor, and he drew her into his arms. He held her close and firmly. It felt so good and questionably right. She felt her heart rate increasing again. It was rarely steady around him. They said nothing as they moved to Lisa Bassenge and The J-Chestra's rendition of the soft jazz song, *Perhaps, Perhaps, Perhaps*.

She was surprised that he was such a good dancer. He moved with grace, and she let him lead. Rhys Jared was certainly a man of many surprises. He made her feel things she had never felt before, not even with David. She had to admit that she was deeply attracted to RJ and knew that she did not yet feel that same pull with Adam. However, she did like Adam; shouldn't that be enough? Eva looked up at him to find him already staring down at her, their eyes locking in that singular way they always did. A familiar tone broke their connection. Welcoming the distraction, Eva turned her head to gaze at where a dancing couple was making conversation with another dancing pair, one of whom was the distinguished Alexander Fairchild. The business mogul made his millions as a developer and business investor. He was probably in his 60s but was still a very attractive man who obviously took good care of himself. A charming man who she had never seen in anything other than a suit or tux. St Benedict was lucky to have him as a benefactor. Even though he was not a church going person himself, his support for St Benedict went back over a decade, long before she joined the church herself. Eva made a mental note to say hello and a big thank you to him before the night was over.

After the period of dance, there were a couple more performances on stage, and then it was time to read out how much was raked out in total and how much each organisation received. Eva was still under the sweet and soothing spell of her lengthy but silent dance with RJ that the applauses from the other guests in the room seemed distant sounds. It was only when RJ touched her hand softly, sending a warm tingly feeling all the way up her arm, that she came back to reality.

RJ was giving her that endearing smile. "£138,750. St Benedict did well."

The impact of what he said took a few seconds to hit her before her eyes widened with surprised elation.

"St Benedict is getting £138,750? Oh my goodness. That's the highest we have ever received. Thank you, Jesus," she cried out, instinctively throwing her arms around RJ in an excited hug.

She felt RJ tense even as she did too. Slowly, she pulled away from him with an embarrassed smile. The other guests at their table smiled their congratulations at both of them. Avoiding RJ's stare, she let her eyes scan the room in search of Alexander Fairchild's table. As if sensing it, she spotted him making his way towards their table. The charismatic way he walked seemed familiar. She stood up as he approached them.

"Mr Fairchild!" she greeted.

His handsome face projected a full smile as she accepted his peck on both cheeks. "Eva da Silva. What a pleasure; you look stunning," he replied.

Eva blushed. "Thank you. I wasn't sure you would remember me."

He crooked an eyebrow. "How could I not? I don't forget a beautiful face. And like I said last time, please… call me Alex."

Eva smiled in response. "Alex, on behalf of St Benedict, thank you so much for once again doing this. £138,750 is a lot of money and would go above and beyond in supporting the church's projects."

He nodded. "I'm glad to hear that." His eyes strayed to RJ who sat quietly, his eyes focused on nothing in particular.

Eva noticed. "Oh and this is Rhys Jared. He…" she didn't know what to say. This wasn't exactly a date. "… accompanied me tonight," she said.

Alex gave a half smile. "Rhys Jared," he repeated.

RJ's attention was now on Alex. He did not bother to get up. Both men stared at each other, neither extending a hand of handshake. Eva felt uncomfortable. Two obviously proud men sizing each other up.

It was Alex who broke the uneasy silence first. "It was good of you to come, Rhys Jared. Tell me; do you attend St Benedict church?"

When RJ did not immediately answer, Alex said, "I only ask because it's usually the church members who represent the church at these functions, and I have never seen you at one before. Do you attend then?"

RJ's steely stare hinted mischief. "No! Do you?"

When Alex's face hardened slightly, RJ went on, "I only ask because you are such a gracious sponsor of the church. Do you attend, by any chance?"

Eva decided to put a stop to this awkward exchange. Why were men such annoying babies sometimes? No matter how handsome, powerful, wealthy, or mysterious, they always need a pacifier to quench their weeping pride.

"No, Alex doesn't attend St Benedict," she informed RJ who didn't seem to care much for the answer.

Alex looked RJ over, and suddenly seemed satisfied. His full smile returned.

"It was nice to see you again, Eva. Please extend my greetings to the reverend. I trust the church will put the money to valuable use."

"Of course. I will be sure to tell him. It was nice seeing you too," Eva said as she offered her cheeks once again for a kiss.

Alex glanced at RJ. "Rhys Jared…"

RJ stood then. "Please, call me RJ."

Alex eyed him, but his smile didn't waiver. "Take care of yourself, RJ."

"Likewise, Alex," RJ said.

"I don't recall asking you to call me that," retorted Alex.

This took Eva by surprise, and for a moment she froze in confusion. RJ tensed quietly beside her.

Slowly, a mischievous chuckle escaped from Alex as his eyes displayed that of humour, implying that he had only been jesting. Eva gave a sigh of relief, a hand on her chest as she went along, laughing in response. She felt RJ relax beside her.

With a farewell grin, Alex patted her on the arm, gave RJ a brief nod and walked away from them.

Eva let her head fall back onto the headrest. RJ had offered to take her home, and she had accepted. He was just as surprised as she was that she had not objected.

Her eyes took in the night scenery outside, observing frequent colourful lights decorating some trees and a few streets. Another hint, besides the few TV adverts like that of the John Lewis, that Christmas was not too far off now. She glanced at his side profile. He was so good looking. If he sensed her staring at him, he did not show it. His attention was focused on the road. They hadn't spoken for half of the journey, and she let her mind wander. While he was still a mystery to her, for some reason, she was not as wary of him as she used to be. Even though she knew that she ought to be. This man was capable of impacting her life in a way she wasn't sure she was ready for. She felt it deep in her spirit. He had shown confusing aspects to his personality tonight. Charming, great dancer, charitable, engaging, rude, guarded, bold… and territorial?

"I started off as, what you would call, a loan shark…" His calm voice suddenly broke her thoughts. She took in a deep breath but did not say anything, letting him continue.

His gaze never left the road. "… at first, it was one person who needed financial assistance. His store had been robbed. I gave him the money. Told him to keep it. Then it was a lady who had been beaten up and duped of everything she had by her boyfriend. The man I had helped previously had referred her to me. I couldn't say no to her either. Then there was a young man and his young family who needed help to open up a shop and couldn't get a bank loan. The man had only ever worked in construction, had been injured and wasn't able to get a job." RJ broke off to check that the right side of the road was free before he took a left turn. Then he went on,

"Before I knew it, I was overwhelmed. There were just too many people in need of financial help, and I couldn't just keep giving it to them. I thought, if I made it a loan and started charging interest, it would keep the fakes at bay and ensure I continue to have money to help others.

"In the space of two years, it got bigger than I expected or wanted. It wasn't just the working class coming to me now, it was everyone. And of course. Not all of them wanted to or could pay back. I had a few of my... my friends to help collect the money owed. I never charged exorbitantly, we were never violent or aggressive. In fact, we lost a lot of money because of it. Anyway, it was illegal, whichever way you look at it. Then at the beginning of this year, I had an idea. I had knowledge of accounting and finance, why not go legal and start up a proper money lending company."

Eva turned to look at him then. He kept his eyes on the road.

"So, I went to see my lawyer and we drafted a business plan. We put all the requirements in place and applied to the FCA for authorisation to start up a consumer credit lending firm. My plan was to try to make it less stringent for people to borrow money. I even found an office which I paid for outright." He paused again to finally glance at her.

She smiled at him. He had applied to the Financial Conduct Authority to legalise his business. Eva felt an enormous sense of relief well up in her. She thought about how she had overreacted earlier about the possibility of him being a loan shark and now his explanation made her feel more... more ashamed... more compassionate. Maybe that was how he knew Betty Blythe. Maybe she had once had to borrow money from him.

"It took about three months to put everything in order and make the application, and another six months to get the FCA's approval.

"Unfortunately, a few days after the approval came though, I got... well... I had my... err accident and haven't had the opportunity to move things further since." He finished. There was an air of sadness around him, but she detected resentment in his eyes.

Eva suddenly noticed that the car was not moving and realised that he was parked in front of her flat building. It was a lovely building and she always marvelled at how beautiful it looked at night through the glow from the streetlights and the ones emanating from the various flats.

She slowly turned back to him. "Thank you for bringing me home," she said.

He turned his body to face her. His bow tie hung loose from his shirt collar. "You're welcome," he replied, his eyes not leaving her.

She thought again and then said, "Thank you for explaining things to me. I know you didn't have to. I don't condemn you now, and I'm sorry I did before. Most of all, I'm glad you finally did the right thing."

He looked down but said nothing.

Awkwardly, she sought for something to say to fill the silence.

"You know, the accident was a minor setback. You survived for a reason. God knows your heart and has great plans for you. Your business will be successful, and you will help loads of people. I will be praying for you." Eva said again. She really had to stop before she frightened him away by sounding preachy. Frighten him away? Did that mean she did not want him away from her?

He remained silent, watching her, but a shadow of a smile was on his mouth. "Okay then. Goodnight, RJ," she said, opening the car door.

"Eva…?" he called before she could step out. She stopped and turned to face him.

"Since I know where you live now, don't you think it's about time you gave me your number?" he asked.

Eva smiled and then gave it to him. They soon said their goodnights and he drove off.

Chapter Sixteen

Laughter and shouting roused him from his sleep induced state. What was all that racket? Only half his body was resting in bed as the bottom half was hanging off it; his feet resting on the floor. He sat up. The sudden thud sound on the floor reminded him that he had fallen asleep whilst reading a book. He picked it up from where it had dropped on the floor and then glanced over at John's small bedside table. It had only one item on it, a small clock radio. The time was just after midnight. He looked around the room he shared with three others, and there was no one in there but him. Again, there was a wave of cheering and singing. He was still wearing his jeans and T-shirt as he had not changed for bed yet. He got up and made his way out of the room. From the corridor, he could hear music and more laughter. What could be going on now? There was always something happening in this crazy house. The noise and music got louder as he approached the TV and snooker room. The door was open, so he walked right in. There they all were, laughing, and drinking. Otty was in a corner, dancing weirdly by himself. Drunk again, obviously. Oscar was standing in front of the TV, smoking what seemed like weed, a glass of gin in his other hand. All the other guys were chatting cheerfully at the top of their lungs; all under the influence of alcohol.

Nick was behind the bar, talking excitedly with Meltdown. He noticed Danny standing in front of the doorway and beckoned to him, yelling, unnecessarily, at the top of his lungs. "Ah, if it ain't young Danny boy. Come 'ere."

Danny quietly walked over to the bar. Meltdown observed him quietly. The punk never smiled.

"Now I know you 'ave always observed the pointless no alcohol rule that was once imposed on you. Guess what? T'night is your lucky night. Drink and be merry wiv us. You'll be eighteen in what? Two? Three months anyway."

The other guys whistled and hooted at that. Danny's eyebrows went up. Really? He could have alcohol? What was going on here? How would RJ, who had always been very strict about him not drinking alcohol until he was eighteen, feel about this? He was going to be eighteen years old in February anyway. Danny wondered what they could possibly be celebrating. Well, as long as it put Nick in a good mood, it was definitely worth celebrating. Besides, RJ wasn't here.

Danny considered for a moment, and they all waited patiently for him to say something. "I'll take errr. I'll have errr a… Smirnoff?"

"Smirnooooofffff!" the men shouted in unison.

Danny smiled uncomfortably. Nick slammed his hand on the bar surface with excitedly determination. "The lad wants a Smirnoff, 'es getting a Smirnoff!"

In a matter of seconds, Nick was slamming open the cork of the Smirnoff bottle using the edge of the bar, then he handed it over to Danny. Once again, apart from the blaring music, the room was quiet.

Danny nervously brought the opening of the bottle to his lips. He knew the smell already from being around the guys when they were drinking it. He loved the smell of vodka. Without waiting anymore, he took a long hard swig of the drink, trying to impress the guys. When he came up for air, he coughed a little. He had taken in too much too fast and some of it had gone down the wrong way.

"Whooooo hoooooo," shouted John as all the other guys raised their bottles and glasses in Danny's direction, jeering at and hailing him playfully.

Rog – short for Roger, gave him a slightly hard pat in the back. He was a huge muscly fella and Danny felt it. The attention on him soon died down and Danny walked over to where Oscar now sat in front of the TV. He had downed his drink and was grassing up again. This was the only room in the house that smoking was permitted.

Danny was not sure if he would be allowed another drink, and so he wasn't going to rush but savour it. It tasted so good and made him feel good too. Although, this was Nick they were talking about and not RJ. Nick did not care a hoot whether or not Danny was of drinking age, or if he drank and got drunk. However, Danny did not want to take that chance. Besides, even though RJ was not here to see, Danny still felt a little guilty.

"So, what are we celebrating?" Danny asked Oscar, dropping beside him on the sofa.

Oscar cast a quick backward glance at where Nick was talking at the bar with a couple of the guys. He let out a skilled puff. "Nick and some of us went over to the poker place Otty and I talked about. Nick won 120 grand," He said, devoid of the joy the others had.

Danny's eyes opened wide in shock "What? In one night? That's crazy. I think I need to learn me how to play some poker."

Oscar chortled. "Nick is very good, but then again, the other players at the table were absolute rubbish."

Danny knew Nick was desperate to get enough money to buy into the drugs business. He did not want to be a part of it, and he knew quite a number of the men would rather not as well. RJ certainly was not happy about it from the very little Oscar had told him.

"He will be going back there, won't he?" Danny asked, knowing the answer.

Oscar cleared his throat. "You can count on it. He needs just over the same win to have enough."

Danny sighed sombrely, then took a sip of his drink.

Oscar gave him a puzzled look. "Smirnoff? Most lads go for beer first."

"Well, I'm not most guys," Danny replied, looking very pleased with his choice. At that moment, Danny reminded Oscar of RJ.

Mark Fischer did not usually get calls this late, but he could never ignore them as it might have something to do with work. It was almost 1am! The sound of his ringing phone caused his wife to stir in the bed beside him. He hurriedly but quietly picked up his mobile phone and left the room. In the bathroom, with the door firmly shut, he hit 'answer' before he could check the caller ID.

"Hello. Fischer!" he answered.

"Can you explain to me how and why I was blindsided by Rhys' presence at the FairCorp annual fund-raising gala?" Alexander Fairchild's cool but firm voice was heard at the other end of the line.

"What?" Fischer was shocked.

The brief silence at the other end of the line alerted Fischer further to Fairchild's underlying anger which he was working hard to keep a reign on.

"The very fact that you are unaware of this is not very encouraging," Alex stated.

Fischer was still lost for words. It was strange that RJ would visit the fundraiser at all, much less now that he has obviously been trying to keep a low profile.

When Fischer remained silent, Alex said, "Not only was he there, but he showed up with a woman from a church I sponsor. I happen to know that woman. Needless to say, he is either involved with her or the church… or perhaps both. Why don't I know what the hell is going on?" Fairchild never raised his voice, but the hidden icy edge to his voice was worse.

Fischer sighed. "You did ask us to remain cautious and not be too intrusive. We're trying to give him his privacy, just like you asked. The last place we would have expected him to show up was at the fundraiser!"

"Well, now I'm ordering you to be more intrusive and even more cautious. I want answers, Fischer, and when I want something, I need it!"

"Okay, Mr Fairchild. Consider it done." Once off the phone, Fischer proceeded to ring up his partner, Tom.

It was Sunday morning and Eva was reluctant to get out of bed. She was used to having late nights and still being up early for work. For some reason, however, she felt really tired. She wanted to stay in bed and daydream about RJ. Oh my! Did she just think that? Forgive me Lord. She was definitely going to church. She still had about 15 minutes before she had to be out of bed to get ready.

She had managed to change to her PJs last night but could not be bothered to wipe off her makeup. She stretched as she basked in the daylight that escaped through the spaces between her blinds and rested on the span of her queen-sized bed. It was RJ she had thought of before falling asleep last night, and him, the first thing when she woke up this morning.

What was that man doing to her? She could not get him out of her thoughts.

She said a short morning prayer, and then reached for her phone afterwards. She had not had a chance to check it for the better part of the day and practically all night yesterday. She had quite a lot of missed calls and messages. One was from RJ. She sat up in bed. It was a text message. It read: *"Sweet dreams, earth angel!"*

Her heart leaped. He sent this just after 1am. She smiled. Should she reply? What was she to say? She pondered for several moments then decided to check her other messages and probably come back to that one.

There was a missed call from Adam and a text message asking how her weekend was going… basically wanting to know what she was doing. She continued to go through her phone.

Two missed calls and voice messages from Evan. One message asked why she was not picking up her calls and that he was coming over to hers. The second said he was right at the front door of her apartment and wanted to know where she was. She had totally forgotten that he had tried to reach her yesterday. She meant to call him back but had totally forgot.

She had been in a mad rush yesterday trying to get ready for the evening. She immediately dialled his number.

It rang once before he picked up. "Eva, where in the world have you been?" Evan asked immediately. He sounded worried.

"Why? What's happened?" Eva replied anxiously. He sounded like he was driving.

"I don't know; you tell me. I couldn't reach you yesterday," he said.

Eva exhaled in relief, unaware that she had been holding her breath.

"Goodness! You scared me, Evan. I was busy getting ready for the charity event that raises money for St Benedict every year. You know, the one. It was last night. Sorry I was unreachable," she explained.

"Yes, I remember. But not cool, Eva. The whole day? Not cool!" He scolded, even though he sounded a bit more relaxed than he did when he first answered the phone.

"I said I was sorry. You don't know how long it takes to prep for these things. There just aren't enough hours in the day," she said, wondering what his problem was.

"Women!" Evan sighed.

There was something in the way he said that. Concern welled up in Eva again. "What's up? Why have you been trying to reach me?" she enquired.

Evan did not respond immediately. She heard his car indicator going.

A few seconds later, the sound of the indicator stopped, and he said, "Do you know what could be going on with Rachel?"

Eva closed her eyes. Not this. She was hoping she could keep out of it and let them work things out themselves. What did he want to know? What did he already know? Should she tell him about Rachel having dinner with another man? Evan would not normally open up about any issues in his relationship, so this must be really important. She had to be careful with her response. She opened her eyes again.

"What do you mean?" she asked.

"Oh don't give me that, Eva. You know! She has been acting strange lately and she happened to think that there was something you had told me." Evan replied, irritated.

She frowned. What did Rachel think she could have told Evan? She obviously did not know that she and Adam had seen her at the restaurant, so what could she be referring to? Was it the marriage concerns that Rachel had shared with her? Rachel had been indirectly asking her to talk to Evan about it, but she did not think it was her place to do so. She remembered advising Rachel to be open about it with Evan. Had Rachel still expected her to discuss it with Evan?

"For the love of God, are you women trying to drive me crazy?" Evan asked frustratingly. "Is there some kind of training you go on about how to drive a poor bloke, who you have deliberately left in the dark, mad, by keeping him waiting endlessly for a frigging answer?"

Eva was taken aback by Evan's spurt of anger. This was so unlike him. He was genuinely annoyed.

She was quickly taken over by the need to help him, to calm him down. "She did talk to me a few weeks ago about… well about you not having brought up the prospect of marriage."

Eva was a bit apprehensive. "She thinks you might not have plans to marry her in future. I… I think she feels a bit inadequate, for some reason."

There was silence at the other end. "Evan. Evan? Are you there?" she asked.

"Yes, I just pulled over at a convenient place to take this in," came his reply.

Eva waited a few seconds then said. "I think she wanted me to bring it up with you, but I thought it was best that she does it, and I asked her to. I guess she was worried about the possible negative effect such a talk might have on your relationship."

"Well, not talking about it isn't having a brilliant effect either, is it?" he responded sardonically.

Eva sighed. "What are you going to do about it?"

"I'm on my way to hers now… to have that talk," he said.

"Wouldn't she be going to church?" Eva asked, noting as she glanced at her dressing table clock, that she should have been out of bed ten minutes ago.

"That's why I left early; to catch her before she leaves for church," he answered.

RJ had just finished with his push-ups and stretches when Ben arrived. He knew he went to sleep late last night, but he was never one to lie in. He was an early riser. Besides, he could not sleep anyway. His mind had been taken over by Eva da Silva. He had never thought about a woman the way he thought about her. Thoughts of her were now an intrusion into his already complicated life. Yet, he had enjoyed spending time with her last night... despite a couple of problems that threatened to destabilise him. Man, she was so very easy on the eyes.

The glorious aroma of eggs and bacon welcomed him as he walked into the living room. Lisa was in the kitchen making fried eggs, and Ben was sitting on one of the sofas, reading a newspaper. He was old fashioned like that.

"Hey, RJ, ask Ben here why we're never over at his for a meal?" Lisa requested, pointing the spatula in Ben's direction.

"Because Ben doesn't cook," RJ replied wryly instead.

Ben chuckled. "You're welcome anytime, peach, if you don't mind cooking."

Lisa frowned and put her free hand on her waist. "Who's the peach? And why do I have to cook? Can't you order in?"

Ben considered this, but only for a second. "Actually, not a bad idea."

RJ joined Ben in the living room.

"How did it go last night?" he asked.

"I was about to ask you the same thing," Ben said with a grin.

RJ did not feel like going into it. "It was an interesting night."

"Did you encounter any issues?" enquired Ben.

"No not really. Well, nothing I couldn't handle."

"You like this angel of yours, don't you? Was she worth going to the trouble of getting tuxed up and going to the thing?" Lisa teasingly asked.

Did he like this angel of his? Without a doubt! Had she been worth the trouble? Absolutely! Hell, he could not stop thinking about her.

"Sure," was RJ's brief response.

Ben and Lisa exchanged a look. He's mad about her, Lisa mouthed to Ben, and he smiled.

"So yesterday?" asked RJ wanting to change the topic. He didn't need more reasons to keep thinking about Eva.

Ben sat up and moved to the edge of the chair. "It all went as planned. Nick's got himself £120,000 now. Oscar got in touch last night. Apparently, Nick's been on top of the world."

RJ nodded. "Good. He needs £130,000 more to make the mark, and then some for the money issues Oscar hinted that Nick might be having regarding the house and other expenses. Any idea when he intends to go back?"

"Oktapod gave him three weeks. One week has gone by, so he has two left. According to Oscar, Meltdown suggested that they go to the poker house this Friday, but Nick insisted that they had to keep up appearances and skip a week. He does not want to come across as desperate. He's confident they can make that and more next week Friday."

RJ looked at Ben quizzically. "Really? Even though he is desperate? That's cutting it a bit close. Isn't the money due the Monday after?"

"Yup. Nick's a very confident man." Ben stated scratching the back of his head.

Lisa could not help listening and joining in on their conversation.

"So wait; we know Nick's very good at poker and will most likely make the money he needs on that day, so what's the whole point? Don't you need to stop him?"

Ben turned to look at her as she dished out their breakfast.

"That's the whole point. Lure him. Get him close, get him overconfident, and then bam." Ben slammed his left fist into his right palm.

"Wait! Are you saying that that the two of you set the poker house up? Sweet lord! Is that your poker place?" Lisa's eyes shone with admiration.

RJ coughed. "Temporary poker house. It was set up for one and only one thing."

This was getting better by the minute.

"And the players?" Lisa asked.

"Ours," Ben replied with a wink.

Lisa shook her head in amazement. "So is it open every day of the week?" she asked again.

"No. Wednesdays, Fridays and Saturdays. Nick wouldn't want to play on Wednesday, I think. It's expected that the turn up is more and chances higher on weekends."

RJ looked at Ben, eager to finalise the plans and getting a bit impatient with Lisa's constant interruptions. "Since he's skipping a week, we go by his schedule. The next play day is next Friday? Well, we make sure he falls a little shy of the target."

Lisa interjected again. Her head was fully immersed in their plan now and she needed to reason it out.

"So sorry, guys, but that leaves one more day – Saturday for Nick to try again. Whether or not your players are good or terrible at poker, Nick is very, very good and can still make the score. Hello?" She said waving her hands in the air in a questioning motion.

Ben made a sound that was a cross between a snort and a chuckle.

"Yes, Nick is very good. But he'll also be playing against the best on the last day."

Lisa looked confused. The best? Who could…? No…!

Slowly, she turned to RJ. "No! RJ? I thought you quit! This is a bad idea!" She said, shaking her head in disbelief and apprehension.

RJ stood up abruptly. He had had enough of Lisa and her interruptions. Ben should not have overindulged her. They will have to finalise things later… when Lisa was not there to give her thoughts.

Chapter Seventeen

Karen watched as Sunita ascended the stairs carrying a tray laden with a plate of omelette, sausages, and toast. She turned back to the TV, taking another spoon of her porridge. She was sitting cross-legged on the floor in front of the TV with her porridge bowl balanced between her thighs. She still had on the oversized sleeping shirt that she usually went to bed in at night. Sunday was her lazy day. This time in the morning was when she watched her recorded TV programme, Love Island.

She could hear Sunita from upstairs trying to coax Rachel into eating something, and she rolled her eyes. Karen heard a door open, and then inaudible conversation before a door was shut again and Sunita came back downstairs.

"What's up now? Whatever Evan did, there are three bouquets of flowers on the dining table that obviously show her he's sorry." Karen quipped.

Sunita sighed. "Don't start, Karen. This is serious for her. She's quite sad. She didn't eat any dinner yesterday but has, thankfully, accepted breakfast. That's positive."

Karen rolled her eyes again. "I could have had the eggs and sausages if she didn't want it. That would have been positive too," she muttered under her breath.

Sunita gave Karen a look that pleaded with her to be more understanding.

"I guess she isn't going to church this morning then. It's a bit unusual for her." Karen tried to lay off a bit. She guessed she could try harder.

"Obviously not," Sunita replied, picking up one of the sofa pillows from the carpeted floor and placing it back on the sofa.

The doorbell rang and both Sunita and Karen were jolted by the sudden sound. It was unusual to have guests on a Sunday morning, especially this morning. Sunita went to open the door.

Evan walked in wearing joggers and a thick hoodie. He was not his usual jovial self and didn't have the usual mischievous generous smile to offer, but he was still as good looking as ever, Karen thought.

Karen and Sunita both greeted him. "Hey Sunita… Karen," he greeted back.

She did not know what to say, and judging by Sunita's silence, neither did she. They did not know the details, but they obviously knew something was wrong.

"I saw Rachel's car outside. It looks like I caught her before she left for church," he said quietly.

"She isn't going to church today." Sunita offered. He looked at Sunita and gave an 'I-see' nod.

"How is she?" he suddenly asked. He seemed to be trying to assess the situation first.

"In her room all day yesterday and this morning; wanting to be alone." Sunita explained. A look of concern slowly crept into his eyes. "Is it okay if I go up and see her?"

"Of course, it is," Sunita replied.

Evan smiled a thank you and began moving towards the staircase.

Karen could not bear to see Evan like this. She felt the need to cheer him up and put a smile on his face. Whatever the situation, he was obviously hurting too and was trying to make things right. "To be honest, I'm sure you'll be alright. No woman can resist beautiful flowers like those," Karen said, gesturing towards the dining table.

Sunita's eyes widened. Evan halted abruptly. He appeared puzzled and looked towards the table where the three vases stood with their lovely array of flowers.

"Err, no. Those are not for Rachel," Sunita said awkwardly with a smile. She hurriedly went to the table attempting to pick up two of the vases.

Karen frowned in confusion. "Oh? I could have sworn you said yesterday that they were from Evan."

Sunita glared annoyingly at Rachel. "No, I didn't. You just assumed." Her tone was uncharacteristically harsh.

Karen watched Sunita struggle uneasily to carry the two large vases. Did she really misunderstand the conversation about the flowers yesterday?

"Here, let me help." Evan went over to where Sunita was trying to balance the vases in her arms.

Sunita shook her head. "Oh no. Don… don't worry. I… I've got this," What was wrong with Sunita? Karen thought.

For some reason, Evan walked more purposefully towards Sunita and grabbed one of the vases from her. Sunita went still as he withdrew a note from it. Karen watched as the look on his face slowly became unreadable.

Then he peered at the one Sunita carried and read the note in that one too. Finally, he reached for the last vase on the table and pulled out the note in that bunch. Karen did not like the look on Evan's face nor the ghastly one on Sunita's. Who in the world were those flowers from?

At that moment, Rachel came downstairs. She was wearing her night robe but had managed to freshen up a bit and brush her hair. "I thought I heard Evan's voice. Did he leave?" she enquired softly.

She stopped uncomfortably, aware of the quietly tensed atmosphere in the living room. Evan looked at her but said nothing.

Sunita cast an apologetic look at Rachel, who obviously did not understand what was going on. She saw the vases in Sunita and Evan's arms and thought he had brought her flowers.

She smiled faintly and asked, "Are those for me?"

Sunita was about to say something, but Evan cut her off. "Yes, Rachel. They are for you."

His tone was laced with anger and none of the three women in the room missed it. The smile disappeared from Rachel's face.

"Who's Patrick?" Evan suddenly asked. His eyes not leaving Rachel's face.

Karen frowned. Patrick? Who the hell was Patrick? Unless he looked like Henry Cavill, Rachel needed to have her head examined.

Rachel looked like she wanted the floor to open up and swallow her. Her face displayed a host of terrified emotions, but she did not answer.

Evan placed the vase he had been carrying back onto the table. "I guess this explains all of your inexplicable, unexplainable and illogical behaviour."

Dipping both hands in his jogger pockets, he quietly made his way past Rachel, to the door, and walked out of the house.

Rachel slammed her eyes shut tightly.

"Oh, Rachel. I'm so sorry." Sunita exclaimed, putting the vase down and rushing towards Rachel as she burst into tears.

"What the hell just happened?" Karen asked from where she still sat cross legged on the floor.

As the congregants streamed out of the church, several of them engaged in conversation, Eva spotted Joyce looking at her just before she said something to her husband, Ian and came hurrying towards her. Eva did not break her stride until she got to her car.

"Thought you could escape without filling me in?" Joyce asked in between breaths as she approached Eva.

Eva smiled derisively. "I wouldn't even dream of it."

Joyce waved away Eva's tone. "So how did it go? You best hurry; Ian is a bit impatient this morning."

"It was beautiful, as usual. You heard how much we will be receiving from the church announcement this morning…"

"Oh please, Eva…" Joyce said, cutting her off. "…I meant how did it go with him?"

Eva sighed. Can she never get a moment when she wasn't thinking about RJ? However, it was a topic she seemed to be drawn to herself.

"Actually, it went really well with RJ. He's not what I originally thought. I got to see a few different sides to him," she answered.

Joyce smiled with apparent joy. "You see; I told you. How did he look? Were you swept off your feet?"

Eva could not help but smile too. "He looked so amazing in a tux, Joyce. I'm not sure about being swept off my feet, though. This isn't a fairy tale."

Joyce's smile widened. "Are you sure?"

Eva ignored her. "There's something about him, though. I can't put my finger on it."

"Why, what happened?" Joyce asked curiously, the smile leaving her face.

"I don't know. He was charming, a gentleman, but also displayed some unreasonably rude behaviour," Eva replied.

"How so?" Joyce asked, pretending not to hear Ian calling her from a distance.

"Okay, there was an instance where he and Alex Fairchild butted heads, for some reason. There was this air of hostility between them. It was the weirdest thing. The butting of heads wasn't extremely obvious, but it was there," Eva explained.

Joyce took on a mischievous look. "Oh my, Eva; two men sparring over you. Two very attractive men at that."

Eva stood watching her in shock. How could Joyce even think that both men's hostility was about her?

Joyce frowned. "Don't look at me like that. It's not impossible."

"Alex must be in his sixties!" Eva said, still in shock.

"So what? A man is a man, even one in his sixties. Besides, sixty isn't old. What world are you living in? Two men, no matter what age, can still desire a beautiful woman. Their egos can make them butt heads to stake some kind of imaginary or physical claim to her." Joyce said as a matter of fact.

Eva's jaw dropped. Where did Joyce come up with all this stuff? "Anyway, Alex, despite being extremely attractive, is about my dad's age so, no thank you," she stated.

"We weren't going for Alex anyway Eva, were we?" grinned Joyce with a wink.

They both turned at the sound of Ian's voice again. He was walking towards them and didn't look too happy.

"I better dash. Speak later." Joyce gave Eva a quick hug.

Rachel sat quietly in the passenger seat of Eva's car, which was still parked in the office car park. She waited patiently for Eva to take in everything she had just related to her. When Eva had asked to speak to her after work, Rachel knew she had to talk to someone. Sunita was a good friend, but Eva, well, Eva was more, close to family. Being the only child of parents who lived in Coton in the Elms, a village in the county of Derbyshire, she craved having something in the way of family around her. She knew she had not looked herself today and felt uncomfortable when she kept getting enquiries as to her health. Apparently, she had lost some weight, which was ironic. To think that she had wanted to lose weight, but certainly not under these circumstances.

"How did you know we saw you that night at the restaurant? Did you see us?" Eva asked curiously.

"Oh, no. I didn't! Adam let it slip sometime last week. When Evan rang me… the manner in which he questioned me, I was so sure you had told him." Replied Rachel, her eyes welling up with tears.

Eva looked empathetic. "Rachel, you should know that I wouldn't do anything to hurt you. Yes, Evan is my brother, and I did wonder if I should tell him, but I would have come to you first. To be honest, I was hoping I wouldn't have to do anything and you two would work it out yourselves. I didn't want to meddle. I'm so sorry that I wasn't supportive enough."

Rachel nodded. She believed that now. She was the one who got herself into the mess she was currently in.

"It's not you, Eva, it's all me. My fear of losing Evan evaporated all rational thought, and I have been spiralling since. I got paranoid and started making bad decisions. And now, I think I've actually lost him. Patrick was a big mistake… a way of making myself feel good and desirable. To prepare myself mentally for the fact that Evan might not want to marry me and would break up with me some day. It makes no sense now, but it sure did then. I've been so stupid." The tears began to drop onto Rachel's cheeks.

Eva gave her a comforting hug and Rachel tried to compose herself. A hand tapped on Eva's side window that almost made her jump. It was Adam. Eva wound her window down.

"You okay? You don't have car trouble, do you?" he asked, bending a little to peer through the open window.

"Not at all. Rachel and I just lost track of time talking, that's all," Eva answered.

Adam smiled. "You've been a bit busy lately; I haven't been able to get a hold of you. Did you see my text message? I've been out on a couple of sales meetings most of the day so not had a chance to catch you before now."

Rachel noticed an uneasy expression flit across Eva's pretty face, but she quickly replaced it with a smile. *That smile,* Rachel thought… Eva did not even know she did it, but that smile could render a man totally enamoured.

"Oh yes, I saw it. I'm sorry I didn't get back to you. It was a very busy weekend. Is it okay if we talked later?" Eva responded.

The look of disappointment was evident on Adam's face. "Hope not too much later; I've missed you," he said reaching in and giving her a peck on the cheek.

"Sorry about that," Eva said awkwardly after Adam had left.

"Don't be. So, are you two dating now?" Rachel asked.

"No. Not really. It's well… It isn't official or anything. I'm not sure yet. It's complicated." Eva was looking even more uncomfortable.

Rachel hardly ever saw Eva so uncertain. "Why is it complicated? You're both single and you both like each other, right?"

Eva sighed. "Well, he's a sweet guy, but I'm not sure I'm where he's at right now. Besides…" Eva paused, looking like she had suddenly come to a realisation.

"Besides…?" Rachel urged her on.

Eva came back from wherever her mind had briefly gone to. "Besides, there might be someone else."

Rachel was surprised. "You think there's someone else he's interested in?" Being with Eva was helping her forget her predicament.

Eva shyly put a hand loosely over her mouth. "Not him. Me!" Rachel's eyes shot wide open. "Really?"

Eva hurriedly waived Rachel's question off. "Okay, forget about me, and let's deal with your situation. This is about you. It's Rachel's time."

It would have been nice to have forgotten for a bit longer, Rachel thought. "So, what are you going to do?" Eva asked.

"I don't know what I can do. I betrayed him and was even a pain long before that," Rachel answered hopelessly.

Eva studied Rachel's face intently. "That was it, right? There isn't much more to this, is there?"

Rachel frowned, confused. "What do you mean?"

Eva looked even more closely. "You know…?"

Rachel felt a hole boring through her face. However, she suddenly understood. "Oh no. We met up jogging a couple of times. Exchanged a few text messages and then went out for dinner that one time. We've never been alone in a closed space, and we have never discussed anything sexual… regarding feelings or anything like that. I think the flowers where the first gesture connected to that."

Although, saying that, everything that had transpired between her and Patrick so far that she had just mentioned to Eva, had been inappropriate. Plus, she had known that Patrick liked her. Why else would he have invited her to dinner? Dinner had definitely been inappropriate!

Eva looked relieved. "Look, don't lose hope. Have you forgotten your faith? We all miss our way now and again, but as long as we realise our wrongdoing and are remorseful, God is faithful to forgive and help us at out time of need."

Rachel smiled through fresh tears. Why did she ever think to resent Eva? Eva was her own person, and she was hers. She had a friend and sister in Eva, no matter what, and she knew that.

"I love him so much Eva." Rachel burst out.

Eva handed her some more tissues from the small box on her dashboard. "I know you do. All is not lost. I will speak to Evan when I can, and you and I will pray, but you must not give up, Rachel. You have to win that man of yours back. Okay?"

A renewed hope and strength came over Rachel. "Okay," she nodded, dabbing away her tears.

It was already mid-week and Eva had not heard from RJ. He had her number now; why hadn't he called? She was still trying to accept the fact that she actually liked and was definitely attracted to him. It had dawned on her on Monday when she was speaking with Rachel. She really did not need to be obsessing over the man right now. She was swamped at work this week, was worried about a brother who will not return her calls while guiltily avoiding Adam's. Why was she evading Adam? She only just realised that she was subconsciously doing it.

She had left the office a little later this evening and was driving straight to church for the midweek service. When her phone started to ring, she knew instinctively that it was Adam, even though her heart wished that it was RJ. He wanted to see her tonight. It was not an emergency, only because they had not spent time or even really talked with each other in days due to their busy work schedule. Eva wondered why that fact was a problem for him. Were they dating? People did not really ask these days; it was just assumed. Had she written him off? He was a nice guy and had done nothing wrong. She needed to be sensible and not let RJ confuse her. She asked him if he was interested in joining her for church and they could go out for dinner after, or he could just meet her after church, if he wasn't up to attending the service. Adam had opted to join her for the service, which had surprised her. That was a good sign. She smiled. She really should not be writing Adam off; not even subconsciously.

Adam did not turn up for the service. She had waited for him outside for a bit to offer some support as he was not really a church person. He did not show up after church either. She waited an extra twenty minutes in her car after service as she tried to ring him. He did not pick up all three times, and he had not sent her any message to let her know what was happening. Sighing heavily and then finishing it off with a yawn, Eva gave up.

As she drove home, she thought that it was just as well that he had not shown up. She was tired and had a lot on her mind. Plus, Adam was proving to be a very unreliable person. Once she got home, she would eat the leftover shepherd's pie in the fridge, ring Rachel to find out how she was holding up, then try Evan again before calling it a night.

She spoke with Rachel as she ate her dinner. Eva had not had the chance to speak with her since Monday, and work was so busy for everyone. Rachel had not tried calling Evan and Eva scolded her for that. No, Evan did not need time to calm down as Rachel suggested. Eva knew her brother very well. Giving him time to think, and possibly move on, was not what Rachel should be doing. If neither of them could reach him by Friday, the best thing was for Rachel to come over to their parents' house on Saturday. Eva would suggest to her parents that they have a family lunch, and she would invite Rachel. She just had to make sure Evan did not know Rachel would be there.

Once she was in bed, she tried ringing Evan but was not lucky. However, she received a WhatsApp message from him instead.

Evan: *"Did you know about Patrick?"*

Eva's heart sank. That was the question she did not want him asking her; not like this. She wanted to bring it up herself; speak to him about it...explain herself.

Eva: *"Kind of, but it's not what you think, Evan. Can you please pick up my call? You're being childish!"* She decided to use a bit of bravado, not very hopeful that it will work. He had every reason to be upset with her. He was hurting and she wanted to be there for him... for Rachel too. She gave it a minute and when he did not respond or call her, she tried him again. He did not pick up.

She groaned and placed her phone on her bedside table, turned off her bedside lamp and settled into her bed. The buzz of her phone made her jump. Hopefully, Evan had changed his mind and was ready to talk. She reached for her phone and checked the text message she had received.

"Would like to see you again. How about Friday evening? Just tell me where and when. Sweet dreams, angel. RJ."

Her heart fluttered. She had been looking forward to him contacting her for the past few days and he had not. The one time she was not even thinking about him, he gets in touch. Everything about this man was always unanticipated, even the way he came into her life was sudden.

Of course, she wanted to see him again too. She was looking forward to seeing him on Friday. Eva fancied going to the cinema. Maybe they could see a movie and then go for drinks afterwards. She would look for a good film showing that would be right up his street.

She figured he would love a good action-thriller. She was more of a romantic-comedy person herself but would have to compromise. What was wrong with her? Getting all schoolgirl and giddy over a simple text from a man she still knew very little about. She would decide what film and send him the details later. Right now, she had to go to sleep. She was not going to answer immediately. Eva smiled. He kept her waiting a few days, it would be nice to give him a taste of his own medicine. At least he had only until tomorrow evening to wait.

Chapter Eighteen

RJ dipped his left hand in his jacket pocket to keep it warm from the cold. His other hand held the mobile phone to his right ear. It was eight degrees today, but he had to get out of the flat or he would go crazy. It was so cold. At times like this, he wished he had not given up smoking a while back. He stood outside the block of flats, his hoodie over his head. Man, did he miss his house!

As he waited for Oscar to find a quiet spot where he could talk freely, RJ quickly checked his phone to see if he had received any reply from Eva yet. There was nothing. What was wrong with that woman, was she trying to test his limits? He did not know why but he had to see her again.

He could not get her out of his mind. It took all his will power not to ring her the very next morning after the night at the fundraiser. He did not want to scare her away, plus he had a few things to take care of. If he had not heard anything from her by tonight, he was going to ring her. No more playing it cool!

Oscar's voice came back on the line. "In the kitchen now. No one's here."

"Great. As we were saying, how are you lot doing for money?" asked RJ.

"You know that carwash business you invested in last year. Well, Nick talked to the owner; you remember Jim, right? Well, we get some monthly payments from the profits. It's not much, but it's something. We also get commission from referrals. Nick allows us to do our own hustling too, but we always need to let him know what we're up to," Oscar said.

RJ cursed. "What? Nick knows damn well the money I gave Jim wasn't to invest. It was a start-up loan he never paid back, and that's because I heard later that the business was for money laundering. I didn't want the money back after that."

"Maybe he's blackmailing Jim?" Oscar asked.

"Who knows?" RJ sounded irritated. "How about Danny Boy? How's he doing?"

"He's fine. He doesn't ask for or need much. I know he has a lot of questions, but I don't reveal much," replied Oscar.

"I would find a way to send you two some money, but that would be too risky for you both. We don't want Nick, Meltdown or any of the other lads asking questions." RJ sounded regretful.

"That's fine. I should… oh hey… nothing…" Oscar's voice trailed off just before the line was cut off.

Someone must have interrupted Oscar. RJ tried not to worry too much about it. Oscar knew how to take care of himself. RJ needed to plan for the weekend after.

"Well, are you going to answer me?" Meltdown stood at the entrance of the kitchen; his head corked suspiciously to the side.

While Nick was a ruthless man, Meltdown was a smart fox with piercing grey eyes. He was a man of few words whose calculating persona was often confused with calmness. The deep scar running across his cheek hinted at a vicious man who should not be trifled with.

Oscar swore in his head. Standing in the kitchen facing the bare part of the wall did not look good. He struggled to think of a plausible response. Meltdown walked further into the kitchen and Oscar turned to face him.

Meltdown gave Oscar a cold stare. "You said you were doing nothing when I asked you, yet it wasn't nothing, 'cos you were on your bleeding phone now, weren't you? So, I ask again; what are you up to?"

Come on Oscar, he willed himself. *Come up with something… anything.* He swallowed. Meltdown's wicked penetrating stare was not helping.

"Did you order the pizza already?" A low voice broke the silence that was almost reaching the point of awkward. Oscar looked beyond Meltdown as he also turned to notice Danny boy at the doorway.

Danny boy looked pointedly at Oscar, his enquiring expression bordering on impatience. "Pizza?" asked Meltdown, looking from Daniel to Oscar.

Oscar nodded uncertainly, forcing a smile.

"I have been craving Papa John's pizza. I don't have any money, so Oscar here decided to order a large for me and him to share." Danny boy explained.

Meltdown frowned, then turned to Oscar, a brow lifting. "Really? So why didn't you just say so?"

"Err…" but Oscar was cut off.

161

"Sorry MD, but we didn't want to share. I haven't had one in a while and I figured if the other guys knew about it, we would have to. Oscar was just helping me out," Danny boy said, looking down dejectedly.

Oscar held his breath, and he knew Danny boy was doing the same thing. He just hoped and prayed Meltdown did not think to check his phone. It was something he could do, and he and Nick had done with the men in the past.

If Meltdown checked his phone, then there was going to be trouble... for him and Danny boy.

There was a bit of silence as Meltdown looked away from Danny boy to study Oscar's face. Oscar tried hard to keep a straight face and let nothing slip.

"So, did you?" Meltdown suddenly asked.

"Did I what?" Oscar asked uneasily.

"Order the blimming pizza," Meltdown said in calm exasperation.

"Oh yes. Sure. It will be delivered in forty-five minutes." Oscar nodded emphatically with a smile.

Meltdown glared at Oscar just before he turned and then walked towards the door. Danny boy stepped into the kitchen freeing the way for him to get past.

"Selfish hogs; the two of you," Meltdown said as he left the kitchen.

Danny boy walked to the doorway to peer into the hallway. "He's gone," he confirmed, breathing out a sigh of relief. Oscar was so relieved too. He could not believe that he had clammed up like that. He shuddered to think of how things might have panned out if the lad had not shown up and stepped up. Danny boy was alright!

"Nice one," Oscar said, extending his hand and they both shared a fist-bump. He then began punching some buttons on his phone.

"Who are you calling?" Danny boy asked. "Papa John's," replied Oscar.

Eva put the kettle on to boil and set about putting tea bags in the mugs that required them. She spied the coffee jar and realised it was empty. Who on earth would put an empty jar of coffee back in the cupboard? Eva shook her head and brought it out to place it on the counter. It would help remind her to inform Jane in Facilities.

Adam strolled into the office kitchenette with a broad smile on his face "Eva! You're looking lovely today, as usual. Those trousers look good on you," he said.

Eva turned to him briefly and smiled back. She really wasn't in the mood to have a conversation with Adam. "Thank you. How are you?"

Adam came to stand beside her and then leaned against the kitchen worktop. "I hardly ever see you. I've really been missing you."

Eva frowned reaching past him to get the kettle. "Really?" It was hard to believe since he had stood her up on Wednesday and still had not explained why.

Adam drew his head back in an expression of shock. "I'm surprised you would even question it. I'm sure you know I like you and love spending time with you."

Eva finished stirring the teas and placed all five on a tray.

Pam from her team walked in. "There you are. I see Adam's the cause of the delay."

Adam and Pam exchanged greetings. Eva gave Pam an apologetic smile. Taking her mug off, she handed the tray to her.

"So sorry. Please can you tell the two caffeine junkies in our team that we're out of coffee?"

Pam nodded as she took the tray from Eva. Once they were both alone again, Adam turned Eva to face him. "What's wrong? Are you doubting me?"

Eva slowly pulled away. "We're at work, Adam."

He sighed and let her go. "Fine. Just in case I haven't told you, I like you, okay? Very much!" Eva licked her lips, not very comfortable discussing such things in the office.

"I'm hoping we can go out tomorrow after work. Some of my friends are meeting up at this club; I was wondering if you'd like to go with me?" Adam asked.

Eva sipped on her tea. "I'm busy tomorrow, Adam."

"You are? What plans have you made?" He sounded disappointed but curious.

"Meeting with a friend too. At least I'm telling you as it is… not giving you false hopes and then disappointing you later without any explanation whatsoever," Eva replied, the words tumbling out of her mouth unexpectedly. She had not meant for it to come out like that, even though she was planning to bring it up with him at some point.

Adam's eyes widened in understanding and his shoulder drooped. He looked lost for words, and Eva marvelled at how he could still have nothing to say. She was glad when Rachel entered the kitchen just then.

"Hey Rachel. I was hoping to speak with you," she quickly said, then glancing back at Adam, she said, "Sorry, Adam. Talk later?"

He nodded slowly and without a word, walked out. Rachel looked at Eva, a questioning look in her eyes.

Eva waved her hand. "Don't ask! Anyway, how did it go with Evan? Did you ring him yet?"

Rachel shook her head soberly. "I tried calling him several times, but he didn't pick up. He did send me a text message right after my last try. Can't remember the last time we communicated via text."

"What did he say?" asked Eva.

"It read: *'Please stop. Will call back later'.* " Rachel replied, trying to cover up the hurt in her voice as she moved to make herself a cup of tea.

Eva's heart went out to Rachel. She had messed up but her relationship with Evan was still salvageable. Evan just needs to sit down and talk things through with Rachel.

"My mum is thrilled with the idea of lunch. She would have preferred Sunday, then she can make a proper roast dinner. However, I did mention that there was nothing wrong with a Saturday roast dinner," Eva said.

She remembered how her mum was open to the idea of a meal, but not warm to a Saturday roast. 'Who does that?' her mum had asked.

'Anyone who can… since anyone actually can,' she had replied to her mum. Some traditions can be bent; surely! There was a reason why Sunday was not an option. If all went well on Saturday, Evan and Rachel would need Sunday to further mend things instead of having work on Monday to Friday breaking the smooth flow of making-up. Eva had suggested that her mum call Evan to tell him; she was sure he would be picking up his parents' calls. Eva would let her mum know on Saturday morning that Rachel would be joining them. Mum loved Rachel and would not mind at all. She just did not want Evan suspecting that Rachel would be there. The last thing she wanted is for her mum mentioning it, as it would be natural to do.

Rachel seemed uncertain. "Are you really sure that would be a good idea? Evan obviously doesn't want to see me."

Eva stopped halfway from sipping some more of her tea. "How is it obvious?"

Rachel looked oddly confused. "Well, the not picking up my calls, for one!" She almost laughed in derision.

"Well, that doesn't make it obvious to me. Human beings can be silly and tend do the opposite of what they really want sometimes. You, of all people, should know that." Eva winked at Rachel and took another sip of her tea.

When RJ finally received Eva's reply late Thursday night, he had let out a long breath he was unaware he had been holding in. What was it about that gorgeous woman that rattled him so? He could not wait to see her again. Being around her was a breath of fresh air and made him forget how complicated his life was at the moment. It was ironic, as she would probably pose a whole different complication of her own. The aromatic smell of Thai green curry and chilli prawns teased a particular sensory organ. Guessing that Eva would be coming here straight from the office still dressed in work clothes, RJ had dressed smart casual. He zipped up his River Island grey funnel neck wool coat and pushed his flat cap lower over his forehead as he approached the entry of the Ritzy Cinema. There was a reason for why Eva's choice of Brixton Village was both good and bad. Good, because they were spoilt for choice regarding a good meal for dinner. Bad, because it was smack in the middle of Brixton and the chances of him being spotted here was high. It was a good thing it was dark. However, the Christmas lights that decorated most areas defeated that purpose. He was not a fan of the holiday, but that didn't stop it from coming every year. He checked his watch. She had given 6.15pm as the meeting time. It was 6:18pm.

"You haven't been waiting long, have you?" Eva's voice behind him sounded so sweet.

"Not really," he replied, turning to face her. She looked beautiful as usual, despite coming straight from an obviously long day at the office. Her long glossy funnel coat was left open with the belt hanging down from the loops, and he could see that she had on a fitted collared white shirt with long sleeves tucked into high-waisted flared trousers. Her hair was beautifully unruly, and she looked adorable. He could not take his eyes off her. Instinctively, she pushed back a handful of tendrils. He must have been staring too hard. He lowered his eyes.

"Oh, my goodness, it smells amazing out here." Her eyes brightened in delight.

RJ smiled. "I know. I wasn't hungry until I got here."

She laughed. "Or would you rather we skipped the cinema and go straight to dinner?"

"Nah. It's okay. It's Friday, we have a long night ahead of us; we ought to slip in a movie." Why in the world was he assuming she wanted to spend most of her night with him?

She nodded and then tilted her head sweetly. "I wasn't sure which film you would prefer so I haven't purchased any ticket yet. However, I have narrowed it down to two films; one is a fantasy-thriller, and the other is romantic-adventure. They both start in ten minutes. Your pick."

She stood there looking up at him expectantly, a warm and lovely glow to her face and sparkling eyes. He knew his control was slipping, and he was happy to lose it, even if it was for a moment. RJ took a step closer to Eva and slowly cupped her face.

"I pick this," he said leaning down and inching his face closer to hers. The intended but inactive kiss was hanging in the air.

She said nothing. He felt her tense, but then her eyes remained warm. That seemed to be the answer he was hoping for. Finally, he brought his lips to hers, and it was like magic. It was warm, sweet like honey, like her... and she responded, she was kissing him back. He didn't know how long they kissed for, but it took all of his willpower to pull away from her. They stood there, gazing at each other in silence. Someone had to break the silence.

"Well, romantic-adventure it is. We better hurry; need to grab me some of those peanut M&M'S." He pulled the door open for her.

She looked flushed, then offered him another of her gorgeous smiles before she walked into the building.

Eva was very aware of RJ's strongly appealing male presence beside her. He looked devastatingly handsome and smelt like tobacco or was it old spices? There was a hint of almond there too. She wondered what perfume or aftershave he used. The movie they were watching was very interesting and the perfect choice, but she kept getting distracted with thoughts of the man sitting beside her. How in the world could he be so focused on the film when all she could do was rewind their kiss over and over again in her head? It was so unexpected but welcomed. She was still reeling from it; it had been soft and beautiful. He was such a good kisser. She had struggled to compose herself while he purchased their tickets and paid for their snacks. She stole a side glance as he tossed a handful of M&M'S in his mouth. She looked at her bag of crisps and dipped in to take one that she immediately put in her mouth.

As they exited the building after the movie was over, Eva was basking in the euphoria of the great and romantic ending of the film. She shivered a little and she was not sure if it was from the cold. RJ noticed and put an arm around her.

"How about we get something to eat?" he asked.

Eva was definitely starving, and the smells of various foods were inviting. It was such a busy night with the usual TGIF vibe.

Eva suggested a nice Thai restaurant and RJ was quick to agree. She was glad that they were on the same page. He asked the waiter if there was a dark cosy little corner available, and he was in luck. The butterflies in Eva's stomach fluttered wildly like they were high on something. Not long later, and they were settled with their meals.

"So, what exactly do you do in the church? Are you like a preacher or something?" RJ enquired.

Eva laughed. "Do I come across as a preacher?"

"So far? No!" replied RJ.

"I'm a church usher. I also help with a lot of organising and admin stuff. I'm head of the volunteer group," she informed.

He seemed to consider this. "I see."

Eva had questions of her own. "So how's it going with the setting up of your consumer credit business?"

RJ leaned forward, placed his elbows on the table and clasped his hands together. "That's still in the pipeline, but some urgent things came up that I have to take care of first."

Eva nodded. She was curious but didn't want to pry. She still had more questions, though. She was liking this man; really liking him. She owed it to herself to find out more about him. "So, you said you were lending people money, what were you doing to earn money?"

RJ swallowed the food he had been chewing and then took a sip of his wine. "I use to own a pub, but I sold it."

Eva was surprised. "Really? How did you come about owning a pub and why did you sell it?"

RJ frowned and then chuckled. "Jeez Eva! Is this a crime investigation or a job interview for a political position?"

Eva grimaced, feeling apologetic for putting him on the spot and making him feel uncomfortable. "Oh no. I'm sorry. I have a very curious and inquisitive mind. My dad said I should have been a lawyer, and my brother said I should have gone into journalism."

"Too right!" RJ grinned. "Anyway, I acquired money from this and that; gambling was one. Then I decided to give all that up and buy a pub. It was making money, but I had to sell it as people started to take advantage of my liberality."

"Oh okay. Well, I do hope you can get back to officially starting your business," Eva said. When she first found him unconscious on the church steps, she had immediately assumed him to be a gang member. However, there were things about him that did not add up, like the night of the fundraiser. Still, the more he opened up to her, the more she wasn't sure… and she didn't know how to ask. She had already asked too many things that almost came across as insulting.

Putting another fork of food in his mouth, RJ threw a question at her. "So what do you do?" He raised a hand to stop her before she could answer. "Hold on; I have another question… since we're barraging each other here…" She laughed at that, and he smiled before he continued, "…does your whole family go to St Benedict?"

Eva waited some extra seconds in case he wanted to throw another question in there. "To answer your first question, I'm in marketing and advertising. You know, creative design and all. And for your second question, once my brother and I were in uni, it was easy to drift away and eventually find other churches we fitted into. I found St Benedict."

RJ suddenly fell quiet and stared emptily at his glass of wine. "You know, I used to go to church as a child. My dad never went, but my mum always took me."

Eva could not believe he was sharing something so personal about himself without her having to ask.

"So, what happened?" she asked softly.

He suddenly looked like he had snapped out of whatever it was that had come over him and looked at her with a smile. "Well, I stopped… obviously."

Chapter Nineteen

It was just going on 10pm. To Eva, the night was still young for a Friday, and she really did not want it to end. As she strolled leisurely with RJ, on their way to where she had parked her car, he gently reached for her waist from behind and drew her closer to him. It felt strange but right.

"So did you enjoy the movie?" RJ broke the comfortable silence.

"Of course, I did. I'm a sucker for romantic films. Didn't you?" replied Eva.

"I did, but I could tell that you really, really enjoyed it, especially the extremely corny end scene." His deep voice hinting at amusement.

Eva cast him a quick 'are-you-serious?' look. "What's not to like? The race against time to the airport to stop the person you're in love with from getting on that plane and flying out of your life forever." She gestured dramatically.

RJ laughed. "Well, when you put it that way, it doesn't sound corny at all."

Eva jabbed RJ in his side playfully. RJ quickly turned her to face him as she laughed. She had been waiting for them to kiss again… anticipating it. She was not disappointed. She loved how male he smelt and tasted. She felt safe and warm in his arms. She loved the way he lifted her slightly, so she did not have to stretch too hard to meet his deep kiss. It was easy to forget that they were out in public, but Eva was a private person. She broke their kiss. RJ stared down at her, his deep blue eyes full of desire.

"That's my car over there," Eva said, pointing to where her car was parked.

Quietly, they both walked to the vehicle. No longer in his warm embrace, the cold air hit harder, so she hurriedly unlocked the car and slipped in. She switched on the car engine, turned up the heating, and waited a few seconds for RJ to join her. She was hoping to spend a bit more time with him. When he still had not joined her in the car as she expected, she reached over to the passenger side and opened the door.

"You getting in?" she asked, but it sounded like an order.

RJ got into the passenger seat and shut the door. He turned to face her, and before she knew it, they were back in each other's arms. There was an urgency to their kiss, a deep craving to get closer… to explore… to know. She was not sure how many minutes they had been in the car, but she knew it was getting hot and heavy. She felt RJ's hand moving up and down her back, and then slowly moving towards the front of her shirt. Eva knew she had to stop it before it went too far, but her self-control seemed strangely weak. RJ's fingers began fumbling with the top button of her shirt and Eva had to summon all her willpower to pull away. Breathing hard, they both stared at each other.

"I'm sorry, but I had to stop," Eva said, relaxing into her seat.

RJ took off his cap and ran a hand through his jet-black hair. "I had a feeling you might. You're a virgin, aren't you?"

Eva shot him a sharp glance. "What does that have to do with anything?"

RJ sighed. "Let me guess; you're saving yourself for your wedding night!"

Eva looked away. "Well, chastity before marriage is ideal."

RJ humphed, "So I was right, then."

Eva shook her head slowly. "I said that is the ideal, but no; you're not right."

RJ let his head drop back. "You don't want to wait until your wedding night, then?"

"I wish I had," Eva said quietly and regretfully.

RJ's head snapped back forward in surprise. Frowning, he turned to her. "You mean you're not a virgin?"

Eva took a breath before saying, "No, I'm not." The silence was deafening.

RJ suddenly chuckled harshly. "No way! A saint like yourself, and you've already let someone pop that cherry?"

Swiftly and without thinking, Eva turned to face him and slapped him across the cheek. How dare he speak to her like that? His words hurt her, and it was almost like he was trying to shame her. How can a man be so wonderful one minute, and then a jerk, the next? She adjusted herself in her seat and put on her seat belt. RJ, who had not reacted at all when she slapped him; not even to touch the reddening spot on his face, got the message. Without giving away any expression, he quietly got out of her car. Once he was out, Eva quickly put her car in reverse gear and pulled out just before turning towards the road and driving off without looking at him.

RJ stood there in the cold after Eva drove off. He was angry… and it wasn't because of the slap he had just received. What had just happened and why had he let it happen? He had been out of line to say that to her. He did not want to admit it, but he knew why he was angry. It was jealousy. Jealousy had welled up inside him. Why? Because he would have liked to have been her first. She was like his pure angel, and the thought of her with another man infuriated him. It made no sense; he had no right to be. Such a beautiful woman; he should have known that men would have been flocking to be with her. What made it even weirder was that, she wasn't quite the prude he thought she was. As he began walking to the area where his car was parked, his phone started to ring. He was in no mood to take calls, but checking his phone, he saw it was Ben. He picked it up.

"Yes?" RJ's tone was cold.

"What has you all up in a twist?" Ben asked curiously, not missing the tone.

"Who else?" RJ sighed, finally rubbing his still stinging cheek. What had she whacked him with? Her hand or a cricket bat?

Ben chuckled. "She's not taking any of your nonsense, is she?"

RJ looked irritated. "You don't even know what happened."

"No, I don't. But I do know you, and I'm pretty sure you deserved whatever it was she dished out."

RJ was pretty sure he did too. That did not stop him from being less inclined to fill Ben in. The man always had some type of weird insight and had the annoying knack of almost always being right.

Eva had intended to go straight home but found herself parking near the church. She had not been this upset in a long time. Why had she let that man get to her so? Hitting a man, or anyone for that matter, was something she had vowed never to do. The guilt of letting her anger get the better of her was what had brought her to the church. She unlocked the big doors, let herself in, and shut it behind her. Someone had forgotten to put off the lights in the section where the pulpit was. She was grateful for that. Walking briskly to the altar, she positioned herself in the line of the cross and knelt on the kneeling steps. In her hurry, she failed to notice Reverend Bainbridge sitting in one of the pews.

"Forgive me, Lord; I struck a man," she said remorsefully. The reverend's eyebrows shot up.

"Oh, but he is sooo infuriating," she said, standing up with indignation and beginning to pace.

"However, it was wrong of me, Lord; I let my anger get the better of me," she quickly knelt again.

The reverend's face relaxed, and he watched in amusement.

"Why though? Why did you bring this insufferable man into my life to provoke me so?" Eva stood up again restlessly.

Suddenly sombre, she knelt again. "I know you said that we can be angry but should not sin."

However, irritation began creeping into her voice one again. "Ooooh but this man is very trying. He is the embodiment of testing. He insulted me and made fun of me not being a virgin…"

At that point, the reverend couldn't help but clear his throat.

Eva quickly swung round. She had thought she was alone in the church. Spotting the reverend, her eyes widened in embarrassment and shock. She was mortified and didn't know what to say.

"Reverend Bainbridge! I err… didn't know… I was errr…"

Reverend Bainbridge stood up uncomfortably. "Please… erm… don't let me interrupt your one-sided chat with God."

Eva stared on wide-eyed as he carefully made his way to a door in a corner of the room.

"I came in through the back of the church so don't forget to lock up the front on your way out," he said quietly and then exited the room, leaving Eva looking awkwardly on.

How in the world had she not noticed him there… seated in the pew? Had she been so overwhelmed with emotion? Finally, and still in shock, she turned back to the cross, adjusted herself properly on her knees.

"I regret hitting him, Lord. I'm so sorry. Please forgive me, and please… please make the reverend forget all he just heard," she said miserably.

By the time Eva arrived home, it was almost 11:30 pm. She was exhausted and in a very sober mood. She used her car keys to remotely lock the doors and proceeded to make her way to the block of flats. As she walked past the parked cars, she noticed a figure leaning against a car. She paused. The neighbourhood was relatively safe, and the streetlights were adequate, but the figure happened to be positioned at a spot that just missed the glow. She always meant to get pepper spray, and kicked herself for never getting round to it. She clutched tightly at the straps of her handbag, ready to swing it hard, if necessary. The figure stood up straight and took a step forward. Eva was ready to scream and swing out when the lights illuminated RJ's face. She heaved a sigh of relief. He stood there, looking as sober as she felt. His hands pushed his open coat apart in order to nestle deep into this jeans pockets. Wasn't he cold? He did have on a thick long-sleeved pullover. He was not wearing the cap he had on earlier. She only had to take a few more steps to be right where he stood. He looked down at her, the blue depths of his eyes revealing anguish.

"You scared me." Eva found her voice.

"I hurt you," he said softly.

"I hit you," she said back.

"I deserved it. I was out of line, and I'm sorry." He took a step closer to her.

"And I'm sorry I hit you," she replied.

He reached out and pulled her closer. He then used his hand to push some of her curls away from her face as she stared up at him.

"I was... jealous. Don't ask me why. I just was," he said looking at her face but avoiding her eyes.

He was jealous? Of what? Whoever it was she had lost her virginity to? RJ was certainly not a virgin, and now, thinking about all the women he has ever been with or even within the past month, she felt slightly sick. She had thought a man like him would prefer it if she was not a virgin, but she was getting the impression that RJ had wanted her to be a virgin.

She looked down. "Does this change things?"

"How and why should it?" He gently titled her chin up so her eyes could meet his. "You're still my earth angel."

She was relieved. She brought his head down to hers and kissed him deeply. His arms went around her hips and hers circled his neck as they kissed each other deeply. She wanted this man. She wanted him in her life, in her world. The feel of him, the taste of him! This time he was the one who broke their embrace. They were both breathing heavily.

"You don't want to know what I feel like doing to you right now, Eva. We better stop now."

Eva knew what. She wanted it too, but she had resolved years ago that the next time she had sex would be with her husband. It was not easy… especially now with someone like RJ in her life. Was God testing her? She had to be strong, even though she felt like inviting him up into her flat.

She sighed. "You're right."

"I just needed to see you tonight to apologise. I couldn't go to sleep knowing that I hurt you. You didn't deserve that, especially as you were being so honest with me."

A thought suddenly occurred to her. "Did you come straight here?"

He nodded. "Yes. I have been waiting for you for a while now. Checked around and didn't see your car so knew you hadn't come home. I was a little worried and contemplated calling you but wasn't sure you would pick up my call. Where did you go?"

"Church," she replied.

He chuckled. "Why am I not surprised? You went to get back-up? I'm not going to get struck by lightning any moment now, am I?"

Eva found this funny and laughed. "No. I went to find peace."

His face soon took on a more serious expression. "And, did you find it?"

"Yes," she replied.

"So, we're good?" he asked.

She smiled. "Absolutely!"

He smiled too, kissed her on the lips and then released her so he could walk towards his car. "I'll call you," he said, starting the engine.

Feeling excited, like a teenager over her first crush, she watched him drive off. What was she doing? He was not even a Christian. He was obviously born a Christian, and he did say his mother used to take him to church when he was a child. RJ was a lost soul. He called her his angel. Well, maybe she could help save him.

Rachel rang the de Silva's doorbell. Eva was already there and had assured her that Evan had not arrived yet. She had not seen his car in the quick scan she had done with her eyes when she was looking for a spot to park. She was relieved. She needed some time to relax and gather some courage to see him again.

Abigail de Silva was happy to see her. She gushed about how she had not seen Rachel in a while and noted her little loss of weight. Timi was in the sitting room watching TV. He offered Rachel an understanding smile, knowing how overwhelming his wife could be. Even though Eva and Evan shared some of their mother's looks, it was their dad they really looked like – the same big eyes, same full eyebrows. Abigail practically dragged Rachel into the kitchen. The smell of roasted vegetables, chicken and potatoes was invitingly strong. Eva was in there. She had an apron on and was busy taking a tray of roasted vegetables out of the oven.

She took off the oven gloves and looked at Rachel. "Hey, you. Food's practically ready. Just need to set the table. You wouldn't mind sorting that, would you?"

Rachel did not mind at all. This was not the first time she had helped with setting the table at the de Silva's house. She knew her way around their kitchen and dining room. Even though there was a smaller dining section in the kitchen, Rachel knew that they would be using the main dining room. There was a massive cabinet unit in there where the proper china, drinking glasses and cutlery were kept. She liked that she had something to keep her occupied; that way, she did not have to think about Evan and her nerves wouldn't be all over the place.

She had tried to look her best in a turtle-neck blouse on fitted flared jeans. Her hair was pulled back in a ponytail, and she had hoop earrings and light make up on. What would he say when he saw her? What would she say to him?

"Evan's here," Rachel heard Abigail call from the living room.

Her heart began to pound loudly as she set a table knife by the last table mat. She smoothened her hair and looked for how to further keep herself busy in there even though she had practically placed everything needed on the table. She needed to help bring the food into the dining room from the kitchen, but she was not sure she was ready to go out there yet. Abigail came in carrying a dish which she placed on the table. Rachel could hear Evan talking with his dad.

"Evan's here," Abigail repeated to Rachel with a smile, just before walking out of the room again. It was obvious his parents did not know what had been happening between Evan and her. This didn't surprise her; Evan wasn't likely to share that with them; not unless she and he were completely over. Did that mean they were not completely over? A feeling of hope ignited in Rachel.

"Mmmm! Smells good. I'm starving." This was Evan, making his way into the kitchen.

"You're always starving when you come here." Abigail laughed.

There was a bit of silence, and then Eva said "What? So you're not going to say hello to me now?"

"Of course I am, you're my sister," Evan said.

"I must not have been these past few days," Eva retorted.

"Oh shush," Evan responded. Rachel could imagine that he was giving Eva a hug.

"Look I'm sorry, okay? It was a difficult situation to be in. I didn't know how to tell you. I also didn't want to be a tittle-tattle; she is like a sister to me, and I hoped she would tell you herself. I just didn't want to get all up in your business. You know I love you and will always look out for you," Eva explained.

"Alright, Eva. It's okay," Evan said resignedly.

"You alright?" asked Abigail.

Rachel jumped. She had been facing the window, intently focused on listening in on Eva and Evan's conversation that she had not heard Abigail come in.

Rachel turned to Abigail with a smile. "Of course. Just waiting for everyone to come in here."

Abigail dropped a bowl of stuffing and small jar of mint sauce on the table. "Evan and Eva, can you bring whatever's left from the kitchen? And your dad too when you go past the living room," she called.

Rachel rubbed her hands together uneasily. This is it. Soon, there were sounds of footsteps coming into the dining room. Eva came in first, shooting Rachel a quick look of support before dropping some more food on the table. Timi was next, holding a bottle of red wine and making his way to the head of the table. Eva came to stand by Rachel, obviously intending to sit beside her. Abigail sat at the other end of the table. Evan came in last, carrying a jug of gravy and a tray of several small-sized Yorkshire puddings.

Rachel took in a deep breath. Seeing her, he suddenly stopped. He locked eyes with her for a moment. He was looking incredibly handsome. He had obviously gone home first to change and shower after his Saturday cricket game.

Rachel felt Eva pull her to join her in sitting down. She did slowly.

"For pity's sake, put the food on the table, Evan and sit down. You can devour Rachel with your eyes after lunch," Abigail exclaimed in irritation. "Don't you see each other enough?" she asked again rhetorically, as Evan slowly sat down in a chair at the other side of the table, opposite Rachel.

Timi was busy trying to open the bottle of wine, oblivious of what was going on.

Finally glancing at Eva, Evan said, "Always looking out for me, huh?" He did not sound happy.

Eva guiltily looked away from him and bowed her head as their mum said the grace. Once the prayers were said, they all began dishing out.

"What a nice spread. I bet it all tastes as good as it smells and looks," Rachel said, trying to abate her unease.

Eva smiled thankfully, while Abigail beamed.

"I was just telling Rachel here that she's lost a little weight. She looks lovely. Not that she wasn't before. I guess she just looks different," Abigail said, passing Evan the roasted potatoes.

Evan took the dish from his mother without a change in his cold expression. "She's certainly different, alright!"

Rachel shot him a hurt look as Eva shot Evan a harsh glare.

"Weight loss or not, I'm still me, though." Rachel laughed, hoping Evan got her message too.

"Of course, dear." Abigail said with a smile.

"Wine, anyone?" Timi asked, attempting to pour some into his wine glass.

Abigail reached out to assist him, and he avoided her hand. "I can pour my own wine, thank you very much."

"Alright. No need to be testy," Abigail said, displeased.

"I wonder why… telling the children to bring me into the dining room like I'm some really old man or invalid." Timi mumbled under his breath.

Trying to smoothen things, Rachel took the wine bottle from Timi after he was done. "Thank you. Looks like my favourite wine too." She began pouring some into her glass.

"Careful there. I remember what happened the last time I saw you drinking," Evan said dryly.

Rachel sighed. Evan was not going to make this easy, was he? She did regret that wedding party… the fact that she drank a little more than usual.

"Oh my; don't tell me she spilt wine on herself or something?" Abigail laughed, not even contemplating the other option. It was not like Rachel at all.

Eva looked at Rachel, hand over her mouth in surprised humour. "You didn't, did you?"

Rachel smiled back.

"Not at all; thank heavens."

"No spills. But she certainly did a number on herself," Evan quipped, reaching for more mint sauce.

Rachel was finding it difficult to stay in control. "No, I didn't. Don't kid, Evan," she said. She had been slightly tipsy, but she was not going to let him imply that she had been drunk.

She felt Eva place a steadying hand on her knee. Rachel tried to relax.

"Did I mention that my church got the funding needed again this year? We will be sending a number of people to Africa on missionary work in January as planned," Eva said, obviously trying to change the topic.

Everyone was pleased to hear that and expressed it.

"So, are you still opting to go?" Timi asked. The look in his eyes showed that he was torn. He obviously wanted his daughter to serve God in any way she can, but she was his baby girl, and not having her around for six months to a year would be tough.

"That was the plan, but I haven't made up my mind yet," Eva replied.

In the past, when Eva had talked about it, it had seemed like it was a sure thing. Now she was not sure? Rachel wondered if it had anything to do with Adam or even the other man in her life.

"Whatever you decide dear, you know we'll always support you," Abigail said.

Evan was not very talkative and even though Rachel was sure he would miss his sister if she went to Africa, she knew that wasn't why he was quiet.

Abigail suddenly clapped her hands together loudly, startling Rachel "What are we doing for Christmas this year? Evan, come first weekend in December, I need your help with putting up some lights on the front of the house. You'll need a ladder."

"Why does he need to come over to do that? I can do it," Timi stated with a frown. "I did it last year."

Abigail rolled her eyebrows. "Oh goodness!" she said, ignoring him.

"I don't know yet. What do you have planned, Mum?" Eva asked.

"I was hoping we could have you all over, especially if you'll be going to Africa. It will be nice for us all to spend it together. Rachel, what are your plans? I know you and Evan spent it at your mum and dad's last year."

"I haven't really thought about it, to be honest," Rachel replied.

"She might be going there with someone else this time around. Who knows?" Evan stated with a wry smile.

This brought sudden silence to the table as Timi and Abigail looked up at him in bewilderment. Eva was speechless. No doubt deciding that the whole lunch thing might have been a bad idea.

Rachel felt very uncomfortable. She could not just sit there without saying anything. There was nothing between Patrick and her. She had contacted him and gently let him know that he was a lovely man, but she would not be going into a relationship with him. She apologised for leading him on... because that was what she had done. She had known deep down that nothing would come of them, but she had used him and inadvertently led him on. He had been disappointed but had taken it well.

"I do not intend to go to my parents' with anyone else," Rachel said slowly, her eyes fixed on Evan.

Evan gave a sardonic smile, not caring that they were not alone. "Other than Patrick, you mean?"

"Evan, there's no need for that..."

Eva began but was cut off by Rachel. "It was one dinner, Evan. Patrick and I are not a thing!"

Evan's smile disappeared. "Well, dinner and three bouquets of flowers seem to suggest otherwise. You don't just go to dinner with another man out of the blue. It's a consequence of a build-up. And unless it was a business meeting, an old friend from school or a family member, I don't see why it should have happened at all..."

"Evan please..." Rachel began, but Evan was not done.

"And that number of bouquets would suggest an appreciation for something much more!"

"Evan!!" Eva and Abigail shrieked in unison.

Rachel stood up abruptly, unable to hold back the tears she had been fighting off.

She looked at Eva. "I'm sorry; I can't do this." She turned to Timi and Abigail. "I'm so sorry." Then she pushed back her chair and hurriedly left the dining room.

"I raised you better than that." Rachel heard Timi admonish. She assumed it was directed at Evan.

179

There was a flurry of footsteps behind her. "No! Go back, Evan. You've said enough," Eva yelled.

Rachel grabbed her coat and opened the front door just as Eva caught up with her.

"Rachel, I am so sorry. I had no idea it was going to go this way. Please come back, let's talk it out now... instead of around it," Eva begged.

Rachel shook her head. "No. It hurts too much, Eva. I don't blame you for trying. I wanted to do this. The funny thing is, I'm not even angry with him. This was all my fault, and now it's over."

"No, it wasn't okay for him to speak to you like that. Rachel, it doesn't have to be over. Please don't give up," Eva called out since Rachel was already making her way to her car.

Rachel could see that Eva wanted to follow her, but she did not have her coat on, and it was cold. There was no point her trying to get it because she would be gone before Eva had a chance to put it on. As Rachel got into her car, she noticed Abigail had joined Eva at the doorway. She felt bad that she had left during the meal and with a plate still half full of food. Abigail didn't deserve this. Not able to bring herself to wave goodbye, she drove off.

Chapter Twenty

The few days that followed were both bitter and sweet for Eva. She and RJ were getting closer. They had met up for drinks at a nearby pub on Sunday evening, and he had popped in to see her at work during lunch time on Tuesday. They communicated via text and WhatsApp outside her working hours and talked on the phone in the evenings. She already knew she was falling for him hard, and Joyce practically screaming it in excitement after the evening service on Wednesday, made it even more real.

"Oh thank you, Lord. Eva, this is the one. Look how you're blushing just talking about him? Girl, you are head over heels." Joyce had looked pleased with herself; like it had been her who had engineered the whole thing.

Seeing RJ leaning against his car and patiently waiting for her, got Joyce even more thrilled. The woman was obviously a hopeless romantic, and to be honest, so was Eva.

She had avoided catching Reverend Bainbridge's attention or speaking with him ever since last Friday's embarrassing mess. What must he think of her!

The bitter part was that she knew both Evan and Rachel were hurting but did not know what she could do about it... except pray. Evan hadn't been himself at all after Rachel had rushed out. Their mum had tried to get him to talk about it, but he had not. Their dad had empathised; however, he had asked Evan never to disrespect a woman like that again, especially when he did not have the facts. She knew from the look Evan gave her before leaving that he partially blamed her for how things had panned out.

Eva did feel responsible for how things got from bad to worse on Saturday and decided to keep away and give Rachel and Evan some space. On Sunday Eva had asked how Rachel was in a text message and had subsequently sent her a couple of encouraging bible passages. Rachel had responded with appreciation, but that had been it. Even at work they hardly spoke, but merely smiled at each other when they happen to see each other. With Evan, she had sent him a message on WhatsApp apologising and letting him know she was there for him if he needed to talk.

On Thursday, there had been an uncomfortable situation with Adam. She had just stepped outside the office building to meet RJ at the car park as they had made plans to have lunch together, when she heard Adam call out her name. It looked like he had been running to catch up with her. Eva could see RJ's car already parked but stopped to speak with Adam briefly. They had not really communicated since the day she told him that she couldn't go clubbing with him and his friends. She was not sure if he had been sulking, but she hadn't felt the urge to placate him or resume whatever relationship they had had or were on the path to having.

"Hey Adam. How are you?" Eva asked as he stood in front of her.

"The thing is, Eva; I feel like you are punishing me, and it hurts. I really do like you," he said folding his arms across his chest.

Eva was surprised. "Sorry?"

"You know, the silent treatment! You and I haven't talked in days," he stated, unfolding his arms, and stepping even closer to her.

Eva looked confused. "I haven't been giving you the silent treatment. Why would you say that?"

"Because you haven't said a word to me since the day you turned down my invite to take you out clubbing," he replied, lifting a finger up to gesture the number one.

Eva did not know what to say. She quickly looked to see if RJ was still there, hating that she was keeping him waiting and aware that she was losing precious minutes of her lunch time.

"Adam, first of all, clubs aren't my scene… not since my uni days. Second, I did tell you I had already made plans for that evening. Third, you haven't said a word to me since then either. I guess we have both been preoccupied."

Adam's face relaxed and he sighed. "Okay; you're right. I apologise for overreacting. Anyway, I have missed you and would love to spend some time with you."

"Is there a problem here?" RJ's voice disrupted Eva's thoughts on how to come up with a suitable response.

Adam's gaze went past Eva to settle on RJ. Being over six-feet tall, RJ was several inches taller than Adam. He was also in better shape, even though Adam had a good physique too. While RJ wasn't dressed in a coat, shirt, and tie like Adam, he managed to pull off his coat, hooded top and fitted jeans ensemble just as well. Besides, Eva had seen the man in a tux before and there was definitely no competition. What was she doing? Was she just physically comparing the two men?

Eva snapped out of it just as Adam asked, "Sorry, who are you?"

RJ squinted and was about to say something when Eva quickly interjected, "No, there's no problem at all. Just having a quick chat with my colleague here, Adam."

Adam's face didn't look too happy as his gaze shifted back to Eva. "Think about what I said. Talk to you later." Then he turned and walked back into the office building.

Eva knew she and Adam needed to have a proper talk. She turned to face RJ. He had a peculiar look on his handsome face.

"What is it?" Eva asked. Why did all his looks give her butterflies?

"Adam! I recall him ringing you once. Late one night... we were outside the church. Same guy?" RJ asked.

Goodness! He had such a good memory. "Yes, same one. Now let's go," She affirmed and grabbed his hand.

A burst of electricity shot through her at the contact, and she quickly let go. Even though they had made out several times, touching him still felt like touching an open live wire. It bothered her that she could not speak to or touch this man without feeling so sexually charged and drawn to him.

Reaching out quickly, he grasped her hand back in his and said, "I don't burn. I promise." Eva swallowed hard. Oh, if only he knew.

Eva was keeping a look out for Adam. She did not want to miss him after work. She had been feeling guilty. Had she led him on and then left him hanging? Whatever the case, the man needed to know where he stood... where she stood. She had known from the start that there was no connection between them but had tried to keep an open mind. Then she started to get put off by the unreliable and undependable vibe he was giving off. Now with RJ in the picture, she knew there was nothing and could never be anything between Adam and her. She did not know what to call what she had with RJ, but it was definitely more than something, and that was enough to require her having that talk with Adam.

It was just after 6pm when she noticed him walking towards the office exit with a colleague from Sales. Eva hurriedly packed up for the day and rushed to join them.

"Have you got a minute, Adam?" she asked.

Adam nodded when he saw her. "Sure." He said goodnight to his teammate, and soon she had his full attention. She walked beside him until they were outside the building.

Eva cleared her throat. "I thought it was time we talked?"

"Who was that guy earlier today, Eva?" Adam asked abruptly.

Eva was taken aback, and she needed a few seconds to respond to that. "He's a friend," she replied.

"Just a friend?" Adam threw another unexpected question her way.

"Well, probably not just a friend. Not sure what we are." She answered, not quite comfortable with the line of questioning.

"Like what we are… or were?" Adam asked unnervingly.

Eva sighed. "Look, Adam. I liked you too. You are a really good guy. However, I was never sure about us. To be honest, I'm not sure we're right for each other."

"How do you know that?" Adam looked upset.

Eva tried to say it as gently as possible. "Because of how I felt? That spark just wasn't there for me. Furthermore, the times you had to be at church…"

"I knew it! The church thing. So you can't date a man that isn't a Christian and that doesn't go to church?" Adam sounded a little annoyed.

Eva gave a tired shrug "Well, I wouldn't put it that way. It was more to do with you breaking commitments to me that require you having to be even near the vicinity of a church… or my church. It shows a total disregard for what's important to me, as well as a lack of enough respect for me by not bothering to let me know you won't be able to make it, and why."

He shifted on his feet. "So, this guy that's not just a friend, is he a church goer?"

"No," Eva answered, but before Adam could respond to that, she added, "However, that's not the point. Adam, I just didn't feel it with you from the beginning, and much less now with him in the picture. I am truly sorry if I hurt you, but I never meant to. I would have said something earlier if I had thought you and I had gotten to that point, but we hadn't… at least I didn't think so."

Adam looked down regretfully. She felt awful for making him feel the way he felt right now.

He looked up. "Okay. Eva. I'm here though; just in case. Don't know for how long, but I'm here."

Eva stretched out her arms and went in for a hug. He accepted the hug and held her there for almost a minute, like he did not want to let her go. She felt she owed him a bit of patience. Finally releasing her, he planted a kiss on her cheek. Then together, they quietly walked to the car park.

Rachel's sadness had made her numb to the world. She was not expecting Evan to ring her, and she didn't think she had any right ringing him. She could tell Eva was feeling guilty, but Rachel really did not want her to. Eva had been very nice and supportive, and Rachel appreciated the encouraging messages Eva had sent her. However, she needed some time alone and Eva seemed to understand that and was giving it to her. Sunita, on the other hand, had been so sweet, offering to make her dinners and being so helpful and attentive. Rachel appreciated it all, she really did, but she did not want Sunita inconveniencing herself for her.

She was not a baby, and she was not dying either. At first, Karen had treated her like she had lost her mind, but now, Rachel could see the sympathy in her eyes and in the way she spoke to her. She was not sure which one of Karen's treatment of her she preferred. Probably neither?

Rachel was trying to come to terms with the fact that she had lost Evan. The very thing she wanted to keep forever, was what she had practically thrown away. It had really hurt that Evan would suggest or even imply that she had had sex with Patrick! But then again, she was the one who had sown those doubts in him. She just had to focus on work and keep praying to God to forgive her and get her through this.

She had come home early that Thursday night because she wanted to get into the kitchen to sort out her own dinner before Sunita did, and probably make some for Sunita herself.

Sunita had been surprised, and after much convincing, left her alone in the kitchen to make some spaghetti carbonara.

As she busied herself, she could hear Karen in the living room saying something to Sunita in hushed tones. She suspected it was about her but ignored it. When Rachel was finally done cooking and had dished out, she came out to place two plates on the table intending to go back to the kitchen to get the third plate. She was grateful that Sunita had already laid out the table mats and cutlery. Her two housemates were already seated at the table.

On her way to get the third plate, she heard Karen ask Sunita, "So are they truly broken up now; her and Evan?" It was meant to be in low tones but somehow fell short.

Sunita did not respond, obviously realising that it was not an appropriate question for Karen to be asking when Rachel was obviously in earshot.

Rachel stopped and turned to answer Karen herself. "Quite possibly." She was about to head back into the kitchen but decided to add with a smile that didn't reach her eyes "He's all yours now, Karen. I know how much you've always wished that he was with you and not me. After all, he's the perfect catch."

Karen gasped as Sunita sighed and bowed her head.

Rachel placed her hands on her hips. "What? Am I out of line? Have I been mistaken all this time? You haven't been lusting after my boyfriend and thinking you deserve him more than I do... did?"

"Stop it, Rachel," Sunita demanded gently. "You keep talking like Evan is this big prize. What about you? You're also a great catch for any man."

Rachel ignored Sunita and continued to glare down at Karen who seemed lost for words.

Uncomfortable, Karen avoided Rachel's eyes before sighing and then looking straight at her. "Alright fine! Of course I have imagined it being me with him. What woman in her right mind wouldn't be attracted to Evan? He is hot in every way. And yes, I have wondered why he was with you."

Sunita shot Karen a surprised frown and Rachel's face took on an 'I-knew-it' look.

Nevertheless, Karen went on, "However, he was with you, Rachel... for whatever reason, and what I think or want doesn't matter. Besides, whatever you may think of me, I certainly wasn't rooting for or expecting you to break up."

Sunita smiled softly and put a hand over Karen's as it rested on the table. Rachel's face softened and her eyes glistened with tears.

"If anything, I'm pissed off at you for messing it up," Karen suddenly added.

Sunita's head drew back in shock, and she slapped Karen's hand. Leave it to Karen to spoil the rare moment that she had surprisingly created. However, Rachel could not help smiling a little even as her eyes welled up fully with tears. She wiped them away with the back of her hand. "I'll go get the last plate," she said, walking back into the kitchen.

As Alexander Fairchild settled into the spacious backseat of the maroon-coloured Mercedes S-Class Maybach, his mobile phone rang.

It wouldn't be a Friday if he didn't have a hundred calls to deal with, he thought. Calmly, he retrieved it from his coat pocket as the driver started the engine and put the car in gear.

"Fairchild," Alex answered.

"Fischer here," came the voice from the other end of the line.

Alex crossed his legs; the ankle of one leg on the knee of the other. "What do you have for me?"

"RJ is definitely seeing that woman – Eva da Silva. He doesn't seem to be involved in the church in any way; he certainly doesn't attend services." Fischer informed.

Alex took this in. "I see. So how serious is it?"

"It looks to be in the very early stages," replied Fischer.

Alex adjusted in his chair. "Let me rephrase: how serious is he?"

There was a short silence on the other end as Fischer considered this before answering.

"It's difficult to tell, but I think she has got his attention. It's different from his past relationships. However, like I said, it's still early days."

Alex nodded slowly, lost in thought. "Mr Fairchild?" Fischer called.

"Yes, Fischer?" he replied.

"There's something else; something very important that you need to know." Said Fischer.

Resting his head back into the headrest, Alex said calmly "I'm listening."

Daniel and the three other men in the bar and TV room with him jumped as Nick barged into the room with Meltdown in tow. Quickly reaching the bar, Nick

187

started to pour himself some brandy. Meltdown popped himself on one of the bar stools.

"Rubbish! Rubbish, I say. Who the 'ell were those men? They bloody ruined my game t'night," Nick yelled.

Danny wondered why Nick always had to shout. Things had obviously gone wrong for him tonight and the house would have to pay for it.

"I think they were just lucky," Meltdown said, equally sounding upset.

Otty chose that moment to change the TV channel. Nick's attention was drawn to where Danny and the other three men sat on the settees in front of the TV.

"Clear outta here; the lot of you," He shouted, slamming the whiskey glass on the bar counter. All three men stood up. Danny was surprised the glass did not break. It was the norm with Nick, breaking every bottle and every glass. He did not know how much more of this hell he could take.

He and the other men left the room and shut the door behind them. Otty and the other two guys grumbled and went upstairs. Danny was initially behind them but then he saw Oscar sneaking towards the door of the room they had just left. He watched as Oscar put his ear gently to the door to eavesdrop. Danny turned and walked quietly to stand beside him.

Oscar was stunned by Danny's close presence. He said nothing but was clearly annoyed with him for joining and startling him. He put a finger to his lips indicating that Danny was to keep silent.

"I almost lost everything; I won t'night." Nick's voice came through the door loudly enough, it was unnecessary to place their ears to it. However, Meltdown was a man who spoke mostly in low cold tones, they might have to listen more attentively.

"Yes, but you didn't. In fact, you made £95,500," Meltdown reminded.

"And what is that in our grand scheme? I should 'ave the full amount and even more right now. I must 'ave the money for Guri on Monday. I must!"

"We still have Saturday, boss. If we can make £35,000 at the very least, then we've done it, and I'm sure we can win more than that. We will make it up tomorrow. I'm sure of it," stated Meltdown.

There was some quietness from the other side of the door, then Nick said, "Alright. Tomorrow. Let's do it. We'll make up the short fall. We 'ave to."

Oscar moved away from the door at that point. Danny looked at him questioningly.

When Oscar said nothing, but began walking away, Danny followed him. "So what does all that mean?"

Oscar halted in exasperation. "Dammit, Danny boy. The less you know, the better!" Without saying another word, Oscar took out his mobile phone and walked off.

Chapter Twenty-One

———————～———————

Despite the seven-degree weather that Saturday morning, lots of people were out shopping. Eva noted that, like her, so many were working through their Christmas lists. She did not like to take any chances; it was always wise to get the best whilst they were still available and reasonably priced. However, it was more to do with her being an extremely organised person. She liked to get things out of the way and avoid the last minute rush. She had decided to shop around Oxford Street since she would be meeting up with an old friend for coffee in Knightsbridge at noon. It was the street they had picked since they had decided to meet halfway between where they both lived. She and Sally didn't see each other often, but when they did, it was almost like time hadn't past. Traffic and parking had been a nightmare and Eva wondered why she had not bothered taking the trains. Then she remembered that it was because of all the shopping she was going to be lugging about.

Eva had practically done most of her shopping. She had decided to get something for Rachel. No matter what, she would always be like a sister to her. One person she had not been sure about shopping for was RJ. It was weird; should she get him something? That would assume that they were more than just friends. Weren't they more than just friends, though? She would think so, but she did not know what he thought. She had not invited him over to hers to visit yet and vice versa. Who knew where this budding "friendship" will be by Christmas?

She knew she really liked him and would like to see where this was going. She was also mindful of the fact that he had to want more too. Not to mention the fact that he was not a man who believed or had faith in God. That was a huge challenge and problem, but she had prayed about it and was willing to see how God was going to use her or make things… them align. That got her thinking about the church's missionary trip in Africa in about two months. January was

190

just around the corner. She had never questioned whether or not she was going. If this thing between her and RJ was real, would it make sense to leave now? She was not sure now. It all depended on where they are closer to the time. She felt guilty for wavering on her decision, but she could not help it.

It had been nice seeing Sally again. Her friend had broken the good news to her about her long-time boyfriend proposing to her. Eva had a feeling that there was a reason why Sally had wanted them to meet. It was great news and she thought it was sweet that her friend had wanted to tell her in person. A spring wedding next year sounded lovely.

After her tea with Sally, Eva began heading back to where she parked her car. As she rounded the corner, she observed a familiar looking face. The elderly woman was looking at her too, an expression of recognition on her face. She was wearing a button down expensive looking coat with a furry collar scarf around her neck. Where had she seen this face recently?

Then it came to her. The fundraiser. It was Betty Blythe! She remembered just as the woman approached her. She could not help remembering how rude RJ had been to her and hoped the woman didn't remember it; or worse – bring it up!

"Hello, dear. Now what's that lovely name of yours again... Eva? Yes, Eva. Fancy seeing you here. Do you live around here?" she asked, giving Eva a sweet smile.

Eva instinctively smiled back. "Hello, Mrs Blythe..."

"Nonsense. Call me Betty," chastised the woman.

"Betty. No, I don't. I live in Kennington."

"Ah. I see. I live not too far from here." She noticed the shopping bags in Eva's hands. "I see you have been doing some shopping. I was just heading to Harrods."

"Oh nice. I've had a lovely time. I hope your shopping goes smoothly too," Eva said. Not breaking her smile, Betty nodded in gratitude.

Eva was about to bid her goodbye when Betty said, "It was nice seeing you and Rhys together at the fundraiser the other day. I'm sure his father was happy to see him there, and with a beautiful girl like you beside him, too."

Eva was surprised. *RJ's father?* "No. He was actually there with me. I was representing my church at the fundraiser," Eva explained with a frown.

Betty's eyebrows rose. "Really? I thought he had surprisingly come to support his father. What a coincidence."

Eva was confused. What was Betty on about? "I'm sorry, Betty. You say RJ's father was there? You know his father?"

Betty appeared offended. "Of course I know his father, and there's no mistaking that he was there."

The woman looked serious. Eva's frown deepened. "Who is RJ's father?"

Betty looked amazed that Eva would even ask that. "Why, Alexander Fairchild, dear."

Muttering something about not understanding how RJ can be so calm, considering the risk he was going to be taking tonight, Lisa left the flat to get some groceries. Ben and RJ looked at the items of disguise spread out on the sofa. RJ was expected to wear brown coloured contacts, a thick beard, a pair of glasses, a body suit that would give him a bit of a punch on the belly and a hat. Of course, he had to dress up in suspenders and a tweed jacket. The idea was to come across as an old-fashioned businessman. Ben joked that he was sure RJ would very much look the part. However, on a more serious note, he was not sure if RJ could act the part. He suggested that RJ take the walking stick as well; just to add to the character. After Oscar had confirmed to them last night that Nick and Meltdown would definitely be coming back tonight to win the balance, they had to speed up getting everything ready. Ben gathered everything up and took them into the bedroom, leaving RJ to pick up his buzzing phone.

RJ was surprised that Eva was calling. Did he have plans with her today? He could have sworn that he had told her he was going to be busy attending to some things today and would probably see her tomorrow. However, he could do with hearing her voice. He wanted to hear her voice every day. She brought peace to his chaotic world. What was this woman doing to him? He thought as he swiped the button to answer.

Five minutes later Ben comes out of the room to find RJ pacing. He stopped, waiting for RJ to explain what had happened.

Pausing, RJ said, "Eva's on her way here."

On the phone, she had sounded upset about something which had bothered him. Was she okay? She did not want to talk about it over the phone and had asked for his address so she could come to him. Of course, he had offered to go to her instead; he did not really want her coming here. However, she insisted on coming to him and seemed to be getting more upset by his delay in giving her his address. He was really disturbed now and had gone into protective mode. He did not want Eva upset. He did not want anything upsetting her, so he had agreed. Now he was left wondering what the matter could be.

"You've got it really bad for this one, haven't you?" Ben asked. He was not expecting a response, and he didn't get one.

Once Eva texted to say she was about ten minutes away, Ben decided to make himself scarce.

"Don't miss the plot, RJ. Keep it within time. I'll go see the men. Hope you'll be ready by the time I get back." RJ's nod was enough for Ben.

RJ swung the door open after Eva's first knock.

A lot had been going through Eva's mind since she saw Betty earlier today until now. Initially she had felt sad, but now, she was angry. Why did RJ not deem it fit to tell her? All this time that she had thought him to be probably a gang member or a hustler? To think that the two of them had been right there beside her, they had communicated, and she had not known they were father and son! Now that she thought about it, they did seem so alike.

Same charisma, same deep blue eyes, same jawline. Alexander Fairchild could have had jet-black hair when he was younger, but it was now mixed with grey and kept shorter than RJ's. Eva was hurt. There was so much she did not know about this man, and if they were going to have some kind of relationship at all, she needed answers, and she needed them today!

Arriving at the address he had given her; Eva was even more shocked. Not sure the neighbourhood or block of flats were where she expected him to be living or not. She did not know what to think or expect of him at all. She never looked down on working class neighbourhoods and had visited countless times herself since many of their church members were working class. Working class! She never quite understood that term, especially since almost everyone worked for a living. You are either working or you're not. All working people, regardless of what job they do, where they work or how much they make, deserve to be respected. That's not saying anything against the unemployed as long as their unemployment isn't due to indolence or irresponsibility.

He stood at the doorway now looking at her with what she could only interpret as worry. RJ's usually calm exterior did not seem so calm right now. He stepped aside and let her in. Eva took in her surroundings. There was something off about it. The furniture, everything about it did not fit into the little she knew about RJ. There was something wrong and she felt it in her spirit.

"Are you going to tell me what's bothering you?" RJ enquired, cutting her assessment short.

She turned to face him, not bothering to sit down. "Why did you tell me your name was Rhys Jared?"

The question obviously threw him off because he took a few seconds to respond, "Because it's my name."

For some reason, Eva had expected him to come clean all at once. "So, it isn't, let's say… Rhys Fairchild, by any chance?"

He took in a deep breath and let it out. Then he looked away. She said nothing but waited patiently for him to respond.

"How did you find out?" he asked finally.

"Does it matter?" Eva flayed her arms in frustration.

When he looked at her again, he said, "My name is Rhys Jared Fairchild. I never lied to you, Eva, I just never told you my last name."

Eva was astounded. "Excuse me? I asked you for your name at the fundraiser, and you told me Rhys Jared."

"I was about to tell you, but I think we were interrupted or something, I can't recall," He explained.

"Really? And since then, you have had no other opportunity to tell me? Instead, you kept me believing your last name was Jared." Eva sounded hurt. "And to think that you and Alex Fairchild were kind of butting horns too… the strangeness between the two of you… Why, RJ?"

In response to the hurt in her voice, RJ reached out for her, but Eva pulled away.

"Look, this thing between us… I don't know what it is, but if it is to continue and grow, it has to be premised on truth. I want the truth, RJ." It was a stern plea from Eva.

RJ sighed. He gestured towards the settee, but Eva was not prepared to sit down. Dipping his hands in his jeans pocket, a habit of his that was endearing, and Eva had now grown accustomed to, he began.

"Yes, Alex is my father. However, we're not really on the best of terms. It's a long story that I can't really get into right now. After graduating from Oxford at age twenty-two with a degree in Economics and a Masters in 'Financial Economics', I left home for good. I came into my trust fund at age twenty-one, so it worked out nicely for me."

RJ paused to walk towards the window that looked onto a small slightly run-down playground.

"I wasn't exactly the ideal son. I gambled, got drunk, womanised, moved with the wrong crowd… and generally just did everything except what my dad wanted for me – to join his business. He has or probably had hopes for me to take FairCorp over from him in future. I mean, why else would I have studied what I studied if not to one day run the business development and financial investment corporation?" The last sentence was said with cynicism.

Even though Eva did not want to interrupt him, she could not help but ask, "So you don't want to run FairCorp in future then?"

RJ shrugged, not turning away from the window. "It's not that I don't want to run it, it's that I've never allowed myself to give it much thought. That's mostly in defiance of him, to be honest. Anyway, eventually, I joined a gang… well more like I started a gang."

Eva's face did not register the shock she felt. She had previously wondered if he was part of a gang but had never imagined that he was the leader.

RJ had broken off, probably expecting Eva to say something, but when she did not, he went on, "I met these men in different circumstances. Good men: most, through no fault of their own, found themselves in situations where they had to do anything to survive. I'm certainly not making excuses for them; just saying, some didn't really have great options and didn't even know better to choose good ones, even if they had the choice. They began to rely on me, for some reason." He gave a light sarcastic chuckle. "Then they started getting into all kinds of messes and trouble, and how could I help put them straight when my life wasn't quite stable."

Tapping slowly on the window seal, RJ paused, turned to glance at Eva before turning back to the window.

"Well, unsurprisingly, my father struck one of his harsh blows. He had been trying to get me to stop my 'foolishness' for a while and had employed all kinds of means to get me to 'take my life and future seriously and come home'. My trust fund is tied to several estates and the income that comes from those estates. He found a way to limit the money that comes through, so I have very limited amounts in there to take out and at specific times. I suppose it could have been worse." RJ's low laugh sounded a little harsh. "However, for me, that blow couldn't have come at the worst time, and I was even madder at him. I had people depending on me…looking up to me. I guess… well, I had to become responsible. I quit gambling and bought the pub. That helped for a while, but then it began to suffer. The guys relied too much on the income coming from the pub. A few of the men were not helping to build it but were constantly causing trouble that was threatening to destroy the business. To make it worse, people started to come to me for money. It was beginning to seep into the business. I couldn't let it happen. I thought, if there was no pub, then maybe people would lay off me a bit, so I sold it. That didn't help; purely because, the huge financial responsibilities didn't go away, and I hadn't really thought about what I was going to do to bring in money. No matter what, we needed a source of income. So I started gambling again." He shook his head sadly in regret.

Eva wished she could go to him and put her arm around him.

"Anyway, the gambling worked but I just knew that I couldn't go on like this. I had to quit again… for good. And I had to stop the illegal lending, I had to make it legit somehow. Well… I guess you know the rest."

When he finished, Eva did not know where her anger had disappeared to. He revealed way more than she was expecting, but a lot of it made sense. She was not here to judge him or his choices. It was clear that revealing to her that Alex was his father would have meant her asking a lot of questions that would have rehashed all he had just explained. Maybe he had not been ready for any of that. She could understand his reluctance to do so, but she was not going to justify pretence, lies or a lack of transparency…especially not now that they had gotten a little close.

She sighed, contemplating whether to stay where she was or join him where he stood by the window "I appreciate you opening up to me. I wish you had done so earlier, but at least you have explained it all now."

He turned to look at her and there was a strange look in his eyes. Eva wondered what it meant. "You have explained it all, right?" she found herself asking.

The lock on the door turned, the door opened, and Lisa walked in with two bags of groceries. She stopped briefly when she saw Eva standing in the middle of her tiny living room. RJ closed his eyes and calmly buried his forehead in his hand.

Eva, unable to think for a moment, just stared on at Lisa.

Lisa eyed her in irritation. Walking into the open plan kitchen, she said "Oi, don't look at me like that. This is my house."

Once she said that, it was too much for Eva to take. Without looking at RJ, she quietly walked to the front door and walked out. As she went down the stairs, Eva did not know whether to laugh or cry. She was not going to cry! Who was that woman? The woman had said it was her house and Eva believed it. Hadn't she felt uneasy in the flat when she first walked in? Something in her spirit had told her that it was not really RJ's. Here was another thing for RJ to explain away. She wondered what he was going to say now. He had been bad news ever since she met him. Her gut had told her that right from the beginning. Why, oh why hadn't she listened to her spirit instead of letting Joyce get in her head? Lord, was this a test?

Eva got into her car and was about to start the engine when the door of the passenger's side flung open, and RJ got in beside her.

"Excuse me?" Eva said in anger and surprise.

RJ raised his arms up in peace. "Eva, listen to me. Please listen to me," he said when she started the engine and gestured for him to get out.

"I thought I already had. Now you want to explain why you live with another woman! Unless she is your sister or mother, then don't bother," Eva said, surprised that her voice, though a little emotional, came out evenly. What she really wanted to do was yell at him.

"My mother died years ago, and I'm my father's only child," RJ informed, but it didn't shake Eva's resolve.

RJ's pleading eyes aligned with his words. "It's not what you think, Eva. I can't let you leave without clarifying the situation. Please, you're hurting, and I don't want you to."

"I thought you had clarified all that needed to be clarified upstairs. In your words, I know the rest, right?" Eva retorted.

"Give me a break, Eva, I'm trying. My life is this great big mess of a rollercoaster ride, and I don't know how to open up. I'm trying, okay?" His slightly raised tone was not what silenced Eva. It was the pained look in his eyes as he watched her.

Quietly, Eva turned off the engine and sat back in her seat.

RJ studied her expressionless face for a moment, then said, "Thank you. I told you before that a few of my men were more trouble than others; well, there were two men in particular. I met Nick and his mate, Meltdown earlier on during my gambling and betting days. Nick said he was inspired by my poker skills and wanted to join my poker team...with Meltdown too, of course. I didn't have a team then, so we started one. It was fun. It's weird because, starting a poker team soon turned into starting a gang. Not all the men who joined after played or could play poker.

"When I bought the pub, Nick started to borrow money a lot, and he wasn't paying back. He worked at the pub, and drinks and money started going missing. He brought in all sorts of friends, and they would get away with not paying for their drinks. Eventually, he started getting involved in some shady stuff; one of them was buying drugs and reselling them… which he got into trouble for with main suppliers. The pub was always his cover and was often being financially sapped for his mistakes. Meltdown always supported him and tended to do his bidding. By the way, Meltdown's real name is Melvin Banks, but we call him Meltdown 'cos he's capable of causing so much trouble and disaster…. just like Nick.

"Nick knew I had money… everyone did, but no one knows I have a trust fund… except Ben, a very close friend of mine. They thought it was all from the gambling, and a lot of it was, especially when my trust fund became limited.

"I sold the pub mostly because of Nick; to keep him from ruining it. I still have shares in it. However, he doesn't know that. The money lending soon got out of hand, and I couldn't cope, so I went back to gambling. Nick loved the loan shark idea and wanted to milk it and unleash terror on the poor borrowers, but I wasn't having any of it. That's when I decided to start a proper lending business. Nick and Meltdown weren't too happy. Nick always had this big idea about me becoming this drug lord in London and he would be my second in command. He kind of was my second in command; a very troublesome one. I'm not an upstanding citizen, but there was no way I was going to go into the drug business. Nick felt, if I couldn't concede to running a loan shark business, then surely, I could do the other. He went ahead and met with this Albanian kingpin and tried to set up a meeting which I never attended 'cos I wasn't interested. Not only did I not want to do that, I also didn't want to mess up the lives of the other men who depended on me. There's… there's this young lad who has his whole future ahead of him…"

Eva instinctively knew who RJ was talking about. "Daniel?"

He cast her a side glance. "Yes… Daniel. I figured I could send him to school or something."

RJ looked away again. "Anyway, this brings me to the night… the night you found me. I had recently received my FCA approval and was excited about setting everything in motion…"

RJ had just left Ben's pub after having a celebratory beer on him. He could have had more, but he still had to ride his bike back home. He and Ben had met and become really good friends some years back. Ben was a bit older, but that meant he was always the sensible one of the two of them, and he was constantly there for RJ when he needed him. Ben had once been the head of a relatively large gang many years ago but had turned his life around. He had never been married and did well on his own, especially as he had a good head for business. The former members of his gang were still very loyal to him and would do anything for him. He did have some men he paid to keep his pub secure, and RJ could understand why.

RJ parked his sports bike in front of the five-bedroom house he had been renting for the past six months. This was where he housed all eleven of his men. However, he did not think it wise to live with them; not only did he enjoy his own space, but the men needed the extra room. He lived in his own house not too far from here. Nick was there to keep charge of things anyway. They were due to move in a week or two anyway, so he had already paid his last rent for the month. It was just as well as the people who lived in the neighbourhood were not too happy about the likes of the men living in the area. No matter how many times he had told Nick to keep things on the down low, it was always one drunken party, one fist fight between the men, and one weed-smoking galore after another. It was a tough job trying to whip guys like these into shape, but it wasn't impossible. Nick was the main hindrance. He was such a bad egg; RJ did not know what to do. At the beginning, Nick and Meltdown were so much fun, and they still were, but they had grown a bit too puffed up now and it was getting harder and harder to control them. Now that he had gotten his FCA approval and could start up his business, he would make sure they all benefitted from it.

He could finally start to do right by each and every man. He will get them all set up in either the business or something else. Those who needed to go to school, like Danny boy, would do so.

RJ had secured a massive house that had an adjoining bungalow. It had cost him an arm and a leg, but it was perfect. The men would move into the house while he could use the bungalow for the business. Hopefully, as time went by, they would all move out and go their own way, and as the business expanded, he could convert and use the rest of the building. When he left home eighth years ago, he never thought he would have this massive responsibility... and over mostly grown men. Nevertheless, they had become family to him, and he felt responsible for them.

RJ got off the bike and took off his helmet. He was happy the house was quiet tonight, which was rare. He liked to check up on the guys every day to see how they were doing and to make sure they were not getting into any trouble. Mostly, he liked to check up on Danny boy. He would really prefer to have the boy live with him and not with the guys, but he knew that would cause some discord among the men and start raising questions. He made his way to the back of the house so he could get in through the garden, which was where all of them went in from. Oscar was sitting on a bench in the garden having a smoke. Beside him was Rog.

"Evening, boss," they greeted when they saw him.

RJ nodded; glad they weren't smoking weed tonight. Walking into the house, he spotted Danny boy playing checkers with Otty. The lad smiled, always happy to see RJ. They both greeted him. He could hear the voices of two men chatting in the kitchen. He was looking for Nick and he definitely was not in the kitchen.

"Hope you're not cheating, Otty? Be careful with him," RJ warned Daniel as he made his way upstairs.

He met Nick on his way downstairs. The man looked like he was in a hurry. "Just the man I was looking for. What's going on?" RJ asked.

"'Ey, boss. Dunno. Meltdown was out, but 'e is on 'is way back. Says it's serious," Nick responded as RJ followed him back downstairs.

They both went through the garden and RJ was back in front of the house.

"Meltdown gave no indication of what the problem might be?" RJ remained his usual calm self, but definitely felt a bit anxious. Not knowing what was happening could be unnerving.

"No. 'E just said to wait for 'im outside. 'E ain't too far," Nick replied.

"RJ, are you leaving already?" Danny boy asked. He had followed them and now came to stand between Ben and RJ.

"You get back in the 'ouse, Danny boy," Nick immediately ordered.

"Why? What's wrong?" Danny boy grimaced, looking from RJ to Nick.

"This ain't none of your bleeding business. Always whining 'n tagging along like a sore puppy," Nick growled.

RJ gave Nick a look. "Hey, Nick, lay off the lad a tad, okay?"

A van suddenly sped onto the driveway. Meltdown was at the wheel. "Hey, boss, you're going to want to see this," he quickly yelled out.

RJ hoped this had nothing to do with the Streatham gang again. He thought he had settled everything once and for all. Nick and his racist views and comments practically started a war with the gang of mostly black men some months back.

"Did you see John in the house?" asked the agitated Meltdown.

RJ had not had the chance to see all the men since he only arrived a few minutes ago, so he looked at Nick for answers.

Nick shook his head. "Come to think of it, I 'aven't seen that punk for hours."

Danny boy scowled in confusion. "John? I thought I saw…"

"You and Nick need to get in, boss. I saw something; I think John might be in trouble," Meltdown shouted.

RJ didn't like this. He didn't like this one bit. What could John have possibly gotten himself into?

Nick pulled the back of the van door open. "We best get going, boss." Turning to Danny, he barked, "You, do as you're told n' get back in the f-ing 'ouse."

Meltdown was impatient and was revving the van's engine, causing a hell of a racquet, while Nick was screaming at Danny. The poor boy looked scared out of his mind. Instinctively, RJ pushed Danny boy into the van and hopped in behind him. As they sat down, Nick looked furiously at Danny boy just before he swung the door shut. Quickly walking to the front passenger's side, Nick got in the vehicle and joined Meltdown at the front.

Meltdown hit the accelerator and they were on their way.

Danny boy sat quietly looking guilty and worried. Meltdown kept casting him looks from the rear-view mirror. The van was moving too fast, and the last thing RJ needed was police trouble.

"Hey MD, slow down," he ordered. When the vehicle slowed down a little, RJ asked, "So what exactly did you see? Are you sure it was John?"

Meltdown and Nick shared a look. "Positive." Meltdown answered. RJ caught that look and instantly felt uneasy.

"I… err… I don't think it's John. I think he was in the loo," Danny said, a little scared.

"Oh shu'up, peanut! What do you know?" Nick hissed.

Danny glanced at RJ who seemed even calmer than normal. "So where are we going, MD?" RJ called out again.

He got no response. RJ stared at Danny boy for a while and then knew he had to get him out of the vehicle. Banging the ceiling of the van, he said coolly, "Stop the van."

The two men in front didn't respond, but once again, Meltdown glared at them from the rear-view mirror.

"Stop now," RJ called louder now. "Pull over and let Danny out... let him find his way back home. I'll stay in the van."

Danny began shifting nervously in his seat. RJ placed a hand on his knee to calm him.

RJ took his phone out of the pocket of his hooded top. He wasn't sure who to call. The police? Probably not. He wasn't exactly keen on Fischer getting on the case. His finger hovered over a particular number before he chose to call Ben instead. As he was about to hit the call button, the van braked suddenly causing him to drop his phone. Damn! RJ scrambled to his knees to find it. Daniel hurriedly brought out his phone. Meltdown swung open the door, grabbed it from him and slammed it several times on the edge of the van's door before tossing the smashed-up phone in the van. RJ's hand found his phone and picked it up just as Meltdown roughly grabbed Danny boy.

"Let me go," the lad shouted.

RJ stood up and immediately threw a blow at Meltdown's temple. The man's grip on Danny loosened and he stumbled in pain.

Danny boy was visibly shaken as he fell silent in fear.

"Get your filthy hands off him, Meltdown," RJ ordered. His cool tone meant he was furious, and it was best not to mess with him then.

Nick suddenly approached him from the corner, but RJ was too quick for him. Turning swiftly, he landed a punch on Nick's neck. Nick held on to the assaulted area, growling in pain.

RJ turned to Meltdown, who still held onto Danny. He moved slowly towards him, and Meltdown backed up, dragging Danny with him whilst holding a hand over his mouth with the other hand.

"How dare you both pull this stunt? After everything I've done for you?" RJ asked, rolling up the sleeves of his hooded top. The weather was cold, but he could not feel it. He felt only heat... anger.

He knew Nick and Meltdown were capable of something like this, but he never really thought they would do it… not to him. Or maybe he just did not want to believe it. His number one concern now was Danny boy. Why in the world had he brought him along? Probably because he wanted the boy with him as much as possible. Had he really thought the situation was so dire? Of course not, or he would not have dragged Danny with him. Nick and Meltdown had always been prone to the dramatics.

Nick laughed harshly, but obviously trying to keep his tone low. RJ had no idea where they were, but that was currently not on his attention list.

"After all you 'ave done for us? We can be more than we currently are, but you keep 'olding us down 'n 'olding us back. We ain't allowed to do anything. You sold the bliming pub to that tosser Ben, we can't run a successful loan shark business, we ain't allowed to gamble anymore, we can't smoke weed." Nick broke off uncomfortably when RJ took a step towards him.

"Now you want us to go like corporate 'n shit! We're a f-ing gang, RJ! We're so toothless when we can be strong 'n respected. That deal wiv Oktapod is our chance and you're bloody standing in the way." Nick spat out.

RJ gave a half smirk. "Again with the drug business. I should have known this was about that. I thought you wanted to have opportunities in life and become something… something respectable, and I was working towards that for all of us. But you and Meltdown are just bad eggs Nick. If it's so important to you, then leave; you and Meltdown, leave the guys and I for good and go do your thing, your drug project. Leave the rest of us alone."

Nick glowered. "I 'ate you, RJ. I 'ate you n' everything you stand for. You're get'ing what you deserve tonight."

RJ immediately rushed towards Nick as the stocky man struggled to get something out of his inner jacket. Reaching him before he was able to, RJ grabbed Nick by his jacket collar, pulled him towards him and began raining his face with one hand punches.

Meltdown, who had been quiet in the corner with Danny, finally spoke, "Stop or Danny gets it."

RJ stopped abruptly, still holding on to Nick, and turned. Meltdown had a knife to Danny's throat. The lad was quivering. This enraged RJ further. He wanted to rush over to Meltdown and lengthen the scar on his face, but he could not take any chances.

Calmly, RJ said, "Let the boy go. He's not the one you want. Like you, he's just another one of the gang."

Meltdown gave an evil smile. "You're right. He's not the one we want."

Before RJ could respond to that or realise what's going on, he felt a sharp blow to his left side. He looked back at Nick, wondering what the man had done. Nick pulled out of RJ's hold, and RJ suddenly felt powerless to hold on. Something was wrong, that was no ordinary blow. RJ looked down. There was a big knife lodged in his side. Sticky wetness was beginning to soak the area as explicable pain shot through him. Nick placed his hand on the blade again and pushed it in deeper, his face expressing the amount of energy he was exerting. RJ felt the life being knocked out of him through shear pain.

Nick was saying something, but RJ could not hear. He was feeling dizzy and could barely see Danny's mouth open wide as he flayed his legs and was soon able to get free of Meltdown's grasp. RJ dropped to his knees and Danny was quickly beside him. The boy was saying something, his mouth wide open and tears pouring down his face. He saw Meltdown grab Danny again, put a hand over his mouth and drag him to the van. Nick quickly crouched beside him and pulled the knife out of his side. The pain from this was too much for RJ to bear, he immediately lost consciousness.

Chapter Twenty-Two

"Obviously, those two expect me to be dead. They were staking out my house some time ago, and have probably stopped, but I can't take any chances and risk them finding out that I'm actually alive. Lisa is an old friend that has been kind enough to put me up for as long as it takes," RJ quietly concluded.

The silence that ensued when he finished was prolonged. This was beyond anything Eva had ever expected. She felt overwhelmed by what he had just revealed to her. She knew that gang life was terrible and dangerous, but she never heard about one first-hand. God, please grant her the strength to handle this. She finally turned to him and found him watching her anxiously.

She had a lot to say yet struggled to find what to say. To be honest, she did not want to say anything at all. She just felt like praying. This was a bit much and way out of her comfort zone.

She looked down at her hands. "So… why did you put up with Nick and Meltdown at all… for that long?" It was an irrelevant question, but she felt he wanted her to say something.

RJ gave a deep sigh, appearing to give this some thought "I guess because I didn't want to give up on them. They were friends of mine… quite helpful at the beginning, and I really wanted to help them too."

Eva looked up at him curiously. "But how?"

"By giving them the opportunities that I had but they never did. By showing them the right way to go. It didn't start off that way, but eventually, that's the turn I decided to take. I know it's weird that I would mess up my opportunities and then hope to create some for others. But you learn things on the streets, out there in the real world. You grow up…well some people do. I guess I grew up."

When she remained quiet, he went on, "Nick and Meltdown were hustlers when I met them, I hoped to get them out of that life, get them into commerce, business…either mine or theirs someday. I could always give them the start-up money. Like Otty, now he was a skilled thief. Getting him out of that life was the best thing I ever did for him. He's very skilled at cutting hair. He's the gang's official barber. My plan was to help him open his own barber's shop."

Eva noticed the excitement in RJ's voice, the passion in his eyes.

"John, well, he's good with accounting. I planned to get him to work for me part time while he takes an online accounting course or as many as he needs to get fully certified. Then he can work for me full time. Oscar – I believe you have met him. He loves the ladies. He's been known to be forceful with women especially when he's been drinking too much. Almost raped a girl once, but we got that sorted. Anyway, he was actually going to school. Like the others, he's from a poor family and was putting himself through college. He ran up debts, couldn't pay and I ended up helping him with that problem. He dropped out of school because of his money issues and hasn't been able to find his way back since. I promised to help him with that, and I intend to keep my promise. The rest of the men have similar or unique stories, and I would love to help them too."

Yes, Eva remembered Oscar. How could she forget the way the overeager man came onto her strong, and the look of fear on his face when he saw RJ. That made sense now. He had thought RJ was dead, so seeing him must have been terrifying. Then she remembered one other person.

"And Daniel?" she asked.

RJ's enthusiasm mellowed a bit. "Daniel's an orphan. He came to us just before he turned sixteen; that's almost two years ago. I have taken on the responsibility of sending him to school and taking care of him. If only he will, though. He doesn't want to go to school. He attended primary school and some secondary and that was it. I was still trying to convince him."

"Why not take him to social services or something… get him help instead of keeping him in the gang…which was…is not good for him," Eva enquired, a bit of desperation in her voice.

RJ huffed. "Where do you think he came from? He was in the system. You don't know how messed up the system is. He ran away and came to me… to us. I wanted…want to give him better… especially as… as…" He broke off, shaking his head.

Eva studied RJ's face, his perfect and handsome features. This man who was born with a silver spoon in his mouth, who knew wealth and, in most ways, the life of the poor. It suddenly occurred to her.

"You know what?" she asked.

He turned to her, "Go on."

"You're not that different from your father." She saw him raise an eyebrow as a cynical expression came across his face, and quickly continued, "You have his heart for philanthropy. You both like to help people and you have such strategic minds on how to get that done. It's obvious that, given a few years or more, you could build an empire like your father has. However, he has already built one for you. Why not use that? Faircorp is huge and it is ready. You studied for it, you have matured for it… and guess what? It's practically yours. RJ, you keep calling me your angel, but I think it's you who's the angel."

The look RJ gave her was unreadable. It was intense and she wondered if he was even looking at her at all. His phone rang and he quickly picked it up.

"Yes, damn! I lost track of time. I'm coming up now to get ready," he said before quickly hanging up. Turning to her, he said, "I have to go."

Eva did not like the sense of urgency she was getting from him. Dare she ask?

"Go where?" she dared to ask.

He considered whether or not to tell her, then took a deep breath and said, "Ben and I set Nick and Meltdown up. He's trying to get the gang messed up in drugs and we're trying to make sure he loses the deal."

Eva was flabbergasted. "Wait. What? You're kidding. How?"

"Tonight, they're going to lose all their buy-in money in a poker game."

Eva was still stunned. "How do you know? Are you going to be there? No, RJ. You quit, remember?"

He shook his head and smiled. "Don't worry, it's just one night and that's that. I'll be in disguise."

Eva shook her head too. "No. It won't be over. Don't you see? You keep quitting and then having to resort back to it. Stop this cycle, RJ!"

He took hold of her hand, but she yanked it away from him just before saying,

"You know, I held back asking why you didn't just tell the police everything, why you're letting these two men walk around after attempting to murder you while you hide away. Why won't you just get the police involved now and end things."

RJ's face became stern. "Because it is personal. Because I wanted to handle it on my own. Because I didn't want my father finding out and me ultimately proving him right about the choices I made. Because I didn't want this full-on investigation that would pull the other guys in. Because I'm a lot more like my father than you think – I'm a very proud man."

Eva was panicking. She worried for him. "Pride goes before a fall, RJ. What if you succeed, then what? Are you going to remain 'dead' forever? What if Nick finds out it is you and that you're alive? You need to stop this RJ. It needs to end."

RJ drew close to her and kissed her on the forehead "Promise me that I'll see you tomorrow."

Eva did not know what to say. She was sad. "I don't know. Please, RJ," was her pleading response.

He looked a little disappointed as he gave her a peck on the lips, then quietly got out of the car.

Rachel put on her cardigan before going downstairs. The heating was on, but it was still so cold. She might probably turn up the radiator downstairs. She had just finished reading an encouraging Christian devotional: *And we know that in all things, God works for the good of those who love him, who have been called according to his purpose.* Romans chapter 8 verse 28 was such a reassuring verse, and she had read it alongside Philippians' chapter 4 verse 7: *Do not be anxious about anything, but in every situation, by prayer and petition, with thanksgiving, present your request to God. And the peace of God, which transcends all understanding, will guard your hearts and your minds in Christ Jesus.* She had neglected God and that was why she had made some terrible choices. She just needed to remember to trust God to work it all out for her.

She usually read her devotionals in the mornings but had not had the chance to do so until tonight. There were so many things she had left undone since her little emotional breakdown, but she was trying to get her feelings back on track. This Saturday, she had gone grocery shopping, cleaned her room, done some long overdue laundry, and watched TV with Sunita and her new boyfriend in the afternoon. She was not fully there yet, but it had been a good day and she was grateful for that, at least.

In this positive and peaceful spirit, Rachel decided to give Eva a call. Eva had been really supportive and was sincerely worried about her. Rachel needed to give her a call to appreciate and reassure her. Sunita and Karen were out so it was nice having the whole house to herself. Eva's phone rang until her voice message took over, so she decided to try an hour later, knowing that Eva would most likely ring her back before then. An hour later, still nothing from Eva so Rachel tried again. Once again, it went to voicemail. Rachel sent her a WhatsApp message. Thirty minutes later, Rachel stood up from the settee. It was time to rustle something up for dinner. She checked her phone. Eva had read her message but still had not responded. Normally this sort of thing would not be a cause for concern, but it was unlike Eva.

Besides, Rachel hoped she had not subconsciously pushed Eva away and this was the consequence of that – being ignored. She was going to try one last time. Hopefully, Eva would not think she was badgering her. It rang once and was immediately picked up.

"Can I call you back later, Rachel?" Eva sounded distressed.

Rachel was instantly worried. "Yes, of course. Are you o…?"

The line was cut off before she could finish her sentence. This was rather disturbing. In the number of years she had known Eva, Rachel had never heard her sound like that. Should she just wait for Eva to ring her back later and pray everything was okay? Eva had been there for her when she needed someone, whatever it was, she wanted to be there for her too.

Eva had not been herself for the last few hours. All she could think about was RJ. She did not really have all the details of what he was going to be up to tonight, but she knew it was not safe. How could she feel so much for a man in so short a time? A man that came with tonnes of scary baggage! She had driven home after he got out of her car, not having any recollection of driving. Her phone rang on a couple of times, but it had been lodged somewhere in her handbag and she could not answer it. She had not even remembered to connect it to her car. Getting into her apartment, she checked her phone to see if RJ had tried to reach her. She saw a message from Rachel that she scanned through but didn't digest. In a state of unrest, she decided to ring up Joyce. Rachel's call came in before she could dial Joyce's number. Sparing Rachel only a few seconds; promising to call her back later, Eva rang Joyce right after and told her everything that was going on with RJ.

Joyce had been astounded, but ever the positive soul, had managed to calm her down a bit.

"Eva, this is God at work. He wants to use you," Joyce said.

Eva was a little stupefied. "Really? How? It looks more like he's punishing me."

"Don't be absurd!" Joyce exclaimed. "Sometimes we get tough tasks. The tougher we are, the tougher the tasks. The tougher the task, the tougher we get."

Even though it sounded strange, Eva knew there was some sense in that. Finally, Joyce asked to pray with her.

After her long phone call with Joyce, Eva did not know what to do with herself. She tried ringing RJ, but his number was switched off. Should she call the police? What if RJ hadn't gone ahead with it? Then why was his phone going straight to voicemail. What if she called the police and it made things worse? After all, she did not really know the details of whatever plan RJ had hatched. What if it got RJ in trouble too… or instead?

There was a knock on her door. Without thinking, she ran to it and hurriedly opened it. Evan stood at her door with what looked like some takeaway in his hand.

"Jeez, Eva, is that how you welcome anyone who knocks on your door? Such eagerness… with no thought to safety and security?" Evan quipped.

Eva was not in the mood. She turned away from him, walked into her living room and sank into a couch.

Evan closed the door behind him and walked in. "Hope you haven't had dinner yet; I brought some Indian."

"I'm not hungry," Eva said, reaching for the TV remote control. "You know, you could have called to check if I was in the mood for Indian."

"I did a while ago. You didn't pick up," Evan responded, walking into Eva's kitchen to sort out some plates and cutlery.

He joined her in the living room, a dished-out plate in hand. She cast him a look of annoyance.

Evan frowned. "What? You said you weren't hungry. I did bring a plate out for you. There's a lot still there so you can help yourself when you want."

Eva was wondering why he couldn't just eat at the dining table.

"I find it a little weird that you would attempt to call me and even show up here at all," remarked Eva.

Evan grimaced, struggling to push down the food in his mouth. "I'm still your big brother, you know, Eva."

Eva rolled her eyeballs. "My big brother? Anyway, funny how you remember that when it suits you. You have been avoiding my calls lately and not really communicating with me much."

Evan placed his plate on the glass centre table. "Okay, maybe I overdid it a little, and I'm sorry. But don't forget; you betrayed me so it's understandable that I would avoid speaking with you. It makes no sense that you would do that to me."

Eva looked at him incredulously. "Well, you avoiding me eventually upset me, so maybe it's my turn to play the victim." Tears stung the back of her eyes. She was not the sort who cried much.

Evan's expression switched to that of concern. "Hey, hey, what's this? What's wrong Eva?" She struggled to hold back her tears. Evan moved to sit beside her.

"You used to be able to tell me anything," Evan said gently.

"Not everything," Eva replied.

Evan conceded after a thought. "Yes, but only when it came to the issue of boys." When Eva remained quiet, he said, "So it's a guy, then?"

Eva didn't feel like going through the whole thing, but she wanted to give him something.

"This man I met; I really like him. However, he's involved in a lot of... a lot of serious and overwhelming stuff and I don't know what to do."

"What man? You haven't mentioned any man to me before. When did you meet him?" Evan asked curiously.

Eva was reluctant to tell him, but she did not really have a tight rein on her inhibitions right now.

"Remember that guy I found on St Benedict's doorstep some time ago?" she asked slowly.

Evan did remember. "The one that was half dead?"

Eva nodded.

Evan looked at her in disbelief. "Eva? Are you telling me that you're in a relationship with that guy? How did that happen? I told you to steer clear of him. Of course he would be involved in a lot of unmentionable stuff. People like that are always bad news. Come on, Eva!"

Eva knew Evan was just concerned about her, but his reaction was not what she needed right now. She stood up angrily.

"Where do you get off judging people all the time? You don't even know him or what the 'serious stuff' is. Funny; it's so easy to think you know people, brand them and 'Steer clear' of them. I'm like that too, you see, but I don't want to be like that anymore. How can we claim to be Christians and people of faith when we never give people a chance? Where's the love?"

Evan remained seated but looked up at her. "Eva, are you calling me judgmental? Love, as mentioned in the Bible, doesn't mean you save their lives and then have a relationship with them! I mean, I'm all for giving people chances but…"

Eva laughed in derision, cutting him off.

Evan shot her a frown. "Eva, I believe in giving people chances, and I do!"

"Evan, look how you've been treating Rachel, for goodness sake. Yes, she messed up, but you don't have a clue what's been going on with her or what led her down that path. You've totally refused to give her a chance, sit with her, and talk about it. And that's someone you know and who is absolutely crazy about you. Trust me, she is!" Eva said almost hysterically.

She really did not want to be having this conversation. She wanted to know what was happening with RJ. If Evan was going to respond, he was prevented from doing so by the sound of the doorbell.

Immediately, Eva went to the door and opened it. It was Rachel. What a coincidence. She was carrying a small box that obviously contained a cake or something similar.

"Oh look, Rachel brought dessert," Eva said in high pitch tone, but she wasn't smiling.

Everyone was showing up at her door except the one person she was desperate to see. Eva suddenly had a vision of her parents turning up.

She quickly gave the confused Rachel a hug and pulled her in. Then she picked up a coat from one of those hanging on the hook and her handbag from the small table she had tossed it on earlier. Her car keys were in it.

"There's some Indian in the kitchen. Make yourself at home. I need to go somewhere. Love you guys," Eva said and hurriedly left.

She was going back to RJ's to see if he was there... or back or whatever. Please God. Keep him safe, she prayed.

Nick liked to make an entrance. There were a number of cars parked outside already and a few of the well-dressed gentlemen were making their way through the entrance. This was going to be his night and he was pumped for it. By the end of tonight, he was going to have all the money he needed and then some.

His hair was gelled to perfection and glistened under the glare of the quarter moon. He had decided to wear a suit tonight so he could blend in. This was Saturday night; he expected the rich pricks to be dressed formally as they usually did. He wasn't going to be slack today. This was his big night, and he wanted to go out in style. He had come with every single dime he had, but he planned to leave with everything and so much more. He was feeling extremely lucky.

He brought three of the men along with him. Tony, one of the men, stayed in the van while Meltdown and Rog walked to the entrance with him. The two beefy men at the door stopped them just before Nick said the password.

"Only two of you allowed in. New rules for security reasons," one of them informed, blocking their path in.

Nick glowered. This was a problem. He was confused. He needed Meltdown's observant eye and sharpness. Although Meltdown could manage to hold his own physically and be there for him if it came to it, Nick would stand a better chance under big strong Rog's protection.

Meltdown must have read Nick's mind, because he said, "Take Rog. Don't worry. I'll be out here. I'm sure all will go smoothly."

Inside, the room was smoky and reeked of Cuban tobacco. There was a little bar in the corner where men could purchase expensive drinks and cigars. Nick decided to get a cigar today. Busy night: It looked like there might be about fourteen or more of them at the table. Some men merely stood and observed while others chatted away. He usually kept to himself, as he did not know anyone and did not care to. He was more of an observer himself. He liked to read the people he would be playing against. Rog stood solidly behind him carrying a briefcase, as a lot of the other men's security men or bodyguards did. No one ever acted like they came with bodyguards, but Nick knew that those extra men who stood beside them, looking mean and tough but not playing, were definitely there to protect their bosses. Nick spotted a few return players and some new ones. He did not bother with the ones he had seen before but focussed on the new ones. He remembered the black man who was probably in his forties. He was present yesterday and was a strong player, but Nick was not too worried. From what he could read, no one looked particularly skilfully threatening. One of the unfamiliar faces was that of a man who looked like a Jewish rabbi but clearly, he wasn't, or he wouldn't be here. His pair of glasses and dependence on a walking stick made him come across as weak. He might have a good mind for business, and it would explain why he was obviously wealthy, but Nick's guess was that the man was here to drown his depression on a game he was probably less than good at.

Nick was in high spirits.

Not long after, ten of them were seated at the table. The four remaining men would have to join once seats become available. The dealer, a man who complimented his shirt and trousers attire with a flamboyant waist coat and tie, cleared his throat.

"Now that you're all set; please mind the rules. This is high-hand stud poker. No limits, no rebuys, or buy-backs. Gentlemen, let's play poker."

Chapter Twenty-Three

Seeing Nick again for the first time since the stabbing incident was strange. It took all of RJ's restraint and mental discipline not to run to him and smash his head into one of the poker tables. In addition, Ben's voice was annoyingly stuck in his head: "Keep your cool, and don't take any chances". The Neanderthal's hair was sparkling like he had washed it in stardust, plus he had on a suit. RJ almost laughed; like that could somehow make him look decent or respectable.

RJ was one of those on the side lines for now. He covertly watched Nick sitting at the poker table with confidence.

About an hour later, a man collected his chips and cashed out. The man gave RJ a discreet nod and soon left quietly. Bayo, the black man that stood quietly beside him joined the table and took the vacated seat. There were a couple of sofas and a settee near the bar, but like the others, RJ preferred to stand and watch. It was a long time to be standing, but he needed to study Nick. RJ knew the whole poker thing had to be real. Real players and real games every time. If anything was out of place, if there was any cheating, then Nick would know. The only foul play was in the previous games – the men played to deliberately lose. RJ wanted to make sure that Nick's wins were believable and that his loss today was real. Today, the players were playing to win!

All the players were made up of some of his old friends from school and some of Ben's mates. Some were wealthy and some weren't exactly. However, they all knew how to play poker and they were on board for a chance to play fun poker, probably make some money while helping him and Ben pull one over on Nick. His friends didn't know who Nick was or what he had done, but they were up for some fun. On the other hand, Ben's men, and friends, like the dealer, did it out of loyalty. All the money the men had lost to Nick were given back to them. That meant all the money Nick had won so far was RJ's, and he had every intention of getting it all back. The only real cost of this poker gimmick was renting this venue.

RJ scratched at his beard. It was beginning to feel a bit itchy, and the scratching was not very effective at alleviating the discomfort. He honestly did not know how people who kept full beards did it.

He could not imagine having to deal with this for the next couple of hours or so, but he would have to.

When two other people cashed in forty-five minutes later, two seats became available. RJ was the last man standing. Nick, holding what looked like his third cigar lightly between his fingers, wasn't looking too happy. So far, he was not making headway and had lost almost a £100,000. From the look on his face, he didn't look too confident about his hand.

It was not going to get any easier either. RJ had saved the best players for last. Bayo was a mean player, and tonight, he was not playing to lose.

Thirty minutes; was how long it took before another person left the game and RJ could take the empty seat. He scratched at his beard as he placed his chips on the table, aware that Nick was watching him. Feigning serious concentration, RJ placed a few thick wads of money on the table, and the dealer slid him a stack of poker chips. It was an aggressive game running already and they had just finished playing a hand.

"Place your bets," the dealer stated.

Once the blind bets were placed, the dealer dealt the cards and RJ picked up his two cards. He had an ace and a ten. Not bad, he could work with that. He sniffed and shifted the pair of glasses up his nose, trying to throw Nick off, not wanting to reveal anything.

Ten men seated at the table, the man to Nick's right placed his bet. Nick called it, matching the man's bet. RJ was familiar with this tactic. Nick was probably bluffing to give RJ the impression that he had a strong hand as RJ was the newest to the table. It was going to be a long night.

Rachel was absolutely shocked by Eva's strange behaviour. What could be going on with her? She turned slowly and found Evan seated in the living room, staring at her. She immediately felt uncomfortable.

Quickly, she said, "I had no idea you were going to be here. It wasn't a set up or anything. Eva didn't even…"

"I know," Evan replied before she could finish.

Unsure of what to do next, Rachel quietly walked to the dining table.

"I'll just pop this on here," she said, placing the box of carrot cake on the table. Walking back towards the front door she had to ask, "Is Eva okay?"

Evan shrugged. "She's clearly not herself at the moment, but I'm sure she will be fine."

Rachel paused at the door and nodded. "Well, I better head off." She tried to force a smile but failed. She turned to the door and reached for the handle.

"Rachel, wait," Evan called.

Rachel stopped, turning back to discover he was now on his feet.

"Can we talk?" he asked.

Anxiety surged through Rachel. Her palms felt moist. "Sure," she replied, walking quietly into the living room. The uneasy silence that followed was broken by Evan.

"So… about Patrick?" he enquired.

Rachel's eyes threatened to well up with tears again, but she fought them back.

Not able to control herself, she blurted out, "Nothing happened between Patrick and me. We met on my Saturday morning jogs and started talking. My… err… my insecurities made me say yes when he invited me out to dinner… which, I agree, was a big mistake. He took me back home and that was it. I wasn't expecting him to send flowers. I mean, I knew he liked me, but I wasn't even thinking about him. I was busy wallowing in my insecurities and using him to make myself feel better. That was wrong too. Anyway, I've told him that I'm not interested, and I apologised for giving him the wrong impression."

Evan took in a deep breath then looked down at his feet. "I'm sorry for what I said during lunch at my parents'. I was out of line."

Rachel nodded. She had already forgiven him. She had forgiven him the moment he said what he said on that day. It was nice to hear his apology though.

"I'm the one who should be sorry. I did wrong, and you didn't deserve it. I'm really sorry, Evan. I'm truly, truly sorry," she said.

He looked up at her, a worried look in his eyes. "So, why though, Rachel? Why were you so insecure?"

This time, she looked away from him. Why was she so insecure? Wasn't it obvious?

"Look at me Evan," she said, waving her hand up and down her frame "I'm never going to be less than a size fourteen. I'm not particularly pretty. You have all these beautiful women at your work. All your friends' girlfriends look like models. I try my best to look beautiful for you, and it's never enough. A clear example is the last wedding we attended together. I took my time to look extremely attractive for you, and you looked at me funny and acted weird throughout the car ride to the reception; almost like you suddenly realised I was never going to be good enough for you." Everything came pouring out, as if she had kept it all tightly bottled up until now, which was exactly what she had done.

"To make matters worse…you hadn't… we hadn't…you hadn't… I just felt like I didn't deserve you." She couldn't quite bring herself to say that he hadn't even brought up the issue of marriage.

She looked at Evan and he was watching her in dismay.

"What in the world are you talking about Rachel?" He stepped past the centre table and took a few steps closer to her.

"Your size? You think when I look at you, I see your size? Rachel, to me, you are beautiful; you're the whole package. You're beautiful inside and out. I love your personality, your smile, how your face radiates, the way you look at me, the way you make me feel. You have a good heart. To be honest, since the day you agreed to go out with me, I have been questioning whether or not I deserve you." He stopped, almost like he was trying to remember something.

Shocked, Rachel was getting overwhelmed with emotion.

"The day I picked you up for the wedding…" he paused for a moment. "How can I forget that day. You looked absolutely breath-taking. It was then it hit me, it hadn't even crossed my mind before, but it was then it hit me; I'm going to marry this woman… and then I freaked out. I thought, wow… this is it. She is the one. Then a frightening thought crept in. What if I'm not the one for her? I was so lost in my own head, my own thoughts. I'm sorry if I made you feel inadequate. Far from it, you are way more than I ever hoped for."

His expression suddenly changed as he went on, "You started to confuse me though right from that day. Your behaviour changed. You were drinking way more than usual and, to make matters worse, you were flirting with Scott! Things started to go downhill from there on," he finished.

Rachel burst into sobs, and Evan quickly went to her and pulled her into his arms. "I wa-was ac-acting out. I-I'm s-sorry," she said between sobs.

He held her tightly. "Rachel, I love you. I have always told you I love you. Maybe I did not say it enough? Rachel, I love you, okay? You are truly beautiful, and I'm absolutely crazy about you."

Rachel felt like her heart would explode. She tried to smile through her sobs and succeeded. "I love you too, Evan. Way more than you can imagine… more than even I imagined. And you're definitely the one for me."

Evan kissed her then. It was such a sweet and possessive kiss, and she tingled all over. She always enjoyed his kisses.

He broke the kiss. "I think maybe we need to work on our communication skills," he said, chuckling.

Rachel laughed too, wiping her tears away. She was feeling over the moon.

Pulling away from her a little, he said, "Have you had dinner? If not, hope you're in the mood for Indian. I need to warm up my food." He was looking at his plate, with its now cold content, resting on the centre piece.

She nodded smiling warmly at him. He smiled back.

"I say we eat something, tackle whatever's in that box of yours, and then try giving that sister of mine a ring. By then she would have had enough time to sort out whatever it is she flew out of here to go sort out," suggested Evan.

It sounded like a good idea to Rachel.

Several rounds later and there were four men left seated at the table. Some guys had remained behind to quietly watch the rest of the game. Nick was tired and extremely hungry, but he was good at this. It was not his first rodeo. He had the stamina for long poker games, so long as he won at the end of it, and he had a good feeling about this one. Yes, it had been a bit rough at the start; the men today played even better that normal. He had been a little surprised the last time he played; not coming away with more than he hoped. But then again, he had not brought enough cash to put on the table. This time around, nothing was going to stop him. He brought £215,000, the sum so far of his total winnings at this poker joint. He was not going to add anything extra. Not that he had that much extra to add. At this rate though, he was probably going to leave with, at least, double that.

The southern Asian guy to his right had been restless, and Nick knew that he was not feeling lucky anymore. The black guy had not called or raised in a while. The fact that he kept folding was a sign that card hand was on a losing streak. The funny looking bearded man was another kettle of fish. Other than perpetually scratching at his beard, Nick could not really read him. He had been scratching right from the beginning, so Nick did not know if that was a sign of nerves, or he just had lice. *A rich punk like that ought to take better care of himself,* Nick thought. There was something he could go on, though. The bearded man had a lot of chips in front of him, he kept betting, calling, and even raising, but he always folded. To Nick, it was either a sign of more money than sense or a guy who did not care… probably just here to throw money away. Nick looked up and caught the bearded man staring at him. It was the first time he had looked at Nick, which Nick had found odd. Everyone looked at everyone all the time, but the man had seemed not to care or was cleverly avoiding him. He held Nick's stare for a moment, then looked away. Nick felt uneasy. There was something about the man that seemed familiar and discomforting at the same time. Was this his tactic? To make him uncomfortable?

Nick had made some of the money he had lost back. He had chips worth £95,500 in front of him and was hoping to win the £105,000 currently in the pot. Nick waited for the dealer to place the Turn card; it was the fourth card he was placing in the middle of the table. Nick was going to make Full House – which was a great card hand, so he bet £50,000. The black guy considered for a while before folding. The Asian man, looking defeated, folded as well, and the bearded man immediately folded. Nick smiled as the dealer slid the chips in the pot towards him. He caught Rog beaming at him from a corner of the room that had a great view of the table. Then he started shaking his head slowly from side to side. What was the idiot on about? Nick did not need any distractions. That is why he would have preferred to have Meltdown in here instead. Looking away and pushing Rog's shenanigans out of his mind, he brought his attention back to the table. He had £200,500 back of his previous £215,000. He could easily make £50,000 to over a £100,000 in the next round. The Asian man chose to quit at that time. Nice. There were just three of them left now.

The dealer took the cards back in the muck, and after shuffling, said, "Place your bets."

The black man bet £20,000. The bearded man bet the big blind, which was double that. The dealer dealt out the two hole cards to each of the three players.

Nick called it, matching the bearded man's £40,000. He had the potential to get an awesome hand – Four of a Kind.

The dealer then deals the three flop cards on the table. The black man obviously had a bad hand because he checked and did not place any bets. The bearded man also checked. Nick wondered if the bearded man was just copying whatever the black man was doing.

However, he must know something about poker to have lasted this long in the game, or maybe he was just lucky. He had seen luck like that before, but that kind of luck never lasted! Nick was close. However, to throw the guys off, he checked and did not bet either.

Nick studied both men, trying to get a feel of what hands they might have. The black man cracked his neck. First time he had done anything like that since the start of the game. To Nick, this meant good news – the heat was on for the bloke. He looked at the bearded man again. The guy was eyeing him above his rimmed glasses and scratching his beard again like he would like to yank every strand out. *Why grow a beard if you are not comfortable with it,* Nick thought? There was something about this man that rubbed him the wrong way.

Nick practically held his breath when the dealer placed the Turn card on the table. Things were looking even better. He was expecting the black man to fold, but he did not. Instead, he bet another £50,500. Maybe the man's hand had improved, or maybe he was semi-bluffing. They both looked at the bearded man. He raised by an additional £50,500. Nick was not surprised. Of course copycat here would do that. Nick re-raised by £60,000. Both men looked at him, as Nick expected they would.

The dealer dealt the fifth card, the River. They were headed for a showdown.

The black man suddenly bet £70,500. Nick was confused and almost frowned but managed to check himself and maintain an unreadable face. The man was relentless. The bearded man scratched his beard and raised the bet by moving chips worth £100,500 to the pot. What was going on? That was a big bluff. Did the guy even know what he was doing? Nick tried to keep calm; he did have a pretty good hand, so he should have this in the bag. The black man was just a man who did not like to give up, while the bearded man was a wealthy moron!

Taking a deep breath, Nick confidently pushed all his remaining chips into the pot. He was all-in with precisely £100,500.

It was time for them to show their hands. The black man went first, revealing a flush. Nick breathed out a sigh of relief. It was not as good as his Four of a

Kind. Next was beardy. Not as worried as he had been with the black man, Nick, along with everyone else in the room waited for him to show his hand. Slowly, the man placed them on the table. Straight Flush! Nick could not believe it. He could barely think straight. All the men in the room did not look too hopeful now but were still curious regarding Nick's cards. Worn out and sourly disappointed, Nick cast his cards on the table dejectedly, confirming the bearded man's victory. There were some cheers in the room as people proclaimed that it was a great game. The bearded man did not smile or put on any air of victory. Instead, he sat there staring at Nick with a hint of a smirk on his face. Nick still couldn't' believe it. He never for one second thought he would lose tonight.

As soon as they could, he and Rog exited the property and quietly made their way to where the van was parked. Seeing them, Meltdown nudged the sleeping Tony with his elbow and stepped out of the van. Tony steered, lifted his feet off the dashboard and got out of the van. He went round the vehicle to join Meltdown where he stood with Nick and Rog.

Meltdown ran a hand through his hair. "Wow! Over three hours. That must have been some game."

Tony and Meltdown did not even have to ask how it went; the expressions on Nick and Rog's faces said it all.

Nick rested his forehead on the van. "I lost it all. Bloody 'ell. I lost it all." He said, like it was just beginning to sink in.

There was a moment of silence. Then Meltdown said, "You lost it all? All £215,500?"

Rog nodded. "That's why I tried to tell the boss when he won £205,000 back; I tried to tell him to quit while he was ahead."

Nick immediately turned around and smacked Rog on the face. "Quit without accomplishing what we came for?" he shouted angrily.

The huge guy took a step back, obviously angry to have been struck for expressing himself honestly.

Meltdown placed a calming hand on Nick's shoulder. Suddenly, Nick froze and then tilted his head to the side.

Looking at Rog, he asked, "What did you say again?"

The other three men looked at him in confusion. Rog scowled, not sue if Nick really wanted him to repeat it.

Nick had an odd look in his eyes. "Rog, what was that last thing you said?"

Uncertain what the outcome would be, Rog slowly said, "Quit while you were ahead?"

Nick's eyes narrowed. "Why did you say it? Wait! I mean; what made you think it at all?" Now the three men were looking at Nick like he had lost his mind.

"Well?" Nick asked again.

Rog looked from Meltdown to Tony before his eyes settled back on Nick. He was not comfortable "I don't know…maybe because that's what RJ used to say about poker; quit whilst you're ahead."

Nick started to nod slowly to himself, "Exactly."

"What's going on, boss?" Rog finally asked, getting impatient with Nick's strange behaviour.

Nick had a sick feeling in the pit of his stomach. RJ! For some reason, that was who the bearded man reminded him of. There was no resemblance, the man never even said a word. Yet, there was something about him that had irked Nick Something familiar… The man avoided looking at him, the fact that he kept stealing looks at him. The scratching of the beard. He had thought all sorts of things. It almost looked like the man would like nothing more than to yank his beard off. He certainly did not seem comfortable having it. Now why was that?

Could it be because he was wearing a fake beard? Even if it was fake, so what? Maybe the man just wanted to hide his identity. Some people liked to keep their gambling addictions a secret. However, Nick had a strong nagging feeling that was not going away. He had to talk to Meltdown about this.

Nick relaxed his face and turned to Meltdown. "Nothing. Let's 'ead 'ome. I'm sure we're all starving."

Eva had been sitting in her car for about twenty minutes. She dialled RJ's mobile phone ten minutes before she arrived. The fact that he had not picked up was a sign that he was probably not back at the Lisa woman's flat. She could not go up to the woman's home without RJ there.

Besides, it was almost 11:00 pm. She knew she ought to turn off her engine, but she needed the heating on. She cranked up the heat and changed the radio station to Hearts FM. She just needed to hear something about love; something sweet. She was on the alert for any car that approached, slowed down, and parked, hoping it was RJ's.

How ridiculous was it that she was seated in her car, engine running at an hour to midnight across the street of a block of flats waiting for, and worried sick over a man she barely knew, but who she had somehow grown to care about in such a short period of time! What was she thinking? She was contemplating driving back home when her phone started ringing. She quickly grabbed it. It was Evan. Before she could pick up the call, she saw the glare from the headlights of two cars as they approached. One of them took an empty parking slot and the other pulled up beside the parked car.

Eva cut off the incoming call on her phone. A tall familiar figure got out of the car. It was RJ. She breathed out a sigh of relief. He leaned towards the driver's seat of the other car, talking to the person behind the wheel.

Eva turned off her engine and got out of her car and began walking towards RJ. Realising that a figure approached him, RJ turned quickly, straightening.

He squinted when she got closer. "Eva? Is that you?" he asked, walking to meet her. "What are you doing here?" He sounded extremely worried.

"I was concerned for you. I drove back here," she said quietly.

His deep blue eyes were bright in the dark as he studied her face with an unreadable look in his eyes. Without saying a word, he put his arms around her and drew her into a deep kiss. She was sucked in. It felt so good and safe being in his arms. He tasted like whisky. She slowly let her arms circle his neck and she lost herself in his kiss. The blinking of lights from the other car, broke them apart. The car slowly moved to park on the side with double yellow lines. RJ put his arms across Eva's shoulder possessively as a muscular built man of average height stepped out of the car. He walked calmly to where they stood.

Looking at Eva, he grinned. "A bit late to be smooching in the dark."

RJ chuckled lightly. "Eva, this is Ben Sharpe."

So, this was the Ben RJ had mentioned when he was opening up to her earlier that day. She smiled at him.

"Nice to finally meet RJ's angel in person." Ben smiled back. Eva blushed. The man then turned to RJ.

"I'll go up briefly to say hello to Lisa. I'm pretty sure she's still up waiting for you to get back," Ben said, walking away from them.

So, Lisa was waiting up for RJ? Eva wondered what sort of relationship RJ really had with the woman. What was wrong with her? Was she jealous? She couldn't believe it. It was an emotion she was unfamiliar with, and she didn't like it. She looked up at RJ and found him staring down at her. It was dark but lights from somewhere helped to make out his features. It was like he read the expression she did not even realise she had on her face.

"Lisa has been a friend for years. She used to be on the down and rough and I helped her get her life straight. I think Ben's got a thing for her. She probably feels the same way but doesn't know it yet. Either that or she does know it but enjoys playing dumb."

This explanation reassured Eva, plus she could not help but be fascinated by this man and his willingness and desire to help people. He had such a good heart and did not even know it.

She knew then for a fact that their meeting was not an accident. She noticed a few faint red marks on the edge of his jaw and reached out to touch it.

"It's nothing. Bad reaction to a stuffy prickly beard," he explained, even though she had not asked any question.

Sighing, he stated, "Eva, much as it is awesome seeing you tonight, you really shouldn't have come. It's late."

Eva blinked. "I have been trying to reach you. I... I was very scared. I thought this Nick guy might have realised who you were and..."

He took his phone out of his pocket. It was on silent. He took it off silent and then checked his missed calls. There were several from Eva. He put it back in his pocket and turned her to face him.

"I told you it was going to be fine. You need to learn to trust me. Anyway, Nick won't be doing any drug deals anytime soon. I just need to finish planning how to bring him and Meltdown down before they hatch up another plan, and without involving the other guys," RJ interjected.

Eva couldn't believe it. She started to panic again. What was wrong with this man?

"RJ, are you serious? Is this how your life is going to be all the time? Dangerous plots, schemes, and lord knows what else?" she asked.

He raised an enquiring eyebrow, but she went on, "I'm not comfortable with this; this life of yours. How do you plan to bring them down? Will it be illegal and risky? You need to go to the police and inform then about how Nick and this other guy tried to kill you. They are dangerous men. They've tried to kill before, and they could attempt it again with someone else and actually succeed."

Her rant was cut short by the ringing of his mobile phone. He took it out of his pocket and checked to see who the caller was. His forehead creased into a frown that worried her.

"I need to get this," he said just before picking the call.

"Danny boy?" He answered curiously. "Danny? You there?" he asked again when there was no answer from the other end.

Eva watched as RJ's stance change. His body seemed on the alert. He was clenching and unclenching his right hand. She too became anxious. Presumably, it was Daniel on the phone.

"RJ," Danny finally said. His voice was strained.

Straining hard enough, Eva could hear the other end of the line. "What is it, Danny? Talk to me." RJ's calm voice was unusually raised.

There was some noise at the other end of the line and Nick's voice took over. "You sneaky bugger, RJ."

RJ took in a deep breath.

"I must admit, you 'ad me there, RJ. I was so sure you were dead. 'N the game? Friggin 'ell, you were good. That disguise too…brilliant stuff, RJ. You can't stay away from the game, can you? I know 'ow much you love poker." Nick's laugh sounded evil.

Eva gasped.

"What do you want?" RJ asked quietly. He stood perfectly still except for the fisting and un-fisting of his left hand.

"I'll ring back in thirty minutes to tell you where to bring me £300,000. I'm just asking for what you took from me today, plus some extras for all the damned trouble you put me through. I must 'ave the money tonight, RJ, or else…" Nick broke off so the sound of Danny in pain was clear. Then the line was cut off.

Eva's hand clasped her mouth in shock and fear. RJ stood thinking for a second. His face was hard, and his blue eyes were steely.

"Oh my goodness, is Daniel in danger? Nick recognised you, didn't he? Now we just have to call the police," Eva said shakily.

RJ grabbed her hand, pulling her along as he quickly walked towards the building. It was almost like a race up the flight of stairs. RJ practically burst into the flat. Ben and Lisa, who were sitting on the settee, jumped. RJ closed the door and locked it behind him. Ben recognised that something was up. He stood up and Lisa joined him on her feet.

RJ looked pointedly at Ben. "Nick just called me using Danny boy's mobile phone." Lisa shrieked and Ben's eyes widened.

"What?" Ben exclaimed.

RJ shook his head from side to side. "He figured it out. I don't know how he figured it out, but he did. Now the son of a bitch is threatening to hurt Danny boy if I don't bring him £300,000."

Ben appeared to be rooted in shock while Lisa remained frozen to the spot. "Did he say where to meet him?" Ben enquired, rubbing his chin.

"He said he'll ring back in 30 minutes," RJ replied.

Eva could not keep quiet any longer. "That should give you enough time to get the police involved."

RJ glanced at her. "Yes, of course, but not right now. He might hurt Danny. We need to be careful."

Ben instinctively walked towards the window. "We don't even know at what point he discovered it was you. What if he followed us back here?"

Eva clutched her chest in trepidation while Lisa went quickly to the window Ben was peering through and shut the blinds.

"I knew this was a bad idea, you two. I told you," Lisa said, obviously scared.

Eva stretched out her arms. "So now what? You want us to wait for him to call back first so we know his location; then we can make a move?" Eva was hoping they could ring the police once they knew where the terrible men were.

"No need to wait," RJ stated, and the two women looked at him in surprise. "We're going to them now."

"What? Why do you have to go to them? Besides, how can you go to them when you don't know where they are?" Eva asked incredulously.

RJ pulled his phone out of his pocket again and started to punch some buttons. Finally, he said, "I know where they are right this minute."

The women looked confused.

"Some time ago, I made Danny wear a tracker. A band around his wrist. He has it on now – good lad." RJ said, waving his phone.

Ben went into the kitchen and grabbed two of Lisa's sharpest knives. Eva recoiled in shock.

"I have a baseball bat," Lisa offered and disappeared into the inner room to emerge with the object.

Eva felt the utmost disbelief. It was like she had stepped into a different world.

"You keep it… just in case. It's unlikely you'll need it, though. Please keep the door locked and do not open it for anyone… unless you're absolutely sure of who it is," RJ directed.

"I still don't understand why you have to go. Please don't go. What if you all get injured badly, or worse... killed? Wait for him to give you the location, and then call the police. Don't do this... at least not alone," Eva begged.

RJ moved to Eva and pulled her to him. "Wise suggestion. However, I can't risk them hurting Danny boy, and getting the police involved might do that... I don't know."

Eva continued to stare up at him disapprovingly.

"Look, I'm sorry you're being caught up in all of this. Please stay here and don't go anywhere. They're currently on the move, but once we get their final destination, I'll text it to you. Then you can call the police. Is that okay?" RJ implored.

Eva nodded reluctantly and he planted a kiss on her forehead. "It will be fine. Trust me."

"And the £300,000 Nick asked for?" Lisa queried.

"We still have all of the cash from the game in the boot of my car," Ben replied.

"You do know he has no intention of letting you or Danny boy go, right? He intends to take the money and get rid of you once and for all," Lisa said miserably, addressing RJ.

RJ nodded and Eva burst into prayer in her head.

The two men walked to the door. Lisa suddenly ran towards Ben and kissed him smack on the lips. Ben seemed surprised at first, but then kissed her back. RJ and Eva exchanged a look. RJ's phone started to ring again. He did not pick it up right away. He ordered Lisa to lock the door immediately behind them, and then he and Ben were gone.

Chapter Twenty-Four

———————～———————

Less than an hour before.........

Oscar was on the lookout. He was anxious to know how everything went. They had been gone a long time. He knew how long poker games can go on for, but that did not stop him from feeling a little apprehensive. When he finally heard voices and what sounded like Rog's voice, he quickly made his way to the front door. Rog walked in looking tired, and he and Tony speedily went past him, no doubt heading for the kitchen. Otty had made a big pot of tasteless pasta, but Oscar was sure that Rog and Tony could not care less about the taste. Nick and Meltdown ignored him, and Oscar followed them. They were going to the lounge.

"Hey, Oz, can you get Danny boy in 'ere?" Nick asked, shutting the door in Oscar's face as he and Meltdown went into the lounge.

Judging by their demeanour, RJ's plan obviously went well, but why was Nick asking for Danny? Trying to listen in, it was more difficult than normal. Nick was whispering. He couldn't make out a word of what Nick said, but he did hear Meltdown's cool voice, a little agitatedly say, "What the f**k? Are you serious? It can't be."

Oscar frowned. Something was obviously wrong. Reluctantly, he left the door to go get Danny. The lad was sitting up in bed playing a game on his phone when Oscar came to get him. Danny looked worried.

"Did I do something? How's his mood? Is it bad?" The boy asked all at once.

Oscar did not know how to answer him. He did not know why Nick was asking for him and he certainly was not going to tell him that Nick was in a bad mood. Oscar said nothing.

Danny shoved the phone under his pillow and stood up nervously to follow Oscar. When Oscar opened the lounge door so Danny could go in, the lad hesitated.

Nick's face was serious, and he had a glass of vodka in his hand. Meltdown's face was colder than ever.

"C'mon in, laddie," Nick urged.

Danny slowly walked in just as Meltdown left the room and shut the door behind him. Oscar could not hang around the door in order not to make Meltdown suspicious, so he moved away. As soon as Meltdown disappeared, he moved back to the door. However, he was not comfortable standing there being as Meltdown could return any minute now. He spotted John and quickly went to engage him in a conversation about what Otty made for supper. Oscar did not want to be away from the vicinity of the lounge. Although, he did not know for how long he could carry on a conversation with John about food.

"Look, I don't care. Me, I'm actually going for more. Don't kid yourself Oscar, you sound like you're still hungry." Laughed John.

Just then, Meltdown appeared. He was taking menacing and purposeful strides. Oscar and John quickly moved away from his path. Meltdown went into the lounge.

John thought that was his cue to disappear and he quickly walked away. Oscar hovered. Then Nick came out of the room. Behind him was Meltdown. He had a hand lightly in Danny boy's back nudging him forward. Oscar tried to catch Danny boy's eyes, but the lad deliberately avoided looking at him.

"We'll be back in a bit," Nick said, obviously addressing Oscar.

When they left the house, Oscar ran to a window where he could get a clear view of the van. However, they chose to use Meltdown's old Volkswagen golf. Oscar watched as Meltdown got into the driver's seat while Nick and Danny boy got in the back seat of the car. They must have been in the car for up to twenty minutes before Meltdown started the car and drive off.

Oscar began to pace. The youngster was in trouble. Had Nick seen through RJ's disguise?

Otty came downstairs. "Hey, any idea what's going on with Meltdown. Did Danny cross him or something?" he asked.

"Why?" Oscar asked, trying to act calm.

"Well, he came into the room and frantically started going through Danny's things. He found the lad's mobile phone under his pillow and then took it…"

Oscar did not wait to hear the rest. A few steps away was the door to the loo and he quickly ran in there.

He heard Otty yell, "Crikey, you could have said you needed to go. Punk!"

Oscar took out his phone from his back pocket and dialled RJ. It rang for a while but then it was finally picked up.

Not waiting for RJ to speak, Oscar said, "RJ, I think Nick and Meltdown know. They found your phone with Danny, and they've gone… taken him somewhere. I don't know where."

"I know," RJ's voice said calmly. "Nick called me. Wants me to bring money to him at a location he will reveal in the next twenty minutes or so." It sounded like RJ was getting into a car. In the background, Oscar heard a voice saying something to RJ. It was Ben's.

"They didn't take the van. So if you're looking for them, you need to look out for Meltdown's beat up car," Oscar informed.

"Got it. Thanks Oscar. Look, I have to go. I'll text you the location once I know," RJ said.

After Oscar got off the phone, he knew what he had to do. He could not just sit here and do nothing. He found Otty and asked him to help gather all the guys in the lounge.

One by one they all walked in wondering what Oscar had to say.

"Look, I'm tired mate. What's this all about?" asked Tony, walking in with Rog. They made up the final numbers.

Oscar stared at them all, a little overwhelmed.

"Oi? Get on with it," Otty snapped impatiently.

Oscar took in a deep breath and said, "There's something big that you all need to know."

Eva watched as Lisa sat there on the settee with the baseball bat in her hand. She was too restless to sit down. She was hungry too, but she really should not be thinking about food right now. Her mind went to the Indian that Evan had brought. Regret came in the form of a rumbling tummy.

Lisa looked at her. "I have some store-bought sandwiches in the fridge." Had her belly been that loud?

"Thanks," she said, walking over to the old fridge and picking out a prawn and mayo sandwich. "So do you play baseball?" she asked Lisa.

"Of course not!" Lisa scowled, then turned to give Eva a funny look. "Who in this country plays baseball?"

Well, Eva did not really think she did but had asked anyway. It was partly to make conversation and partly out of curiosity since she owned a baseball bat.

Eva sighed "What a night. I can't believe this is happening right now. I never imagined being part of this mess." She was not aware that she had said it aloud.

Lisa shot her a look of irritation. "Didn't you already go home? If you had stayed home, then you definitely wouldn't have been part of this mess."

Eva's face went red, and she tried to calm down. "When I said that; I meant my relationship with RJ and how complicated his life is."

Lisa ignored her. Eva leaned on the kitchen counter and decided to check her phone for any messages. None from RJ yet. Several from Evan and Rachel wondering where she was and if she was okay. She also listened to an angry and concerned voicemail from Evan. He said he knew she was a grown woman, but it was late, and he was worried about her, especially as she had not been herself when she left her apartment earlier. Eva felt guilty for worrying both of them. However, she certainly could not ring either one of them now. They would want to know where she was and what was going on. She could not tell them because they would freak out, especially Evan. On the other hand, she could not lie either. So, for now, feeling like a terrible person, she would have to put off getting back to them.

Lisa stood up and sauntered in the direction of the window. Eva decided to say a short prayer in her head. She remembered the sharp knives that Ben had picked up from the kitchen and her stomach twisted. She had seen first-hand the damage a knife can do. RJ had been very lucky. She needed to pray for the safety of Daniel, RJ, Ben… for all their safety.

This also included Nick and the other guy. She would pray for God to touch their hearts.

Lisa, suddenly dashing over to a side of the wall to slam her hand on the lights switch, interrupted her prayer as the room was bathed in darkness.

Eva's head snapped up. "What? What?"

"Shhhh," responded Lisa almost aggressively rushing to join Eva in the kitchen and stooping behind the counter.

Eva instinctively ducked too. "What's going on?" she asked in a whisper.

"I just peered through the blinds and saw two suspicious looking men looking directly up at the window. I don't think they saw me, but I can't be too sure." Lisa whispered back.

"So you turn off the lights?" Eva asked hysterically. "Your flat isn't suddenly going to disappear because you turned the lights off… and neither are we."

"Well maybe they'll think we've gone to sleep or something… look I don't know. I panicked and it's the first thing that came to me," Lisa retorted, rummaging through one of the kitchen drawers.

"What are you looking for? All that clanging around is causing a racquet," Eva asked in frustration and fear.

At that point, Lisa found what she was looking for and tossed it to Eva who managed to catch it despite the lack of warning. It was a pair of scissors. Eva gave Lisa a curious look.

"I have the baseball bat; you have the scissors. Defence weapons," Lisa explained, like it made total sense.

The sound of a text message coming though on her phone startled them even more. It was either Evan, Rachel, or RJ's text message. Her phone! At least she could call the police if things were as dire as she and Lisa feared.

Lisa quickly whispered to her, "My phone… in room. Get yours… hurry."

She had left it lying on the counter, so she tried to get over her apprehension and steady her shaking hand as she reached up to search for it on the counter. The sound of footsteps and whispered voices outside the front door pushed both women to the brink of absolute dread and terror. Eva quickly pulled her hand back. They both looked at each other. Lisa held the bat tightly with both hands and Eva did not even remember the scissors in her hand. Her free hand covered her mouth to hold back the scream that was threatening to come out. There was a knock on the door. Eva's eyes widened. Lisa shut hers tight. There was another knock, louder this time. Eva knew the bell was not working because she had tried it earlier on in the day; it probably needed a change of batteries. Someone tried the door handle. Eva felt like she could not breathe. Lord, please protect us. Lord, please protect us, she kept chanting in her head. Almost immediately, a banging sound could be heard. Their eyes communicated confusion. However, not for long as they quickly realised that it was the sound of a weight being hurled against the door. Eva noticed that she was not the only one shaking from fear. Lisa's eyes remained closed.

Suddenly the door gave and was pushed open. Eva stopped breathing, her hand back over her mouth. Several footsteps sounded in the room. There were at least two people walking around. Footsteps disappeared into the inner house. A few minutes later, they were back in the living room. Eva could not tell what they were doing now because the sounds of the footsteps stopped. It was so quiet you could hear a pin drop. Eva and Lisa stayed still. The unexpectedly blaring of her phone as it started to ring almost made Eva lose it. Lisa's eyes flew open now and she gave a defeated sigh. The footsteps resumed and started to come towards were both women were crouched. The blasted phone didn't stop ringing. It stopped when someone picked it up and cut off the incoming call. Eva was very aware of a shadow looming over her. Slowly turning to see, she accompanied it with a scream.

Ben had been driving as fast as he could without running past speed limits. It frustrated RJ that Ben cared about that even now, but to be honest, it was the fastest that he had experienced Ben driving. They had been able to find short cuts and routes to link close to where Nick and Meltdown were. They were probably about ten minutes away from them on route. Based on their current course, RJ tried to make out where Nick could be headed. If he were Nick, where would be a good place to make a monetary exchange quietly and discreetly and also get rid of someone or more? Think RJ, think. Could it have been where they were taking him initially on the night he had been stabbed? Obviously, where it all happened hadn't been their original plan and they must have been forced to flee the scene instantly because Danny boy must have made a ruckus and there were residential houses in the neighbourhood. Come to think of it, they would be approaching that area in a bit. Where there any abandoned buildings or houses not far from there? The only place he could think of was the New Cross area; the one with the abandoned warehouse.

When Nick rang back, ten minutes later than was expected, he confirmed RJ's thoughts. It was the area of the warehouse and RJ was supposed to be there in forty minutes. Well, he was going to be there way before that time, thought RJ.

"Oh 'n RJ…" Nick said just before hanging up, "… I know you ain't stupid enough to involve the bobbies."

"Let me guess; he said not to involve the police, right?" Ben asked curiously when RJ got off the phone.

Nodding, RJ googled the area and got a postcode. He went to text messages, typed in the postcode and description, then sent the message to Oscar and Eva.

Tracking Danny's wristband, he could see that they would be arriving there in five minutes. That meant he and Ben should arrive in fifteen minutes. That would be twenty-five minutes ahead of the time expected.

Not long after, they arrived at the location and parked some distance away. They put their phones on silent and get out of the car. Ben hands RJ a knife. RJ slips it partially into the back of his jeans and underneath his jacket.

"Toss me the car keys. Hopefully, I can lure one of them to the car," RJ whispered.

Ben quietly threw him the car keys. Guided by the tracking on his phone, they quietly made their way to the location of the two men and Danny boy. RJ could not let himself think about what those two might have done to Danny. If they hurt him in any way... or worse, then he was sure he would get locked up for double murder. RJ would wring Meltdown's cold neck first before ending Nick slowly and painfully.

As they got closer to the building area where there were some roofless structures, RJ and Ben heard voices. It was quite dark there as there was no source of light. They watched as Nick placed one torchlight on the floor and then lit a cigarette. Quickly RJ and Ben moved away from the glare of the light and hid in the dark behind the wall where they had a good view of the men. Dropping a duffel bag, Meltdown pushed a gagged and shaking Danny onto the ground and began to tie his hands behind his back and then his legs together with a rope. Danny boy was bleeding from what looked like a deep cut on the side of his forehead. The sight angered RJ and he tensed, but Ben placed a calming hand on his shoulder.

Nick reached into the duffel bag and pulled out a fat bladed knife. He inspected it and then looked around. Finding a stone, he proceeded to sharpen the knife with it.

RJ stirred again, and Ben held him back whispering, "Stay here, I'll check if there's a way round the back. Text me if you need to."

A few minutes later, RJ peeked and saw that Ben found a way through to the other side. He was hiding behind an opening but peeked briefly so RJ could see him. That meant, they were both on either side of the clearing and roofless structure while Nick, Meltdown and Danny boy were in the middle. Meltdown checked his watch then walked to what was left of what used to be a window.

"There are some overgrown shrubs and grass on the other side by the old railway lines. Perfect spot to get rid of the bodies," Meltdown said.

Nick nodded approvingly and Danny struggled, making a muffled sound of despair.

Nick looked at Danny boy. "'Tis a shame, kid. I was kinda fond of you. You only 'ave yourself 'n RJ to blame for this."

RJ shook his head. It was incredible how cruel people can be. Two men he had always been good to, that he had taken care of, and now, they were discussing killing him and an innocent youngster with no feeling or hesitation. He took out his phone and sent a quick message to Ben.

RJ: *"I'll step out shortly. They don't know you're here so you can hold back until when necessary."*

In less than a minute, there was a response.

Ben: *"Okay, but don't do anything foolish. I'll be guided by the consequences of your decisions."*

Five minutes later, and RJ stepped back and the sound of his shoes hitting rubble was loud enough to alert Meltdown and Nick.

"Who's there?" called Nick. Meltdown quickly pulled out another knife from the bag and moved towards were Danny lay.

"It's me." RJ slowly moved out of the shadows, into the light and the view of the men. Meltdown looked at his watch again.

"You're early," Nick said.

RJ shrugged. "Fastest I've ever driven. I'm probably in trouble for breaking several speed limits."

Nick grinned crookedly. "That's the least of your worries, mate."

RJ nodded. "Exactly." Then his eyes drifted to where Danny's body lay on the ground. "Is he alright?"

Meltdown pressed the tip of his blade to his thumb slightly. "Depends. Where's the money?"

"I have it in the boot of my car. The notes haven't been stacked yet. They're loose in several small sacks. I couldn't take any chances carrying it just in case I got accosted by the wrong men." RJ replied.

Nick gave a sigh. "'N where's your car?"

"A quarter of a mile away or so. Didn't know exactly where you were parked," replied RJ.

Nick waved his knife branding hand. "Go bring your car closer. 'Ave to count the dosh too."

236

RJ turned and went to get the car while Nick walked a little after him, stopping where Meltdown's car was parked so he could direct RJ to park beside it. When RJ was parked beside the beat-up VW, he popped open the boot of the car and came out. Ben's car was a Mercedes Benz CLA.

Nick whistled. "Nice. Purchase or rental?"

RJ didn't answer as he walked to the boot. Nick followed him, holding on to the knife firmly.

They were a little distance from Meltdown and out of his view, so Nick shouted loudly enough for Meltdown to hear him, "Off the boy if you so much as suspect I'm in danger."

Meltdown yelled back an acknowledgment. Nick moved closer to RJ, standing behind him as RJ bent to untie one of the many sacks in the boot. Nick leaned in to see the denomination of notes in order to figure out how best to count the money.

"It's mostly £50 notes, so should be easy to count," RJ said.

As Nick leaned in further, RJ quickly shot his elbow back hard into Nick's chest. Nick howled in pain, stumbling back as one hand clutched his chest. Instantly, RJ turned and delivered Nick a hook in the jaw. Nick stumbled back further but remained on his feet, his right hand still grasping the big knife.

Meltdown heard the commotion and instinctively moved forward to see what was going on. Ben used that opportunity to get out his knife and sneak up fast behind him. He was only a couple of paces away from Meltdown when the guy suddenly decided to turn back so he could get to Danny boy. Meltdown's surprise was flitting as he immediately took a fighting stance and whirled the knife in his hand to get a better grip. Ben and Meltdown both swayed from side to side, each looking for an opening advantage in order to strike.

The muffled and twisting sounds of Daniel on the ground could be heard. Each time Ben reached to grab hold of Meltdown; the tall lanky man lashed out with his blade. Finally, Ben had had enough. Tossing his knife aside onto the ground, he took a wide step and grabbed hold of Meltdown's shoulder. Meltdown took this opening and without losing a second, slashed Ben on the left arm near his shoulder.

Ben was close enough already and using his strong grip on Meltdown's shoulder, spun him the other way so the man had his back to him, and instantaneously pulled Meltdown backwards into his sturdy body. Then he put his strong muscular arms around Meltdown's chest in a bear hug, and started to squeeze hard.

Meltdown, still holding his knife began to flay his arms and kicked out, and Ben slightly lifted him off the ground, but held on tight, squeezing harder. His arm was already oozing out a lot of blood. Meltdown was slowly beginning to feel the effect of the air being squeezed out of his lungs, but he was not ready to give up. He continued to struggle. Ben tried to hold on tight, but the injured arm was losing blood and the pain threatened to weaken his hold.

Meanwhile, Nick was determined to keep RJ from getting any more shots at him. He kept lunging forward with his knife, now and again tossing it from one hand to the other. Nick spat out blood. This was from the impact to his jaw which had caused his teeth to slam against the side of his tongue.

"Why RJ? Why do you always 'ave to rock the friggin' boat, eh?" Nick screamed out in frustration as he lunged forward again with his weapon and RJ dodged it.

Watching and calculating, RJ replied, "Because it's my 'friggin' boat, Nick."

Nick shot his knife out again, but RJ swiftly caught his arm just below the wrist. He kicked Nick in the chest again. The move provoked a sharp but minor pain from the almost healed knife wound that Nick had dealt him some time ago. No way was he going to let the man dip a blade into him a second time. Nick, struggling from the pain in his chest, wrestled with RJ to keep possession of the knife. As RJ continued to aggressively twist Nick's wrist, suddenly Nick lost his grip, and the knife was sent flying backwards. With the knife now out of Nick's hand, RJ freely punched Nick in the eye. Nick clutched at his eye but recovered quickly and attempted to throw one back at RJ, but RJ intercepted and blocked it with one arm whilst repeating the punch again with the other.

"You have never been a match for me, Nick," RJ said, a little out of breath.

Both men were panting. Nick's right eye was red; the skin around it was swollen and sore.

"You 'ave been nothing but trouble for me, RJ. Nothing but trouble. You're a troublemaker." Nick shoved RJ.

"No!" RJ pushes Nick to the ground; face up. Pulling out the knife from where it rested at his back, he squatted across Nick, ignoring the pain coursing through his side, and placed the blade close to his neck. "You're the troublemaker. I'm more of a trouble shooter."

Suddenly, the glare of headlights was cast on RJ's back and Nick's face and was quickly followed by the sound of a vehicle swerving and screeching to a halt. RJ turned to see who it was. A van door swung open and, one by one, six men jumped down from the vehicle. Rog, who had been driving, and Oscar who had sat in the front passenger's seat came out too.

Just then RJ felt a hard blow to the corner of his mouth. The knife fell out of his hand, and he was instantly pushed off by Nick, who immediately got to his feet and took off into the dark. RJ, who had fallen on his back, quickly sat up. The men were all watching him in amazement… almost waiting. RJ rubbed the side of his mouth and looked at them.

"Find him!" he quietly ordered.

"Yes, boss." The men responded almost in unison as they spread out into the dark in search of Nick. Only Oscar stayed to help RJ up.

Finally up on his feet, RJ suddenly remembered Danny and Ben and turned in the other direction, breaking into a run. Oscar followed him.

The sight of Meltdown struggling in Ben's arms came into view. The tall lanky man was almost out of breath but still continued to flay his arms; his hand stubbornly still holding on to the knife. Ben had his eyes shut in what seemed like being close to a faint. His right arm was completely soaked in blood which had gotten on Meltdown too and was beginning to drip onto the floor. As RJ approached, he could see the injured arm faltering and starting to lose its hold. Danny lay wriggling on the floor obviously horrified by the sight in front of him.

"Untie Danny," RJ directed Oscar as he rushed up to Meltdown, yanked the knife out of his hand and gave him a swift head butt.

The force to his head and the strain on his lungs made Meltdown slump to his knees. Ben, still holding on, dropped to his knees as well. RJ grabbed hold of Ben's arms and tried to pry them apart, being gentle with the right arm.

"It's okay, Ben. You can let go now. It's okay," RJ calmly urged.

RJ was not sure if Ben could even hear him, but slowly, the man released his hold.

Oscar quickly untied Danny and joined RJ beside Ben. RJ gave Danny a quick look over as the lad rubbed his aching wrists and ankles. The cut on his forehead was semi-dried. He had dirt all over him and blood stains on his T-shirt and cheek. Danny then came to crouch beside RJ and Oscar. He was crying. "I'm so sorry, RJ. They found the phone. Nick said if anyone knew if you were still alive, it would be me. There was only one number on there that I had been calling and had been receiving calls from. So Nick called the number. I am so sorry. I didn't tell him anything."

"I know Danny. It's fine. Are you okay?" RJ asked him.

"Yes. Is Ben going to be okay?" Danny responded, wiping at his tears with the back of his hand, suddenly ashamed that he had been crying.

Ben seemed to be in a half state of consciousness and remained on his knees while RJ held on to him.

"His arm has lost a lot of blood, but he'll be fine once we get him into the car and safely to the hospital," RJ replied.

Otty was the first of the men to come back. Rog and Gabe walked back together. John followed. Last were Henry, Jasper and Tony. From the looks on their faces, it was obvious that they had not been able to find Nick.

The blaring of sirens from police cars seemed faint at first but was slowly getting louder.

Eva's work, no doubt, RJ thought. He quickly turned to Oscar. "You and the rest of the guys, get into the van and get out of here… quickly."

"We're not leaving you, boss," Gabe said adamantly.

RJ managed a half smile. Up until now, apart from Oscar, he wasn't sure if any of the guys were still loyal to him.

"I just don't want to get you all involved… not in this scene. Just go back to the house. I'll see you all tomorrow," RJ said more authoritatively.

Oscar nodded and the men began making their way to the van. Otty turned suddenly. "Great to have you back, boss," he said.

"Yeah," the others echoed.

RJ nodded. He just wanted them to get out of there quickly. Finally, he heard the van start up and hurriedly drive away. Hopefully, they could find another route out of here without being seen. The sirens were really loud now, and RJ knew they had arrived and were parking.

Meltdown was out cold while Ben was still the same. RJ nudged Danny who then stood up from his crouching position and walked out to meet the police officers.

As he finished relaying the night's events and what led to it, RJ's attention remained on the figure of a man who sat quietly in the backseat of a conspicuous car. Constable Fischer closed his notepad and followed RJ's gaze.

Officer Tom Cohen had spoken to Danny and was letting him rest at the back of his police car while they waited for the ambulance to arrive. Meltdown and Ben needed medical attention and Danny's cut to the head needed to be stitched. Meltdown was under arrest and there was going to be a nationwide search for Nick. RJ knew that Meltdown was never going to snitch on Nick, even if he had an idea where the man could be. They were going to be charged with attempted murder, kidnap, and assault.

A few minutes later and two ambulances arrived. RJ tapped Ben comfortingly on the knee as he was lifted into the vehicle on a stretcher. Meltdown was lifted into the other one. Finally, the figure at the back of the car got out slowly and walked towards RJ and Fischer.

"Hello, Rhys," Alex greeted. He was clad in a long expensive looking coat.

Not surprised, RJ said, "Hi, Dad."

Alexander Fairchild took a deep breath, looked down and then looked up again. "Gambling again, Rhys? Really?"

RJ looked away. "I'm not gambling again. It was just the one time, and it was for a reason."

"When Fischer told me you had opened up a gambling parlour… and were cooking up some scheme…." Alex began.

"Still having Fischer spy on me, I see. I've always known. Just didn't realise to what extent," RJ interjected angrily.

Fischer stood there silently, a little uncomfortable.

RJ wondered which one of his friends or Ben's was the contact. Probably more than one.

Alex dipped his hands in his coat pocket. "It wasn't as intense at first. It was just to keep an eye on you since you never contact me. You left me no choice. How else am I supposed to know how you're doing? It was only after you got yourself stabbed… and then started seeing Eva da Silva."

"Oh, of course," RJ retorted sarcastically. Then he frowned. "So it wasn't Eva who rang you then?" He looked inquiringly from Fischer to Alex.

Fischer shook his head. "No. Since we had been informed by our contacts about the poker house, I'm sure it's not surprising that we followed you there today and followed you back to where you have been staying – Lisa Simms'."

RJ looked confused. "If you were following me, then why did it take you long to get here?"

An indignant expression came across Alex's face, and he looked away, expecting Fischer to do the talking.

Fischer coughed uneasily. "Well, not sure what happened, but for some reason, we didn't realise when you and Ben left again, so we missed the two of you. Suddenly Ben's car was gone but the one he gave you to use was still there. We weren't sure if he had left, and you had stayed. We tried to catch a glimpse through the window... in case we could see something – a long shot. Anyway, the blinds were shut, but then there was suspicious movement behind it... and then the lights suddenly went out. We had to investigate it. Our contacts had explained that you were successful at winning a large sum of money back from Nick, so we weren't sure if he had seen through the... err... disguise you were wearing and was out to get you. We didn't know what we had missed. We went up to the flat, the bell didn't seem to work. We knocked but it wasn't answered, so that raised more of a red flag, because we knew there was somebody in there. We eventually had to break the door down."

RJ felt anger boiling up inside him. He could not imagine what Eva and Lisa would have felt. They must have been scared shit out of their minds. He refrained from making a comment and let Fischer continue,

"Well, let's just say we found the ladies armed and hiding. They updated us and Miss Da Silva gave us the location you texted to her. She's safely back at her apartment now. She has confirmed this to us," Fischer finished.

There was silence as RJ digested this information.

Fischer was shuffling uncomfortably. "It's unfortunate that we gave them such a fright, but I really don't know how we missed you and Ben leaving."

Alex turned to Fischer. "You don't know how you missed them? I don't know; let me take a wild guess... maybe through sheer incompetence?" His calm tone contrasted with the annoyance he was obviously feeling. A trait he had passed down to his son.

Without saying another word, Alex walked back to his car and got in the back seat. RJ glanced at Fischer, his anger subsiding. "Don't know why you put up with him."

Fischer shrugged. "You know he's my godfather. My dad has worked in his company for years. He put me through school and has always been there for me. I can't imagine not being there for him." He suddenly smiled, casting RJ a side glance. "Besides, the compensation is good."

RJ nodded. He was tired, but he needed to get to the hospital first to check on Ben and Danny. It had been a long night.

Chapter Twenty-Five

Eva was tired when she woke up around 12 noon. She had been unable to get up for church. It was well after midnight when she arrived home and finally went to sleep at about 3am, and that was because the police officer from last night had updated her on the situation with RJ and the others. This was a deal they had struck if she promised to let him know when she was safely at home, which she had. She had never been so frightened before in her life and had never prayed so much. It was good to know that everyone was alive, and even though Ben was wounded, it was not life threatening.

She had also sent reassuring messages to Evan and Rachel to let them know she was okay. Evan had responded instantly; expressing relief that she was okay and then scolding her for making him worry. Eva would have to fill her family in on the past twenty-four hours of her life. She was not sure they would believe it. Joyce, on the other hand, would bring out the popcorn to hear this story. Reaching for her phone, Eva realised that Rachel had replied to her message earlier this morning: *"We were really worried. However, I'm pleased to hear you're okay. Hope we can catch up later. P/s Evan and I had a talk and are back together {{smiley grin}} Rachel xx."*

Eva beamed. This was brilliant news. Thank you Lord. She quickly replied to Rachel telling her how happy she was to hear this and promised to give her a call in the evening. The final message was from RJ: *"Hey, angel, crazy night, wasn't it? I'm so sorry you had to go through all that. I'll make it up to you. All's good, except Ben got hurt in the arm. Going back to the University Hospital Lewisham to check on him at about 1 pm. See you there, maybe? RJ."*

Eva flew out of bed. She hadn't known Ben long, but it would be nice to see how he's doing. Most of all, she was excited about seeing RJ again. She was going to have a well-deserved bath and then head to the hospital.

Ben was sitting up in bed looking in good spirits. The arm was going to be fine, but he was going to have to take things easy for some time. RJ watched as Lisa squeezed Ben's hand affectionately. It was good. The man needed a woman in his life. Ben must have said something funny because Danny and Lisa burst out laughing. It was good to see Danny laughing. He had a patch of bandage covering the area of his forehead where he had been given stitches. When RJ tried to imagine, as described by Danny, how Meltdown had knocked the side of his head with the base of the knife handle, rage welled up inside him.

Meltdown had received treatment last night but had been taken to the police station this morning. He hoped the police found Nick. Not that he thought the man would dare to come anywhere near him, Danny, or the other guys again, but they all had to be careful. In the mid-morning, before coming to the hospital, RJ and Danny had popped over to where the men lived. It was great seeing them again, especially knowing that his fears had been unfounded. Each one of them had seemed genuinely pleased to see him and had expressed disgust and shock at what Nick and Meltdown had done. Nick had been RJ's second in command, so they had to transfer their allegiance to him after RJ's supposed death. RJ understood that. The men were also glad to see that Danny was okay. He explained to the men that he wanted Danny to come live with him, and they thought it was a great idea.

Danny had been over the moon as he packed up the few things he owned. RJ was also finally moving back home. He and Danny had gone back to his house after he had received his stitches. It was good to be back at his house and to sleep in his bed after what seemed like forever.

Once he and Danny left the hospital, they were heading to Lisa's to pick up the few belongings RJ had at hers.

The right-side curtain was drawn open and all four of them turned to see who it was. The imposing figure of Alexander Fairchild stood there. RJ was surprised to see him here. He had hoped it had been Eva. Alex gave a firm nod, which was supposed to be a general greeting to everyone. All three of them except RJ nodded back.

"You alright there, Ben?" Alex asked, directing his attention to Ben. Ben gave a genuine smile. "I've been better, but I'll bounce back."

He had thick bandages around the wounded area of his arm. The pain extended to the side of his chest, so he tried not to move much. It was strange seeing such a usually strong and sturdy looking guy wearing one of those patient gowns.

"Good," Alex said, a surprising look of admiration in his eyes for the middle-aged man.

Giving RJ a look that indicated he would like to see him, he smiled at the others and walked out of the enclosure. RJ followed him, pulling the curtain back shut after him. After walking for a distance, Alex stopped and faced RJ. His eyes paused briefly over the slightly red spot at the side of RJ's mouth where Nick and struck him.

"I see you're working really hard to get your money's worth out of those boxing classes you took during college," Alex stated.

RJ smirked. "That's not why I took those classes."

"You could have fooled me," Alex's stare was unwavering.

RJ was getting impatient with the man. He remembered why he took those classes. He realised he had a lot of rage in him, anger issues and he thought taking up boxing would help to vent and release them. It was quite effective.

"Did you want something?" RJ asked in derision.

Just then Eva appeared at the entrance to the ward. RJ's pulse rate went up. Damn, that woman was beautiful. Alex followed his gaze, and then raised an eyebrow when he saw who it was.

Eva spotted them and came to say hello. He couldn't take his eyes off her as she talked briefly with his father. Then she turned those beautiful light brown eyes to him, searching his face. There was something in those eyes… something.

"I'll quickly go check on Ben. See you in a bit," she said. He watched as she walked towards Ben's curtained corner.

"She's a good one, RJ, and she deserves a good man. Don't mess about unless it's for the long haul," Alex said.

RJ frowned and turned to Alex. The man was right. Eva was a good woman, but was he a good man? She was a sweet, sensible, beautiful, faithful, God-fearing woman. He remembered another woman that used to be God fearing…. A strange feeling came over him. He shook it off.

"So, Dad…?" he asked, leaving the question hanging.

"Oh, yes…" Alex started, his faint blue eyes resting unflinchingly on his son "… as it's only about two weeks away, I hope it's not too soon to ask if you could join me at Castle Fair for Christmas breakfast… or dinner?"

Castle Fair – the name given to the mansion in Knightsbridge that he grew up in. He hadn't been there in years. His memories of the beautiful home dredged up mixed feelings inside him. He did miss his room, though. RJ sighed.

"Not too sure about Christmas. However, I just might do New Year's. If I do, I won't be coming alone, though," RJ replied.

Alex gave a half smile. "That's fine; as long as you show up."

He patted his son on the arm and calmly strode off. RJ turned and Eva was right beside him.

He smiled. "Hey, you."

She smiled back. "Poor Daniel with the plaster on his forehead. Ben's not doing too badly. He says he's going to be discharged tomorrow apparently. I'm just relieved that the whole fiasco is over, and nobody died."

RJ grinned. "Me too."

She lifted a hand and gently touched the small bruise by the side of his mouth.

Something stirred in RJ, and he looked down at her. He couldn't hide his deep attraction for her and… whatever else was lurking deep in his heart. Whatever it was… it scared him.

Suddenly, she stood on tiptoe and kissed him on the lips. He groaned. He wanted this woman, and he wanted her badly. She wasn't making it easy for him to keep his hungry desires to himself. He took in a deep breath, trying to control himself before kissing her back. If he responded the way he wanted to… with the fierce need within him, he would definitely scare her off. Besides, they were in a hospital ward with other patients and other people.

Eva broke the kiss and licked her lips. "I'm going to be decorating my house today. I usually do it earlier, but I have been so busy and tired. I think I'm up for it now."

He raised an eyebrow. "Hmm nice." It was more to do with the act of her moistening her lips.

She seemed unsure as she said, "I was kind of hoping you could come over later for dinner?" Then she quickly added, "Daniel can come too, if you like."

It was the first time she was inviting him to her house. That was a big step… a dangerous step as he was definitely not going to be going over there with Danny boy. He gave a mischievous grin.

Eva studied his face. "Is that a yes?"

He laughed and ran a hand through her mass of curls. They were in a corner of the ward, but people could still see them. He didn't care, though.

"A yes to dinner tonight, a no to Danny tagging along," he replied.

She smiled excitedly. "Great! Also, I was thinking, what are you doing on Christmas day? In case you're free, we'll be having a big spread at my parent's. Also, the Sunday before Christmas we're having Carol service at church. It's always so beautiful, the lights, the music. Maybe you and Daniel…"

RJ was struggling to take it all in. Christmas at her parent's house? She wanted him to meet her parents already? She must be serious if she was inviting him to theirs for an occasion like Christmas. When she mentioned church, it all became a little too much for him. Was he up for this? Did he deserve her? Could he do the whole church thing?

His expression must have changed because she stopped to stare at him.

"RJ, I hope I'm not overwhelming you with this, but…well… you must know that I really like you. In fact, I actually think I'm falling…"

"Look Eva…" He cut her off, not sure he could handle what she wanted to say. He didn't think he deserved or was ready for the frilly life she lived. He had too much pent-up rage and darkness in him. She was this warm, lovely person with so much light within and around her. His father's words drifted into his head "Don't mess about". He didn't know what to say or how to say it.

She stared directly into his eyes, waiting for him to finish what he started to say, but the silent empty look he gave her back must have said it all. He saw the sadness slowly seep into her beautiful brown eyes and the disappointment creep onto her face, and his heart broke.

"I see," she said.

The awkward silence persisted again. Finally, she stretched forward lifting herself once again onto the tip of her toes and gave him a gentle peck on the cheek.

"Take care of yourself, RJ," she said then hurriedly walked away.

He tried to convince himself that he was doing the right thing letting her go; that he wasn't good enough for her, but it didn't help alleviate the pain he felt in his heart.

The days leading to Christmas weren't as exciting for Eva as they usually were. She knew she was falling for RJ, but she didn't realise how deep it went. She was hurt when he communicated to her, in no words at all, that he didn't want to pursue anything serious with her. In fact, she had been devastated but had summoned all her strength to compose herself. From the way he treated her and acted around her, she was almost sure he felt the same way about her that she did about him... or at least close. Did she move too fast inviting him to her parents'?

Was it the church? Maybe it was too much too soon all at once. Eva had prayed about it, and in the end, she felt God tell her that RJ was probably battling demons that only God can help him deal with. She couldn't force it. She could only pray for him and leave him in God's care.

He hadn't contacted her since the last time they spoke at the hospital, and she decided to refrain from contacting him too.

As she had expected, her family had been astounded when she filled them in on the night at Lisa's and the whole saga with RJ, Daniel, Nick, and the others. It had been a lot to take in. Added to the fact was that Nick's profile had been on the news as the police were on the hunt for him and welcomed anyone who had seen him or had any information that would help in finding and apprehending him. Eva was seeing Nick's face for the first time. The man looked brutal yet had his hair styled like Jason Priestly from the old teen series 'Beverley Hills 90210'.

Evan wasn't too pleased about it all, but from all Eva had said, he had to admit that RJ didn't seem that bad after all... despite the mess he had been involved in. Her parents couldn't believe that RJ was the son of Alexander Fairchild. They had all thanked God everything had worked out and she, along with everyone, else was safe.

Noting how she felt about him, everyone said the same thing: maybe it was for the best. Her mum and Rachel had tried to encourage her, and her dad had assured her that if things had worked out between her and RJ, he would have been happy to meet him. They wanted a good Christian man for her but were not people who judged. It wasn't impossible for God to provide the man first, then make him a good one of faith in due time. Eva was comforted by the support of her family, coupled with the knowledge that Evan and Rachel were back together and looking closer and stronger than ever.

Joyce had been totally captivated when Eva had told her what happened. She said it was the best movie she had never watched, except the ending wasn't to her liking. She did remind Eva that things always work out according to God's plan. Joyce's bubbly, funny and positive nature always manages to lift her mood.

The Carol service in church had been beautiful. Reverend Bainbridge's sermon was centred on love and how the birth of Jesus Christ was God's show of love to the world; that Christmas wasn't the only period to show love, but it was a season that served as a reminder to always show and spread the ultimate act that gives and brings joy. He also tied it in with the missionary trip to Zimbabwe on the 2nd of January.

Reverend Bainbridge:

"In second Timothy, chapter 2, verse 2, Paul says: '*And what you have heard from me in the presence of many witnesses, entrust to faithful men who will be able to teach others also.*' This is in line with Christ's instruction in Mark chapter 16, verse 15 – '*Go into all the world and preach the gospel to all creation.*' That is our mission; to teach and help, to preach love and show love. The gospel is about love. Christ is love. How can we not show and share the good news of love… of Christ which we have seen and received?"

"What does first Peter, chapter 4 verse 10 say? '*As each has received a gift, use it to serve one another, as good stewards of God's varied grace*'. We need to reach far and wide with our love. However, this doesn't mean we always have to go far to show our love. We can do so here as well."

Eva had initially subconsciously decided not to go on the trip anymore because of RJ. She felt she needed to stay to develop their relationship and help him in getting his life back on track.

However, there was no need to stay anymore. The reverend's sermon had served as motivation to do what she had planned to do before meeting RJ. Some time ago, she had brought it to the attention of the management at work that she might need to take a six-month sabbatical to do some charity work in Africa. Much to her delight, they had shown great support and had applauded her for it. She had brought it up again and they had signed off on it. So she was going to be busy working around Christmas to get some projects finished and to sort out her handing over before the new year. It was just as well, to get her mind off RJ.

Christmas itself had been a lovely affair. Rachel had joined their family for a wonderful day of cooking, eating, and watching old classics on TV. Eva was sad on the inside but tried really hard to put up a happy front and hoped she succeeded at it. She didn't want to bring down anyone's mood. Against her better judgment, she sent RJ a brief text message wishing him a merry Christmas.

Almost immediately, his response came back. Her heartbeat raced as she read his response: "*Merry Christmas to you too, Eva. RJ.*"

She was glad he responded at all, but disappointed it wasn't more.

At the end of the evening, Evan accosted her in the kitchen and informed her that he was planning to propose to Rachel. Eva couldn't believe it. Unfortunately, she couldn't jump up and down with joy because Evan cautioned her. It was a surprise, and he didn't want Rachel to know.

"I'm a little nervous, but I know it's what I want. Details are still in the pipeline, so I'm not quite sure how it will go exactly. However, it's going to be special because I want her to know she's special," Evan said.

Eva smiled. "Aww. I'm so excited for you." Then added with a pout, "No hints on how you're going to propose?"

"No. I'll let Rachel have the joy of telling you how it all happened." Evan winked.

Eva did express her fears that the wedding might take place while she was in Africa. Evan assured her that he was sure Rachel wouldn't dream of having a wedding without Eva present. Besides, Eva was his twin sister, and he definitely wanted her there.

RJ and Danny had celebrated with Ben and Lisa into the new year, which was a Friday. Then later in the afternoon, they had headed over to Castle Fair to have dinner with Alex Fairchild. RJ didn't realise how much he had missed the big house. It had come as a shock to the men, Lisa, and Danny that Alex was his father. He knew the truth had to come out someday. This new knowledge seemed to provoke a different level of respect and admiration from them and not the reaction he had feared he would get in the past; the one where they joked and called him rich boy whilst throwing phrases like 'silver spoon' and the like around.

Danny had been mesmerized by the size and beauty of Castle Fair, and RJ understood why. It was quite grand with marble floors, beautiful paintings, artwork, and sparkling chandeliers. Every piece of furniture looking expensive, spotless, and perfectly in place.

Wandering off upstairs and leaving Danny to watch a film on the TV room's massive screen, RJ decided to look around himself; see if there had been any changes since the last time he was home. Alex, unsurprisingly, had been in his study for a while, taking a work call. Even now… on New Year's Day, the man was still working. No change there!

Dinner had been pleasant enough, RJ thought. His dear father hadn't made any of the comments that were bound to elicit a negative feeling or reaction from him. This was good. Alex had also been very kind and polite with Danny.

His thoughts remaining on Danny, RJ reminded himself that he had to sort out the issue of school and give the lad a stable life. There were so many things in RJ's head that he wished he could just get out, but he didn't know when or how to. It wasn't as easy as it was a few days ago when he sat with the other guys after their big M&S purchased Christmas meal to discuss their futures and what they wanted to do with their lives. He had spoken to them candidly about things needing to change and how all of them had to grow up and look responsibly to the future. It was quite a fruitful talk, and he was impressed with their reaction and what their thoughts were.

RJ might be busy starting up his business, but he was going to help them in any and every way he could.

Lisa had been the most shocked about him. She said she kind of knew there was something about RJ; something he was hiding, but him coming from money was the last thing she expected, even though it kind of made sense. She also said that it was a shame about him and Eva not working out.

"I can see why you're so into her. She's beautiful. And to be fair, she's alright too." Lisa wasn't one who gave many compliments, so this was something coming from her.

Eva! Not a day had gone by that he hadn't thought of her. He was aching for her. He missed her. How in the world did she manage to get under his skin like this? He had never felt this way about a woman before… never, and he had had loads of women stream through his life! He tried to shrug off the sober feeling within him. The feeling had been there since the day she walked away from him at the hospital, and he hadn't stopped her… even though he had wanted to. When she had sent him a message on Christmas day, he hadn't realised how desperately he had been hoping to hear or read from her.

He had quickly responded, hoping she would send another message, whilst hoping she wouldn't either. He knew that if she had sent another message… saying anything remotely close to her feelings or his, then his resolve would break.

However, she hadn't sent another message and that had been that. Lisa and Ben, whose arm was healing a little slowly but nicely, were now very much into each other. Not surprisingly, they had told him that they thought he was making a big mistake. Danny's mind too was occupied with thoughts of Eva, and he kept asking about her. Not wanting to go into it, RJ had always found a way to change the subject.

Besides Eva, another thing that occupied Danny's mind was Nick. The lad worried about their safety and if it was possible that Nick would come after RJ again. RJ knew Nick. With the publicity he was getting and the nationwide search for him, the bloke wouldn't even attempt to come anywhere near either of them. Nick loved his life more than anything and wouldn't risk getting caught. He explained this to Danny who seemed to be reassured by that. RJ remembered the first few days after the night of the kidnap incident; the constant trips to the police station and statements that had to be given. He was glad that was all over for him and Danny... for now. Of course, the police had to speak with the other guys too, to find out if they knew where Nick could be.

As he moved from room to room, RJ thought the house still looked great and felt like home. There hadn't been a woman living in the house for years, so the feminine touches here and there could only be the work of Heather, the housemaid. She had been working for his father for over a decade.

He didn't know why but he found himself stopping at the door of a bedroom he hadn't been in since the tragic night seventeen years ago. Eight years ago, he hadn't had the courage to enter this room, but now, maybe after being away for so long... after all he had experienced, he had gained a new kind of strength; one he certainly didn't have before. He took a deep breath before opening the door and walking in. The furniture in the once elegant room was still the same, but the bedding had been stripped, and he knew without opening the wardrobes that they were devoid of any clothing. He remembered his father giving it all away to charity almost a year after her death. A lovely painting of her still hung up on the wall. He walked up to it and studied it. She was so beautiful.

"Didn't expect to see you in here," Alex said quietly.

RJ hadn't noticed when Alex appeared in the doorway. He didn't turn around but continued to stare at the painting.

"The best painting of your mother. I couldn't take it down from the wall," Alex said again, stepping into the room.

RJ sighed. "I shouldn't be in here."

"Why not? I know you avoided this room all those years because you missed her, but surely..." Alex was saying.

"It wasn't because I missed her that I couldn't come in here..." RJ said, cutting him off. He was struggling with several emotions.

Alex paused for a bit before saying, "Okay. Do you want to tell me why then?"

RJ debated, but ultimately decided to talk. Quietly, he walked to the big four-poster bed and sat on it. Strange, such a beautiful bed but his mother hardly ever slept in it as she used to sleep in Alex's bed. He always wondered what the point was. He remembered her telling him that everyone needed their own 'little space'.

RJ leaned forward, rested his elbows on his knees, and clasped his hands together.

"The night that Mum died, I heard the two of you having an argument. She had just come back home after so long away on that church retreat. She had been gone so long and had only just come back, and you angrily asked her to leave. I heard you tell her to get out," RJ said, unable to look at his dad's face.

Alex stood rooted to the spot; he didn't say anything, so RJ continued,

"I didn't want her to go. I had missed her. Not long after, I heard her going downstairs. I know I was supposed to be in bed, but I had snuck out of my room and was hiding... listening. When she left the house and got into her car, I couldn't let her leave; it was her home too. And so, I followed her. She was behind the wheel and was manoeuvring out of the driveway when I rushed out in front of her car to stop her." RJ stopped and looked up at Alex with eyes that moistened with tears that would never drop.

Alex's face had gone white as he stared back at his son.

"I killed her, Dad. I killed her." RJ said shakily. "She swerved to avoid me, and that's when her car hit that huge mermaid fountain structure that used to be there," RJ finished, burying his head in his hands.

"My goodness, Rhys. You were at the scene? You were thirteen!" Alex stated quickly walking to the bed and sitting beside RJ.

"I was so scared, so ashamed. I hurriedly ran back into the house and to my room. I'm a murderer, and I kept the truth from you all this time," RJ said; the pain in his voice evident.

"RJ..." Alex began.

"There's more, Dad. More I have to tell you. You have to let me finish before I lose the courage," RJ interrupted.

Alex kept quiet.

RJ continued, "I hated myself for what I had done and didn't think I deserved to be happy. I hated you too, for telling her to leave; kicking her out of the house just because the church thing kept her away for so long.

"If you hadn't kicked her out, then I wouldn't have tried to stop her leaving. I hated the church… for taking her away on that damn retreat…and I hated God for letting her die even though she was devoted to him. That's why I refused to go to church for her funeral. That's why I've been so full of rage. That's why I couldn't come into her room; the shame… the guilt."

Alex grabbed hold of RJ's hand. "RJ, listen to me."

"No no. There's more. Let me finish," RJ pleaded.

Fiercely, Alex turned RJ to face him. "No! You listen to me, RJ. There are things you need to know."

Chapter Twenty-Six

Alex had his son's attention now. RJ remained quiet as his father began talking.

"You have been angry with me, and I have been angry with myself. Angry about so many wrong decisions I made in the past. I could have handled things better, I shouldn't have kept so much from you, and definitely not for this long." Alex broke off for a second when RJ looked at him with interest.

"Bethany never went away on a church retreat like I told you. She had run off with a man named Michael. I don't know how she met him, but she fancied herself in love with him. I did some digging and found out that he was a recovering alcoholic in a struggling band. Bethany stopped going to church because of him. I remember the reverend trying to talk to her, but she wouldn't listen. I don't know what it was about this man, but she decided he was of more value to her than you, me… what I had to offer her, and God."

Other than the frown crease on his forehead, RJ's eyes held no expression. He stayed quiet as his father continued.

"I told you she went away on a church retreat because I didn't want to hurt you. You were twelve then. I had no idea she was going to be gone for a year. I thought, once whatever strange fascination she had for this fellow wore off, she would be back home. I loved her enough to take her back." Alex sighed.

"She did come back, but as you know, after a whole year. I remember the afternoon she strode in, acting like nothing had happened; like she had never left. You were so excited, and she was suddenly the devoted mother again. I wanted to be happy, but it all seemed so strange. Anyway, after you had gone to bed, I decided to confront her about it. Turns out she had gotten pregnant at some point and had a baby with this Michael, which was painful considering she and I had been trying to have another child for years. She went on about how Michael had relapsed with his drinking and had gotten worse, how she had made a big mistake and wanted to come back. The baby was only a month old, and she wanted to come back! I asked her where the baby was, and she said at home with Michael. I didn't understand how she could have left the baby with Michael." Alex's mind must have been transported back to that time because a puzzled look appeared on his face.

"I told her no; she couldn't just abandon her baby with a drunk and waltz back in here like she didn't have one. It never even occurred to me that she might have been suffering from post-natal depression. I told her that I didn't know who she had become and that she couldn't just abandon her baby. I then asked her to leave, and she just kept on pleading.

"That's when I lost my cool and yelled at her to get out. I know I hurt her, but believe me RJ, I was hurting too. Anyway, she didn't leave immediately although I had strictly told her not to go to your room to say anything. I thought she was packing some more of the tonne of stuff that she had previously left behind, but as it turns out, she was helping herself to one of the bottles of gin that she had taken from the bar."

Alex glanced at a stunned RJ. He was obviously finding the revelation tremendous.

"Your mum was drunk when she got behind the wheel of the car RJ. That's what the coroner's report said. She was extremely intoxicated and shouldn't have been driving in that state. That's why she lost control of the car. If she was sober, she would have been able to control the car when you stepped in front of it. She might have had to swerve suddenly, but she wouldn't have had to hit that fountain. Trust me; not where it was situated. So, you see, you were not responsible for you mother's death, and it's unfortunate that you blamed yourself for it all this time. It pains me to know that."

RJ sucked in his breath and let it out heavily. His heart felt like lead, as a sense of sadness and relief washed over him all at once.

Alex grabbed him and gave him a hug, patting him in the back and RJ welcomed, unusually, his father's comfort.

After several seconds, Alex pulled away. He stood up and walked towards the exquisitely carved dressing table. He paused there and began again.

"I figured Michael would need help raising the baby, and I approached him, offering my financial assistance. He refused my offer of help, claiming that I had killed Bethany. I don't know how he took care of that baby on his own, but four years later, he died from complications with his kidney. He took his hatred for me to the grave because his dying wish was that I wasn't to adopt his child. Of course, that had been my plan but then I had to respect his wishes and I think child services felt the same way."

"The child was placed in the care of Emma Colindale, a lonely but sweet woman who had gone through a bad divorce and had no children of her own. I communicated with her every year or so and helped out financially. Unfortunately, Emma's unstable and jealous ex-husband found out that I was in regular contact with her and often sent her money. He thought we were in a relationship. I discovered only years later that he had hung her from a fan and tried to make it look like a suicide. I tried to find out what had become of the child but was advised by my friend in child services that he was in a good home now, and to stop beating myself up about him. He assured me that the boy was fine, and I was to move on... and I did... for a while." Alex shook his head slowly. "Another bad decision of mine. So, I don't know what became of the boy," Alex finished regretfully.

"I do," RJ said suddenly.

Alex turned round swiftly. Blue eyes glazed with naked curiosity fixed on RJ.

"The lad's downstairs watching TV," RJ stated, responding to his father's unasked question.

Head jerking back in shock, Alex's eyebrows rose in disbelief. "What?"

"I told you I had more to say," RJ said with a weak smile.

Alex shook his head vehemently. "It can't be. Bethany's son's name was Daniel. Daniel Grange... Dan..." He stopped; a flash of realisation shot across his face as it suddenly dawned on him.

RJ nodded. "Yeah... Danny... Danny Grange. Well, in fairness, you didn't know his last name until now."

Alex looked lost. "How is it even possible?"

This night was proving way too overwhelming... for both of them.

"I was eighteen when I overheard a telephone conversation between you and that Emma woman about Daniel," RJ started to explain, then paused when he caught the look on his father face.

"Okay, I was eavesdropping. I couldn't believe I had a half sibling. Only, I thought he was yours. I didn't realise he was Mum's until now. I didn't even care how he had come about... maybe you got some woman pregnant during that time Mum was away... I didn't care. I just wanted to see him.

258

"I snooped around your desk and found information on where Emma lived. When I left home eight years ago, I decided to find him.

"It was amazing seeing him. From a distance, I used to watch nine-year-old Danny arrive in school almost every day, and sometimes, follow him home. I was looking out for him. I considered myself his guardian angel." He broke off, his mind going back to something Eva had said to him the afternoon before Danny was kidnapped.

Shaking off the thought of Eva, he went on.

"Then all of a sudden, I just stopped seeing him. He wasn't going to school anymore. At first I thought he was ill or something, until I decided to stakeout the house. After asking around the neighbourhood, I discovered that Emma had been found dead, and naturally, Danny was moved to another foster home. I was crushed. I tried to find him, but there was no way of knowing where he could be. It's not like child services would just give you the information. I wasn't Alexander Fairchild, after all."

RJ gave a half smile when Alex raised an eyebrow at him.

"One amazing day… years later, I see this lad walk into a local grocery store close to where a couple of my men and I were doing some business. He looked so familiar. I wasn't sure at first, and he was a few years older, but it was Danny. It was unbelievable. He was almost sixteen and living with this terrible foster couple down the road from thc grocery store. I was so excited to see him. However, he didn't look very healthy or happy, so I resumed watching him again. I started going to that area every other day just to see if I could catch him coming out of the house or something. He attended a local school but skipped classes a lot. I used to watch him walk to the local playground, sit on the swing, and read a book. He loves reading."

RJ broke off when Alex walked up to the bed and sat beside him again, obviously intrigued by all RJ was revealing.

"There was this day… I was driving with one of my men, Gabe in the car. I decided to take the route through where Danny lived so I could go past the house. That was when we saw it; Danny's foster dad beating him up at the corner of the house. You might have missed it if you were not deliberately looking out like I was. It was a narrow path leading to the back garden of the house. I couldn't help it… I wasn't thinking; I found a place to park and five minutes later, Gabe and I were knocking on the door of the house. As soon as the man opened the door, Gabe put a black bag over his head, placed his hand over his mouth, and we dragged him to that same corner and gave him the beating we thought he deserved. I know it was wrong, but Danny was my brother, and that man had beaten the hell out of him. Turns out it was for coming home late from school, even though Danny had explained to him that he had stayed behind to get help with one of his assignments. Anyway, we didn't realise that Danny was in the garden and had seen the whole thing. That was the day he took an interest in us. So, when he recognised Gabe, who happened to be in the neighbourhood picking up something from the store one day, he followed him. It took Gabe two bus journeys and some walking to get back home, and Danny had followed him all the way. This was to find out where Gabe stayed, and then he went back to his foster home. A few days later, he packed up all he had in a bag, ran away from his foster home, and showed up where the men lived.

"He came to us to find a home, a family… to get protection. He didn't want to go back there or to another foster home because he had been treated badly and physically abused in each and every one of them since leaving Emma's… and…and I was not going to turn him away," RJ ended with a defiant tone.

Alex was in shock. "So you've had him for almost two years?"

RJ nodded and then said, "I don't know what story his foster parents gave child services, but I can tell you this, if Danny was ever reported missing, I didn't hear or read about it."

"Neither did I," Alex said frowning.

They both sat there in silence for a few minutes, lost in their own thoughts. RJ looked at his watch. He didn't realise that he and Alex had been talking for so long. They had barely said ten words to each other over the years.

Finally, Alex said, "Rhys, I'm glad you finally opened up to me, and we had this talk. We still have so much more to catch up on and to talk about; plans moving forward. Can I invite you and Danny to stay the night?"

RJ looked at his dad. He was right. They had a lot more to discuss, and it was getting late. It was strange being back here, but it still felt like home. RJ nodded and Alex smiled, standing up.

"So, does Daniel know you're his half-brother?" Alex asked.

RJ shook his head. "No. I haven't been able to tell him yet. It's a lot to tell and, until now, I didn't have answers to a lot of the questions I know he will have."

Alex nodded in understanding and walked to the bedroom door.

"Now might be a good time, don't you think?" he said, walking calmly out of the room.

He knew his father well enough to know that it wasn't really a request. Sighing deeply, RJ stood up and followed him out of the room.

RJ woke up that Saturday morning feeling tired, but unburdened and freer. Danny had slept in his old room, and he was in one of the spare bedrooms. Last night had been an emotional one for all three of them, especially Danny. The lad just couldn't get around the fact that he was family. He had been so happy and so very curious, just like RJ thought he would be. RJ was glad to have his father there with him for support and to help answer some of the questions. If he felt hurt for being put in the care of social services, or for being abandoned by Alex or for RJ keeping the truth from him all this time, it was suppressed and overtaken by the joy and excitement he felt to know that he had a true family and was finally at home.

RJ and his father had a good talk until well past midnight; both of them enjoying one of Alex's expensive bottles of whiskey. The many revelations had been quite heavy, but they needed to come out. Accepting that he wasn't responsible for his mother's death hadn't made the memory less painful, but it had freed him of the guilt he had carried with him for more than half of his life. And all this time that he had thought Danny was Alex's only to discover that he was actually his mother's. True, Danny didn't look like Alex, but RJ did see certain features of himself in Danny that he thought were from Alex, but now it made sense; they were features they both got from their mother. He recalled hating his father even more back then… thinking he had abandoned his son and put him in foster care out of shame. It was good to know the truth and to be able to let go of all the hate. In a way, he preferred it that Danny was his mother's son. It meant; he still had a part of her with him.

He and his father had talked about Faircorp and RJ needing to step up and take his place in the business. They then talked about RJ's plans for the men, his consumer lending business, Danny, and school plans for him. Alex was very good at solving problems and putting things in perspective. He wanted to take responsibility for Danny and his education and asked RJ to leave it to him. If anyone could get Danny to go to school, it would be Alex.

261

Although, due to recent developments, RJ was sure Danny wouldn't put up much of a fuss anymore. Danny's eighteenth birthday was in a couple of weeks and Alex wanted to be able to throw him a big one. However, RJ reminded his father that Danny knew very few people, so it might mean more to have a smaller event that counted. Of course, RJ, Alex, the men, Lisa, and Ben would be the guests. When Alex had asked about Eva, RJ had told him how he had ended things.

"Good grief, Rhys, when I told you not to mess her about, I didn't mean break it off with her. I was actually suggesting that you take it seriously with her." Alex had exclaimed.

After everything that had come to light in the last fourteen hours, things had become clearer, and RJ now had a better outlook. He knew then that he had made a big mistake and had to contact Eva. It had been too late to call her then since it was past midnight, but he couldn't wait to call her this morning. He looked at the time and it was 9am. He thought that was a good time to ring her. He couldn't wait to hear her voice. When her phone rang until it went to voicemail, he decided not to leave a message and hoped she would ring him back. He was a little anxious over breakfast but was still expectant. However, when he hadn't heard from her by 11am, he tried her number again. Still, she didn't pick up. Was she so upset with him that she had decided to cut him off completely? She had sent him a message on Christmas, hadn't she? She couldn't be that upset with him. He couldn't bear the thought of having lost her completely. He and Danny were both quiet on the drive back home from Castle Fair.

They were both were preoccupied in their own thoughts. Danny was, no doubt, thinking about how much his life was going to change and RJ was thinking about Eva. He had to speak to her, to see her.

On getting to the house, he tried calling her again. He wasn't one to leave voice messages, but he did: *"Please pick up your phone, angel."* Then he quickly followed up with a WhatsApp message: *"Eva, can you please get back to me, it's important!"* Then he started to think. Who else could he call? He really didn't know much about her. Did he know anyone she knew? What was the name of that friend of hers from the church again? Joyce? Yes Joyce! But he had no way of reaching her. RJ decided he had to go over to her house. Deciding to take his bike, he kitted up. When Danny saw RJ come out of his room all geared up and grabbing the keys to his bike, he got up from the sofa and followed him outside.

RJ opened the garage. He walked to the beautiful black Ducati V4 S superbike parked in the corner and spent a few minutes checking and prepping it. Then he pushed it out of the garage.

"Where are you going?" Danny finally asked.

"To get Eva." RJ responded, getting on the bike, and putting on his helmet.

Danny smiled. "Well, it's about time."

RJ knew Danny wasn't stupid. He was old enough to know that things hadn't been right between him, and Eva. Hopefully, RJ would be able to fix that today.

As he rode to hers, he kept thinking of what he was going to say and how he was going to say it. What if she didn't want to see him? What if she had moved on… probably with the Adam guy from her work. He could tell there had been something there. Jealousy and annoyance had coursed through him the day he had come to her work to pick her up for lunch and had witnessed the bloke pathetically trying to work himself into her life. That same feeling surged through him again at the thought and he increased his speed.

On arrival, RJ noticed her car wasn't in her parking slot. He felt a little disappointed. That meant she wasn't home but was still going to try her flat… just in case. He had never been to her apartment, but he did know the number as she had mentioned it before. After ringing the doorbell and knocking a couple of times, RJ finally had to accept the fact that she wasn't home. Where could she be? He didn't have enough information about her family to be able to contact any one of them. This was his fault. While she was trying to get to know him, he had been afraid to get too close to her, even though he liked her… likes her a lot. He felt so much for her, and he couldn't wait to tell her, to put things right. There was only one place he could think of checking for her next.

Arriving at St Benedict, RJ was already disappointed. He had scanned around, and he couldn't see her car parked anywhere. There were a few cars parked in the church's limited car park, so he knew there were people in the building. He walked to the church and slowly climbed up the steps to the huge doors of the entrance. The last time he climbed these steps, he was between life and death, and this was where Eva had found him and rescued him. He hadn't been inside a church since he was almost twelve. His father hadn't been one who attended church much, but he always made appearance during major events and holidays. His mum used to attend and took him along with her every time. Taking a deep breath, he pushed open one half of the door and quietly stepped in. There were two people arranging vases of flowers around the church. One person was seated on a pew, praying. Someone else was sweeping a corner of the room. RJ stood there, not knowing what to say or do.

"Can I help you?" A man asked gently.

He had just come out of a side room and had moved towards the altar. He had a smile on his face. RJ swallowed and then walked down the aisle to where the man stood by the altar, attracting the attention of the others in the room. It didn't help that the massive stained glass cross on the wall behind the altar was intimidating.

"Hello…" greeted the man when RJ was finally in front of him. "My name is James. I'm the Parish secretary here. How can I help you?"

"Hi. I'm looking for Eva da Silva?" RJ asked, unsure if the man would be able to help him.

James looked surprised. "Eva? She and the others should already be at Heathrow by now."

Heathrow? Why would Eva be at Heathrow Airport, RJ thought, trying to remain his cool and calm self.

"Heathrow Airport?" RJ asked, the confusion he was feeling was evident on his face.

James nodded. "Their flight to Bulawayo, Zimbabwe. It's today. Didn't she tell you?" James, obviously wondering why RJ did not have this information, was suddenly curious. "I'm sorry, who are you again?" he asked RJ.

RJ's mind was in a whirl. "Why is she going to Zimbabwe?" he asked, ignoring James' question.

"Missionary work… for six months," James replied, studying RJ strangely.

RJ placed his palm on his forehead and shut his eyes. Eva had never mentioned anything to him about missionary work in Zimbabwe. Was it last minute? Calm down RJ and think, think.

"If I must say, you're looking rather distressed. Is anything the matter?" James asked again.

This drew more attention from the others in the church. RJ couldn't give up. Maybe he could still do something.

"I just need to catch her before she leaves. It's important," RJ replied. "What time is the flight?" RJ asked desperately.

"Oh, I see. Err, I'm not sure now… I think it's about 2pm or so…or probably earlier than that." James looked like he was trying hard to remember.

RJ checked his watch. It was 1.05pm. That wasn't good.

One of the ladies doing the flower arrangement said, "It's 3:00pm! The KLM flight departs at 3:00pm."

Three o'clock? RJ could just still make it.

"Thank you. Thank you both." He gushed as he almost bolted out of the church, trying not to run as James and the others in the church stared on after him.

RJ was aware of the attention he was attracting as he rode on the motorway. He had never ridden to Heathrow on a bike before, but it was the best form of transportation at the moment, and he was happy he happened to be riding it. It was a fast machine, and he rode it like he had never done since he purchased it. He went as fast as he could possibly go, making sure to be mindful of speed limits. Luckily, he was able to avoid all the nasty traffic. Buying the bike was one of the best decisions he had ever made, he thought.

Coming off the M4 and getting close to the Heathrow airport tunnel, RJ realised he had no idea what terminal the KLM plane would be taking off from. He found an awkward side of the road, away from the traffic, to stop. He just couldn't be bothered right now. Quickly, he whipped out his mobile phone. It was freezing. The cold infiltrated his thick motorcycle gear and bit through his gloved hands. RJ pulled off the glove off his right hand and felt the harsh pinch of the cold on his bare palm.

Navigating onto the Heathrow website from his phone's Google browser, he searched for flights and the terminal finder.

"Come on," he said out loud as the page took forever to load. Finally, it came up. He rotated the screen and then enlarged the page to enhance his vision. Terminal 2. Got it. He shoved his phone back in his pocket, He didn't bother to put his glove back on or close his visor as he quickly rode to Terminal 2 motorcycle parking.

At 1.52pm, RJ was parked. With his helmet tucked under his left arm, he ran to the elevator. When it opened, there were a few people in there on their way out. He held back a bit allowing the people to come out. One of them looked a lot like Eva, only he was a man, and he didn't have a mass of curls on his head. The guy's hair was curly but short cropped, and he was taller than Eva, but RJ had no doubt that that was her twin brother, Evan. The guy frowned when he noticed RJ staring at him. His translucent brown eyes intense… just like Eva's.

The woman at his side nudged him to ignore RJ's rude stare as they both came out of the elevator.

RJ turned to them. "Evan?" He called with uncertainty even though he knew it had to be him.

The man stopped and his frown deepened. The woman beside him stood watching curiously.

"Do I know you?" Evan asked.

"Probably not," RJ replied. "My name's RJ and I'm trying to get to your sister."

Evan quirked an eyebrow and studied him for a moment, and for a brief second, RJ thought the guy was going to ignore him.

Evan stepped forward and reached out a hand to RJ. "How're you doing? Nice to finally meet the famous RJ."

RJ was surprised that Eva had even mentioned him to her brother. The woman beside him had a broad smile on her face, he thought her cheeks were going to burst from smiling so much.

RJ quickly took his hand. "I'm sorry, but… I need to get to her… fast."

"Oh yeah, sure. Their party's all checked in and almost done with baggage drop so you do need to hurry before they go into the departure's hall," Evan replied.

RJ nodded and as if on que, the elevator opened again. He stepped in and just before the doors shut…

"Hey, RJ…" Evan called. RJ looked at him.

"Good luck, mate," Evan said with a friendly grin.

"Cheers," RJ said, but the doors had already shut.

Chapter Twenty-Seven

Eva should have been done with her baggage drop by now if she wasn't currently helping Diane. Being an organised person, Eva had practically finished packing her two suitcases two days ago and ensured they weighed within the luggage limit. She didn't understand how Diane could have excess luggage… with both her suitcases. She and Jess, another church member, now had their suitcases open, trying to fit a lot of Diane's things into theirs. They were running quite late. The day had been a very hectic one since the early hours of the morning, and she didn't really get much sleep last night. She had spent the night at her parents' as she wasn't going to see them in a while.

Rachel had come along with Evan to pick her up and bring her to the airport. It had been a bit emotional for her as they shared hugs just before they left not too long ago.

Eva was shocked to see so many bottles of water in one of Diane's suitcases. Did the woman think they didn't have water in Zimbabwe? Besides, they would be there for six months; her bottles of water were bound to run out long before that time. What would she do then?

"I think you better leave the bottles of water behind," Reverend Bainbridge gently suggested.

It was almost like he had been reading Eva's mind. It was the sensible thing to do. Diane didn't look happy, but Eva and Jess were more than happy to pass the bottles of water to Thomas, who had his arms stretched out to take them. There were nine of them going. Five women and four men. Thomas, one of the clerics at the church, Lucy, one of the church deacons, and Reverend Bainbridge had been kind enough to come to the airport to see them off and assist them in any way they could.

All the rushing and bending was making Eva feel a little warm, even though it was cool in there. She stood up straight and took off her coat and proceeded to tie it round her waist. She had on a grey checked patterned high waist, button front, and wide-leg suspender jumpsuit. Her white chiffon blouse was long sleeved and gathered around her neck and wrists. Once they arrived in Bulawayo they would spend one night in a hotel before heading to the village the next morning. She was certainly not going to be dressing like this there. She had packed a lot of casual and light clothing for warm weather.

"Can I at least keep one or two bottles?" Eva heard Diane ask, clearly upset.

However, the sound of her voice and the firm responses she got faded away as Eva spotted a figure running into view and then stopping to scan around. It was a very handsome man with unmistakable piercing blue eyes, even from a distance. His jet-black hair was a little unruly. He had on black leather pants that clung to lean legs and disappeared into heavy black and silver designed boots. The black leather jacket he wore had silver stripped designs on the sides of the sleeves and was zipped up at the front. He had only one black leather gloved hand and the bare hand clutched a black helmet. It wasn't only her attention this sexy and attractive looking man had caught. He was getting a lot of stares from other people at the airport.

"Wow. Who is that?" Jess exclaimed in awe, straightening up to stand beside Eva.

RJ!

His eyes suddenly found and locked on hers. Eva's heart began to pound loudly in her chest, and she feared Jess might be able to hear it. He started to walk towards them.

"Oh my goodness, he's coming this way," Jess said excitedly.

"Err, ladies, we aren't quite done here. We need to hurry. There's very little time left." Reverend Bainbridge tried to get their attention back.

Eva said nothing. Could it really be him? RJ was here. Why was he here?

Soon he was standing right in front of her. Jess was confused now and looked from RJ to Eva and back.

"Hi, angel," he said, unable to take his eyes off her. Eva was dumbfounded.

RJ went on, "Eva... I've been a fool... but I'd be a bigger fool if I let you get on that plane today."

"What's going on here?" asked the reverend.

RJ turned to him. "I apologise... Reverend..." he added, noting the white collar round the elderly man's neck.

RJ looked at Eva again. "… I cannot let Eva go with you today. Maybe sometime when I can come along with her, but for now, I need her here with me… please," he added at the end.

Eva sucked in her breath. Was this really happening? She turned to the reverend.

"Err this is RJ… Rhys Fairchild…" She began to introduce as the others, including nearby passengers who were not in their party, watched.

The reverend obviously recognised the surname as that of the church's benefactor. Eva continued, "He's also the man I helped that day on the steps of the church." The reverend remembered that too.

Leaning close to Eva the reverend asked, "Is he, by any chance, the infuriating and insufferable man you were talking to God about some time ago?"

Eva blushed and nodded. Clearly the reverend hadn't forgotten that incident like she had hoped.

The reverend quickly turned to Jess and Diane. "Do you have any more room in your suitcase Jess? We need to transfer Diane's things from Eva's suitcase into yours. Diane, hurry, you go and sort out your baggage drop. Thomas, we need to cancel Eva's ticket."

Everybody started moving fast. Eva was shocked. She turned to the reverend. "Excuse me, Reverend? What about the work? The mission to help and sav…"

The reverend looked at her with kind eyes and placed gentle hands on her shoulders. "It looks like you already have a mission to complete here, Eva. Like I said, we don't always have to go far to show our love, we can do so here as well. We have enough people to handle the work there. You finish what you started here."

Eva's eyes welled up with tears. "Thank you, Reverend."

The reverend glanced briefly at RJ who stood there waiting patiently and then he looked at Eva and grinned. "No! Thank you. Let's hope he keeps his word and actually goes along with you on the next missionary trip. That would be a huge testimony."

Eva smiled and hugged the reverend. Then she went and hugged the members of the missionary trip. Thomas placed her suitcases beside her as Jess ran quickly to drop off her bags. Eva wouldn't be surprised if the flight was already boarding.

She finally faced RJ. He looked relieved as he stared at her. She still didn't know what to say to him. He stepped closer to her and handed her his helmet.

She took it slowly, confused. He then went off to find an empty trolley, arriving minutes later to help place her suitcases on them.

"Shall we?" he asked.

She slowly followed him as he wheeled the trolley away from the others.

"What a waste. Would we get away with just a cancellation fee?" Eva asked, feeling guilty.

"Probably not. You might have lost the whole cost of the ticket. Don't worry, I'll give a big donation to the church to make up for it. It's my fault, after all," RJ replied.

She went quiet again. She still wasn't sure about all of this. When she woke up this morning, she thought she was travelling to Africa, even though her heart was aching. Now, she didn't know what she was doing and how she was feeling.

RJ must have sensed her retreating into herself because he stopped pushing the trolley and finally came to stand in front of her.

He grabbed her hand. "Eva, the first time I saw you, I thought you were the most beautiful woman I had ever seen… and I still think that. I wanted you instantly. I wanted you to be mine, but I didn't want to want you. Yet, I couldn't get you out of my mind or stay away from you. You're such a good person, sweet, kind, sensible, caring. How could any man stay away from you? But the man you rescued that night was a broken man, a troubled man. I had a whole load of baggage from my past, and I even got you mixed up in my crazy life. I didn't think I deserved a woman like you. I didn't think I was worthy of your affection… or God's for that matter. So I let you go. But it was a mistake. In the past twenty-four hours I have been through some overwhelming emotional stuff that I can't begin to talk about right now. However, I will tell you all of it, and as usual with me, there's always a lot to tell."

He broke off to take a deep breath as Eva's eyes stayed fixed on his.

He brought her hand to his lips and kissed it. "You saved my life and gave me a second chance… the opportunity to turn things around and get it right, and I'm doing that. But I want you right beside me as I do. I am so sorry for the day at the hospital when I let you go. I panicked, I thought I was doing the right thing… even though it felt terrible. I haven't felt happy since that day. I need you in my life, Eva. You make me want to be a better person."

When he stopped talking, Eva was shaking with emotion. "Eva?" he said, drawing her into his arms.

It felt good being in his arms. He was warm and strong and smelt good. His words had brought joy to her heart even as she wanted to reassure him that he was a good person too, that he was a kind person. She pulled away from him a little; enough to see his face but remain in his arms. He looked down at her, trying to read her eyes… her expression.

"RJ, God loves you. He loves everyone, no matter what. No one is deserving of the kind of love he has for us, but he still loves us regardless," she said softly.

He gave a slight grin. "You don't know how very reassuring that is, Eva. How about you, though? Do you still want me, regardless?"

Eva smiled back. "Well, I'm not getting on the plane with the others, am I? Do you think I would have done that otherwise?"

He took in a deep breath and pulled her closer to him again, resting her head on his chest. "Eva, you've hooked me, reeled me in big time and now, you've got me," he said.

Eva thought her heart would burst for joy. "You hooked me first, RJ… when I came to visit you at the hospital… with your devilishly blue eyes and your sarcastic charm."

He chuckled.

"I thought you were bad news and everything within me told me to stay away from you, but somehow, I couldn't. I was as drawn to you as you were to me," Eva confessed and went on, "The last time I saw you at the hospital, I wanted to tell you I was falling for you. It was fast, but it was real. It is real."

"I know. I knew what you were about to say, and I stopped you from saying it because I knew if you had said it, then I wouldn't be able to let you go." Gently, he pushed her away from him so he could look into her eyes. "I wouldn't be able to let you go because I had fallen for you too… hard!"

Eva smiled, and he kissed her.

"You have no idea how miserable I was over Christmas and up until now," she said.

"I'm sorry. If it's any consolation, so was I," RJ replied.

Eva gave him another hug then said, looking him over. "Did you ride here on a bike or something?" She couldn't imagine that he would have.

"Yes," answered RJ.

Her eyes widened in surprise. "Really? You own a bike? You rode all the way here on a bike? In this crazy cold?"

"Yes. Yes. Yes and yes," was his response.

Eva shook her head. "Unbelievable!"

"It wasn't planned. When you didn't pick up my calls or respond to my text messages, I had to go over to yours, and I needed something fast. I still checked your apartment even though I didn't see your car parked outside…" he started to explain.

"That's because it's parked at my brother's, Evan," Eva interjected.

"Oh, I met him, by the way," RJ informed.

"Really? Where? Was he the one who told you I was at the airport?" Eva asked in surprise.

RJ shook his head. "No. I met Evan at the terminal's parking lot. I knew he was Evan straight away. He wished me luck getting to you."

Interesting, Eva thought, smiling. She liked that.

"It was James from your church who told me where you were. When you weren't at home, the only other place I knew to check was the church. The people present there were busy but were kind enough to help me with information regarding your whereabouts," explained RJ.

Eva was amused and astonished at the same time. "You mean you went into the church and did not spontaneously combust into flames?" She exclaimed.

RJ, observing her with a side grin, laughed. "Well I figured; if he was willing to save me on the church steps, then he wasn't about to finish me off in the church."

Eva smiled and nodded.

"So… about Zimbabwe…?" RJ didn't need to finish the question.

"It's something I have always wanted to do and will do at some point in future. It's missionary work to help build and support the churches in the villages. This one is to Zimbabwe. The next one is Kenya, and so on. I had planned to be part of the team going there, but then you came along, and I decided to shelve the idea for the time being. However, when things didn't work out between us, I thought I might as well go… I also hoped it would help me get my mind of you."

RJ stared at her. "You have such a good heart. I'm sorry yet glad you didn't go now."

She said nothing but stared back at him. He looked around the airport, almost like he had forgotten they were there.

"We better start heading off. Maybe we can put your suitcases in storage and come back for them tomorrow?" he suggested mischievously.

Eva gave him a stupefied look. "If you think I'm riding all the way home on your bike, you are gravely mistaken."

RJ laughed. He grabbed hold of the trolley again and started to push it.

"Come on. I'll get you a taxi. I can't leave my bike here, so I'm going to have to ride it back," he said.

Eva felt bad for him, plus she was disappointed that they wouldn't be together in the taxi. Yet, all in all, she was happy. Happier than she had ever felt in her life. She wondered what her family would think about this. Oh and Joyce! She couldn't wait to tell Joyce about all that transpired today. Eva couldn't even begin to imagine what the woman's reaction was going to be.

As they made their way to the car park, Eva turned to RJ. "You do realise something, don't you?"

"What?" he asked in return, wondering what sort of question that was.

"What you did today… coming all this way here… to the airport, to stop me from getting on the plane… it was pretty corny," she said; a hint of mischief in the smile on her face.

He threw his head back and chuckled. "Well I'm glad my girl happens to like corny."

His rich chuckle was music to her ears. Eva liked that he called her his girl. As they approached the elevator, she placed RJ's helmet on the suitcases stacked on the trolley, untied her coat from around her waist, and put it on.

Two weeks ago…

Ardian knocked on the door for the third time and waited patiently again as he had done previously between the first two knocks.

Finally, there was an angry groan from inside the room. "I gave strict instructions that I was not to be disturbed. This better be important." The strongly accented voice came from inside the room.

Ardian knew this was his invitation to come in. He opened the door and was immediately bathed in the instrumental sound of 'Toka E Diellit', a classical number by famous Albanian composer Aleksander Peci. Guri was seated, eyes closed, in a reclined chair. A bit of white powdery substance was spread on the table in front of him. He appeared to be on a substance and music high. Ardian walked in, half shutting the door, and then stood patiently waiting to be acknowledged by his boss.

A minute later, when the song had finished, Guri opened his eyes. He lifted his arm, and with the remote control in his hand, he stopped the source of music which was coming from the TV screen hanging from a corner of the wall. Slowly, he sat up, bringing his chair back to its upright position. He cast Ardian a look.

"What is it?" Guri asked, sniffing as he wiped his nose with the back of his wrist.

"You won't believe who we found lurking in the bushes outside, near the fence. Romeo sniffed him out," Ardian began, extremely proud of the energetic black German shepherd.

Guri said nothing but inclined his head inquiringly. Ardian turned, walked to the door, and opened it. A 6'5" muscular man held Nick Payne closely and tightly by the arm. At Ardian's nod, he pushed Nick into the room.

It definitely got Guri's attention. His eyes took on one of surprise and pleasure. Guri leaned forward in his chair, studying Nick. The man looked terrible. Gone was the smooth fold-back hair style. He looked slightly gaunt, but Guri suspected it was more to do with the strain he was currently under than malnutrition. The man also stank like a skunk's bottom.

Guri's hand instantly covered his huge nose. "Miresia Ime! Nick, did you shit yourself?"

Nick looked tired and uncomfortable. Guri wondered when last the man had experienced a proper shower or bath.

"As I said, boss, we found him lurking around in the bushes," Ardian repeated.

Nick tried to shake free of the tall man, but it was fruitless. So, he settled for standing with his legs slightly apart to give an air of fearlessness and confidence.

"I wasn't lurking. I was trying to ge'in to see you," Nick said.

Guri frowned. "To see me? Why? There's a manhunt for you, Nick. Are you not aware of this?"

Nick looked sober. "'Course I'm aware. 'Tis why I'm 'ere to see you."

Guri sat back in his chair, interlocked his fingers, and rested his hands on his chest. It was a gesture that implied he was all ears.

"All this 'appened b'cos I wanted to go into business wiv you. RJ was trying to mess that up. I still want to work wiv you… or for you." Nick said loudly with gusto.

Guri remained quiet. A quirk of an eyebrow was his only reaction.

Nick shifted uncomfortably on his feet, losing his stance of self-confidence.

"I was err… thinking; if you could 'elp me… you know… get to Australia… or maybe Spain, I could 'elp with your business over there. I could 'ead your operations… I'd do a damn good job."

Guri frowned and sat up, once again leaning forward in his chair.

"Help you? Do you realise that, because of you, the police are making my operations across the city difficult? The investigation into your case, which includes kidnapping a young man for ransom so you can use the pay out to buy into a famous drug cartel, is costing my business. You cast a huge light on my affairs, and I have had to shut down a number of my operations." Guri shouted violently.

Nick said nothing as Guri stood up.

"To make things even worse, I find out that RJ isn't dead, but survived your murder attempt on his life."

Guri stopped to unlock one of table drawers. He pulled it out and rummaged through for something. Finding it, he picked it up and shut the drawer.

He then walked around the desk and paused. "Nick, let me tell you about our code of conduct in the Oktapod."

Nick stayed silent as his concentration was fixed on whatever it was that Guri held in his hand. His twitching face betraying the feeling of fear that was beginning to stir inside him.

Guri continued. "We are terribly loyal and will not take kindly to anybody who hurts or tries to hurt one of our own. Imagine my surprise when I found out that you… Nick, tried to kill RJ, your own boss? That kind of thing cannot and should not be tolerated anywhere."

There was a slight pause just before Guri gave Nick a deadly stare.

"You came lurking around the wrong place, Nick," Guri said and quietly gave Ardian a look, prompting the man to walk towards the door.

Nick suddenly began to struggle in the tall man's arms, but the much-stronger man tightened his hold, pulling Nick's arms back and holding him firmly in place.

Guri slowly put on a heavy gold-plated brass knuckle with two rows of sharp blades, and then equally slowly, began walking towards Nick.

"Did I ever tell you about the time we made an example of one who dared to test our loyalty code? It happened to be a Judas in our midst; a traitor. We hunted him down, gutted him like a fish and fed him to the seagulls," Guri said.

Nick began to shout and plead as Ardian slowly shut the door.

The End